DIRE STRAIT

Cover Aircraft Picture acknowledgement Boeing P8

DIRE STRAIT

a Down Under mystery

By

TONY BLACKMAN

This book is entirely a work of fiction. All characters, companies, organizations and agencies are either the product of the author's imagination or, if real, used factiously without any intent to describe their actual conduct. Descriptions of certain aircraft electronics and equipment have been altered to protect proprietary information. Mention of real aircraft incidents are all in the public domain.

Dire Strait ISBN 978-0-9553856-8-1

First Published 2013
© 2013 by Anthony Blackman. All rights reserved.
Published by Blackman Associates
2 Thames Point
London SW6 2SX

Previous books by Tony Blackman

Flight Testing to Win (Autobiography paperback)
ISBN 978-0-9553856-4-3, 0-9553856-4-4
Published Blackman Associates September 2005

Vulcan Test Pilot
ISBN 978-1-906502-30-0
Published Grub Street June 2007

Tony Blackman Test Pilot(Autobiography revised and enlarged, hard cover)
ISBN 978-1-906502-28-7
Published Grub Street June 2009

Vulcan Owner's Workshop Manual
ISBN 978-184425-831-4
Published Haynes 2010

Nimrod Rise and Fall
ISBN 978-1-90811779-3
Published Grub Street October 2011

Victor Boys
ISBN 978-1-908117-45-8
Published Grub Street October 2012

FICTION
Blind Landing
ISBN 978-0-9553856-1-2
Published Blackman Associates

The Final Flight
ISBN 978-0-9553856-0-5, 0-9553856-0-1
Published Blackman Associates

The Right Choice
ISBN 978-0-9553856-2-9, 0-9553856-2-8
Published Blackman Associates

Flight to St Antony
ISBN 978-0-9553856-6-7 0-9553856-6-0
Published Blackman Associates

Now You See It
ISBN 978-0-9553856-7-4, 0-9553856-7-9
Published Blackman Associates

.

To Margaret, my long suffering wife, without whose first class ideas, enormous help, continuous encouragement and amazing editing skills, this book would never have seen the light of day.

Acknowledgements

This book could not have been completed without the help of specialist advisers. I should like to acknowledge with thanks the support and advice I have received from Henry Barton, Deborah Blackman, Joe Kennedy, Charles Masefield, Justin Morris, Karen Mow and many others. I must apologise to any who I inadvertently have not mentioned.

Despite all the help I have received, there will inevitably be inaccuracies, errors and omissions in the book for which I must be held entirely responsible.

Author's Note

I felt able to write this book as a result of the research I had to make in order to publish **Nimrod Rise and Fall**. There can be little doubt that the detection of submarines is getting harder and harder as their engines and propulsion systems get quieter and quieter. There is an appendix which explains how the information from the many sensors on the aircraft in this book is stored and analysed in its mission memory; the mission system is, of course, mythical but matches very closely mission systems being used in the real world. Clearly new effective ways of detecting submarines need to be developed since the world depends on safe marine transportation.

Some of the technology in the book is ahead of current capabilities and regulations but it can't be long before pilotless aircraft are allowed to fly in airways as suggested in the book. Perhaps long range unmanned nuclear submarines will take rather longer to develop but their time will surely come.

Anthony L Blackman OBE, MA, FRAeS

About the Author

Tony Blackman was educated at Oundle School and Trinity College Cambridge, where he obtained an honours degree in Physics. After joining the Royal Air Force, he learnt to fly, trained as a test pilot and then joined A.V.Roe and Co.Ltd where he became Chief Test Pilot.

Tony was an expert in aviation electronics and was invited by Smiths Industries to join their Aerospace Board, initially as Technical Operations Director. He helped develop the then new large electronic displays and Flight Management Systems.

After leaving Smiths Industries, he was invited to join the Board of the UK Civil Aviation Authority as Technical Member.

Tony is a Fellow of the American Society of Experimental Test Pilots, a Fellow of the Royal Institute of Navigation and a Liveryman of the Guild of Air Pilots and Air Navigators.

He now lives in London writing books.

DRAMATIS PERSONAE

Peter Talbert	Aviation Insurance Expert-
Charlie Simpson	Peter's wife, Procurement Director Australian National Gallery

Boeing P8-U RAF CREW

Sergeant Bill Bailey	P8-U Acoustics Two 'ACOUSTICS2'
Flight Lieutenant Mary French	P8-U Radar Operator 'RADAR'
Flight Lieutenant Tim Hadley	P8-U Routine Navigator 'TACCO2'
Flying Officer Jane Murphy	P8-U Communications 'IM'
Flight Sergeant Walt McIntosh	P8-U Acoustics One 'ACOUSTICS'
Flight Lieutenant Pat O'Connor	P8-U Second Pilot 'P2'
Flight Sergeant Stan Orwin	P8-U ESM Operator 'ESM'
Flight Lieutenant John Sefton	P8-U First Pilot 'P1'
Squadron Leader Greg Tucker	P8-U Captain and Tactical Navigator
Flight Sergeant Wyn Williams	Crew Chief

Australian Politicians etc

Group Captain Bob Acton	RAAF Canberra Operations Officer
Dominic Brown	RAAF Security
Commander Tom Benson	Captain HMAS *Rankin*
Jessica Butt	Director, ASIO
Mark Coburn	Inspector, ATSB
Flight Lieutenant Fred Cooper	RAAF No 10 Squadron Acoustics
Robert Covelli	Senior Inspector ATSB
John Dempster	RAAF Procurement
Sarah Johnson	ASIO communication expert
Squadron Leader Buck Luckmore	RAAF Townsville Duty Officer
Philip Morgan	Australian Prime Minister
Squadron Leader Shane Morris	RAAF No 10 Squadron Navigator
Wing Commander Alan Nguyen	RAAF Operations Officer
Vin Partridge	Secretary of the Department of Defence
Dick Skipton	Boomerang Airlines
Geoff Smith	Minister for Foreign Affairs and Trade
Jack Smithson	Minister for Defence
Lucy White	Member for Wakefield, South Australia
General Max Wilson	Chief of the Defence Force

The Rest

Jeff Almond	*Total Systems* expert
Randy Bercholz	Boeing, Los Angeles
Harry Brown	Chief Secretary in MOD
Walter Brownland	A&AEE submarine systems engineer
Rupert Carstairs	Deputy Director, Cheltenham

Maureen Chester	UK Defence Minister
Jill Evans	Peter and Charlie's Nanny
Martin Foster	Deputy Head of Air Accident Investigation Branch
Robert Fotheringay	UK High Commissioner, Canberra
Matt Fraser	CIA executive
Wing Commander Charles Grainger	UK Air Advisor, Canberra
Hank Goodall	CIA operative
Tyler Hammond	Submarine expert, Seattle
Liz Mansell	Mike's wife and dress designer
Mike Mansell	Owner, Antipodean Airline Insurance
Roger O'Kane	Avionics designer, Independant Transport Aircraft Company
Brett Nelson	Head of Operations, US Secretary of State
Clive Perkins	UK Senior Civil Servant in High Commission
Jeremy Prentice	Al Jazeera reporter
Jim Sherburn	Commander of the *Audacious*
Alastair Smedley	Foreign Secretary
Wing Commander Brian Spencer	Squadron Commander at Waddington
George Swinburne	First Sea Lord
Stephen Wentworth	UK High Commission Staff Security
Brigadier Timothy Whetstone	Defence Advisor, UK High Commission

ACRONYMS AND DEFINITIONS

Acronym	In full
AAIB	Air Accident Investigation Branch
Active Sonobuoy	A submersible buoy that pings and listens for underwater reflections
ADF	Australian Defence Force
AIP	Air Independent Propulsion. Makes submarine almost undetectable http://en.wikipedia.org/wiki/Air-independent_propulsion
AMI International	Expert Naval Intelligence firm
APU	Auxiliary Power Units
ARDU	Aircraft Research and Development Unit
ASIO	Australian Security Intelligence Organisation
ATA	Actual time of arrival
ATC	Air Traffic Control
ATIS	Automatic Terminal Information Service
ATSB	Australian Transport Safety Bureau.
CAA	Civil Aviation Authority

CASA	Civil Air Safety Agency, Australia
DARPA	Defense Advanced Research Projects Agency
DGAC	French Directorate of Civil Aviation
DME	Distance Measuring Equipment
DoD	Department of Defence (US)
EASA	European Aerospace Safety Agency
ELT	Aircraft Emergency Locator Transmitter
ETA	Estimated Time of Arrival.
EWSP	Electronic Warfare Self Protection system
FAA	Federal Aviation Agency
FMS	Flight Management System
GPS	Global Positioning System
Laser buoy	A device that detects submarines using reflected light
NTSB	National Transportation Safety Board
MSS	Mission Support System
Passive Sonobuoy	A submersible buoy that listens for underwater sounds
Ping	Sending a discrete sound from an active sonobuoy in order to get echo and so calculate distance.
PNG	Papua New Guinea
Qinetiq	UK Defence Firm
RAF	Royal Air Force
RAAF	Royal Australian Air Force
RCAF	Royal Canadian Air Force
RCC	Rescue Coordination Centre
RNZAF	Royal New Zealand Air Force
RF	Radio Frequency
Sonobuoy	A device which detects submarines using sound
SRG	Safety Regulation Group, UK CAA
TCAS	Traffic Collision Avoidance System
Transponder	Aircraft beacon which can be seen by Air Traffic---secondary radar
USAF	United States Air Force

Book Specific Acronyms

ASC	Australian Submarine Corporation
EA	European Aerospace
ITAC	Independant Transport Aircraft Company
OZOPS	Australian Air Force Operations
SAB	South Australian Boats

CONTENTS

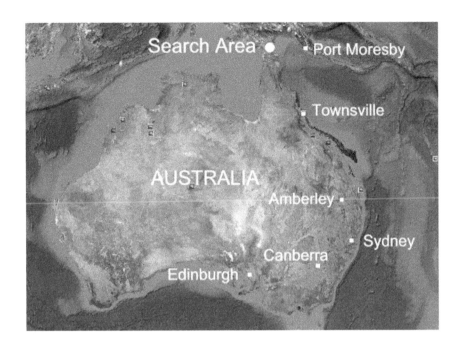

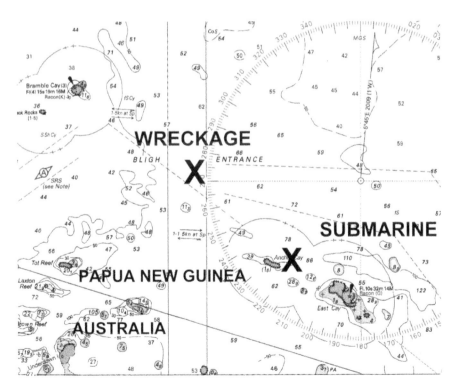

Torres Strait - Submarine locations and Australia PNG dividing line

13

Prologue

Jack Smithson picked up his scrambler phone.

"Jack?" He recognised the voice immediately; it was Geoff Smith, Australian Minister for Foreign Affairs and Trade, not one of his favourite Cabinet colleagues. "Jack, what the bloody hell have you people been up to? One of your patrols has just blown up a boat full of asylum seekers. You're meant to be Minister for Defence not Offence. We'll be cut to ribbons in the House, not to mention the media."

Looking out from his office towards the Old Parliament Buildings in Canberra Jack suddenly felt himself getting warm in spite of the air conditioning. "I've no idea what you're talking about, Geoff." As he spoke he saw his door open and Vin Partridge, his Departmental Secretary, come into the room holding a piece of paper. He reached out and took it.

Geoff was not about to stop. "Jack, clearly your communication system is not much good either. Apparently one of your patrols looking for asylum seekers fired on a suspected boat which sank. You'd better find out what happened as the PM will need to make a statement."

The phone went dead and Jack took his jacket off before reading the signal which Vin had given him. 'One of our patrol boats intercepted a suspected asylum seeker vessel in the Torres Strait in the middle of the night. It was actually a large high speed inflatable dinghy which started firing at our boat. The Captain returned the fire and the vessel suddenly exploded, disintegrated and then sank. Only mutilated bodies have been recovered and are being examined for identification.' The message was signed by Max Wilson, the Chief of the Defence Force.

"Vin, how the hell did Geoff Smith get to hear what happened before I did? You'd better get Max over here straightaway."

Vin disappeared and returned almost immediately. "The PM's office has been on the phone. He wants you to call him." He paused. "Apparently there was a guy from Foreign Affairs on our boat as a spectator and he signalled direct to his office before the boat's captain could issue a report. Max is coming over from his office in Russell as soon as he can. Shall I get the PM?"

"Yes, please."

A moment later Jack heard the PM's voice when he lifted his phone. "Jack, Geoff tells me one of your patrols has blown up a suspected boatload of asylum seekers?"

"PM, I'm just getting full details in as fast as I can. It wasn't an asylum boat, that's for sure. I'll call you when I get the full story."

"Well the press will soon get hold of it and we must have an answer."

"They'll only get hold of the story quickly if Geoff leaks it to them, PM. You know my views. If it is not too late can you stop him stirring things up?"

"Jack, you're being paranoid about Geoff. He wouldn't do that." There was a moment's silence. "I've just heard The Australian has the story of the asylum boat on its web site."

"Yes, Philip." He put his receiver down but it rang almost immediately. It was the PM again.

"Whatever you may think of Geoff and his relations with the press, Jack, it's even more important that I have a draft statement immediately, quashing the asylum connotation."

Jack put his phone down and still felt uncomfortably warm even though the air conditioning was churning out cold air. There was a knock on the door and Max Wilson pulled a chair over to sit next to Vin Partridge. "Minister, I've just been talking to the captain of the patrol boat. As you know his job was to check boats coming from Indonesia as well as from Papua New Guinea. It was at night but through his infra red glasses he saw a small boat steaming south at about twenty knots and quite correctly decided he'd better investigate. As he closed in, the boat started machine gunning our vessel; all our man could do was to return the fire and suddenly the boat, an inflatable, exploded violently and sank. Our boat was very close by this time and got covered with debris. There was no trace left of the inflatable on the surface but after a few minutes, even though it was still dark, they managed to find the remains of five bodies which they took back to their frigate. Apparently the bodies have no obvious means of identification and they're being taken back to Cairns for close examination."

"Alright then, what had we better say to the press?"

"Why not write down the exact facts and say we are investigating the identity of the boat and of the passengers, missing out all other details."

"If the boat was not an asylum boat they are bound to ask what it was doing out there at night."

Vin looked at Smithson. "But surely, Minister, we have no idea what the boat was doing, do we?"

Smithson nodded. "I suppose you're right. Better make sure the PM's Office knows exactly what happened and then come back. And Max, stop that guy from Foreign Affairs communicating with his Office. Take his phone away and if your people can't do that, isolate him so he doesn't know what we're doing or finding out." Max looked slightly worried. "I mean that, Max. We've got to control the information to the press at this time. No ifs or buts. If the guy complains then so be it. He can put in a formal complaint when he gets back."

A few minutes later when they had both returned Jack looked at them. "Now then, what happens next? What chance have we got of finding the wreckage of the boat?"

Max was ready with an answer. "Minister, it was a type of inflatable. We'll look of course though in view of the severity of the explosion I don't suppose there will be much left; the Navy tells me the depth there is only about thirty metres which will help a bit. They're proposing to use their French small unmanned sub to try to locate any wreckage and then recover it depending on what they find. Luckily the skipper of our boat made a careful note of the GPS position which should help enormously."

"Couldn't they just use a TV camera from a surface boat since we know pretty well where the wreckage is?"

"Don't know, Minister. I'm no expert. There may be a problem if we want to examine the wreckage closely. The sub will be more delicate."

"Alright, tell the Navy to go ahead as quickly as they can but no press or non-military experts to be with them." He stopped for emphasis. "I don't have to tell you how important it is to find out if it really was just coincidence that the boat was searching in this particular area."

Chapter 1

Charlie was already home from the National Gallery and was dealing with our son Peter and Francie, our two year old daughter, when I got back from the office. She looked great in spite of a long day negotiating painting exhibitions all over the World.

"Liz and Mike are coming over latish this evening. I said you'd meet them at the airport."

"Splendid. What time? Is Walter coming as well? Peter would like that."

"Not this time. It's mid-week and they both have to be at school."

Liz and Mike were great friends and we loved having them over. They were the first couple we had got to know when we came to Australia. Liz's dressmaking business in Sydney was flourishing and I still felt the financial shock every time Charlie bought one of her dresses. Mike's business was negotiating the insurance of aircraft and the cargo that they carried. They both worked really hard and had a splendid house overlooking Sydney Harbour.

My aviation insurance investigative work fitted in perfectly with Mike's though I had turned down the opportunity to be his business partner when we had first arrived in Australia a few years before.

Using our mobiles I timed my arrival at the airport so that I was able to pick them up without having to park, though I was still finding it difficult to allow for Canberra's traffic lights and the interminable time they seemed to take to change. Ten minutes later we were at our home at Kingston by Lake Burley Griffin. Like us, Liz and Mike had already eaten and so we settled for brandy and decaf coffee before going to bed. We discussed children and education for a bit and then I enquired why they had come at such short notice.

"It's a Government insurance job." Mike was explaining. "You know the RAAF aircraft they lost very recently? The one they've just made an announcement about, a Boeing P8-A?" I nodded as the loss had been reported in all the papers but with very little detail except that it had happened in the Torres Strait. "Well the

RAAF were renting a very expensive analysis kit from *Discover The World Inc* in San Diego which allegedly was on board the aircraft which was lost and unfortunately we were insuring it. I've come over to discuss the matter with them."

Liz joined in. "And I needed to check on some business issues with one of our customers so we decided we'd both come and maybe stay to-morrow night as well if we may. Have a meal somewhere or go to the cinema or the theatre, if there's anything on here."

I couldn't help smiling. "Despite what you may think there's always lots going on in Canberra. The problem will be getting seats at short notice. I'll have a look."

Mike looked at me. "By the way do you happen to know anything about the accident?"

I shook my head. "Not a thing. Military aviation is not my scene. I did think it strange though that the RAAF said they didn't know what had happened nor exactly where the event occurred. Surely there would have been a Mayday call on a satellite frequency or at the very least an emergency locator beacon on the water. Must have been an explosion."

"I agree. That's what I want to talk about though they weren't at all keen for me to come over." A pause. "By the way I think there was an RAF P8-U on the RAAF side of the field when we taxied in."

Charlie butted in. "Can't you two talk of something else for a change? It's always aircraft and you never look for a simple explanation of anything."

"My darling, if an aircraft is lost these days it can never be simple. Aircraft are so safe, even military ones."

"Well you'll have to sort it out in the morning."

We went to bed but I didn't go straight to sleep. I hadn't given the loss of the RAAF much thought but it was clearly a very serious matter with the loss of ten lives.

"Darling, solved it yet?"

I nudged her and I could smell her with a trace of perfume. "You should be asleep."

"So should you. It's nothing to do with you."

"What isn't?"

"Don't try that game on me, my love. You've switched on to the loss of that P8-A."

"How on earth did you know it was a P8-A?"

"The papers have talked of nothing else. It must be horrible for the families suddenly in peace time to lose their husbands..."

"...or wives or girl friends. You're right. It's particularly strange for the P8-A as it is so reliable."

"Was there no warning?"

"Apparently not."

"What are you going to do?"

"Nothing. It's not my problem."

"Let's get some sleep then." She rolled away from me to make sure but it was some time later before I dropped off.

In the morning we all had breakfast with Peter and Francie before Liz and Mike went off in a taxi. Charlie took Francie off to her nursery and Peter went down the road to a neighbour who took him to school. I drove off to my office but out of curiosity I went the long way round by the airport to try to see the aircraft on the military side. As Mike had said there was a Boeing P8-U there in RAF colours, parked some way away from the RAAF terminal.

Mike called me towards the end of the morning and suggested we met for lunch. Being a member of the RAF Club in London I had reciprocal rights at the Commonwealth Club so I had suggested that we meet there because it would be quiet. We sat in the shade at a bar table outside and got a couple of beers; for once I wasn't in a hurry but I could see that Mike was waiting to tell me about his morning meeting with the Australian Defence Force.

"Where was your meeting, Mike?"

"It was in one of the Russell suite of offices; only a Government could afford so many buildings. John Dempster was the guy's name; he met me in the lobby and we went up to an empty meeting office. I pointed out that *Discover The World Inc* wanted to be paid for the loss of their equipment, that we couldn't meet their claim without evidence of loss and that, under the terms of the agreement, I needed to know why the aircraft crashed because the RAAF might be liable for the loss if the aircraft had been involved in military action."

"That must have stopped the show."

"You're right. How did you know? Dempster looked a bit uncomfortable."

"I think there's a lot more to come out than we've heard. Anyway I interrupted you."

"I said we needed full details, time, place and what happened. Dempster argued and said surely a letter from the Australian Defence Force would be good enough, after all the papers were full of it. He didn't seem to understand, or chose not to, that we needed evidence that the equipment was actually on that particular plane. He added that the loss was almost certainly due to pilot error flying too low and hitting the water and so there was no way that the RAAF would be liable, but somehow I got the feeling that he was reciting the party line if you know what I mean. After a bit, as we were not making any progress, I said that we would have to proceed through our solicitors."

"That must have gone down well."

"Not exactly. He looked uncertain and then another guy came into the room. He didn't give me his card but he said his name was Dominic Brown; he was smartly dressed with a tie and spoke rather quietly. Dempster seemed relieved and quickly brought Brown up to speed; he then immediately asked me if a copy of the load sheet would do. I said it might be alright but clearly I needed to see it. I also needed to know what actually happened in case the RAAF were liable as per the terms of the agreement." He paused. "You know Peter I don't think he liked my saying that and I think he was wondering how to satisfy me that the loss was just an accident. He seemed to be very much up to speed, even before he had heard the whole story."

"Well that's not surprising, is it? He'd been listening and probably watching your whole discussion with Dempster. The room was clearly bugged and had a camera."

Mike stared in disbelief. "Peter, why would he do that? It can't be that important."

"I'm not so sure about that. As I said, it looks to me as if there may be more to the aircraft's disappearance than has appeared in the press. Maybe there was a Mayday call or an emergency beacon. The Australians must know by now why the aircraft crashed."

"Charlie's right about you. You always complicate a simple situation."

"Mike, the Boeing P8s are very reliable aircraft. They are based on millions and millions of hours on the 737. They don't just disappear. Wasn't it in this area a month or so ago that a RAN patrol boat sank some inflatable? I'm coming to the conclusion that there's a lot more about this disappearance than has been advertised."

"It could be just as the man said, pilot error. Flying too low and hitting the sea. Maybe the visibility was very poor, a thunderstorm perhaps."

"Maybe, but that's what they all say when the pilot isn't there to defend himself. Anyway let me know when you get the load sheet. Are they faxing it to you?"

"You have to be joking. I'm only going to be allowed to see it if I sign a confidentiality slip and I'm not sure if I'm going to be allowed to have a copy of it."

"Will that satisfy your people?"

"I don't know. I think that we have to know exactly how the aircraft crashed. I'll have to talk to our solicitors."

"So what happens next?"

"They promised me they would have the load sheet in a couple of days. I'll have to come back to look at it and make notes."

"Well you can use my spare office this afternoon. I think you're doing exactly the right thing making sure it was on the aircraft and making sure you know what went wrong."

We went back to my office in Marcus Clarke street in the City and out of curiosity I called Mark Coburn of the Australian Transport Safety Bureau and asked him if they had been consulted.

"Peter, I've no idea. It's a military aircraft and they don't normally call us in. Why not call my boss, Robert Covelli?"

I realised I was wasting a lot of time on something that did not concern me and tried to forget the whole thing, though it was difficult to do so with Mike in the next office and staying with us. Luckily I had an important and unusual job that was exercising me in that there appeared to be a problem on the certification of the latest aircraft for British Airways. The European certification authority, EASA, had signed it off but the airline had complained to the UK CAA that the indication of system failures on the displays was not satisfactory. The airline had asked me to support their case and I was trying to get to grips with the problem. I think the airline had asked for my help because they knew that I had had discussions on this subject with both Boeing and Airbus. In my view it was absolutely vital, but very difficult, to get all possible failures identified, covered completely and accurately. In a severe emergency there could be more than one emergency page telling the pilots what to do and it was difficult sometimes for them to know the correct priorities. British Airways felt that the emergency procedures that were being shown on their latest aircraft needed altering with improved prioritisation; the FAA, the American certification authority, were coming round to the BA view, which was causing the manufacturer some concern and EASA were not sure who to support.

With difficulty I tore myself away from the BA problem and decided to call Robert Covelli at the ATSB. "I know it's not really my scene but have you been asked to help with the loss of the RAAF P8-A?"

"No. I did offer but was told our help wasn't needed. Definitely a case of 'don't call us, we'll call you'. Strange really as we don't normally keep any secrets from each other. If it was just flying and hitting the sea we might be able to confirm what happened by looking at the wreckage. Something odd is going on. TOP TOP SECRET or something like that. They've obviously looked at the wreckage by now so they must have a very good idea of what happened."

"I agree."

I collected Mike and we drove home past the airport again; the P8-U was still there with what looked like some guards round it.

Chapter 2

Jane Murphy, the radio operator in the RAF Boeing P8-U reconnaissance aircraft, quickly switched her microphone box to the aircraft's intercom position. "Captain from IM. Got an ops immediate message from OZOPS saying we are to discontinue the Fincastle competition immediately and contact the Australian Rescue Coordination Centre for instructions. They've given me two frequencies to try, one satellite and one HF using the call sign RAFAIR 735."

Greg Tucker, the tactical navigator and aircraft commander wondered for a moment what on earth was going on before replying. He couldn't help feeling disappointed because they were surely in a winning position in the competition searching for submarines off the North Eastern Queensland Coast of Australia against the air forces of Australia, New Zealand and Canada plus the United States Navy; since this was the first time the United States had been allowed into the competition it would have been particularly satisfying to win. His aircraft had found the target submarine in record time thanks to the latest passive sonobuoy underwater detection device made by Ultra, a UK firm specialising in making these buoys; the new device, which had its own GPS onboard, was able to hear submarine noises at a greater range than the normal sonobuoys and indicated fairly accurately from which direction the noise was coming. They had only been allowed six of these new buoys because they cost £30,000 each but they had managed to find the target sub using only three of them. Now, as they were just preparing to go for the kill, Jane had called him with the stop message.

Greg knew there had to be a very good reason to stop such a large and important exercise which had taken many months in the planning and involved so many aircraft and ships. "OK IM. Call the RCC and find out what's up. We should be getting full search. Acoustics, keep tracking but we'll delay dropping the active sonobuoys. P1, keep following the target until we find out what we're to do. All Crew, monitor the satellite radio frequency." Greg selected the satellite radio on his communication box so he would hear Jane calling the RCC.

"RAFAIR 735 to RCC." As he had expected Jane had called the Rescue Coordination Centre immediately using the satellite frequency.

"RCC to RAFAIR 735. Receiving you loud and clear. Confirm that Fincastle competition now stopped. Proceed to 9° 15'S 143° 55'E to commence search for possible survivors and wreckage of Boeing P8-A registration A34-487. Advise search height and how long you can be on station without refuelling, landing at Townsville."

"RCC from 735. Roger."

Greg responded instantly. "Jane, I got that. Crew abandon Fincastle tracking. Tacco2, get course to steer as quickly as possible. P1, climb to flight level 250 and reprogram your Flight Management System for search waypoint with Townsville as destination. We need to know the ETA at search position and time on search. Assume 2,000 ft search height. IM, call RCC with the information when available."

Tim Hadley, Tacco2, sitting next to Greg had already entered the initial search and rescue position into the tactical system so that the pilots could see the course to steer on their displays. John Sefton, the first pilot, opened the throttles to climb power as he turned the aircraft to starboard to follow the heading pointer taking the aircraft to the search area. Pat O'Connor, the second pilot was busy putting the search waypoint into the flight management computer and selecting Townsville as their final destination to calculate their fuel usage. John put the autopilot in and watched Pat entering the data. "Pat, the flight plan will need a diversion airfield so put in Amberley. It's 600 miles away but there's nowhere else closer for a military aircraft to use so we're not going to have much time to search on station."

The pilots had to wait a few seconds for the FMS to calculate the flight tracks to the search waypoint, to Townsville and diversion to Amberley. Pat interrogated the FMS to calculate the search time on station. "Captain from P2. Box shows ETA at search position 0503Z, 93 minutes on station before going to Townsville with Amberley as alternate."

"Thank you. IM from Captain. Check weather at Townsville and Amberley. Tacco2, what time does it get dark at search area?"

"Captain from Tacco2. 0902Z is sunset, just after 7pm local time."

The aircraft reached its cruise altitude of 25,000ft and Greg wondered what had happened for the P8-A to go into the sea. The Boeing manufactured aircraft's safety record was extremely good and the RAAF maintained their aircraft in immaculate condition. He considered asking the RCC for more details than the routine report but clearly nothing would be gained. What he and his team had to do was look for survivors and wreckage. Still they needed confirmation that where they were going was the exact place to start the search plus the time of the mishap, if it was known, so that they could judge the area of search. It was high Summer and there was always the possibility of enormous thunderstorms covering the area. "IM. Find out from the RCC the weather at search area and whether it has changed since the time of the accident?"

"Captain from IM. Got an Ops Immediate from Northwood giving some details of Boeing P8-A loss. Passing it over."

Greg read the signal carefully. 'RAAF A34-487 reported missing west of Port Moresby. Aircraft failed to give routine position report at 0030Z. It was en route to Port Moresby from Townsville. Australian Defence Force surface search ship being despatched immediately plus another P8-A aircraft but need search to start soonest. It has been agreed that your aircraft will start the search being the closest available.' Greg briefed the crew and then got up and went over to look over the radar operator's shoulder at the screen. "Mary, I've looked at the radar on my display. What do you reckon will be the best search height to spot wreckage with the current wind and sea state? We can eyeball it but it will restrict the area we can cover; of course, the higher we can go the better for the radar, give us better endurance as well." Mary French was a very new crew member who had suddenly been substituted into his crew, against his wishes, replacing his regular radar operator and upsetting slightly the crew co-operation; as far as he was concerned she was an unknown quantity and an added responsibility. She was probably in her mid twenties, blonde and curved in all the right places; he couldn't help wishing she looked a little less attractive, not that she encouraged any nonsense from the rest of the crew, not when he was there anyway. However, he had discovered that she was first class at her job and that she knew it.

"Captain, there seems to be very little wind down there and any significant pieces of wreckage should show up on the radar if we search at 2,000 ft. I don't think we need to go any lower." She adjusted the range being displayed on the radar. "You see that echo at 50 miles. I'm sure that it is only a small craft, possibly one of the very small illegal fishing boats they were telling us about at the first Fincastle briefing, but it is showing up really well as you can see. Mind you, there's going to be a lot of returns from reefs and small islands to the south of the search area."

"Good. I hoped you'd say that. As you know 2,000ft is what we assumed when we worked out our search time on station to tell the RCC. Anyway I'm afraid It will only be a short search as we'll need a lot of fuel to get us back to Townsville with Amberley as diversion. We're still waiting to hear which way to start searching."

"Will any of the pieces float under the water?"

"Probably. Why do you ask?"

"Well we've got not only the new passive sonobuoys but also those four new active ones which the manufacturer claims have a phenomenal range and also a great listening capability if the pinging is switched off. With one of those we might be able to pick up the wreckage at quite long distances. At the start of the search you could drop one of the active buoys and see if there are any significant returns. We might find the wreckage a lot quicker."

Greg realised, not for the first time, why Mary had got accelerated promotion to Flight Lieutenant. He wished he had thought of her idea since it could possibly save hours of searching, not that they could do hours. What Mary didn't know was that he had been told only to use these special active buoys if really necessary as they were twice the cost of the new passive buoys and their performance was very secret. He wasn't sure what the powers that be would say if he authorised dropping one in the middle of the Torres Strait; it would be a waste in a way because though the active sonobuoys could listen as well as ping, they wouldn't be able to use the listening capability since all it would be doing was making noises listening for echoes back from the wreckage. However, he decided that in the interests of discovering the wreckage as soon as possible he was justified in using one of the new buoys.

"Captain to IM. Confirm the precise starting point for the search if you can from RCC and confirm their recommendation for the orientation. P1, we're going to start the search by dropping one of the new active sonobuoys. Acoustics, prepare one of those four sonobuoys so that we can search for submerged wreckage at long ranges. You can control the direction of the ping with these buoys, can't you?"

"Acoustics to Captain. Confirm we'll be able to ping directionally, narrow beam."

"Captain from IM. The RCC wants to talk to you."

Greg selected his radio. "Captain to IM. Call them up and I'll take over." He heard IM talking to the RCC and their acknowledgement. "RCC RAFAIR 735 Captain here. Go ahead."

"RCC to 735. Your projected time on station is very short. The RAAF are sending one of their Airbus KC-30As to rendezvous with you. Please confirm that you are able to accept fuel from the aircraft and will then be able to continue searching until 1000Z when a P8-A will be available to take over searching."

"RCC from 735. Stand by."

Greg considered the situation. "Captain to P1. Are we cleared to take on fuel from the KC-30A?"

"P1 to Captain. We don't have formal clearance from Boscombe yet but you remember we did some daylight wet contacts with a Boscombe KC30 without any problems and Pat operated the fuel transfer. I happen to know the RAAF KC30As have the same flying booms and the same arrangement as our latest KC30 tankers; it is the same system as on all the large USAF aircraft and it is much easier for the refuelling pilot since all that is needed is to fly steady formation with the tanker and then the tanker's crew do the rest from a TV screen, moving the boom to connect with the aircraft being refuelled. We'll need to confirm the height and speed but there shouldn't be a problem providing we can do it in daylight and they confirm when I'm in the correct position. I'm not prepared to do it in the dark without more training. You'll have to authorise me, anyway."

Greg reckoned that in a potential life saving situation it would be unreasonable not to agree to take on fuel since John Sefton and Pat had already done wet contacts. He knew Boscombe wouldn't like it and that his future career might be at risk but he felt that that was why he was Captain of a military aircraft. However he decided to keep his bosses informed since they had asked to be advised. "Captain to IM. Send ops immediate message to UK saying that in order to extend search time on station as we've been requested, we have to refuel from an RAAF KC 30A. P1, please advise how much fuel we will need to extend our search until the 1000Z handover to the RAAF P8-A."

Greg reviewed his decisions and called the rescue centre. "735 to RCC. Prepared to take on fuel in daylight from KC 30A. Monitoring Tactical Data Link for orbiting position and orientation, refuelling speed and altitude. Note that our pilot is requesting confirmation when in correct formation position."

"RCC to 735. Copied. Call sign KC30A tanker Dragon67."

"Captain from P1. We're approaching top of descent. We'll need to take on 30,000 lb fuel."

"Captain to IM. Confirm monitoring 121.5 and 406 emergency frequencies for the personal emergency beacons and the aircraft ELT emergency beacon. P1, advise descending. Did you copy tanker call sign, Dragon67?"

"P1 to Captain. Copied and awaiting refuelling information from tanker."

Greg looked at his screen and called Walt McIntosh. "Captain to Acoustics. Are you ready to drop and monitor sonobuoy?"

"Acoustics to Captain. All set. Do we know search pattern?"

"Good point. Captain to IM, have we got a final search plan from the RCC?"

"IM to Captain. I passed details to Tacco 2."

"Fine. Crew. Stand by for start of search. ESM and Acoustics2 after sonobuoy drop take visual look out positions port and starboard."

The aircraft levelled at 2,000ft. "Tacco2 to Acoustics. Stand by to drop sonobuoy…. 5 seconds ….3,2,1,drop">>>

Walt McIntosh looked at his screen, selected pinging and waited for the sonobuoy to start transmitting its info. Suddenly the screen was lit up but with no returns showing; he adjusted the gain to get maximum range and slowly rotated the direction of the pinging hoping for some significant returns. Then suddenly behind them, 180^0 from the direction of the search, he saw returns at nine miles. "Acoustics to Captain. Returns seen on reciprocal course at nine miles."

"Captain to Acoustics. Take us overhead."

"Acoustics to P1. Turn to port."

John Sefton banked the aircraft 30^0 to the left and started to turn back the way they had come. He saw the sea was dark blue but lighter to the south where the water was shoaling; the water seemed to be flat calm.

"Acoustics to P1. Continue turning, range returns 9.5 miles. Keep turning 20^0 more. Roll out, you are now on track to the returns." There was a pause as the aircraft closed the target. "Acoustics to P1, six miles to go. 10^0 left four miles." Walt looked again at the returns. The echoes were very strong, too strong for just wreckage. He switched off the pinger and went to the sonobuoy's listening mode. "ESM from Acoustics. Check recorder functioning. Two miles, left 5^0 Estimate overhead now. 9 degrees 15 minutes South 144 degrees 5 minutes East"

"Port look out, wreckage ahead."

"P1, got wreckage, orbiting. Looking for dinghies."

"Starboard look-out, wreckage my side as well. Can see RAAF markings on part of tail fin."

"Captain to P1. Take over search working along line of wreckage. Tacco2, keep plot."

Greg kept the aircraft searching round the wreckage for an hour trying to find dinghies and listening on the emergency frequencies but with no success. There were medium sized ships entering and leaving the Bligh East Channel and lots of small boats which necessitated careful examination; they mostly looked like fishing boats but could equally have been smugglers of things or people; however, there was no sign of dinghies or life jackets floating on the water. Greg decided to have their Wescam MX20[1] electro/optical camera running to photograph all the boats, in case post flight analysis was able to recognise one of them.

The wreckage had not spread out much at all, probably because there had been very little wind. They had seen enough wreckage to know it was from a Boeing P8-A and they had taken a lot of photographs. Greg made sure IM kept the RCC fully informed.

The KC30A came on frequency. "Dragon67 to RAFAIR 735. Confirm ETA Rendezvous 0530Z. Flying at 20,000 feet, .85 mach."

Greg gave the order to stop searching and climb up to the rendezvous point. He had come to the conclusion that they had done all they could in searching but realised that the RAAF would want them to carry on looking, certainly until it was dark. Mary spotted the aircraft on her radar and vectored the P8-U to the refuelling position. John Sefton came slowly up to the tanker and then throttled back slightly to stop the aircraft moving forward when the formating marks were in line.

"Dragon67 to RAFAIR 735. Confirm now in correct position."

He saw the boom coming down and then extending so that the delivery pipe went into the receptacle. Pat opened the cocks to the main tanks and the fuel started to flow.

The tanker called after five minutes. "Dragon67 to 735. Approaching 30,000 lb transferred. Cutting off fuel." The tanker switched off the flow and Pat closed the refuelling cocks of the main tanks; John saw the boom retract and then go back up flush with the underside of the aircraft. Once again he was amazed not only how simple it was but how quickly the fuel was transferred.

The aircraft descended to continue searching for survivors visually while Jane monitored the personal rescue transmitter frequency and the aircraft emergency transmitter frequency but without any success.

"RCC to RAFAIR 735. Intentions after Townsville?"

"RAFAIR 735 to RCC. Standby"

Jane called Greg on the intercom for instructions. He had been considering the situation and now a decision was required.

---

[1] See explanation in Appendix

Amberely was their base for the Fincastle competition and all their gear was there but he felt that they were all tired and needed a rest. It would be a very late arrival at Amberley by the time they had refuelled at Townsville.

"Captain to crew, I think we'd better stop at Townsville to-night. We've all had a long day. IM, let the RCC know and make sure they are arranging accommodation."

"RCC to RAFAIR 735. Advise position for RESCUE 50 to continue search."

"RAFAIR 735 to RCC. Our position 9° 27'S 144° 30'E"

"RCC to 735. You will be clear to proceed to Townsville at 0745Z. Call ATC for climb clearance."

"Captain from Radar. There seems to be a large ship just over fifteen miles from here between two reefs. It's been there all the time and hasn't moved."

Greg switched his display to radar. "Captain to Radar. Can see roughly where you mean. Take us overhead."

Jane was starting to call the RCC but Greg stopped her. "Captain to IM. Stop call to RCC." He paused making sure Jane had stopped. "IM, they may not want us to stop searching by the wreckage even though we've done everything we can so there's no need to tell them what we're doing."

The search was stopped and Mary called out the headings to the pilots but Pat had already selected the radar display on to one of their screens and John was tracking towards the boat. The visibility was dropping fast as the sun set but the ship was just visible. "P2 to Captain. Can't see identification marks on ship. May we use searchlight?"

"Captain to P2. No to searchlight. We don't want to draw attention to ourselves. The Wescam MX20 will photograph it all with its infra red capability and that way we'll have a good record in the mission memory. Just do the best you can visually."

John turned the aircraft again so they slowly approached the boat from its stern. They still couldn't make out the name or nationality of the vessel.

"Captain from IM. Can't get any response from ship on distress frequencies."

"Captain to IM. Pity. They could have helped in the search. We'll do one more run and let the MX20 have another go photographing the ship."

"Captain to P1. One more pass, please."

As they came over again ESM called out "ESM to Captain. Can't be certain but I think there's a helicopter on the stern."

"What type, can you see?"

"Not sure. Too dark but I don't think there were any markings."

Greg saw it was getting dark and hard to search visually. He could see white waves to the east of the boat which he guessed were breaking over the reef "Captain to crew. Prepare to climb to cruise altitude to go to Townsville."

"Acoustics to Captain. I think we should drop some passive sonobuoys near the initial search point before climbing up."

"Captain to Acoustics. Any particular reason? We're about 10 miles away from there and we should be starting our climb."

"Acoustics to Captain. I've been thinking. There must be a large submarine down there."

Chapter 3

Greg had to make an instant decision. The RCC was expecting them to be climbing up and setting course for Townsville and they would be late if they went back to the wreckage. However, he knew Walt well enough to know he wouldn't have suggested going back unless he was sure that there had been a submarine underneath the wreckage.

"Captain to Tacco2. Set course for initial wreckage position. P1 follow command heading"

"Captain to Acoustics. Prepare two passive buoys.

"Radar to Captain. Contact ahead. File 102 assesses high confidence Snort ahead. IM, track 2315 unknown."

Greg was delighted with contact even though the pilots hadn't reported seeing a mast or periscope. As they approached the spot Greg ordered the release of the buoys to give the maximum chance for Walt to detect the submarine again.

"Acoustics to Captain. Good RF. Getting weak contact, stand by."

There was a pause while the aircraft orbited and Walt tried to improve the contact.

"Acoustics from Captain. Any update?"

"Acoustics to Captain. Possible sub, type unknown. Audio indicates flooding tanks. Radar, he's diving."

"Mark, Mark! Phosphorescence disturbance in water, right 10 o'clock 200 yards. Possible submerging antenna."

"Radar to Captain. Sinker"

Greg hearing Radar confirming the sub was submerging decided to leave as quickly as possible. He would have loved to have spent more time investigating the contact and possibly determining whether it was Hostile or Friendly but he didn't have the fuel or the authority. "Captain to P1. Get climb clearance from ATC and set course Townsville."

Greg was delighted that they had been able to confirm Walt's earlier suspicions not only acoustically but also with the radar, not to mention a visual confirmation.

As they flew to Townsville Greg went over to Walt who explained to him that when they first arrived at the wreckage the returns were so loud he had switched the pinger off and looked at the returns on his screen. He was sure there was a large submarine underneath which was why he had asked Greg to return and use the new passive buoys to see if the submarine could be recognised from their mission database. However, he was not able to match the noise from the sub to anything in his database of submarine noises; he felt it was a modern one as it was very very quiet, but probably not nuclear. Walt told him that there was a problem as the Mission Support System had gone unserviceable so that the mission memory drive would need to go back to UK to be analysed to see if there were any new submarines in the UK databases and to get the MX20 photos downloaded. He was hoping to get a replacement from UK in two or three days.

Thinking about their arrival at Townsville Greg was very nervous of starting a hornet's nest by telling the RAAF of Walt's suspicions until the flight had been analysed at their Waddington base. Walt might be able to replay their flight after they had landed at Amberley using the Mission Support System, assuming Walt could fix it, but they already knew the submarine was not in their database so it was important that UK looked at the sonobuoy records as quickly as possible. Consequently, just as they started their descent, he told the crew not to discuss any details of the flight with anyone until he gave permission.

He saw Mary talking to Jane off the intercom, which he discouraged in flight. He went over to Mary who had clearly started the conversation.

"Well done on the radar contact." He looked at Jane and then back at Mary. "Is there a problem?"

"I just wondered If we're not going back to Amberley whether the RCC were letting our hotel know?"

Greg knew it was a fair question and perhaps he should have made sure that Jane had told the RCC to tell Amberley since they might not know from where they were operating. He looked at Mary who smiled at him which he realised he rather enjoyed and smiled back. However, he didn't like having to be reminded, even though she did it very nicely. He moved over to Jane and instructed her to contact RCC and confirm that their hotel had been informed they weren't coming back that night.

It was 9pm when they landed and Greg suddenly realised he was very hungry and he guessed that he wasn't alone; they hadn't expected the flight to have lasted so long and had run out of serious food on board by the time they had refuelled. He went up to the flight deck and was glad to see that they were being marshalled close to the civil terminal with all the ramp lights on; they could see an RAAF Officer coming towards them. Jane opened the door the moment John had applied the brakes to bring the aircraft to a halt and then she operated the switch to lower the steps.

Squadron Leader Buck Luckmore climbed up and introduced himself to Greg. "I'm the Duty Officer. As there is very little traffic, air traffic agreed you could park on the civil side to-night since I expect you'll be off early to-morrow." He paused. "Do you need any ground power?"

"No, thank you. We're running our APU and hopefully we'll be able to shut the aircraft up in a few minutes. We're too tired to go back to our base at Amberley to-night. Did you get a message requesting accommodation?"

"Yes, I've managed to get six twin rooms at the Beach House Hotel which is fairly close but in the town. Glad you decided to stay the night as we wouldn't have been able to refuel you until to-morrow morning anyway."

"That's great. We'll be about thirty minutes and then we'll be ready to go."

"No worries. I'll order three taxis. They should be here by the time you're done."

Greg made sure that Pat had put the locks in the undercarriage legs and then, on an impulse, he got Stan to give him the mission removable memory drive they had used in flight and to put a new memory drive into the acoustic recorder. He locked the aircraft door, went down the steps and then raised them from the controls in the nose wheel bay, locking the covering flap for the controls with the same key. He kept one key of the aircraft for himself and gave the other to John so that he could organise the refuelling in the morning.

As they walked over to the terminal and the taxis, Luckmore asked Greg what they had been doing; he clearly had not been told about the loss of the aircraft but Greg decided that he would let Buck learn what had happened on the news rather than get involved with an explanation straightaway. As they drove into the town he realised that now that the Fincastle competition had been scrubbed there was no longer any time pressure, and they could even leave Amberley a day or two earlier which might be nice as this would give them extra time at Richmond Air Force Base in Sydney. They were being positioned there for a great publicity exercise since Prince William was due to arrive from the UK and the plan was to fly him and Kate around Sydney Harbour accompanied by all the media.

The taxis pulled up at the hotel and Greg reckoned it looked exactly what they required, practical but not palatial. He checked that it was not too late to have food and with popular acclaim he ordered steak sandwiches and beer all round. He chose a room for himself, got Mary and Jane to choose theirs and then left the others to sort themselves out. He announced that breakfast would be at 8am and, when the sandwiches arrived, he took his and his beer up to his room; it looked like millions of others all over the world. He dumped his bag, got out his laptop and connected to the internet. After a bite of the sandwich which proved to be much better than he had anticipated, he decided all his communications could wait until it was finished. Refreshed, he logged on and found there were three messages, one to call the RAAF Central Operations room in Canberra, the second to call the RAF Air Advisor at the High Commission also in Canberra and the last one to call the CO of his Squadron in Waddington. He looked at his watch and decided it would be midday in UK and a good time to call his boss, Brian Spencer. He decided to use Skype to get connected rather than use the special phone he carried for secure communications and got straight through. "Greg here, Sir."

"Greg, good to hear from you. Where are you and what are you doing? I got a message from Northwood that the Fincastle had been stopped."

"Right. We've just landed in Townsville and are going to bed. Did they tell you why the Fincastle was cancelled?"

"No. They made it all sound hush hush for some reason."

"Didn't they tell you that the RAAF had lost one of their P8-As and we were sent to search for the wreckage and survivors since we were the closest resource they had?"

"No, they didn't. Did you find it?"

"Yes. Terrible sight. Lot of wreckage close together but we couldn't find any survivors. We spent hours searching."

"How did you manage that? You must have been very short of fuel."

"They sent one of their new KC30As to refuel us."

"Surely Boscombe hasn't cleared us yet to refuel from the KC30? We're not permitted to take on fuel from that aircraft."

"You're absolutely right Sir. But my crew had done some actual refuelling from the Boscombe test KC30 without any problems. What should I have done? We knew the Australian KC30 had the same standard flight refuelling centre boom as our aircraft."

There was a pause. "Did the refuelling work out OK?"

"Perfectly. John Sefton did a super job."

"Good decision. You know I'll back you up if anyone tries to query what you did."

"Well Sir. There's something else. Could be very significant. I'm not sure I should tell you over this line."

"Send me a secure message when you can. You must be exhausted."

"Yes, we are a bit tired and as you can imagine the operations people want to talk to me now, in Canberra for some reason not in maritime operations at Williamstown or Edinburgh. We'll need to go back to Amberley to collect our kit but don't know what happens after that."

"OK Greg, I'll try and help though it's Northwood's decision. I'll call them while you get some sleep and sort out what happens after Amberley. However you'd better talk to the RAAF people in Canberra. Don't forget to send me the message you didn't want to discuss over the phone and don't forget William and Kate in Sydney."

"Is that still going to be on, Sir?"

"Looks like it. Somehow we've got to persuade the Aussies to stay in the Commonwealth and those two are our trump card."

There was a lightening of Brian's tone. "Do you want me to come out to help?"

"I'm not sure that will be necessary, Sir. We'll probably be able to manage. We'll tell you all about it when we get back." A pause. "If you need me I'm in room 514. Hotel 61745743498. Talk to you in the morning."

Greg decided that before emailing Brian he had better talk to RAAF Ops at Canberra. He got through to the duty ops officer and discovered that he had already spoken to Buck Luckmore. He thanked Greg for all his efforts and said that it was the Australian Defence Force's policy not to discuss the loss of their Boeing P8-A with the press at this time and would he kindly explain that to all his crew. There was about to be a statement issued by the ADF dealing with the loss of the aircraft. He went on to explain that it had been arranged with Northwood that they were to fly direct to Canberra in the morning as it had been agreed that they were to be debriefed immediately in Canberra. Greg pointed out that they needed to go to Amberley first but the Ops guy in Canberra said that it was important that they flew straight to Canberra and didn't talk to anyone else.

Greg disengaged as quickly as he could and then sent a brief secure note to Northwood copied to Brian "There was a large sub underneath the wreckage of the P8-A and Acoustics couldn't recognise what it was. MSS at Amberley and can't transmit secure copy from here so propose sending mission memory drive back to Waddington for analysis ASAP."

He had a shower, lay on his bed and went fast asleep.

***

It was 7.15 when Greg woke up and he decided he'd better log on and look at his messages. There was a scrambled one from Brian "Keep your mouths shut. Northwood want Waddington to analyse memory drive ASAP. On no account mention it to RAAF until we've analysed it. Expect flight to Canberra."

The next one was from Northwood ops directing him to take the aircraft to Canberra and talk to the Air Advisor before meeting RAAF operations. The last one was from Richmond giving him some trivial details of the William/Kate flight. He rang down to reception and arranged a special room where they could all have breakfast together. He rang John Sefton and asked him to tell the crew where they needed to go to eat and then he showered and got dressed.

In the breakfast, room before the meal started, he told them all again how important it was not to discuss yesterday's events with anyone without his permission since, for some reason, the RAAF had yet to issue a statement. They needed to be particularly careful at the airport in case there were any reporters about. In addition there was to be no discussion on Walt's statement that there might have been a submarine near the wreckage. He made it clear that it would not be possible to analyse the sonobuoy's responses in the normal way to check if Walt was correct because the mission memory drive would have to go back to Waddington.

He looked at them all. "Something else. We've got a problem. Apparently we're being sent to Canberra direct for a special debriefing which needs to be done immediately." He raised his hands. "I know we've all got our kit in the hotel in Amberley. I'm not sure what we should do." He looked round. "Any ideas."

"Sir," Bill Bailey chipped in, "I could fly down to Amberley from the civil airport and collect all the gear. Presumably we could ship it to Canberra but it would take a long time. Would the RAAF help us? Otherwise it would take probably one or two nights."

Greg thought about it. "Sounds good. I could try and argue with Northwood about going to Amberley but not sure I'd get anywhere."

Mary put her hand up. "I was chatting to a guy from the RAAF Transport Unit who was here last night. They fly freight from Amberley to Canberra almost every night. Perhaps they would take our gear to Canberra."

"That's a good thought. I wonder who to ask?"

Mary carried on. "I might be able to help. I have his number. Shall I call him."

There was an appreciative jeer from the rest of the crew.

"Off you go. Tell someone what you want for breakfast."

She disappeared but came back after ten minutes.

"Hope I did the right thing, Sir. I said I'd go to Amberley and get all the gear from the hotel. Kev will arrange for a truck to pick it and me up and take it all to the aircraft so that it should be in

Canberra to-morrow morning. I thought you wouldn't need me to operate the radar just for the transit to Canberra."

Greg couldn't help smiling. "Yes, you did do the right thing. Who is Kev, the magician, who can apparently arrange everything and when do we see you again?"

"Kev is the pilot of the KC30 and he says in the circumstances I can travel on the plane as well."

Greg tried to reply over the whistles from the crew. Mary was unmoved. "That's absolutely great, Mary. Well done."

Walt held his hand up. "Mary will have to collect the MSS from my room as well as all my gear." He looked at her and grinned. "Two heavy suitcases. Maybe she'll need Kev to help."

The moment breakfast was finished Greg despatched all the crew to the airport and to plan for a 1200 local time departure for Canberra. Up in his room he rang the Air Advisor, Wing Commander Charles Grainger, who confirmed that the aircraft should go direct to Canberra from Townsville as RAAF Central Operations wanted to talk to the crew urgently. Grainger told him that he had arranged rooms in the Novotel since he thought the crew would prefer to be there as it was conveniently placed for the restaurants and shops rather than close to the Commission.

Greg got a cab to take him to the post office after checking out and, to his surprise, he saw Mary French also going in but not in uniform. He couldn't help noticing that her bra was doing a great job underneath a very smart and very thin jumper.

"I thought you were going down with the crew to the airport, Mary?"

She looked at him steadily and it was he who decided to look away. "Yes Sir. But because we did not return to Amberley last night Jane and I needed some stuff from the chemist and I'm taking the opportunity to send a letter home."

"OK. What time is your flight?"

"Noon, Sir. I've checked in already and I've only got this small bag with my uniform and personal things."

Greg was a bit surprised she was not wearing uniform and had got a change of clothes but looking at her and the length of her skirt they clearly hadn't taken up a lot of room in her bag. The heat was almost overpowering and he envied her and wished he didn't have to wear uniform. He waited until she was standing in line to get a stamp for her letter and quickly chose a padded envelope large enough to accommodate the mission memory drive. He sealed it all up, addressed it to Brian Spencer without any comment at all and took his turn in the queue to post the drive to UK intending to declare the contents to be of no commercial value. However, looking at the size of the envelope, he decided that it would be safer if he used the High Commission and got the Air Advisor to send the module with the diplomatic mail. So when his turn came he just paid for the envelope and put it in his bag. As he did so he realised that Mary had been watching him but he decided to make no comment. She got her stamp and asked to share his taxi to the airport. Sitting next to her in the taxi he detected a faint smell of some perfume which surprised him since he was sure that she knew it was not permitted when his crew was on duty. He found the perfume and her bare legs showing well above the knee a little disturbing which was the last thing he needed; he'd had a turbulent marriage which ended in an argumentative divorce a few months previously and he was very cautious about getting involved again. Of course, at that moment Mary was not in the crew and as she was taking a commercial flight he couldn't complain but he found himself wondering if Kev liked perfume.

At the airport Mary left for the civil terminal and Greg found the crew waiting in the RAAF briefing room. He got Tim to file the flight plan for Canberra while John was finishing supervising the refuelling. They went out to the aircraft and left at 1205 arriving four hours later at 5pm local time and were then marshalled to what seemed like a remote part of the airfield.

John looked at Pat. "Where the hell are they taking us?"

"I think the problem could be that the RAAF ramp is full. Maybe because of the Royal visit. You remember originally we were meant to be going straight to the RAAF airfield at Richmond?"

"Well I hope they've got transport."

"John, I think I can see cars and a bus coming this way."

Greg came up to the flight deck to size up the situation. Jane opened the door and lowered the steps. He went down the steps to be greeted first by the UK Air Advisor who was dressed in uniform; he told Greg that the RAAF were taking the loss of the Boeing P8-A not only extremely seriously but also with a high level of security. They had just issued a statement to the press saying that an aircraft had been lost in the Coral Sea with all the crew, near and to the west of Port Moresby.

"Not very precise."

"That's the way the RAAF want it. By the way they didn't mention that you had found the wreckage. I'm sure there's something going on they're not telling us."

"Which reminds me, Sir. I have a package which needs to be sent in the diplomatic bag as fast as we can get it back to the UK."

Grainger looked at him. "May I ask what is in it?"

Greg didn't hesitate in his reply since it was a question he had been expecting but he wasn't prepared to answer with all the Australians about. "It's just the recording of our flight, Sir. Just routine but better if it is transported securely."

Grainger would have liked to have known why it was so important and so secure but he knew now wasn't the time. "OK Greg. I can do that. Now let me introduce you to Group Captain Bob Acton, who is co-ordinating this terrible accident."

They shook hands and Bob explained "Greg, we'd like you all to stay in the RAAF Defence Academy accommodation overnight for debriefing."

Greg realised from his tone of voice that the request was virtually an order. He hesitated. "We're booked in the Novotel, Sir. Thank you for your offer but we'd prefer to go straight there." Greg could see that wasn't the answer that Bob wanted or expected. He could also see that Charles Grainger was looking unhappy and indicating that he should come over and talk to him.

"Greg, I told you the RAAF are extremely sensitive on the loss of this aircraft. They can't order you to go with them but it would save a lot of friction if you agreed."

Greg considered the situation and turned to Bob Acton. "OK Sir. We'll accept your offer of the Academy. However I'm sure you understand that I need to have a chat with the Air Advisor here in the aircraft before we go with you. The other requirement is that I should talk to the UK before we start the debriefing."

Bob Acton didn't look too pleased. "Of course you must talk to Charles, here," he said in a very doubtful manner, "but we would like to do the debriefing straightaway. How are you going to talk to UK?"

"Well I have a phone which I can use that plugs into your system."

Bob considered the situation. "OK. I'm sure we can organise that."

"Fine. We'll have to go back to the aircraft to get all our gear. Won't take long."

He turned and went up the steps and was relieved to see the Air Advisor following him. He told Pat O'Connor to shut the door and he called the crew together. He explained that it would be difficult to avoid the debriefing before going up to the hotel but he reminded them that no-one was to talk about the submarine unless he gave them permission. He then took his nav bag to the flight deck and asked Charles Grainger to join him. "Sir," he reached down to his bag, "this is the package to go in the diplomatic bag to the UK as soon as possible. Normally we could copy memory or even send it using our Mission Support System but it is in Amberley and needs repairing; anyway I'm not sure what facilities you've got in the High Commission. I've marked it so the addressee will know if the packet has been opened. It is very important that the RAAF do not know anything at all about what's in this package."

"Greg, why are you treating this memory with such secrecy?"

"Well Sir, you heard of our suspicions that there was a submarine by the wreckage. We don't want the RAAF taking action and rushing off to try to analyse the mission memory until we know a bit more. Actually I don't believe that their MSS or their fixed equipment could interface with our system but I don't want to take any chances. For us it's standing orders to ensure the mission memory is transmitted and analysed at our base. Obviously this particular mission memory is extremely important as the submarine seems to be a new one, not only to us, but also to the UK."

Charles recognised that Greg was absolutely correct in the way he was proposing to deal with the mission memory. "Greg, we'd better be careful. They might see me with the package. My brief case is in the car."

"You're right, Sir. It will go in with the security stuff in my bag which we're taking with us of course and we'll give it to you later after the debriefing."

They went down the steps again to meet Bob Acton. "Greg, let's go to the briefing room now, we've got a room from which you can telephone."

He went up the steps yet again and told the crew to take all their gear and disembark. Greg led the way carrying his bag and the security bag; the rest of the crew followed him down but this time Greg kept both keys of the aircraft. He just wished he knew why the RAAF couldn't wait until the morning for the de-briefing.

The bus took them to an Australian Defence location in Russell. They all signed in and went into a briefing room. Greg was shown into an office where he could plug in his mobile phone which had a built-in scrambler. He got connected to Northwood Operations and asked for the operations officer dealing with their Australian trip. To his surprise he was put through to an Air Commodore who checked the conversation was being scrambled.

"Tucker, good to hear from you. Saw your signal. This could be very serious. We need to understand if there really was a submarine and, if there was one, from where it came. I gather your mission system didn't recognise it, hostile or friendly. What have you told the Australians?"

Greg decided not to argue about whether there had been a submarine under the wreckage. "Nothing yet Sir. They are mad keen for a debriefing which I'm finding very hard to refuse. I've told my crew not to mention the submarine and explained to them that the mission memory will have to go back to Waddington before the sub is confirmed."

"Well we're not altogether surprised with this situation. We've known for some time from our key guy in the High Commission that something strange has been going on in the Torres Strait which we don't understand. We clearly need to talk to the Australians but let's look at this mission memory drive first." A pause. "You'd better tell the Australian briefing officer that you've been told to wait until the morning for the debriefing. We're

having to consult with our politicians, Tucker, and that takes time."
He added in a hurry. "But don't mention that."

"It's going to be very difficult to explain, Sir."

"Well you'll just have to do the best you can, Tucker. And
Tucker, we need the mission information as quickly as possible."

"Well Sir, normally as you know we could copy the memory
and send it digitally to Northwood and Waddington from our
Mission Support System but it's in Amberley at the moment so the
Air Advisor is arranging for the mission memory drive to go in the
diplomatic bag, Sir."

"Tell him to get it off as soon as he can and advise us."

"Yes, Sir."

Greg rang off without saying anything else but full of questions
he didn't ask. He didn't know what to say for the best. He looked
at Bob Acton. "Sir, I'm in a fix. I've been instructed to delay the
debriefing until to-morrow morning."

"Greg, that's ridiculous."

"I know, but like you, I have to do what I'm told."

Despite the difficulty Bob was very good and arranged for the
whole crew to be taken to the hotel. Charles followed the bus and
went up to Greg's room after Greg had checked in and took the
drive.

"With any luck I'll be able to get it on the morning flight to
London."

"That would be great. The Air Commodore I spoke to said to
get it away as quickly as possible and for you to advise him when
it's on its way. It needs to be got to Waddington for analysis
without delay."

Charles said good night and Greg realised it was still quite
early. He sent a secure signal to Northwood, copied to Brian at
Waddington, saying exactly what he had done with the parcel and
went down to the bar. They had already started a kitty and he put
his fifteen dollars in but warned them they had to be fit and ready
for an early start in the morning. He didn't stay down there long
and went back up to his room and to bed.

* * *

In the morning they all met for breakfast where John had
organised a large table. Halfway through Mary appeared, wearing

45

uniform, with a tall red haired man in an RAAF Flight Lieutenant's uniform; Greg spotted he had a pilot's badge and assumed correctly that this was Kev as Mary introduced him "Thank you so much for helping us."

"It was no problem, Sir. Glad to be of help. Mary here did most of the work getting all the gear from the rooms. The van with it all in will be here in a moment."

Kev agreed to join them for breakfast and brought up two chairs. After breakfast the gear arrived including, Walt was pleased to see the MSS though he knew he had some work to do to get it working. Kev made his farewells and Mary started to go back with him to his car. However Greg decided that Mary, even if she had been up all night, had better attend the debriefing. He took his bags up to his room; looking around he realised with a mixture of surprise and some alarm that someone had been searching through all his gear but to his relief he found nothing was missing. He thought about telling the hotel but reckoned he would be wasting his time.

An RAAF van duly arrived and took them back to the building in Russell. The security seemed just as great as the previous night; they all had to sign in before entering a windowless room. An RAAF Wing Commander Alan Nguyen introduced himself and went through the time table of the Boeing P8-A A34-487 flight from when it left Townsville bound for Port Moresby, to when it failed to give its routine position report. "We started to get worried thirty minutes later when again there was no report and you guys were the closest to the likely spot where the aircraft could have had an accident. So a rapid decision was made to cancel the Fincastle and get you to help. We really appreciated the rapid response time and the speed at which you found the wreckage. Incidentally the wreckage was so concentrated in one place that you might easily have missed it. Your initial search track in fact took you away from the wreckage but you still spotted the wreckage immediately and of course we would like to know how you managed that." He paused. "We wanted to talk with you all to see if you had noticed anything unusual. What was the weather like? We believe there were thunderstorms about. At the moment we think the aircraft must have hit the water for some reason, maybe in a storm but we'll know more very shortly when we've examined the wreckage."

There was a long pause and Greg decided he'd better join in. "We found the wreckage but as you know we couldn't find any bodies or even dinghies. We saw lots of returns on our radar varying from ships in the main channel to others which turned out mostly to be small craft which looked like fishing boats but, of course, we had to check each one as best we could. However, just before we left we saw a ship about ten miles away from where the main wreckage was located in shallow water near the reefs south of the channel; we decided to have a look but we could not identify it in any way. Jane, our IM, tried contacting them but there was no response. We thought they might have seen or heard something."

Nguyen not surprisingly seemed very interested. "Nothing on the stern? No flags? Are you sure?"

"We had a very good look though it was getting dark." Greg pointed at Stan Orwin. "You were one of our visual look-outs, what did you see?"

"Nothing Sir. It looked as if there were no marks at all. Just a helicopter on the rear deck."

Nguyen broke in. "Did you take any photos."

"Yes we did with our hand held cameras and the MX20. The pictures should be on our mission memory as well as on the hand held cameras' memories. We haven't had a chance to look at anything yet. Problem is that our Mission Support System has only just arrived from Amberley and it needs fixing so we're not set up to use it yet. Because we're having to send the mission memory drive to the UK we won't be able to see the good pictures from the MX20 until they've been downloaded at Waddington. Then they will be able to send them to us."

"Well where are the other pictures?"

"Still on the memory sticks in the cameras."

Nguyen looked at Greg. "Can we see them?"

"Of course." He gave one of the aircraft keys to Stan and Nguyen arranged for Stan to get the camera memory sticks. "There will be numerous shots of the wreckage and all the boats we inspected. Stan you had better bring all the memory sticks over. As

I said the MX20 pictures will also be on the mission memory but that will have to go back to the UK for analysis since we can't do it here."

Nguyen carried on after Stan had departed. "We need to see the MX20 as soon as possible. Can't we use our MSS mission analysis recorder?"

"You're very welcome to try but our mission system is rather different from yours, I believe, since it is a later build and we have different radar and acoustic equipment."

"Well we'd like the avionics people from ARDU, our Aircraft Research and Development Unit to come up from Edinburgh Field with a portable mission analysis box to have a go, if we may."

Greg nodded, hoping he would sound convincing. "Well it would be very useful if it did work but we'll have to wait until they send the mission memory back from UK."

Nguyen carried on. "As I mentioned we are very interested in the speed you people found the wreckage, bearing in mind a lot of it was semi-submerged; did you use any special techniques? We know you people have the very latest Ultra sonobuoys."

To Greg's surprise Mary answered, cleverly avoiding any allusion to the sonobuoys. "We've got a very good radar and we chose the optimum height for search."

Nguyen carried on questioning for a few more minutes and then his phone rang. He listened and came over to Greg. "Your man Stan says the aircraft has been broken into, the door lock has been forced and the portable camera memory sticks have been taken".

Chapter 4

Greg could hardly believe what he'd heard about the loss of the camera memories. It clearly wasn't his day."Alan, can you get me over there as soon as possible?"

"Sure, I'll take you over."

They went over to Alan's car while the rest of the crew remained in the briefing room. About twenty minutes later they got to the aircraft, still positioned a long way from the RAAF facilities; it was being air conditioned from a truck and the temperature was just about bearable. Stan tried to speak to Greg without Nguyen hearing but it proved impossible and Greg decided he didn't want to stir up trouble by sending Nguyen away. "Well Sir, as you can see the cover for the steps controls has been forced open so that the stairs could be lowered and the aircraft door lock has been broken."

"What's been taken?"

"The hand held cameras are still here but their memory sticks have gone."

"What about the mission memory drive with all the pictures from the MX20."

"That's been taken as well."

"Any of the aircraft's documents?"

"Nothing else seem to have been taken, Sir, but I haven't made a complete check against the inventory."

"Well carry on Stan and let me know if you come across anything else."

Nguyen looked at Stan. "I'm arranging for the police to come over and inspect the aircraft. You will need to explain exactly where the thieves went. I expect they will want to take a lot of fingerprints so don't touch things any more where they've been."

Nguyen looked at Greg thoughtfully and then at Stan. "I think we need to have a serious talk. Let's go back to the briefing room."

"Sounds good. We can decide what to do. Meantime we need some repairs to our door if you can help us with that and, of course, real security round the aircraft. Would it help if we moved it?"

49

"Yes, it would but we've got no room on our ramp. I'm arranging for a special guard from now on."

On the way back Nguyen looked at Greg. "Forgive me for saying this but I don't believe you guys are telling us the whole story. Something happened when you were doing the search which you are holding back. You must admit this break-in is too remarkable a coincidence. The robbers knew exactly what they wanted. I think they were looking for more than you've told me. They've even taken the mission memory."

Greg looked back at Nguyen. "Maybe we would be more forthcoming with you if you were being open with us. We get the feeling from the way you scrambled us to find the aircraft and the accuracy of the initial search position that you knew not only that something had gone wrong but roughly where it had occurred. You feared the worst for some reason. I suggest we both confer with our own people and meet again on common ground, if you know what I mean."

As Greg and Nguyen arrived back at the RAAF building Greg got a call from someone called Stephen Wentworth asking him to come to the High Commission, which suited Greg as he was beginning to feel that he was getting out of his depth and needed local help. He briefed the crew and told them that they should all go to the aircraft, look for further signs of the break-in and then return to the hotel. Alan then arranged for a car to take Greg to the High Commission.

Greg felt rather small and unimportant as he went through the first, obviously very strong, sliding security gate and then, when that had closed, through an almost identical second gate. He signed in and walked through splendid well tended grounds into the air conditioned reception area. He tried to relax and get cool in the comfortable upholstered leather chairs. Some minutes later Stephen Wentworth appeared, slightly built, medium height and wearing a very smart dark grey lightweight suit; he led the way up to the top floor past some very imposing offices into a slightly smaller but definitely not insignificant one; there was someone in an outer office who Greg took to be a male assistant or possibly a secretary.

They sat down on a settee and Stephen arranged for coffee and water to appear.

"Well how are things going? Perhaps I should explain that I am the focus for all aspects of intelligence in the High Commission." Greg looked at the card that Stephen held out for him and saw Stephen's job title as Head of Security, UK High Commission. He clearly was up to speed on the P8-U flight and what had happened in Canberra. Greg got the impression that he probably knew a lot more than Charles, on the very basic 'need to know' principle.

"Thank goodness you phoned. I needed to tell someone. The aircraft has been broken into and the memories stolen. Even more concerning my room in the hotel was searched while I was having breakfast."

There was real concern in Stephen Wentworth's voice. "That's incredible. What was actually taken? I thought you gave Charles Grainger the memory drive to send to UK. You call it the mission memory, is that right? He tells me it is on its way to the UK to be analysed."

Greg nodded. "Yes, thank goodness for that. It's the robbery of the camera memories and the fact that my room was searched that is worrying me. Clearly someone wanted to prevent our recordings being analysed. It is the speed of their reaction that is frightening. Did you know that we think there was a submarine right under where the aircraft was lost?"

Stephen nodded. "Obviously the Australians are very worried about the loss of their P8-A. The initial information that I got was that they thought the pilot made a mistake and got too low searching, perhaps in bad weather; apparently every time they think they hear a contact they drop an active sonobuoy, lose height and fly very low level over the sea using their magnetic anomaly detector."

"Well they'll soon know, if they don't know already, what caused the aircraft to crash. There were no thunderstorms about so I don't know why the pilot would make a mistake. I think it's significant that they knew where to find the aircraft."

"You know more about these things than I do but surely the aircraft was probably on a set plan. Again my information says that it had been patrolling the area for some time searching for submarines. They probably had been talking to the aircraft on a strict schedule and that's how they knew roughly where it should have been."

"I suppose you're right. Hitting the water would explain why there was no communication. I know it sounds ridiculous but I wondered whether it could have been shot down."

Stephen looked doubtful. "Surely not. Who would want to do that?"

"Don't know but the wreckage was very close together."

"You know all this regular patrolling by the P8-As up north seemed to start with a boat the RAN intercepted and sank about two months ago."

"What happened then?"

"One of their patrol boats in the middle of the night saw and chased a suspicious small boat which might have been carrying asylum seekers but turned out to be an inflatable. The boat starting firing at them and the RAN boat was forced to return fire. All of a sudden the boat seemed to explode and then sink; later five bodies were recovered."

"Where had the boat come from?"

"The official hand out says they don't know and in spite of two months having gone by we still haven't been told the ethnicity of the bodies though I understand that they were severely mutilated by the explosion."

"Interesting it was an inflatable, perhaps it came from a submarine though from a boat would be more likely. You may well be right linking the searching and loss of the aircraft to something else. Anyway we recorded the sonobuoy returns and hopefully it won't be too long before we know a bit more about the submarine under the wreckage. I've sent it to my boss at Waddington who will arrange for detailed analysis. We should be able to find out if the returns were actually compatible with a submarine being present and furthermore, if there was one, then we should be able to tell whose submarine it was, United States, Russian, Japanese, Chinese, North Korean, you name it. Anyway," he looked at Stephen, "we're convinced that there was a submarine there. We must have alerted them with our active sonobuoy and somehow they knew it was our aircraft and broke in to my room as well as the aircraft to get the memories. It seems unbelievable. By the way, I haven't told anybody that my room had been searched."

Stephen nodded. "Presumably after searching the aircraft they realised they didn't have the memory for the mission recorder so they looked in your room."

"They were taking a hell of a risk. They must have been waiting for me to go down to breakfast."

"How did they know you had the memory? They could have just taken the one in the recorder."

Greg looked at Stephen; it was a question he should have thought of himself. They couldn't possibly have known. He got his mobile out and called Stan. "Any more news on the memories? You haven't found them I suppose?"

"No, Sir. I didn't tell you when Nguyen was with you but there wasn't a memory in the mission recorder for the thieves to take. They must have been very upset."

"What do you mean? I told you to put one in."

"I couldn't. We only had one spare and it was in my bag in Amberley. You'd gone by the time I realised what had happened and I didn't have the chance later to tell you."

"Stan, but how do you know they looked for the mission recorder?"

"There are two screws missing from the cover plate and I found one on the floor."

"No worries, Stan. You've explained something."

Greg looked at Stephen. "Did you follow that? There was no memory module in the recorder. So presumably whoever robbed the aircraft was told to look in my room."

"The Australians knew there had been a robbery. Did they know about your room being searched?"

"No, as I said, nobody knows except you and I."

"Well please don't tell anybody." Stephen considered the situation. "No wonder the Australians are worried. It confirms their view that the aircraft was destroyed in some way. They must know by now how the aircraft crashed since they've looked at the wreckage." He looked at Greg. "Did Northwood explain why the analysis is so important and why they didn't want you to talk to the Australians in detail?"

"No, I assumed it was vital to find out whose submarine it was but I would have thought that could have waited."

Stephen got a fairly small scale Admiralty chart out. "Show me where you found the wreckage and searched."

Greg pointed out the exact position. "You do realize you were outside the Australian Economic Zone."

"What does that mean?"

"Well it means that the P8-A crashed outside Australian territorial waters, except of course that in this case the Australians have an agreement with Papua New Guinea so I imagine the exact location in this area doesn't matter. Mind you as I said, I'm not clear why the aircraft was searching this area."

"What are we going to do about finding out how the Australians are getting on with discovering who did the break-in? Problem is we were, and still are, parked a long way from the RAAF ramp and in an area that is probably outside their routine security arrangements. Nevertheless I can't understand how anybody could wander all over the military ramp without getting caught. More disturbing, how could the people breaking in know that it was the aircraft that did the search? How could they possibly know where the aircraft came from and where it was going?"

"If we knew the latter points I think we'd have a much better chance of finding the robbers. I think we must assume that either the ship you saw or the sub was listening to your radio conversations."

"Our radar operator thought she saw a return which might have been their radio antennae. They could have heard us, I suppose, though a bit unlikely as we were using satellite frequencies; wait a moment, come to think of it, we did call the boat on both VHF and UHF. And of course we spoke to the refuelling tanker on UHF."

"Well then they might have known that you were going to Townsville. One of them, or both I suppose, would have told whoever was controlling them that you had pinged them. Would they have known that you checked them again with the passive sonobuoys?"

"Not unless they were able to listen above the water. Mind you it's a bit of a coincidence that it dived as we approached. Maybe they did hear us or they had a radar antenna up but I would have thought that that was unlikely."

"Well clearly it was vital from their viewpoint, for some reason, that they were not discovered so they needed to find the aircraft and remove the recordings you made. Did you use the same callsign going to Canberra as you did searching for the Boeing aircraft?" Greg nodded. "OK, so it wouldn't be too difficult for them to know where you were going to be."

"But Stephen, their technology must be right up to date. To know that we would be recording them and then know what to do to try to get the memory modules I find very alarming; search the aircraft, take all the camera memories, find the mission recorder memory module missing and then have a go at my room. It was very fortunate I had removed the vital one and given it to Charles."

"You do yourself an injustice."

Greg smiled. "Maybe, but we're clearly dealing with a very capable organisation whose agenda we don't understand. It smacks of 911 and the Trade Center to me."

"You have a point in that either the people on the sub and/or the boat must have people here as well. However I can't believe it is Al Qaeda. Remember every country in the world pretty well has an embassy or some sort of organisation right here. It would be very easy for the operator of the sub to contact Canberra and get their people to enter the aircraft."

"But surely the Australian police should be looking for the people or person who broke in?"

"Yes, but it must be like looking for a needle in a haystack."

"Well they took a lot of finger prints. They might be able to track the thieves down from that."

"Possibly, but somebody who was clever enough to break in and remove the memory sticks would almost certainly be wearing gloves and not be in the Australian finger print database anyway."

***

"Yes, PM," Jack Smithson was not enjoying all the recent calls he was having from the Prime Minister. "We've just heard. Our P8-A was shot down by a missile. It wasn't a mistake by the pilot flying too low."

"But why would anyone want to shoot our aircraft down?"

"Maybe Al Qaeda. They don't like us supporting the Americans in the Middle East."

"We don't have any troops there any more apart from a few instructors. It doesn't make sense. Anyway if it was them they must have a boat. The Navy are still checking for illegal boats?"

"Yes, PM, and they've not spotted anything unusual."

"Jack, that inflatable that your people sank a couple of months ago. Did you decide where that came from?"

"We think it must have come from a submarine, presumably Chinese or possibly North Korean though apparently the experts could not confirm the definite ethnicity from examining the corpses because the bodies were so mutilated by the explosion."

"What was the purpose of the explosives on board the inflatable, Jack?"

"Well, PM, maybe it planned to blow something up?"

"Alright, then maybe it was a submarine that shot our P8-A down."

"You're right PM. We're wondering if the Pom plane saw or detected one."

"But surely they would have told us if they thought there was a sub there?"

"Maybe they were worried it was one of theirs."

"They would know if it was one of theirs, but would they have a sub out here without telling us?"

"They might, PM, if they thought we were hiding something from them."

"Surely they'd ask us first? They wouldn't dare go into our territorial waters without telling us."

"But they might go into PNG's water. Those guys don't tell us everything, especially if money's involved."

"But a Pom sub wouldn't shoot our aircraft down."

"Agree with you there."

"Well what are we going to do? The press are after us. The opposition are smelling blood. We must find out who shot our aircraft down. Jack, I'm looking to you to find out."

"We may need help from the ASIO or from the other lot."

"That's what they are there for."

Chapter 5

Maureen Chester, the UK Minister of Defence, sat at her desk looking at the latest TOP SECRET brief. The paper made it clear that the UK intelligence had suspected for sometime that the Australian Government knew something unusual had been happening somewhere in the Torres Strait ever since one of the Royal Australian Navy patrol boats had destroyed an inflatable about two months previously. Unusually, the Australians had said very little about the boat except that they thought it might have come from China which, allegedly, the Chinese Government had vehemently denied. However, since then, the RAAF had been using their P8-As to search the area on a regular basis. Consequently, with the agreement of Papua New Guinea, which was fortunately a member of the Commonwealth, a Royal Navy fleet submarine, *Audacious*, Astute Class nuclear powered, had been sent to the area; the PNG government was pleased to agree to keep the visit confidential as relations between the Australian and PNG governments were going through a tricky time because of immigration and other matters. The submarine captain had been told to keep in Papua New Guinea waters as far as was possible.

The situation had now escalated in that the RAAF had lost one of their searching aircraft and the UK was involved because it was an RAF P8-U that had been used to search for the wreckage and survivors; it had found not only the wreckage but had discovered that there was almost certainly a submarine beneath it. The crew had recorded the event and the mission memory drive had just arrived in UK which would probably confirm the presence of the submarine and identify the country involved. What was making the situation uncomfortably delicate was the fact that it was just possible that the submarine could be the *Audacious* though very unlikely as the mission system on the RAF aircraft would have recognised it straightaway. Once the memory had been analysed and double checked that the submarine detected was not the *Audacious,* a decision was required on whether the UK should confide completely in the Australians.

The Minister called in Harry Brown, her chief secretary. "Harry, how much did we and do we know about what is happening in the Torres Strait? Do we think there is any connection with that boat that was blown up by the Australian Navy a few weeks back? Isn't the place where the aircraft was lost close to where the Australians sank that other boat which exploded?" Harry was almost scared the way the Minister seemed to remember everything that was put in front of her. He had to be on his toes all the time. "Remarkable coincidence. What are our allies telling us?"

"Well Minister we agree it is a remarkable coincidence but we haven't found a connection yet. To be frank, we don't know what is going on but we certainly need to find out."

"Harry, whenever anybody in this building says to me 'to be frank', for some reason I'm always on my guard."

"Well Minister," he risked a grin as he knew the TV programme 'Yes, Minister' was still compulsive viewing in the corridors of power, "you couldn't possibly expect me to comment. But what is required now is a decision on how frank we are to be with the Australians. At the moment we haven't told them that there was a possibility of there being a submarine underneath the wreckage and, likewise, they haven't told us anything."

"But Harry, the Australians will have examined the wreckage by now. They will know whether the aircraft just hit the sea or whether it was shot down. If it was shot down they will be very cross with us when we tell them about the submarine. I take it that we are not going to tell them that the submarine might be ours?"

"Yes, Minister." the Minister raised her eyebrows, "I mean No, Minister. We're definitely not going to tell them that." He looked at his notes. "Apparently our submarine is trying to keep in deep water so it is most unlikely it is ours. The actual Strait is too shallow for nuclear subs."

The Minister pointed at her brief. "But they are not fools, Harry. This brief says our aircraft was broken into and the camera memories stolen. The Australians must know there was a recording for those clever listening buoys and the radar."

"Of course, Minister. The worrying thing is that someone tried to steal the mission recorder from the aircraft as well as the camera memories but luckily the aircraft captain had realised how important it was and had taken it from the aircraft and got the Air Advisor to send it to the UK. Apparently the Captain's room was searched but he had already got rid of the memory to the Air Advisor. The Australians have been told that the mission memory is on its way back to UK for analysis."

"Well clearly the submarine must have alerted someone and a decision was taken somewhere to raid our aircraft. Harry, this is a very dangerous situation. The submarine clearly wasn't ours though I agree we must check. Apparently we're dealing with very audacious people. People who can organise a break-in into our aircraft with very little notice. Harry, this is a no brainer, we must work rapidly with the Australians to sort it out but I don't want any publicity." She stopped for a moment. "Have you asked them yet why the aircraft crashed?"

"Not yet but we intend to do so. Of course we are in the hands of the Australians, Minister, when it comes to what they tell us and the publicity. And to be quite frank again Minister, we think the Australians are not being open with us."

"Well they probably know that we're not being frank with them. So, no publicity and a complete exchange of information will be the conditions if we are to co-operate. However, if it is confirmed that there was a sub underneath the wreckage then we must tell the Australians straightaway regardless." She thought for a moment. "That P8-U crew and the Captain, they seem to have done a good job. We should recognise it when this problem is sorted."

"Yes, Minister."

Brown went back to his office and called the Head of Operations in Northwood where the Minister's brief had been written. "You can tell our people in Canberra to be ready to work with the Australians providing they are equally confiding with us. Obviously, as a first priority, we need to be finding out why their aircraft crashed. However, we also need to decide how we are going to liaise with the Australians, at what level. Of course we can't do anything with the Australian Defence Force until we know that the submarine wasn't ours and hopefully we've discovered whose submarine it was."

***

Brian Spencer was not surprised when he got a message from MOD in London telling him that there was an urgent package which had come in very late the previous night. He had realised straightaway that the loss of the Boeing P8-A with a submarine on the spot was going to be treated at the top level with the highest level of security. The packet was being flown to Waddington and was going to be with him by mid morning. He had alerted the analysis team to be ready but had given them no indication of where the memory drive had come from. Shortly afterwards operations in Northwood called saying he was to treat the results of the analysis of the package as top secret and to let them know immediately. They reaffirmed that the analysis team must not know from where the module had come.

He met the aircraft, signed for the package and went to the analysis section. The mission memory drive was plugged into the system and then the flight was examined in detail. As a first priority the sonobuoy records were examined but the noises recorded by the passive buoys were clearly not familiar to the analysis team. "Yes, there is a submarine there. It is very quiet and it sounds like an AIP machine. It's definitely not nuclear. In the active echo mode the return is very strong – it must be a big machine. We never would have detected the noise from the sub with a normal sonobuoy. Those new passive ones are spectacular."

"Any idea who made the machine?"

"No idea at all, Sir. I don't think it's French. Could be German."

Brian asked for a full report to be sent to him as soon as possible with a separate file made of all the MX20 photographs when they had been extracted from the mission memory. Back in his office he called Northwood and passed the information on. Then he called the MOD contact in London who had sent him the mission memory to establish where to send the report and photographs. He felt out of the loop and envied Greg and his crew.

***

In Northwood the information was passed to Harry Brown in the Defence Minister's Office and he immediately informed the High Commissioner's office in Canberra. Robert Fotheringay, the new High Commissioner, got the message in the morning from Clive Perkins, his senior civil servant, and they decided to call in

Stephen Wentworth and Brigadier Timothy Whetstone, the Defence Advisor.

"Clive, let me see if I understand the situation properly. We believe that something strange has been going on in the Torres Strait as evidenced by the Australians frequently sending aircraft there to monitor the area. It seemed to start after that inflatable boat had been blown up. Have you asked them what the problem might be?"

Clive looked at Stephen Wentworth who provided the response.

"Well, Sir, my ADF contact says that they've seen Chinese naval boats and French submarines in the area."

"Are they allowed between Australia and Papua New Guinea?"

"There is an international two way route between the two countries. Australia not only looks after their side but helps PNG to look after their waters. However the water is pretty shallow for submerged submarines. Anyway the Australians would need to be informed for any foreign naval boats to get permission to go into their territorial waters."

"It says in this brief that we have suspected for some time that something strange has been going on in the Torres Strait between both Indonesia and Papua New Guinea to the North and Queensland to the South. It seems that on our part, because we had nothing really firm to go on, we sent, as an exercise, one of our nuclear powered fleet submarines, *Audacious*, to cruise round the area and go into PNG waters without telling the Australians. Isn't that a bit unusual?"

Stephen nodded. "Yes, Sir. But our intelligence people felt it was very important to try to find out what was going on. Hopefully the news of our sub won't leak to the Australians."

"Then it says here that a few days ago an RAAF Boeing P8-A crashed in the suspected area and one of our P8-U aircraft discovered not only the wreckage of the Boeing but also a submarine lurking underneath the wreckage. The noise emanating from this submarine has been examined and our experts don't recognise the sub but it might be an AIP type. What does that mean, Timothy?"

"Well High Commissioner, AIP means Air Independent Propulsion so that the submarine is almost undetectable underwater if it's not moving and very hard to find even if it is."

"Well then how did we detect it?"

"Well, Sir, apparently our aircraft used a very special and expensive new sonobuoy to find the wreckage of the P8-A and discovered the submarine at the same time. So It went back and did some more checking with two passive listening sonobuoys of the latest design made by Ultra Electronics; it was able not only to confirm the contact but also record its characteristic noise or signature, since it was clearly a new type and not in the mission memory database."

Even though he knew the loss of the Boeing was very important Robert Fotheringay tried to accelerate the outcome of the meeting as he had another meeting to attend to decide how to organise Prince William's visit to Canberra and Sydney. He looked at them all. "So what are they going to do with this information in Whitehall? Are these AIP submarines very common? How many countries have them? Maybe it was a French one? Don't they have a naval base in Nouema, New Caledonia? Chaleix or something like that? More importantly, when are we going to admit to the Australians that our submarine was in the area? And presumably still is."

Clive recognised the 'let's get the meeting over' signs. "Well Sir, you are right and the French do have a naval base there but there's no reason to believe it's their sub. In fact the experts don't believe it is a French one. We're waiting to hear from London whether or not we should tell the Australians about the submarine our P8-U heard. The experts in the UK are going to make a copy of the memory drive and send the original back in case we want to give it to the Australians though we don't believe they will be able to listen to it with their US manufactured equipment without some help from the US manufacturer. What we will do for sure is to ask them if they would like our help in any way."

Fotheringay turned back to Timothy Whetstone. "What could we do to help?"

"Well Sir, that rather depends on how forthcoming the Australians are. I've been assured that we could make our P8-U, which is currently here in Canberra, available for more searching with our latest sonobuoys in the area; obviously Ultra who make the buoys are very keen that we should do that so that the Australians will see how good they are and start buying them."

"That sounds very sensible."

"Another thing we could do is to send one of our spy planes out."

"Spy planes?"

"I think they are called Airseekers but in fact everybody calls them Boeing Rivet Joints."

"Well Tim, don't we need to be working with them right now?

"Yes, High Commissioner, but I think first we'll have to tell them about the submarine by the wreckage and wait and see what information the ADF releases to the press. Certainly they won't need to know we have a nuclear sub cruising round; anyway, I'm told it's not all that deep where the sub was discovered so it's unlikely to be our sub. Besides, the moment we start telling anything to the Australian politicians everything will leak to the media as it always does. Just like UK."

"You're right there. So who is going to feed the info in if we do tell them about the submarine?"

Stephen joined in again.

"Well Sir, when we have received a copy of the memory drive we propose to give it to the captain of the P8-U to give to the people he has been talking to. We won't have to admit that way what we know and what we are doing. However we will tell them about there being a submarine underneath the P8-A wreckage."

"They aren't going to be terribly pleased that we didn't tell our closest ally straightaway."

Clive responded. "The Foreign Office likes to think that the United States is our closest ally, High Commissioner."

"I've been based in Washington as well as here and there's no contest. That's why I don't like telling lies, certainly not when I'm going to be found out."

"The problem is that the Boeing P8-A may well have been shot down so that's why we must tell them about the sub. If they don't know about it they are bound to search every boat they can find."

"Well if it was shot down then maybe it was that boat without any identification."

Timothy Whetstone chipped in. "I'm told it was far too far away, Sir."

"Not with a missile, surely?"

Clive ignored the remark.

"Sir, London has a decision to make. Whether we tell our friends that there was a submarine down there."

Stephen felt he should try and help. "Well Sir, we really have no alternative but to tell them about the submarine as quickly as possible. We didn't tell them straight away because we had to tell UK first. They will have discovered whether the aircraft was shot down by now or whether the pilot hit the water by mistake."

Robert Fotheringay looked at Stephen for a moment. "You're right of course. Let's do that Clive. You'd better tell London that we believe that we should tell the Australians."

Clive smiled. "Yes, High Commissioner, but don't you think it would be best if you told London?"

"No Clive, you know that would be the wrong chain of communication. You must explain." He stopped. "But wait a moment, Clive. The P8-U crew can't help. Surely they're about to fly Prince William and Kate to Sydney. I've got to meet the Royals here from New Zealand together with the Australian PM and the Governor General and then they are staying in the Royal Suite of the Governor General's place overnight. I'm taking them rubbernecking round this place including the splendid War Memorial before holding a meeting with key businessmen here. The timing won't work."

"That will be alright, Sir. It will take a couple of days before we get the memory drive back. Hopefully nothing else will happen before then."

"Alright. Thank you for telling me and keep me informed. If you find the French are drilling for oil in the middle of the Torres Strait I'd like to know."

Clive put on a dutiful smile.

***

Charles Grainger called Greg at the hotel. "Greg, Prince William comes in to-morrow morning as you know from New Zealand, not to Sydney as originally planned, but here in Canberra. They're staying in the Governor General's House overnight and the plan now is for you to fly the Duke and Duchess to Kingsford Smith Airport from here but only after you've done a tour first round Sydney harbour."

"That sounds fine Sir, but you do know we'll only have four spare seats."

"Can't you leave some of your crew behind? It's a non-operational flight."

"Not very keen. We're a crew and every person has a function in an emergency. I would have thought that will be particularly important for a Royal flight."

Charles decided not to press the point. "Alright I'll find out who you'll be taking. Apparently the flight is planned to last for an hour and a half."

"Fine. I'll need permission to fly over and round Sydney from Air Services Australia."

"Why don't you find out who to call there from your RAAF contacts or from Canberra Flight planning? Do you know where you are going? Have you been to Sydney before?"

"Yes, Sir. Thought we'd start by the airport, look at Bondi beach, fly round the Heads, avoid the Zoo, circle the Bridge, Circular Quay and the Opera House, then up river to Darling Harbour and then round back to the airport."

"Sounds perfect. Wish I was coming with you."

When the phone call was finished Greg went to the airport to check on the state of the aircraft. He had sent the four rear crew down the day before to show some people Nguyen had sent round from where the memories had been taken and generally inspect the aircraft. Luckily Wyn Williams, a crew chief from Waddington who had just arrived as planned to double check on the aircraft's serviceability and readiness for the Royal Flight, had managed to arrange to have the aircraft cleaned so that it looked in mint condition and he had also had both the aircraft door lock and the cover for the steps controls repaired. While Greg was checking all his gear Charles called him on his mobile.

"Australian Security want to crawl all over the aircraft to-morrow morning before the flight."

"No worries, Sir, but they had better be early and they had better not make a mess. It's looking really good at the moment. Have you managed to find out who is flying?"

"Yes, Greg. The Prince, Kate, the High Commissioner and some nameless guy who presumably is a guard."

"No equerry then?"

"The guy's going to be a pilot on this flight. He'll be fine without his equerry."

"Will the guard have a gun on him?"

"I've no idea. Does it matter?"

"Well I suspect there are all sorts of rules about carrying guns but we'll just forget I asked you." He carried on. "Do you want any photos? I'll get the ESM operator to take plenty; we've managed to get replacement memories for the hand held cameras, but we're still waiting for some spare drives for the acoustic recorder to come from Waddington, not that it matters for this trip."

"The British Airways 777 that is carrying the Royal Party and the press will be leaving just after you for Sydney but will land first while you're rubber necking round Sydney."

After Charles had rung off Greg told John Sefton, who had arrived with Pat, about the passengers, what he wanted for the flight and to calculate the fuel required. "You might as well refuel for the round trip so we can get back quickly to Canberra. By the way where are you putting the Prince?"

"Well I thought I'd put him in the right hand seat with Pat in the jump seat to make certain there are no hiccups. That will ensure we can cover all system emergencies because Pat will be able to reach everything."

"Fine. We'll get Kate to sit in the port look-out seat so she gets a good view, the High Commissioner in the Starboard look out and the guard in the spare seat in the sonobuoy area."

***

The next day Greg kept the crew at the hotel. With the Royal Flight about to happen he was absolutely sure the aircraft was being guarded properly and that the repaired lock wouldn't be broken again. Brian sent him a message saying that the original module was being sent back to him but didn't give any details of the analysis. Brian called him before going to bed, scrambling the conversation. "What was on the module, Sir?"

"I'm not sure if you're meant to know, Greg. I think the plot may be for you to give the module to the Australians to see what they discover. Hopefully they will tell you."

"Brian, that doesn't make sense. I don't believe they will be able to use the mission memory module because their system is different from ours."

"Yes, you're right. It was definitely a submarine and probably an AIP machine, identity of country unknown."

"Good Lord. Maybe it's French. They have a base not too far away."

"Apparently our experts don't think it's a French one."

Greg went to bed watching the TV of the Royal Visit. It always amazed him how fascinated the Australians were both with the Royal family and with English football.

In the morning the crew arrived at the airport in plenty of time and John taxied the aircraft to the VIP park. Greg had agreed with Charles that the royal party would use the aircraft's steps since the P8-U was not suitable for moving fingers from the terminal, unlike the British Airway's 777 which was in position to take the rest of the Royal party to Sydney. They arrived on time with lots of photographers. Greg had decided to wait at the bottom of the steps to meet the Prince, who arrived wearing an ordinary lounge suit while Kate sensibly had a trouser suit on. The High Commissioner did the introductions and Greg led the way up.

William decided he wanted to look round the aircraft and was clearly in no hurry. "I haven't been in one of these before."

Greg introduced the crew and each one had to explain what they did. The Prince was clearly very impressed with the size and capability of the displays and the fact that all the crew members could select the other crew members displays though normally they would be using their own specialist display. When they came to the Acoustic displays the High Commissioner looked around "You have a recorder I believe so that you can find submarines and the noises can be analysed later? Where do you keep that?" Walt looked impressed and pointed it out while William looked surprised but said nothing. They moved on to the sonobuoy launch area and the virtues of the various buoys were explained.

The High Commissioner again joined in. "I understand that you've got some very special new buoys."

"Yes, Sir. Ultra have given us their latest buoys to evaluate. This is an active one and this is a passive one."

"I gather that they enabled you to find the wreckage of the RAAF P8."

Walt nodded, wondering how much the High Commissioner knew and whether he was going to mention the suspected submarine. William again looked surprised but Walt couldn't make up his mind whether it was because of the Commissioner's knowledge of the sonobuoy information or whether, being a well trained RAF Officer, William didn't think the High Commissioner should be discussing the matter.

Greg led the way back to the flight deck and noticed that Kate had been talking to Mary and Jane. William accepted the offer of sitting in the right hand seat after checking that everything could be managed by John with Pat in the jump seat. "These pilot displays are amazing and the view outside is so much better than a civil airliner."

John was busy starting the engines but Pat responded. "We need the view to be able to search and track our targets, Sir." They had positioned the aircraft at the end of the terminal so a tractor was not needed and John was able to taxi forward and then turn to get on the taxiway. Greg went back to his seat and for once was able to relax for a bit.

Once the aircraft was clear of the Canberra circuit John offered the wheel to William.

"I wasn't expecting a wheel. I thought the aircraft would have a side stick controller."

"I'm no expert, Sir, but I can't see Boeing ever changing to side sticks or Airbus going back to a control column unless there was some safety reason which required a change. The accident records of both manufacturer's aircraft are fantastically good and both justify their choice of wheels or side stick controllers on the marketing grounds of better pilot interface."

William thought for a moment. "I gather you found the wreckage of that RAAF P8 that was lost the other day. Do you know what happened to it? That was a terrible tragedy."

"We've no idea, Sir, what caused the aircraft to go into the sea. The wreckage was all together though. The Australians should know by now but they seem to be treating the whole affair with the highest security." John couldn't help smiling. "Perhaps they'll tell you in advance of their next press release, Sir. As you can imagine, we searched for a long time for survivors but couldn't find any."

"Did you have dinghies and survival gear on board?"

John remembered that William had spent a lot of time on Search and Rescue helicopters. "No, in fact we didn't. We were taking part in a 'find the submarine' competition and all we had were flare markers."

"Did you win? The Australians are pretty good with their P8-As aren't they?"

"I think we were definitely winning; we had found the target sub and were about to drop the active sonobuoys when we were told we had to stop in order to search for the their P8-A. Apparently we were sent because we were the closest aircraft and had enough fuel to start searching."

"You must have had a lot of fuel on board. The distances round Australia are huge."

"Actually we didn't have that much but the Australians sent a tanker to refuel us."

"Quite a trip for you then by the time you had finished?"

"Yes Sir. But it's a great aircraft. We really love it."

"I believe your sonobuoys are brand new with a very good performance."

"Yes. Ultra have done a marvellous job though we like to think we would have won anyway with our standard buoys."

Greg, listening to the conversation from his seat, wasn't sure how much the Prince would have been told but he decided not to interrupt John.

John took over the aircraft as they approached Sydney and he pointed out the landmarks as they orbited the harbour at 2,000 ft; it was just as well they had been able to negotiate this lower altitude below the standard minimum height because as it was they were only just below a thin layer of cloud. They landed towards the city and taxied to the VIP ramp. William was very appreciative, as was Kate. The Prince's equerry met the Prince at the top of the steps but, before leaving, William and Kate went round the crew thanking each one of them. The person in charge of publicity rushed up the steps after the VIPs had left and asked for the photos and Stan gave him the memory sticks, requesting for them to be returned if possible.

The crew relaxed once the Royal Party had left; the moment John got clearance from Air Traffic they restarted the engines and returned to Canberra where there was a message for Greg to go round to Charles Grainger when he was free. He went straight to the High Commission and they chatted about the flight.

"Greg, here's the memory drive that you sent to Waddington. We'd like you to talk to your contact, give it to him and tell him about the submarine. We've got no more details on the sub like who owns it and what type it was, I'm afraid; just that it's almost certainly AIP and not nuclear.

"He won't be terribly pleased that I didn't tell him straightaway."

"You didn't know straightaway. It all had to be confirmed. Stephen will be getting a file from Waddington with all the pictures taken from the MX20 to give to them."

Chapter 6

I had thought no more about the loss of the Boeing until a day or two later on Charlie's birthday when she had come home early and we were in the Commonwealth Club for a meal. The UK Air Advisor Charles Grainger, who I knew quite well, was there with a group of people who turned out to be the crew of the P8-U that I had seen parked in the airport. He introduced us to them all. They were clearly relaxing after their Royal trip which had taken place the previous day. By chance I found I was talking to John Sefton who explained that he was the first pilot of the aircraft but not the captain.

"How did it go? Did William fly the aircraft?"

"Yes he did. I let him fly from Canberra to the coast before I took over to fly round the harbour. Apparently he was expecting a side stick controller so I explained that both Boeing and Airbus aircraft have excellent accident records and it really didn't matter whether you had a side stick controller or a wheel. I suspect he must have flown recently in various flavours of Airbuses. The P8-U is a lovely aircraft to fly and he spent most of the time trying to understand the advanced displays that we have and the interlink with the navigators' displays in the back. He must have been told that we had found the RAAF Boeing P8-A and, of course, as he was in a Search and Rescue helicopter squadron he was very interested in its loss, what we saw and whether we were carrying dinghies."

I decided not to react to the new piece of information that the P8-U had found the wreckage. "Did you look for survivors?"

"Yes we did but as you must know we had no luck. The wreckage was very close together and if there had been any survivors they would have been near the wreckage, I'm sure."

A rather attractive girl who turned out to be the radar operator had been listening to John talking to me. She looked at me. "Excuse me for mentioning it but I'm not sure that it has been announced that we found their P8-A. It can't matter but the RAAF release on the loss of the aircraft forgot to mention it. I know you're not a news reporter but at the moment it would be better if you didn't advertise our part in the search."

I smiled. "How do you know I'm not a reporter?"

She came straight back. "Because I recognised your name. You're an aviation insurance investigator."

"Yes, you're quite right. But don't worry, I'm not investigating this one. If I were I'd be asking a lot of questions." She raised her eyebrows. "You know the sort of thing. If it was a simple accident why has the reason for the crash not been announced? Why was the position of the accident not clearly stated? Might it have been shot down? Was there any connection with the inflatable dinghy that was sunk in the same area some weeks earlier? And a lot more besides. But as you probably, know I work with the airlines."

I could see she was thinking of developing the conversation but then decided not to. "But I'm sure you would work with Air Forces if they asked you to."

I was just wondering how to deal with this rather perceptive remark when Charlie approached, as if by magic, from the other side of the room. "Trust you to be talking to the prettiest girl in the room." Mary laughed but was completely unembarrassed. Charlie looked at her. "How long are you going to be in Canberra? I work in the National Gallery and can organise a tour if any of you are interested."

"The Gallery sounds a great idea. I wish we knew how long we're going to be here. We were going home after the competition followed by the Royal Flight but I think our stay may be extended."

I looked at Mary. "Competition?"

"Yes, it has been in all the papers. There is a bi-ennial competition between the maritime squadrons of the RAF, RAAF, RNZAF, USN and the RCAF. We were at Amberley doing really well when we had to leave the competition submarine which we had just found to go to look for the lost aircraft."

"So who won the competition?"

"No-one, it was cancelled."

We excused ourselves from the crew and made our way to the dining-room. Charlie looked at me and started chatting as we went along the corridor. "Your mind is racing I can tell. That girl has got you excited." I raised my eyebrows. "Alright, very interested. Is there something that Mike should know?"

"I'm not sure. There's something about the whole accident that is out of the ordinary. When Governments start hiding the truth one has to be suspicious."

"Hiding?"

"The press release never said that it was an RAF aircraft that found the wreckage; it was also very imprecise as to where the wreckage was found or why it crashed, which they must know by now."

"An oversight."

"I don't think so. They are paid not to make oversights. And why isn't the RAF aircraft going back to UK as planned?"

"It's not fair. You are always so suspicious. I could never have an affair with another man, you'd find out straightaway."

"Would I? You go all round the world to exhibitions, looking at and buying paintings."

"And you go all round the world looking at accidents, attending conferences. What was it that Oscar Wilde said 'You can resist anything except temptation'?"

"I'm not sure you've got the quotation quite right."

She grinned and then stopped. "This can't be our table. There are four seats."

"That's right. Liz and Mike are joining us. Didn't I tell you? They only called me this afternoon; they're staying in the Rydges Hotel to-night as Liz has got a breakfast meeting there in the morning."

She hit me in the ribs. "No you jolly well didn't. Confirms what I just said but how lovely." A pause, "but no shop."

"My love, I promise, not much."

She kissed me slowly. "Alright, just this once," and on cue Liz and Mike appeared.

I kept to my promise until towards the end of the meal when Mike raised the subject "I've seen the load sheet of the Boeing. It was definitely on board. We'll have to pay up."

"Why do you say that? I don't believe it was pilot error. We don't know yet why the aircraft was lost. There's more to this than we've been told."

***

On the way back to the hotel Mary asked Greg if she could have a word and suggested they had a drink at the bar but, on reflection, he proposed that they had breakfast together. He went up to his room on reaching the hotel while the rest of the crew went to the bar including Mary. However he had only been in his room a minute or two when there was a knock and Mary wanted to come in. As she sat down in the only chair and took her suit jacket off he couldn't help thinking what a splendid body she had. He sat on the bed trying not to look at her bra thrusting her blouse forward and her attractive black stockings going up to her shortish skirt.

"Mary, what is it that couldn't wait until the morning?" He had tried to sound stern but he had failed completely and it all sounded very friendly.

"That guy, Peter Talbert, we met in the bar. He's an accident investigator and he as good as said he thought the P8-A had been shot down."

"Well you know that's what I've been thinking but it has nothing to do with us."

"Are you sure? I was thinking of the briefing to-morrow. It would be nice to know what really happened. I'm sure the UK would like to know as soon as possible."

"What are you suggesting?"

"Well maybe you should make it clear that we thought the aircraft may have been shot down. They are bound to know by now if it was attacked. If you don't say anything they may duck and weave, Sir."

Greg looked her. She clearly was not a run of the mill radar operator and she had only just managed to squeeze in the 'Sir'.

"Mary, you seem to be telling me what to do. I'm not sure I like that."

She smiled in a very attractive way. "I didn't mean to. It was just an idea. I get a lot of them." He tried to prevent misconstruing what she had just said but she didn't help by looking at him in a way that left him in very little doubt what ideas were going through her mind and he could feel himself responding. "You're right. I'd better go." She stood up and stretched and Greg decided it would only be chivalrous to help her on with her jacket; he certainly didn't find it difficult watching her rear view going out of the door.

With the door closed Greg concentrated on what she'd been saying. Maybe she was right. Perhaps he should stir things up a bit. After all the whole event was indeed very strange and Stephen, not to say his bosses, were bound to question him to find out what he had discovered. He lay on the bed but didn't go straight to sleep; he found himself thinking of Mary, her bra, her black stockings and the skirt pressing against her bottom as she left his room.

In the morning, when he woke up, he had a quick breakfast and then the RAAF bus took him and his crew to the briefing room to be met by Alan Nguyen, but Bob Acton was there as well. Greg started the proceedings. "When we first met I was in a difficult position as we had some information that I was not at liberty to share with you until I had discussed the situation with the UK." He looked at Bob. "However I didn't feel too guilty as you clearly were not telling us your whole story either."

There was absolute silence in the room. Greg carried on. "We found the wreckage of the P8-A very quickly because we dropped one of our latest active sonobuoys and there was enough wreckage to give us a strong return. However we got such a strong return we realised that there was a submarine underneath the wreckage. We dropped some passive sonobuoys as a check but then we had to send the mission memory drive back to UK to be analysed because our Mission Support System was at Amberley and needed repairing; we knew that we needed to let the UK know about the sub as quickly as possible. I gather our experts don't know what exactly it was or who owned it but they think it was probably a large AIP machine and not nuclear."

There was a long silence as the news sank in and it was Alan Nguyen who broke it.

"That's amazing to have a large AIP there. It doesn't make sense. Of course the French have that base in New Caledonia but they wouldn't have it roaming around there without telling us. Maybe it's Chinese."

"Our experts tell us that they don't think the machine was French." Greg then decided to escalate the briefing. "Anyway Sir, if I may comment, why would a French submarine want to shoot your Boeing down?"

Bob Acton reacted strongly. "Wait a moment, who said it was shot down?"

"Well I'm sure you've examined the wreckage by now. It's the only explanation with the wreckage being so close together and near the surface."

Bob considered the situation and clearly came to a decision. "Alright, I suppose it was inevitable you guys would work out what happened. As you know we have put the very minimum in the press and we want to keep it that way at the moment until we've done some more investigation. We thought at first the pilot might have hit the water but we now know it was clearly hit by a missile. We wondered if it had come from a boat but from what you tell us maybe it was shot down by this submarine."

"Well Sir, thank goodness it's not our problem for a change."

"But it's certainly ours. We really need to establish the nationality of the sub."

Greg decided to change the emphasis of the debrief and probe a bit. "Of course what is puzzling the UK is why your P8-A was there and what the submarine was doing there anyway."

Bob wasn't prepared to be interrogated. "Our P8-A was going to Port Moresby."

"At 2,000 ft or what ever altitude it was? If you say so, Sir." He paused and then decided to carry on. "Were you in contact with the aircraft? You were so quick getting us to search for it that it suggests you were talking to it up to the moment it was shot down. But if that was the case you must have known the submarine was there?"

Bob looked at Greg. "Believe me, Squadron Leader, we did not know there was a submarine there. We knew roughly where the P8-A was but there had been no communication for ten minutes. We called the aircraft but there was no reply and we started to get worried."

"But if there had been a submarine there then surely they would have called you?"

"Yes, of course, but we may not have heard it. Communication is very poor there at low level."

"It's a pity we don't have the camera memories, we took pictures of every boat."

***

Stephen Wentworth went into the High Commissioner's office where Robert Fotheringay was reading something on his desk and Clive Perkins was waiting expectantly.

"Stephen, just the man we need. I gather we've just told the Australians that there was an AIP submarine there? What are we going to do, or say if we're asked how we know?"

Stephen wondered what Fotheringay actually understood about what was going on. "That isn't a problem, Sir, since we've just told them we've analysed our recorder. However, you might like to ask sometime why the P8-A aircraft was there." He could see Fotheringay struggling to assimilate the information. "I've just heard from our P8-U captain that at the latest debriefing they admitted that their aircraft had been hit by a missile. They agreed that if the P8-A had seen the sub it would have tried to call operations straight away but of course the communication is not good there at low level. The RAF P8-U captain thinks the Australians are not yet convinced it was the submarine that fired the missile; they are wondering if it was a boat. We can't comment of course as the camera memories are not available."

"It was shot down? Why would anyone want to shoot the aircraft down? Presumably it wasn't doing anything?"

"Well Sir, you've put your finger on it. We don't know what the aircraft was doing. We now know it was shot down with a missile. Presumably a completely unprovoked attack."

"Must be some wild terrorist. Who on earth would want to shoot the aircraft down?"

"We don't know."

"I thought we had ways of finding out about boats by looking at the pictures and matching the pictures to our library of boats. They did take pictures, didn't they?"

"Yes, Sir. But as I said the pictures were stolen."

Stephen reminded him about the break-in.

"But Stephen surely people can't just walk over an airfield and break into aircraft. Don't they have security guards?"

"There are guards but the airfield is large."

"Surely we've got grounds to complain? And anyway they should be finding the people who broke in."

"I agree Sir, but I wouldn't hold your breath. The people or person breaking in will almost certainly come from the country of the people operating the submarine. May I make a suggestion Sir? I think it is time for you to meet the Minster of Defence and see if you can't find out what is the Australian view of the situation. Why the aircraft was there? What did it say before it was shot down."

Robert Fotheringay nodded. "Shall I try and get an appointment?"

"Well Sir, I suggest you give them twenty four hours to absorb the news about the AIP submarine."

***

Jack Smithson, Australian Minister of Defence, sat in his office looking out towards the lake. He was worried. The P8-A had been shot down and there had only been a very guarded release saying that it had crashed somewhere between Townsville and Port Moresby. Now there were problems because the media wanted more details and he wasn't sure what to do for the best. They had had to use the Poms to find the aircraft which, he was forced to admit, they had done very well but they had discovered a submarine as well. Unfortunately they could not identify the machine and just said it was probably an AIP machine.

He wasn't sure how to play the media. It would be necessary to say the aircraft had been shot by a missile but he didn't want to admit that it was impossible to tell whose missile and where it came from. The Chief of the Defence Staff, General Max Wilson, was advising him to ask all the countries that manufactured AIP submarines but the Minister of Foreign Affairs, Geoff Smith, wanted more time to consider all the options; however that was predictable as he was an uncooperative bastard. Jack knew he had to face questions in Parliament that afternoon and he was getting no help from the Prime Minister. He decided it was too early to tell the media about the aircraft being shot down until they had found out who did it.

Predictably In the House of Representatives it was Lucy White, the member for the Wakefield electorate in South Australia where most of the relatives of the crashed crew were living, who asked the questions. "Would the Minister for Defence please explain why the P8-A crashed into the sea with the loss of all the crew?"

"We are not sure yet but an investigation is in progress."

"Have you asked the ATSB for help?"

This was a tricky question as the ATSB would know straightaway that the aircraft had been hit by a missile. "Not yet but the Member for Wakefield can rest assured that they will be consulted if necessary."

"How was the aircraft wreckage discovered?"

"An RAF aircraft happened to be close by and was the first aircraft to arrive. It was followed soon afterwards by one of our P8-As and then one of our frigates arrived to look for survivors and inspect the wreckage."

"Would the Minister explain what the P8-A was doing in the area in which it was found?"

"The aircraft was on a routine flight from Townsville to Port Moresby."

The questioning stopped but Smithson knew a further statement would be required all too soon, especially when they found out that the crash area was way off the direct line from Townsville to Port Moresby.

Back in his office his direct line phone rang.

"Jack, that went alright."

"Yes, Prime Minister. but we'll have to announce what happened eventually. We can't pretend we don't know."

"We need to try to find out who shot it down first and that is your job, Jack."

"I can't act without the support of Geoff."

The phone went dead.

Smithson decided to call Max Wilson. "I think we need to try to find that submarine the Poms found."

"But it may not be there now."

"True but we need to look. Why not get the Poms to go out again?"

"But we can use our P8-As, Minister."

"I think we need to get the Poms working with us and apparently their P8-U has some very good equipment. Didn't I see a confidential paper somewhere saying that they've got some new world beating sonobuoys?"

"Very good idea, Minister, we can regard the flight as an evaluation of the new sonobuoys. We'll put some of our people on board their P8-U to do the assessment. They would have to be there anyhow or the Poms would filter all the information they give us. It would be like getting a needle out of a thorn bush."

"The Poms are our allies."

"The Poms didn't tell us they'd found a submarine. I wonder what else they didn't tell us?"

"They're probably wondering what we haven't told them."

"Yes Minister."

***

I decided to watch the Minister of Defence answering questions on the Boeing. I'd spotted the question in the proceedings by accident and decided it might be interesting. In fact the only thing new was the admission that the RAF P8-U found the Australian aircraft. There was still no explanation of the accident or where it happened. I called Mike. "Did you watch Jack Smithson getting questioned about your aircraft?"

"No, 'fraid not. Was it interesting?"

"You would have found it so but they haven't said yet why the plane went down. I still suspect they were fired at by a sub or a boat."

"Well from an insurance point of view I hope you're right."

"Tell you what, if you know anyone in Air Services Australia it would be very helpful to try and find out if the P8-A filed a flight plan to Port Moresby. Was the flight direct? How long should it have taken?"

"My apologies, I should have told you that I discovered that the aircraft did file a plan but not for a direct flight and it was at low level. Apparently there had been a steep increase in the number of flights starting two months ago, mostly by the aircraft that was shot down carrying the special equipment from *Discover the World Inc.*"

"Did Air Services Australia know what the P8-As had been doing? Did the flight Plan show the waypoints? "

"No. All they knew was that they were operating in and out of Townsville and going towards the Torres Strait."

"Well what you might do is to ask *Discover The World Inc* what their bit of kit did."

***

Greg called his crew together after breakfast. "I've just heard from Northwood. The MoD in London has been asked by the ADF if we could help the RAAF by monitoring the area where we found the Boeing to see if we can find the submarine again and the MoD has agreed. However, the RAAF want to have two of their trained aircrew on the aircraft as supernumerary crew and to be certain that our MSS has been repaired so that there can be an immediate playback after landing. Walt has managed to get the MSS working so we're all set."

Mary put her hand up. "Are we going to arm the anti-missile system, Sir."

Greg looked at her, realising what a valuable crew member she was proving to be. "You just beat me to it, Mary. Wyn Williams has checked that the P8-A EWSP flares and chaff are compatible with our system and he is arranging to load up our dispensers. From now on we must arm the system when we descend to search."

The news of the search was not greeted with unalloyed pleasure. 'How long will we have to be out here' was one of the most frequently asked questions; the other question was 'What can we do that they can't do with their P8-As?'. Greg couldn't help with an answer for the first question but he reminded them of their new sonobuoys which he guessed the Australians were very keen to examine.

He rang Stephen to find out when the flying was going to start.

"Don't know the answer but very shortly. I gather you are going to be based in Townsville. How many of the new sonobuoys have you got left?"

"Three passive and three active. Who wants to know?"

"Northwood. The Australians are aware that you've got some new high performance ones and they've asked if you would do one or two sorties using them. They're thinking of buying some. By the way can you use the Australian sonobuoys?"

"Don't know about Australian sonobuoys. We may need a lot of them wherever they come from but there were a few of our original ones left in Amberley which they could send up. However, if we're going to use a lot of the new ones the UK will have to ship them out quickly."

"Apparently Ultra have already shipped a load commercially with QANTAS to Sydney."

"Amazing. Ultra must be very keen to sell to the ADF. Glad I'm not paying. Apparently they cost a bomb. Who is footing the bill, not that it's anything to do with me?"

"Nor me either and I don't know, but hadn't you better arrange to have some of the Australian sonobuoys as well? You should be hearing from RAAF Maritime or whatever it's called fairly soon I would have thought."

"Depends what sonobuoys they use. We'll check."

Later in the day Alan Nguyen called. "Greg, have you heard from the UK? They've agreed that you can help us search the area with your new sonobuoys close to where the Boeing crashed to see if there are any more submarines in the area."

"Yes Alan, we're all set to help but we've only got three passive and three active sonobuoys left; not sure when the new ones will actually arrive and be available. If we use yours we'll need a lot; I'm checking that they will interface with our equipment but it should be OK."

"I agree, as I'm told we use Ultra sonobuoys as well as American ones so it shouldn't be a problem. Anyway in the P8-U you can use the USN buoys can't you as well as the Ultra ones? That's what we use."

"Yes, I'm sure we can sort something out."

"We plan to send a navigator and an acoustic crewman from Edinburgh No 10 Squadron to fly with you. They'll be going to Townsville."

"Why don't they come here instead so they can learn something on the way up?"

"Good idea. If they come up to-morrow then you can go up once they arrive here. OK?"

"That'll be fine. Names?"

"Navigator Squadron Leader Shane Morris and Acoustics Flight Lieutenant Fred Cooper."

Greg informed Northwood of the plan and got his crew ready for the transit the following day.

Mary waited until the crew had left the room. "What happens if we discover a friendly submarine, Sir?"

Greg considered the question. "Well the system will mark it and say what it is."

"Do we want that? The Australians will see it and it might be one of ours we haven't told them about."

Greg thought about what she was saying. "Well I don't see what we can do about that and we wouldn't have one of our subs out here without telling them."

Mary raised her eyebrows. "If you say so, Sir. I wondered if it was possible for Walt to switch off the routine which identified friendly machines. He could always have a private look on the MSS when the Aussies weren't looking."

"Sometimes I wonder about you, Mary. You think of doing unusual things."

Mary suddenly smiled. "That can be fun sometimes."

Greg found himself grinning in spite of himself and his system definitely was agreeing. He pulled himself together. "Let's ask Walt. It's a great idea. Get hold of him and get him to call me."

She disappeared and Greg went back to his room. Some time later Walt called. "Sir, Mary told me her idea and I'm pretty sure I can do that. I've got the manual on my computer and I'll check it out."

In the morning they were ready to depart when Shane and. Fred arrived at midday from Edinburgh; Greg got Tim and Walt to brief them on emergency procedures and then they left for Townsville where they all stayed in the Beach House Hotel again. However, Greg had only just found his room when he got a telephone call from RAAF operations asking them to take-off at 2100 local time that night and search in the same area as before for submarines. He explained that they would have to use RAAF sonobuoys as the new ones were not available but he was assured that they were now available in Townsville. He alerted the crew and somehow they managed to get the sonobuoys loaded, the aircraft refuelled and galley restocked so that they were airborne at 2113 and on station for the search at 2300.

Greg decided that he would use the new sonobuoys. "Captain to Acoustics. Standby to drop one of the Ultra new passive sonobuoys."

"Acoustics to Captain. Hang on. They're buried on the racks behind the Oz ones. We've got to find them." A minute's delay. "OK, found both active and passive."

"Captain to Acoustics. We'll drop two buoys near and to the south of where we found the submarine last time."

They dropped the buoys and Acoustics soon sounded very excited. "I've got two returns, one 360° and one 250°.

"Captain to Acoustics. OK we'll drop a stick of Aussie buoys. Check the channels please."

There was a pause as the sonobuoys were prepared. Greg positioned the aircraft so that they would have a good chance of locating both the submarines when they got the bearings from the buoys.

"Captain to Tacco 2. Drop buoys on the indicated waypoints, prepare for vectors."

Greg felt John turning the aircraft, more vigorously now to avoid wasting time getting back over the sonobuoys.

"Acoustics to Captain. All sonobuoys serviceable, got good contact on sub to the East, the northerly one much fainter but it sounds like a French Nuclear."

"Captain to Acoustics. Positions of subs plotted."

"Acoustics to Captain. Think both boats may be nuclear and one may be French."

Greg was considering the next move when Mary called "Captain from Radar. Large ship close to where we saw a ship last time near the reef."

"Captain to Radar. OK take us there. IM, take pictures with MX20 camera using the infra red. No searchlights. ESM, identify transmissions if you can and Acoustics2, use handheld camera, not that it will see much."

They came over the ship for the first time. "P2 to Captain. No lights visible at all." Mary steered John for the second run.

"P1 to Captain. Suspect the same ship we saw before with the helicopter but too dark to be sure."

"ESM to Captain. No transmissions."

"Captain to Acoustics. I want to check near the boat. We'll drop one of the new active sonobuoys. Stand by."

The buoy was dropped. "Captain from Acoustics. I've rotated the pinger. I think there's something actually under the ship but there's too big a return from the ship to be sure."

"Captain from Radar. There's another ship ten miles away."

"Captain to Radar. Take us there."

Mary steered the aircraft to the radar return.

"Captain here. Same procedure as for the first boat. ESM, listen to the transmissions."

"ESM to Captain. Looks like an Australian Hobart Class Destroyer."

"Captain from IM. Message from OZOPS. Return to base."

Greg was a bit surprised by the instruction but at least they'd get some sleep. They were back on the ground at Townsville at 0300. Being very cautious before leaving the aircraft Greg told Stan to keep the camera memories and hand them over to the RAAF at the debriefing. He took the mission memory and the aircraft keys. The RAAF had arranged for a debriefing straightaway and the information on the submarines was explained. On the way back to the hotel he chatted to Shane and Fred.

"Did you find that interesting?"

Shane responded straightaway. "Absolutely fascinating and it makes our P8-As look a little bit old fashioned already in spite of the fact we try to keep them up to date. The P8-Us displays and the flexibility of what the operators can look at is amazing."

Fred came in. "I liked that new passive sonobuoy with its position reporting, great sensitivity and accurate bearings. When are we going to know for sure what submarines they were and if there was a sub under the ship?"

"Well we can play back the mission on the MSS in the morning but we probably won't learn anything more than we saw in the plane. We'll transmit the complete mission memory to UK and maybe with their extra facilities and database we could learn something new. Probably take a couple of days before they come back to us."

Back in the hotel he arranged for the crew to meet for breakfast at noon. He went up to his room and a moment later there was a knock on his door. It was Walt. "Greg, I didn't want to say anything with the Aussies there but I think the second submarine was one of ours. I'll be able to confirm it when I run the MSS without the Aussies watching."

Chapter 7

Mike called me in my office. "I've heard from *Discover The World Inc*. They won't tell me what it did. It was classified."

"That's very interesting. I wonder what the RAAF were looking for."

I looked up *Discover the World Inc* in Google and apparently the firm specialised in recording equipment which didn't help a lot. Unlike a normal firm it was necessary to contact them to get any information. I had pushed the whole thing out of my mind when I got a telephone call from Randy Bercholz in Los Angeles. "Peter, what are you doing in Australia? I thought you were a Brit?"

"It's a long story, Randy. How are things with you? Still running after sales support?"

"Not really. I'm semi retired now. I've been asked by Boeing if I could help them with that aircraft that disappeared near Papua New Guinea. I thought of you but I wasn't sure if you dealt with military aircraft. I still remember that great job you did for us on the 737 and the autopilot."

I thought of that prescient girl in the P8-U crew at the Commonwealth Club. "Randy, I'm happy to do any aircraft if it's a job. It's just that I'm not normally asked to do military aircraft."

"Well, we'll pay you your standard fees if you would like to come aboard."

"OK, Randy, you're on. I'll need the normal letter of authorisation. You'd better fax it to me as soon as you can. By the way have you made any progress at all?"

"Not really. The RAAF seem very protective or secretive about the whole thing."

"Did they help you in any way?"

"They showed us a photo of the wreckage which seemed very close together. It's almost as if it exploded. They must have analysed it by now but haven't said anything."

"You're right. The press are getting on to it and there was a question in their parliament. They may have to get their accident people to help. Anyway the moment I get your authentication I'll see what I can do."

I decided not to talk to anybody in the ADF until I had the letter from Boeing. However I did call Robert Covelli again at the ATSB. "Have you heard yet what happened to the P8-A which crashed north of Queensland?"

"Not a word. I reckon they know but are choosing the words for the media very carefully for some reason."

I drove home via the airport. The RAF Boeing P8-U was no longer there. Charlie arrived soon after me and I told her about Randy. "Did you call him or did he call you? You've been trying to get involved with the loss of that aircraft ever since Mike told you about it."

"I almost resent that remark. He called me as it happens. I don't need the business that badly unless you intend to buy more dresses from Liz."

"My love, it's not a matter of money. You can't resist a challenge."

She was right of course and I spent the rest of the day thinking about what might have happened.

In the morning the Boeing fax had arrived so when I got to my office I called the Public Relations department of the ADF and asked to speak with someone who was dealing with the crash of the Boeing. I was given the standard answer by an official but friendly spokeswoman who said that there was no further news.

"That's fine. I've been appointed by Boeing to represent their interest. I had hoped to discuss the matter before I broke the news that the aircraft was shot down by a boat and there was nothing wrong with it."

There was a pause and a rather surly man came to the phone. "What did you say your name was?"

I explained that I was an aviation insurance investigator.

"Well Mr Tarbuck, you had better be careful what you allege. Were you ever in the ADF? You could be prosecuted for breaking news that is covered by the Australian Government Security Classification system."

"I wasn't in the armed forces. I'm just trying to do my job which, in this case, is to find out why the P8-A was shot down."

"I don't know what you're talking about but there's going to be a statement."

"Well I thought it might be better to discuss the matter sensibly rather than have ill informed conjectures all over the front pages of the newspapers."

"Mr Tarbuck, can you give me your contact details?"

I spelt them out very slowly and invited him to look at my web site pages. I could hear him doing just that and there was a change to a more conciliatory tone. "Did you say that you have a letter of appointment from Boeing, Mr Talbert?"

"Yes I did. Shall I fax it to you?"

"That may not be necessary. I see you're based in Canberra. I'll get someone to call you back."

Thirty minutes later Dominic Brown, the guy I remembered who interviewed Mike, came on the line and suggested that I should come round for a chat. His office turned out to be in the new security ASIO building overlooking Parkes Way and the lake but I suggested that it might be better if we met for lunch. He agreed and chose a small place on my street in the Melbourne building. Brown was a tall, lean guy wearing a smart blue shirt and blue trousers; I guessed he had left his tie and jacket in his office. We both ordered sandwiches and water to drink.

"Mr Talbert," I suggested he called me Peter, "I've looked at your web site and clearly you are an expert in accident investigations. I'm sure you didn't get to your position and standing to-day without being a very responsible person. You realise that the loss of the P8-A is a very worrying occurrence besides being a tragedy for the dependants of the crew who were lost. I won't try and pretend that we don't know what happened to our P8-A; as you surmised it was shot down but we haven't established who did it or what was the exact weapon."

"Do you know what boat it was? The RAF P8-U was there fairly soon after the loss and must have seen all the boats in the vicinity."

"No we haven't found a boat yet. There were quite a few small boats about and of course these days small boats can carry very advanced weapons."

"But why would any boat want to shoot down the P8-A?"

Brown was very smooth but I thought I detected some discomfort. "Peter," I noticed the change which put me on my guard since in my experience when a person being interviewed was asked an awkward question he or she always tried to get the interview onto a more personal relationship and, hopefully, avoid answering the question. "A fair question but really not relevant as far as your employer Boeing is concerned. You can reassure them that it was no fault of the aircraft. It is up to us to establish who shot at the aircraft and why it was destroyed."

I looked at Dominic. He was completely correct. "Thanks for being so frank. As you will have guessed I wasn't about to tell the newspapers anything; I just wanted to put Boeing's mind at rest. However I'm sure you'll have to do that shortly after the Minister has made his statement."

"Yes, very shortly probably." He looked at his watch and smiled. "In an hour."

I went back to the Office and watched the Ministerial statement.

"We have now finished examining the wreckage of our P8-A and have come to the conclusion that it was shot down by a missile. We have not as yet determined from where the attack came and exactly what weapon was used."

There was a furore in the chamber and Lucy White had to struggle to get her voice heard. "The Minister for Defence is saying that one of our aircraft has been shot down and we don't know who did it? This is ridiculous and confirms the ineptitude of this Government. We spend a fortune on so called intelligence, erect monstrously expensive new buildings to house an enormous number of 'so-called' experts and then we don't know who is shooting at us. Surely the Minister had better consider his position."

"We think the loss of the aircraft is probably a terrorist attack or possibly fired by an asylum seekers smuggling organisation. We will inform the house the moment we establish what happened."

Some other MP joined in. "The wreckage was found by an RAF aircraft. Would the Minister explain what an RAF aircraft was doing in Australian waters?"

"The aircraft was taking part in a two yearly maritime competition between allied air forces near our North East Coast and very sensibly it was decided to ask the crew to look for the missing aircraft as it was by far the closest resource we had."

"Why didn't we use our own aircraft? We've got enough of them, goodness knows."

"As I just said, the RAF aircraft was the closest at the time and time was clearly critical in order to find any survivors."

"Did the RAF aircraft look for the boat that fired the missile or whatever it was?"

"The aircraft, having found the wreckage, looked for survivors so they looked at everything that floated."

"Then surely it would have spotted boats carrying weapons?"

"These days lethal weapons can be carried in the smallest craft. Let me assure the House that we are doing everything that can be done to find out what happened and we will report to the House the moment we do."

The interrogation came to an end leaving some vital unanswered questions which were not in my area of responsibility. I typed out a report to Boeing explaining that I had completed my terms of reference. I decided to wait twenty four hours before I sent my invoice. To my surprise I got a reply within thirty minutes. "Thank you for the report. A Hank Goodall may contact you. We'll cover any extra expenses incurred."

The message was curious but didn't mean anything to me. However, I decided not to interrogate Randy but wait and see what happened. I didn't have long to wait as my mobile rang. "Peter Talbert?" I agreed. "My name is Hank Goodall." The voice was deep South and very slow. "I work with Randy Bercholz. I wondered if we could meet up?"

"Mr Goodall, no problem. Where are you. Sydney or the States?"

"Canberra. I could be with you in fifteen minutes. I know your address."

"Fine. I look forward to it."

The Canberra Office of Boeing Martin was based in Barton which was 15 minutes away. However after five minutes I looked out into the street from my office and saw a large black Toyota arrive and a medium height guy with a dark blue suit and tie get out. Almost immediately my entry phone rang and as I expected the driver in the car turned out to be Hank Goodall. We chatted for a few minutes.

"Hank, I'll have to leave the office shortly. How can I help you?"

"Well Peter," he looked at me carefully, "as you know I work with Randy."

"Well that's great but I've finished the job for him and am sending him an invoice. There was nothing wrong with the aircraft which was all that Boeing cared about."

"Well we'd like to know a little more about what happened."

I looked at Hank. "Who is we?"

He paused and ignored my question. "What did you think of the Minister's replies in Parliament this afternoon?"

"Why have you come here, Hank? I'm not in any way involved in the whole sad affair."

"Well Peter, I'm not sure about that. Anyway, I wanted to meet you because you've a pretty good track record of working out why aircraft get into trouble."

"Thank you but I'm not an expert on military aircraft and I can't afford to spend my time on things that don't concern me."

"Randy said he'd pay you."

"No he didn't. He just said he'd cover extra expenses which isn't the same thing." I was beginning to get annoyed. "Hank, my guess is that you don't work for Boeing at all. Would you like me to ask them? Who do you work for? The United States Government? Do you have a card?"

To my surprise he showed me a card which said he worked for the US Federal Police. it looked genuine but I decided to photograph it with my phone so he would be in my contacts list.

Hank smiled. "Most people don't do that."

"That may be true but I like to know what I'm getting myself into." I thought for a moment and decided to try and find out a bit more about Hank. "What was the question you asked me?"

"I just wanted to know what you thought of the Minister's replies in Parliament this afternoon."

"He played a dead bat if you know what that means. He did well from an impossible situation."

"What extra questions would you have asked?"

I couldn't help smiling, "Hank, that is a great question. Perhaps you should tell me the answer."

He smiled back. "Well the aircraft was only a few minutes away from Port Moresby. They seem to have alerted the P8-U as if they knew something was wrong."

"I agree. I wondered if it had been reporting regularly and then suddenly stopped. As if it was executing a job or looking at something and then communication was lost."

If Hank wasn't genuine I could be getting myself into tricky waters. It brought home to me that really the whole thing was not my concern. Still I was intrigued by the situation. I decided to carry on. "If we're going into the guessing game it is clear that we're not being told all that the Australians know or, more accurately, what they don't know. Did the P8-U see the boat in question? Was it obvious? What nationality was it? Was it hidden and why don't we know who did it?"

"How could it be hidden? You mean unmarked or a small boat?"

"No. They may have seen an unmarked boat or they may even have seen a submarine."

Hank suddenly turned to me, shook hands and left. I watched him get into his car and drive off. I felt it was time to get some help and called Charles Grainger who suggested I went to his office. The security was just as tight as ever but eventually I got to the lobby and we went along to his office in the main corridor.

"Charles, I'm getting into some difficulty. What do you know about the Boeing that was lost?" I explained about Randy, Boeing and Hank. "Can we check Hank out?"

Charles thought about my problem and then made a telephone call. A Stephen Wentworth appeared who was clearly involved with security. I went through the details again.

"Well Mr Talbert you had better give me all the details on that Police Card."

"How about the limo number?"

"Yes, we can get that straightaway."

He made a telephone call and then looked at me. "Not much joy there. It was from a rental agency and," he raised his hand to forestall my next question, "he paid by cash."

"When will you know about his ID?"

Stephen looked at Charles. "Do you think it is important? I could hurry things along."

Charles nodded. "It could be very important if he's not genuine." He looked at me. "Do you think he was genuine?"

"Well I'm sure he's a spook but where he is from is anybody's guess. He sounded like he came from the deep south. My guess is that he's okay and works for the US Government in some way, probably the CIA, but it is by no means certain. I think he was curious to know what I knew for some reason. I suppose it is just possible that he works for the people who owned the boat or submarine that shot the aircraft down but very unlikely." I saw Charles and Stephen exchanging glances. "Relax, nobody has told me anything but this sort of investigation is what I do for a living. But why would he bother to come and see me if he wasn't genuine? If he is genuine what was he after? And why did he think I might know something?"

Stephen replied straightaway. "Why would he bother to see you if he was genuine? Did you mention the possibility of a submarine?"

"Yes I did. My thinking was that if he wasn't genuine then it wouldn't matter and if he was genuine he would have guessed anyway."

"Peter, this matter has a very very high security grading. Do you have dual nationality?"

"Not yet."

"You might be able to help us but we'd need you to sign the Official Secrets Act. Any problems with doing that?"

"Not at all, but from what little I know of security I thought I needed to be positively vetted?"

Stephen grimaced. "Yes, you're quite right but we can't do that immediately before you sign and it's more important that the fact there was a sub in the area is not spread around."

Charles went to his filing cabinet and produced the forms. I signed them, he and Stephen witnessed my signature and gave me a copy.

Stephen filled me in explaining how the P8-U found a submarine. "The security of this information is TOP SECRET."

I looked at him. "But everyone will guess as I did that there might be a submarine there."

"We don't think so if the RAAF media suggests that there was a boat there."

"But Stephen the crucial thing is clearly who owns the submarine." I thought for a moment. "But you must know that by now. I bet the mission memory with the sonobuoy information has been analysed." He didn't say anything. "Alright, need to know I suppose, but Stephen, why was the aircraft there and what was the sub doing there? There's a lot more to this than meets the eye and to what you're telling me."

"I think you're right and I'd gladly tell you if I knew." Stephen went down to the lobby with me. "They'll take your photo on the way out so you can have a regular pass in future."

Chapter 8

Maureen Chester looked at the latest TOP SECRET brief. It was labelled HARDING but she did not know which source that was and she didn't intend to ask. Apparently the RAF Boeing P8-U which had found the RAAF Boeing wreckage had made another flight under RAAF control to the place where the wreckage had been found. This time they had found not only a French submarine but the same anonymous boat as the time before in the same position and there were still no distinguishing marks; to complicate matters still further there may have been another submarine nearby. A copy of the mission memory was on its way back to be examined in UK because this time apparently the crew had been able to use their special mission playback equipment. The brief noted that the P8-U then discovered a RAN Destroyer not too far away at which point the P8-U was told to return to Townsville.

The Minister called in Harry Brown, her chief secretary. "What's going on out there in the Torres Strait between Australia and Papua New Guinea? It all seems very strange. A French submarine and this time nuclear. Have we asked the French what's going on?"

"Yes, Minister. They said that the submarine was on routine patrol from their base in New Caledonia and they had permission from the PNG Government and, they added, 'just like yours'."

"Do we believe them?"

"Yes, Minister, though we think the Australians would not have given permission if they had been consulted."

"That boat which was in the same position as previously. That must mean something. Surely it can be identified?"

"Not yet, Minister but this time we have all the camera memories."

Maureen Chester thought about that. "Is the camera memory coming back then with the mission recorder memory?"

Harry Brown never ceased to be amazed how quickly the Minister latched on to technical matters. "Perhaps I should rephrase that, Minister. The RAAF have the camera memories. The flight was for their benefit and we had no excuse to keep them;

anyway it was dark so they won't be much use. The difference this time is that with the mission play-back equipment the crew have they can look at the pictures from the infra-red cameras which they couldn't do last time as there was just the one module which came to the UK."

"Well what did we do with the first lot of pictures? Were they any good? Did they tell us anything?"

"Minister, the pictures were excellent from that superb MX20 on the P8."

"Did we make it in the UK, Harry?"

"I'm afraid not. I'm told that we were able to see every boat very clearly but, of course, at that time we didn't know, as we do now, that the Australian P8-A was shot down. We also had some excellent shots of the unmarked boat with the helicopter on, which apparently was originally registered in Panama. We sent copies of these pictures to the Australians as well as to our crew but we are now relooking at the pictures to see if there were any likely gun boats."

"Could a submarine have shot their P8 down?"

Once again Harry was impressed. "I was about to tell you, Minister, that that was being considered."

"Well this recent trip. What was that Australian Navy destroyer doing there?"

"Apparently checking on the other boat."

"Well then we must know what the unmarked boat was doing and whose it was."

"So far, we have not been told."

"Well you'd better ask again. It could be important. And what about the other submarine?"

"We're afraid it might be ours, Minister."

"Get George Swinburne on the phone, Harry."

Brown got through to the First Sea Lord's office and arranged the call.

"George, what orders have you given our submarine in the Torres Strait? I gather our P8 detected it on its last flight and there were two RAAF observers on board the aircraft."

"The Commander has been told to try to monitor movements close to where that inflatable boat was intercepted some time back by the RAN patrol boat but to stay in PNG waters. To be honest, Minister, we had no idea it had been detected. It must be those new sonobuoys from Ultra."

"Well it's all a bit embarrassing, George. We are not meant to hold any secrets from the Australians. We're not sure but they may realise it was our sub."

"Well Minister, we are trying to discover what is going on. We're sure the Australians are holding things back from us."

"We agree there. Can you tell the Commander to be even more covert. Meanwhile you'd better think of a cover story if the Australians find out."

"Yes, Minister."

Maureen put the phone down and turned back to Harry.

"What are they going to say when they find out our sub was there?"

"Nothing, we hope. We are proposing to say that in fact we can't identify the sub. I'm told the Captain cleverly arranged for the system not to identify friendly boats."

"Well let's hope our sub will be a lot more careful. It could have been an RAAF aircraft searching instead of our P8-U and we would have been caught."

"We would then have said that we were trying to help establish what was going on, which is true."

"But surely we should have told them where our submarine was?"

"We felt that something rather unusual was going on and we needed to find out."

"You mean 'is going on' don't you?"

"Yes, Minister."

"I think I need to talk to the Australian Defence Minister to exchange views."

"That sounds a very good idea but I would recommend we wait until we have a bit more information, Minister. Perhaps you should get the views of the Foreign Secretary."

"Harry, that sounds like a no. Alright, but keep me informed. I don't know where you are getting your intelligence from but the source is not doing very well. There is definitely something strange going on."

***

Jack Smithson looked at his TOP SECRET report on the loss of the RAAF P8-A. Apparently the RAF P8-U had been used, as he had suggested, to help find the AIP submarine which had been present when the P8-A was shot down but it had found only a French nuclear submarine instead which claimed to be operating in PNG waters on a routine mission from New Caledonia. It had also found the unmarked boat it had reported last time, another unknown submarine and a RAN destroyer. He called for his Chief Secretary, Vin Partridge.

"Vin, why didn't this report say what was the second submarine the Poms found?"

"Apparently the mission system on their P8 couldn't identify the sub. Our people checked on the mission replay after the flight but that didn't help."

"That's not very good. Max Wilson said when we discussed using the Poms that their system could identify everything."

"Only if the sub or the boat is in its database, Minister. The other problem is that even if we could read their system we don't have such a big database of submarines as the Poms."

"Surely there's another problem as well. They may not tell us the truth or perhaps hide it in some way. For example if they had a sub in the area and it was found by one of their sonobuoys they wouldn't tell us, would they?"

"Minister, the Poms are our allies. We're very close. They wouldn't have a sub in the area without telling us."

"Do we tell the Poms everything, Vin?" A pause when they looked at one another. "We didn't let the Poms go searching by themselves without checking what they were up to, Vin?"

"Certainly not, Minister. We had two crew members on board."

"Well what did they say?"

"They confirmed the French submarine and the sighting of the unmarked boat. They said the new sonobuoys were really great and we ought to get some. They did wonder if the second boat was a Royal Navy sub even though the Poms said they didn't know what it was. They also said that the Poms had discovered something under the unmarked boat, possibly a submarine."

"Well what happens next? That Pom sortie hasn't helped at all except to confirm their sonobuoys are good. How are we going to find out who shot our aircraft down? Surely it can't be that difficult."

"Problem is we don't know whether it was a sub or a boat."

"Well stop using the Poms. Send them home and use our P8-As in future. At least we'll have a chance of recognising what we manage to spot. It's a pity they spotted our Destroyer."

"That's why the RAF sortie was stopped prematurely, Minister, but we want to use them at least once more as their sonobuoys are much better than ours so they cover more ground. As you know we are regarding using the RAF aircraft with the new sonobuoys as an evaluation."

"You'll be asking me to buy these new sonobuoys from the Poms next."

"Yes, Minister."

And they both smiled.

***

Greg looked at his crew over breakfast. They had met as planned for brunch the day before but after a short visit to the aircraft during the day to tidy it up he had let them go to do what they wanted. Back at the hotel after the aircraft had been checked he had received a signal telling him the RAAF wanted them to do another flight searching for submarines the following day. He reckoned that his crew had been sampling the delights of Townsville judging by their expressions though he noticed Mary looked as if she had not stayed up too late. She noticed him looking at her and he looked away quickly, not wanting to be distracted. The take-off time was to be 2200 local time that night, the search time six hours and the area of search had been defined, a rough square south east of the wreckage point of the P8-A.

The RAAF had signalled him that Shane Morris and Fred Cooper would be arriving again in time for the flight but Shane had phoned him later telling him that they wouldn't be able to make it as they had missed their commercial flight from Adelaide. He re-checked with RAAF Operations and he was told to take-off anyway if they hadn't arrived. Wyn Williams, their crew chief, had gone down to Canberra with a copy of the mission from the previous flight and Greg spoke to Charles to check he had got it; in fact Charles told him he had already sent it to be analysed in the UK. He then had a word with Stephen to check if there was anything new. He was just wondering what to do next when there was a knock on the door and he found Mary asking if she could come in. She was wearing very brief red shorts, a white top and a different black bra showing very clearly underneath.

"Can I come in? I've had an idea."

"I thought you'd be down in the Town."

"There isn't really time and I wanted to catch you."

Slowly he looked her up and down and wasn't sure whether he wanted to be caught. "You look great but I'd prefer it if you were wearing working gear."

She returned his gaze, smiled and disappeared. Fifteen minutes later she reappeared wearing uniform with long trousers. "Is that better?"

"Much more comfortable, thank you."

Nothing more was said as she came into the room but they both knew that it was going to be almost impossible to confine their relationship to just work for much longer. Greg closed the door.

Mary sat on the one chair as before and Greg sat on the bed. "Okay Mary, let's have it."

"Is it true Shane and Fred won't be coming with us?" Greg nodded. "Well so far we've only flown over the area doing a low level surface search and an underwater acoustic search. We haven't been able to look down into the water either using our cameras or even visually. The water is quite shallow. There may be something to see."

"I know, but we can't do it this time as it will be dark again. I think they like us to search at night because they think there will be a better chance of finding submarines."

"Possibly, but maybe they don't want us searching in daylight because there is something they don't want us to see. The operational plan is for us to return just as it is getting light. Now if for some reason we had to delay our return for an hour or so we could visually search the original area. The water is very shallow and clear. If there is anything there we should see it."

"The RAAF may not like that."

"Why? They should be delighted if we find something."

He looked at her. He knew she had another suggestion.

"If we had a problem with the sonobuoy release so that we were unable to climb until we had cleared the jam or whatever it was, we would then be able to track exactly over the area in daylight where the aircraft was shot down taking continuous photographs manually, running our MX20 camera and looking down as well."

Greg nodded. "Yes. I expect we could manage all that."

He looked at her thoughtfully, this time thinking very carefully about what she was saying.

"What do you think we might see?"

"I don't know but that strange boat seems to be doing something so we need to look underneath it as well if we can. There was a strong return, you remember." She carried on. "It shouldn't add much to the trip."

Greg considered the situation. "Mary, it's a great idea but we've got to be very careful. What are we going to tell the crew?"

"Well if you told Walt and Pat O'Connor, the rest of the crew don't have to know. It would be routine to take photographs when it was light"

"I'm not at all sure we should be so secretive. We can rely on the guys keeping their mouths shut." He paused. "If your hunch is right and there is something there then the whole crew will know anyway."

It was Mary's turn to nod. "Yes, you're quite right. You'd better brief everyone. Let's hope the Aussies don't change their mind and make us wait until the RAAF guys come."

He thought again. "The cameras' memories? The Australians will see what we've been up to."

"Yes." She nodded. "I thought we might change the camera memories, take our pictures and then refit the originals. We could then transmit the memory pictures to the UK for analysis."

"But the mission recorder will have all the pictures from the MX20 camera and we'll have to replay the mission to the RAAF." He thought for a moment. "I suppose we could brief Walt to turn off the replay at that point and tell them that that was the end of the operational sortie."

"Yes, Sir. That was my solution as well. But we'll need to erase the cockpit voice recorder and the crew intercom recorder."

"I'm not sure we can erase the voice recordings. Anyway it is most unlikely they will have a chance to hear them. After all the aircraft is under our control but the memories are not." He looked at her appreciatively. "You're a bright girl."

"Thank you, Sir"

She got up, looked at him carefully, then came very close to him so that her breasts pressed against him with her hands holding his arms. She kissed him, first on the cheeks, then, as she felt him responding, slowly and sensually on the lips but before he could do anything she was gone leaving only the smell of her perfume behind.

***

I answered the phone. It was Stephen. "How would you like to do a rush job for us, with expenses and pay at your normal rate?"

"Stephen, sounds great. Are you sure you can afford it?"

"Peter, even my lot has discretionary budgets. We want you to visit ASC, the Australian Submarine Corporation, and learn about the latest Australian submarines they want to build. Our expert has been taken ill."

"But why send anybody? It's AIP submarines we need to know about."

"Peter, this is nothing to do with the RAAF P8-A. We want to know what ASC are doing."

"Why not ask them? Anyway why should they tell me?"

"You are our substitute. ASC are briefing potential subcontractors for their new submarine."

"I thought they were buying an American sub not building their own?"

"They probably will do but there is a big political argument going on to decide whether the Australians should build and buy their own manufactured submarines or whether they should buy American."

"Why don't they compromise and be sub-contractors to the Americans?"

"That's another possibility but they'll still need their subcontractors. We wanted to see if there were any opportunities for smaller UK firms who are not represented so, when ASC launched this conference a few weeks ago, we approached them and asked if we could send someone along and they agreed. You are substituting for Jack Bolton. There will be a big bidding package which you will be given and this will help you as they go through each item."

"Why choose me?"

"Because we think you will be good at gathering data and we don't have a lot of choice."

"I thought the Australians were our number one ally. You're inviting me to spy on them."

"Not at all. We are just indulging in routine intelligence gathering to tell our firms in the UK what the opportunities are. Every country does it. There is no national security implication at all."

"When does all this start?"

"To-morrow afternoon. As I said you are a short notice substitute. This is not a cloak and dagger operation. You will be going as yourself and you can explain you are branching out to expand your business. Please make your own travel arrangements but you are booked in at the conference hotel, the Stamford Plaza. You have to sign in by 1800 and the event starts with hosted drinks and a buffet."

"How long will the whole thing last?"

"Two days."

I put the phone down and wondered what I was getting myself into. Back at home I broke the news to Charlie who wasn't too pleased. "You might have checked with me first. We were going out to dinner to-morrow night." She came over to me and shook her head. "I knew you would get involved with the loss of that P8-A."

"It's nothing to do with that."

"'Tell that to the Marines' if you can understand that in English."

Charlie always started emphasising she was an American and I was only a Brit when things were getting taut. "It may interest you to know that that is an English phrase. Your suggestion is a furphy as we say out here."

She came over to me and grinned.

"You're going native."

"Why not. I might take citizenship one day."

"Then your Stephen won't give you any more jobs." She looked at me as if I was losing my grip and shook her head. "Alright I suppose I'll forgive you sometime but I think you're being gullible. Come on, time for a drink."

I decided to book my flight at a more propitious time and joined her for a drink, but later I thought again about what she was saying. Maybe Stephen was stringing me along.

***

I arrived a bit later than I had planned at the Stamford Plaza so that by the time I had checked in and gone up to my room to get rid of my small roller bag the queue at the registration desk was quite long. I noticed that my badge was on the table with all the others so they were either all printed late or Stephen had jumped the gun assuming I was going to agree. The book they gave me was indeed thick, heavy and clearly was going to be a nuisance in the aircraft on the way home as I hadn't checked any bags and it would make my bag very heavy for putting in the overhead lockers. I wrote my name in the space provided on the outside of the book and put it with some others on a table close by. The girl at the desk pointed out where the drinks were taking place and, as I entered, I could see that there were not only a lot of potential bidders but that they came from all over the world. Clearly there was an expectation that the Australian Government really was going to design and build a new submarine to follow on from the diesel-electric-powered Collins.

Not surprisingly there was a complete mix of ethnicity from White Caucasian to Mongolian and Chinese but I knew from experience in Australia that ethnic background was not necessarily a clue to nationality. I looked around and, as I had anticipated, there was no-one there I recognised but there were clearly ASC hosts going round making introductions. As I took what I assumed was a gin and tonic, a smartly dressed ASC badged man came up to me and introduced me to what turned out to be a mixed group of

UK, US and Chinese attendees. I started chatting to a BAE Systems representative who was interested in data communication systems and to a Chinese looking man who came from Shanghai and whose firm made cooling pumps.

I moved on and while I was listening to a lady from a US firm specialising in titanium steel I noticed that the man from Shanghai had taken his phone out; during a pause in the conversation he spoke to me in excellent English. "Mr Talbert, I see from your web site that you are an aviation expert. What brings you here?"

The other members of the group all paused, listening to my response. "I was asked at very short notice to substitute for a friend who was taken ill. Anyway I want to expand my business and represent UK firms so I was delighted to accept his offer."

The Chinese guy smiled politely and the American lady considered my explanation. "You are obviously well up with technology. I specialise in commercial bidding so a lot of the briefing will be a bit of a challenge for me."

"Their book looks very useful."

She nodded. "I'm relying on it."

The BAE man introduced me to a guy from GKN and the Chinese cooling pump man wandered away. We didn't have to wait too long before we all went in to an adjacent room where a buffet was being served. I chatted to one or two other people and then there was a speech of welcome from a senior ASC guy. "The programme is at the front of the books which you all should have and we look forward to briefing you all here in this room to-morrow. We're starting at 0930, giving you all time for breakfast. We plan to show you our manufacturing facilities, of which we are very proud, to-morrow afternoon as a break from presentations." I left soon after he had finished and called Charlie to have a chat.

"Peter my love, do I need to come and check you are not doing anything I wouldn't approve of?"

"I wish you would. Choice would be a fine thing."

"No it certainly would not."

"You know what I mean."

"Yes I certainly do. But have a good meeting. Sit back and think of Stephen."

"I'd prefer to lie back and think of you."

The phone went dead and I went to bed.

In the morning I went down to the coffee shop which was full of people I recognised from the evening before as being attendees of the conference. After a cup of coffee and some fruit I went to the same room as the previous evening carrying the briefing tome. The presentations started on time and were delivered very professionally. I sat next to the BAe man and made a few notes after each talk on the blank pages in the book provided. After lunch we were taken round ASC's facilities as promised. I found them very impressive and, rather like airports, there were a lot of cranes and lorries changing the existing facilities. Clearly, in a developing business investment is always required; however, not surprisingly, our tour did not include the area where the new work was being carried out though we were told it was preparation for building the new submarine. There was a new very high concrete wall at the end of the facility but it was impossible to tell what was on the other side. After about two hours we returned to the briefing room and the presentations recommenced. We worked through until 1800 with one break at 1600. In the evening after a drink I went back to the coffee shop and found myself sitting with some Chinese potential vendors chatting amongst themselves but occasionally switching to English to bring me into the conversation.

The following day was similar to the first except that after the morning presentations we were taken round the design offices and an area fitted with several submarine simulators. We were shown one which had a complete suite of system displays and communication consoles. Back in the hall we had a final round of presentations and I just managed to get the last flight direct to Canberra and was home by 10pm. Charlie was looking very smart. "You look great. Have you been out?"

"Peter, I wonder about you sometimes. I'm welcoming you home. Have a drink."

"I'd better get smartened up then."

"No that won't be necessary though you'll probably feel better if you have a shower."

"Sounds great."

"Then I'll have a debriefing from my spook."

"That won't take long. There was nothing to see."

"Didn't they show you round."

"Of course."

"What didn't they show you?"

"There was a lot of construction going on and a brand new wall at one end."

"Well think about it before you talk to Stephen. He's bound to ask you."

I did think about it as I showered and put on my thin dressing gown hanging on the door.

Back in the living room Charlie gave me a drink as we sat down. I tasted it and gulped. "You've forgotten the tonic."

"I thought you needed a strong one. Let me check."

She pulled herself very close as she leant over to taste and I moved my dressing gown out of the way and put down my gin and tonic.

"You're a smart girl."

"And don't you forget it."

Chapter 9

Greg had got John Sefton to arrange for an RAAF coach to collect the crew. Before that he got Pat and Walt to come to his room and explained what he wanted them to arrange including the memory changes; they discussed the problem and agreed that by removing two fuses it would be possible to achieve what was required so that pressurisation could not take place and that there would be a warning. He took Walt to one side before they left and explained that when playing the mission back to the RAAF he was to stop the play back when the 'fault' occurred.

Out at the aircraft, before there was any electrical power switched on, he briefed the crew on what was going to happen at the end of the flight as he did not want anything to be recorded on the intercom. "What I am going to tell you now is confidential and not to be discussed with anyone else. We want to make a visual check of the area where we found the RAAF P8-A wreckage in daylight, so there is going to be a problem with our sonobuoy pressure release system which prevents us pressurising. It will take an hour or so to fix it by which time it will be daylight. We will then fly over the area with the MX20 running, and with the two visual look-outs using the hand held cameras." He looked at John Sefton. "Obviously you two must look carefully as well and perhaps orbit but that unmarked boat will probably be in the way. You may have to bank away from the boat to make sure the MX20 gets good shots. The water is very shallow and if there is anything to see we should spot it. We will be explaining the pressurisation problem to the RAAF but not telling them anything else and not showing them the mission recorder for this part of the flight so be very careful what you say."

"Captain," as usual he wondered what Mary was going to say, "Should we turn the transponder off while we're taking pictures?"

"Good point. We should be below radar cover so it shouldn't matter but we don't want them to know where we've been so, to be on the safe side," he looked at the pilots, "please switch off the transponder when we get our fault and don't switch it on again until we're through 3,000ft."

The aircraft took off on time and climbed up for the 500 mile transit to the search area. This time the search started to the south west of the previous area and they dropped sonobuoy after sonobuoy without detecting any submarines. At 0430 they had finished searching the programmed area and it was getting light. OZOPS cleared them to climb but, as planned, a fault was declared with their pressurisation system which was reported to OZOPS. Immediately the aircraft turned and returned to the original search area while Pat and Walt discussed the finer points of the simulated failure. Greg manoeuvred the aircraft five miles short of the place where they had found the unmarked boat and the possible submerged vessel; he chose a line so that after going over the area they would fly straight to the place where they found the wreckage and the sub. "Captain to P1. Check transponder off. ESM, check MX20 camera on, looking straight down and run the MAD as well. Acoustics2, go to port visual look out. Tacco2, to starboard look-out position. Use hand held cameras."

As they approached the first point Mary called out. "Radar to Captain. No ship visible ahead."

They flew over the previous position where the ship had been.

"Captain from Tacco2. There seems to be a submerged boat down there, could be a sub but not very large."

"ESM to Captain. Large return on MAD."

"Captain to Acoustics. Flying to original P8-A wreckage position. Acoustics, prepare to drop two passive sonobuoys. ESM, confirm EWSP system armed."

"Captain from ESM. EWSP armed.

Greg watched his screen."Dropping sonobuoy one." And then "dropping sonobuoy two."

They flew over the position of the original wreckage and submerged boat.

"Captain from Acoustics. Definite contact, position established."

Greg watched the aircraft on his screen overfly the contact. He decided to take advantage of the missing unmarked boat.

"Captain to P1. Do 180° and follow command to go back over that sunken boat. Acoustics, prepare to drop two more passive buoys."

He felt the g as John manoeuvred the aircraft and then made the drops as they approached the position of what looked like a sunken sub. "Captain to Acoustics. Report any contact."

He waited as they flew over the submerged boat.

"Acoustics to Captain. No contacts."

Greg checked his watch; it had taken them 90 minutes from when they had told OZOPS they had a problem. "Captain to IM. Advise OZOPS fault cleared, returning to Townsville. P1, alter course and obtain climb clearance. Climb when cleared."

Greg went first to Mary and asked her to collect the hand held camera memories for him. Then he went back to Walt. "Do you know what the first contact was?"

"It was a very quiet submarine. I think it was probably that first AIP machine again it was so quiet; you know, that first one we heard." He stopped for a moment considering the situation. "But there was no sound at all from the place where we could see the small sunken sub or whatever it was but there was a strong MAD return. UK will be able to match sonobuoys returns with the first flight."

Greg decided to go to each crew member telling them there was to be a crew briefing before leaving the aircraft. At Townsville they shut the engines down and assembled near the acoustics stations. He made sure all the electrics in the aircraft had been shut down. "Forget completely visual sightings and the sonobuoys before we climbed up. Remember, once we had the pressurisation problem we did no further work."

Greg collected the camera memories from Mary, making sure the originals had been replaced. There was a crew bus waiting to take them to the briefing room. At the debriefing Greg confirmed that they had searched the agreed area and found no submarines or significant shipping. When questioned about the delayed return he explained about the pressurisation problem which they had finally traced to a double fuse failure. He handed over the original camera memories but kept the camera memories used during the visual runs. It was agreed that Walt would run the MSS in the morning so the RAAF could see the replay of the flight. They were all getting very tired by this time and the bus took them to the hotel.

Before going to sleep Greg called Charles and said he proposed to fly down to see him. He'd had a quick look at the flights and saw he couldn't be in before 10pm so Charles said he'd book him in the Novotel and meet him for breakfast. He also agreed to advise Northwood of Greg's plans so that they knew the aircraft could not fly again with Greg on board until he was back in Townsville. Greg then phoned John Sefton's room and told him what he intended to do; he set his watch alarm, had four hours sleep and went to catch his flight to Canberra. When he finally got to the Novotel he went straight up to his room and slept without waking until 7.30am.

Charles called him in his room while he was getting up and they decided they would have breakfast in his office in the High Commission. While Greg got dressed Charles went to the Mall and bought some croissants and then, as he got back to the hotel, Greg came out with his bag having checked out. At the Commission Charles arranged for Greg to have a pass of his own and then they went up to his office. Before they sat down Charles called Stephen who said he would join in. They were having coffee with croissants when Stephen appeared. "OK for some. Where's my croissant? Just as well I've already had breakfast."

Greg described the second sortie and the decision he had taken to have a quick visual look at the crash area and where the boat had been. Stephen listened and then queried "Why did you want to do that?"

"Well we had only searched under RAAF control at night and we had never had a chance to search visually looking straight down into the water during the day. It was my radar operator who first suggested how we could do it and we hatched the plan of having a technical problem so we couldn't climb. We were particularly fortunate as the unmarked boat wasn't there so we got a better look than we expected. We'll be sending the mission memory back to UK today after we've run though the flight with the RAAF de-briefers."

Charles cut in quickly. "Surely the RAAF would have expected you to have returned low level in that situation? Anyway won't the RAAF see the pictures as well?

"We're going to stop the replay when the 'fault' occurred and in my judgement they wouldn't feel like criticising us for what we did, telling us what to do. As I said the moment it got light we did our run which turned out to be very valuable; the last thing I expected was for us to see visually what looked like a dead submarine. Anyway I made a snap decision and dropped some passive sonobuoys; there was no response from it that we could see but we found another submarine and then came home."

"Any idea whose sub it was?"

"Not yet. The sub apparently was very quiet, maybe the one we heard on the first flight. The people in UK can check for a match. I've brought with me all the hand held camera memories which should go back to UK."

Charles looked at his watch. "Quick. Give them all to me and I'll get them into the diplomatic bag."

He rushed out. Stephen looked at Greg. "Well what did you say to the RAAF people at the debriefing?"

"We told them we hadn't found anything."

"Do you think they believed you?"

"I don't know. They seemed very happy that we hadn't found anything."

"Do you think they knew that you had been over the P8-A wreckage area and the reef?"

"I wouldn't have thought so."

"Greg, what do you think is going on?"

"I've no idea. First time there was this unknown AIP submarine and the nameless boat. Next time there was the French Nuclear sub, another sub which was probably ours and the same boat in the same position," Stephen interrupted "and the Australian destroyer."

Greg carried on "And now we have another sub but maybe it was the first one with confirmation that there is something on the bottom where the unmarked boat was, which looks like a sunken inert sub. But the big boat with its helicopter wasn't there."

"Show me again exactly where this sunken sub was."

Stephen got his Admiralty chart of the area out again and Greg showed him the location between East Cay and Anchor Cay.

"My chart is a bit small scale but the sub looks as if it is definitely in PNG waters."

"It's nearer Anchor Cay than East Cay. It was difficult to be sure but the water seemed to shoal abruptly there."

***

Maureen Chester looked at the latest report on the Australian loss of their P8-A. It was labelled TOP SECRET SPENCER and it looked to her as if it had come from the Doughnut Building at Cheltenham. Apparently there was a library of noises from foreign submarines but it had not been able to identify the AIP submarine. She called in Harry Brown.

"We've spent a fortune on re-housing GCHQ and billions on equipment and this report says that we've still got no idea who was operating the AIP machine?"

"Yes, Minister."

"Surely we should have recorded on our database all the submarines there are?"

"Well Minister, the Defence cut-backs have made it very difficult. We don't have enough resources to monitor 24/7 and we can't immediately record all new submarines."

"I thought we had special trawlers like the Russians with hydrophones to listen out all the time?"

"Well they do a good job but the environments near harbours are always rather noisy with so many other sounds. I'm told it was much better when we had the Nimrods which could drop sonobuoys and get good clean records."

"Well we've just bought Boeing P8-Us."

"Yes, Minister but there has been a big gap between losing the Nimrods and getting the P8s. And we are very limited on how much we can use the P8s and all their very expensive equipment. Each sonobuoy costs as much as a top of the range Mercedes. On occasions with the Nimrods we kept surveillance 24 hours at a time."

"Well what are we going to do?"

"We thought we might ask the French to whom they sold their AIP submarines."

"I thought our analysts didn't think it was a French sub."

"Well they could be wrong. Maybe they changed the engines in some way."

"Will they tell us?"

"They might if we promise not to tell anyone else. We have already told them that one of their subs was there. They are not keen for the Americans to know what they have done in the way of sales because some of the technology was embargoed for onward sale."

"Sounds a good approach. How long will it take to get an answer?"

"We are hoping to hear to-morrow." Harry paused and added. "But Minister, knowing who had French submarines is not going to solve the question."

"You mean who shot the RAAF P8-A down?"

"No, Minister, though it would be nice to know. We need to know why was the submarine there, what was the unidentified boat and what was the sunken submarine."

"But surely we want to help the Australians by finding out how the aircraft was destroyed, who did it and why?"

"Yes, of course. In fact we've got reason to believe that Al Qaeda will be claiming that they shot the aircraft."

"What makes you think that?" There was no answer. "Alright there's not much point in my knowing but as a general comment, Harry, I do hope that our contacts are reliable and not just thinking we're Father Christmas, not that they have one. Anyway, do you believe that Al Qaeda did it? How could they manage it?"

"Apparently they are going to claim they had a boat there."

"But then, why didn't they announce they had shot it down straightaway?"

"Good question, Minister."

Maureen went home and in the morning arrived back at her Office at 0845. She liked to be early to set a good example to her staff but to her surprise Harry Brown was waiting for her. "I thought you might like to know, Minister, that we've had a reply from the French."

"Harry, I know they are an hour ahead but even so." Her secretary brought in two cups of coffee. She smiled. "Sit down Harry, you might as well enjoy it while you tell me what's going on."

"I wish I knew, Minister. The reply has come from their Foreign Office, Ministère des Affaires étrangères et européennes, MAEE, in

English, saying that they had exported or leased quite a few AIP submarines to Venezuela, Pakistan, Iran and China."

"I hadn't thought of leasing. Does that defeat the United States rules on what can be exported? Trust the French to think of that. I wonder if that's a complete list." She thought for a bit. Anyway you'd better say merci beaucoup, Harry."

"I'll be delighted, Minister."

Chapter 10

Greg's crew were getting restless. He'd gone back up to Townsville and received orders to position the aircraft back at Canberra. They had no idea when they could go back to UK and tempers were getting frayed. The general view was that there was not much to do or look at in Canberra and Greg had put the licensed brothels in Fishwyck out of bounds. They'd landed at 1640 and Greg had a message to call Charles who invited him back to the Commonwealth Club for a meal. As he went down to call a taxi he saw Mary having a cup of coffee by herself in the lobby.

"Where are the rest of the crew?"

"Jane isn't feeling too good and the rest have gone next door to the Benchmark. I thought I'd have a quiet evening."

"Would it disturb your evening to come with me to the Commonwealth Club? Charles Grainger invited me down for a meal."

She smiled. "I don't mind being disturbed but I'd better get changed first."

He looked at her. "There's no need." She was wearing a smart jumper and jeans. "You look fine."

She ignored him. "Back in five minutes."

Greg called Charles and explained he was now two and would be a few minutes late. Mary reappeared having exchanged her jumper and jeans for a fairly short yellowish cotton dress and a white cardigan. They called a cab and once again Greg couldn't help admiring her legs with the sheer black stockings as they sat next to each other on the way, though he did wonder if they were tights. They met Charles in the lounge. There was another couple sitting down who got up as they approached. "You remember Peter Talbert and Charlie? They were here last time when you had your whole crew with you."

**

I had spent the morning writing my report on my ASC visit for Stephen. When Charlie came home we decided on the spur of the moment it would be nice to go out for a meal. Our baby sitter was free and as it was a nice evening we thought we'd go back to the Commonwealth Club.

"Luckily I've finished my report for Stephen; I wanted to write something before we spoke."

"I haven't seen what you've actually written but it occurs to me that I shouldn't see it if it's classified."

"It's not exactly riveting stuff. You're very welcome to read it but I wasn't going to show it to you as you'd be bored out of your mind. Problem with security people is that they always like to over classify everything. Come to think of it I wonder whether Stephen realises you are a US citizen?"

"You have to be joking." She came up, pulled me close and kissed me. "He probably knew before you did."

As we made our way to sit down in two comfortable chairs I saw Charles Grainger, the Air Advisor who, after a brief exchange, asked if we'd like to join him and the Captain of the P8-U we had met briefly before.

Charlie smiled. "Only if It is not going to be a working dinner."

"We'll do our best. In fact he's just told me he's bringing his radar operator so we'll be five. Pity my wife couldn't be with us but it's her evening with her reading group and she chairs it."

We ordered some drinks and shortly after they had arrived I saw the Captain and the rather attractive girl I had been talking to last time when the whole crew were there come into the room. Luckily Charles introduced us again, Greg the Captain and Mary the radar operator.

Charlie looked at Mary. "How long are you going to be here?"

"I wish we knew. Canberra's very nice but it would be good to get home." She grinned."My boyfriend is threatening to come out to see what's going on."

"Well my offer to show you round the Gallery still holds." She got a card out of her bag. "Give me a call and I can always organise someone if I'm not free."

I looked at Greg. "But you haven't been sitting on your hands, have you? I drive past the airfield quite frequently and your aircraft was missing."

"We've been up to Townsville and back helping the RAAF but now we're just waiting to go home."

I decided that I had better not explore what they had been doing since they didn't know I was involved and it was important that Charlie was not included in any way. We had a very pleasant evening and Mary seemed to be fairly knowledgeable on painting. As we broke up I encouraged Greg and his crew to go to the War Memorial.

"If you haven't been you must go. They have a wonderful video of an Australian bombing raid in a Lancaster over Germany in the Second World War, 'G for George'. I've tried to get a copy but they guard it jealously. I think it should be compulsory viewing for all UK MPs so that they realise the enormous sacrifices that the Australians and New Zealanders made to support the 'Mother' country."

Mary responded straightaway. "There's the Bomber Command memorial in Green Park. I think that has helped a bit."

"Good point ...."

Charlie butted in. "And the sculpture of the crew is fantastic. I managed to see it last time I was over visiting the Royal Academy."

I grumbled on. "Well I haven't seen it yet and I'd still like the video to be shown in UK. Most of the MPs just don't appreciate how supportive the Australians and New Zealanders were."

We went home and Charlie congratulated me. "That was a nice evening. No shop."

"There was a reason for that, my love."

Charlie smiled. "Of course. You and your secrets. Can I sign the Official Secrets Act?"

"Good question. I must ask Stephen. I can't imagine you can. Maybe you have to sign the US Espionage Act."

***

Peter and Charlie took Greg and Mary back to the hotel. Mary turned to Greg as they got to the bottom of the elevator. "That was a nice evening. Thank you for taking me along."

"My pleasure. What floor are you on?"

"Second. Same as yours."

They got out and discovered their rooms were almost opposite one another in the corridor. They looked at one another, moved closer and then slowly their bodies pressed together. Mary rubbed her face against his cheek and whispered. "Don't you think it would be better if we went inside?"

"What will your boyfriend say?"

"At this very moment what my boyfriend might think is not at the top of my priorities. I'm not sure I care and I definitely get the feeling you agree."

There was a pause as he pulled her even closer with his hands on her bottom and discovered she was indeed wearing stockings not tights.

She moved slightly from side to side. "That's very nice but I do feel that it might be better if we were not in the corridor. Your room or mine?"

"Yours is closer."

They separated slowly, she got her keys out and they went in. Greg looked round; the room was very tidy with bedding turned down. It was a bit cold with the air conditioning on but Mary turned it off before she disappeared into the shower room and a few minutes later returned wearing a thin Novotel dressing gown; she was not wearing shoes and the stockings had disappeared. She was carrying the other dressing gown. "Why don't you put that on?" He moved towards her. "There's no hurry and you'd be more comfortable."

Greg didn't argue but noticed in the shower room that Mary had hung all her clothes up neatly including all her underwear. There wasn't another hanger but he did his best on the towel rail. Back in the bedroom Mary was making two cups of tea but her dressing gown was hanging open showing her well formed rounded breasts.

He came up behind her and pulled her steadily towards him holding her breasts. "Mind the tea. I'll spill it." She managed to turn to face him. "You're right. Maybe the tea can wait. But slowly; I told you," she pushed him gently away, "there's no rush."

They woke up in the middle of the night and Mary suggested they had a shower which he found exciting as she came in with him to help. It was after eight o'clock when he finally woke up and he could hear his mobile phone ringing. Mary was already up wearing some black panties and black stockings half way up her thighs. She had got his phone out of the shower room and leant over, her breasts hanging down, as she passed it to him.

He looked at the number and saw it was Charles."Good morning, Sir."

"I hope I didn't wake you. I think it would be useful if we met up with Peter Talbert. We couldn't talk last night so how about meeting in the High Commission at about 11?"

"Yes, that could be useful but I haven't checked yet whether we've got any news on our return."

"We'll talk about that when we meet."

Mary still leaning over him, took the phone back and put it down. She started to kiss him and stroke his legs and stomach so that he responded.

Greg looked up at her. "Mary, I've got to go to work."

"Yes, I agree but I've never heard it called that before." She stroked him. "Anyway you don't have to be there until 11."

Greg started to kiss her breasts "Hadn't you better put the notice on the door."

"I already have."

Later Greg showered in Mary's room and dashed into his own to shave. He called John Sefton telling him there was still no news and to let the rest of the crew know. He arrived at the Commission with about five minutes to spare, definitely out of breath; the gates seemed to take forever to open and close so he could get through and he was very glad he had a pass to speed up getting into the building.

***

I was at Stephen's office at 0830 as planned. He had obviously read my report on the ASC visit. "Peter, I like this. I'm very glad you went. You mentioned that the simulators were all labelled except for one. Why did you find that interesting?"

"Well the last one seemed to be the newest simulator with what I took to be a lot of advanced equipment. They clearly didn't want us to look at it but they couldn't prevent our seeing it."

"Maybe it was the simulator for the new boat?"

"Possibly, but then surely they would have told us. Incidentally I was very impressed with the system simulators they did show us. Great training for budding submarine operators. It's such a shame that the development of submarines costs so much money. It's difficult for a relatively small country like Australia to develop a competitive submarine on their own incorporating all the latest technology."

"But Peter, that's why they had the bidding conference."

"I know but you can't subcontract new sensors. Apart from anything else there is the security issue. It's alright to give a spec to the Chinese, for example, to make a large piece of metal or deliver a generator or two but they can't or won't deliver a brand new sensing system with interfacing across the other systems in the submarine. You've only got to look at the money DARPA are spending on research to appreciate the extent of the problem."

"You sound as if you should be an advisor to Jack Smithson or their PM." He glanced down at my report again. "I see you noticed the wall. Have you looked on the other side?"

"Not yet. How could I? What's on the other side? What does Google Earth show?"

"The other side is a firm called South Australia Boats, SAB."

"What do they do?"

"Good question. They are providers to the Australian Government of classified equipment."

"That's not much of a help. What does Google show?"

"A lot of covered buildings, but don't know when the pictures were taken."

"Do they have a web site?"

"Absolutely. They show some twelve metre launches but the site suggests that the Government is their only customer."

"But the media won't accept that surely? Maybe in the UK but not here."

"Did you know that they had a D notice system here and after all the wikileaks there's talk of resurrecting it again?"

"No, I didn't. Will it be mandatory?"

"No, only advisory or voluntary but it would be a foolish editor who ignored it. I wonder whether mention of South Australian Boats is off limits?"

"What launch facilities have they got?"

Stephen smiled. "Did I forget to mention that the buildings go right down to the water?"

"I wonder sometimes what else you forget to mention?"

He looked back at me. "Are you thinking of taking out dual nationality?"

"Hardly. I haven't been out five years yet. I like it here very much but my wife is an American as I'm sure you know and we will have to make some big decisions on what we should do in the future. She is internationally well known in the art world and could get a job anywhere I think. And you know I was offered chairmanship of the UK Transport Safety Board?"[2]

He nodded. "Actually I think we could use you in the corridors of power. I mean in the UK."

"Not for me, thank you Stephen. Apart from anything else I don't think my wife would want to change her nationality and it would be uncomfortable to say the least to have access to really TOP SECRET stuff with a non-UK wife."

Stephen glanced at the report again. "You say here that you didn't understand what they were doing with some of the buildings."

"Yes, that's right. They didn't seem to be planning properly for a very large new submarine, but it was probably shortage of money."

"Well they spent enough money on the bidding conference you were at."

"Yes, you're right but I felt I was missing something."

"Well I may get another view later as we're very open with the Americans and I bet they had someone there."

"Stephen, I feel as if you've lifted a tiny curtain so that I can just see the edge of your intelligence world. I'm not used to that environment. In my commercial aviation life each investigation is normally limited and brought to a tidy conclusion with maybe remedial actions to follow. With you it is clearly just a never ending struggle to learn what is happening worldwide and maybe taking some short term limited action until the next problem arises."

We chatted a bit more and then Stephen asked me to send in my invoice. I was feeling a bit unfulfilled which puzzled me as I had completed my job with Stephen, but I realised that what was really

---

[2] *Now You See* it by author

troubling me was that I wanted to know what had happened to the RAAF P8-A with which I wasn't involved and Stephen was. But I needn't have worried.

"Peter, I've asked Charles Grainger and Greg Tucker, the Captain of the RAF P8-U over to talk about the crashed aircraft and the work our P8-U has been doing. I know you had a meal with him last night but obviously you couldn't talk about it then."

Stephen as usual was very well briefed so I wasn't surprised that he realised that with Charlie present there would have been no shop. "But Boeing are happy. It's nothing to do with me."

"Peter, you may see something that we've missed. You're very used to this sort of problem with crashed aircraft."

"Not military aircraft, but I'll willingly stay and listen."

"I hope you can do more than that."

We had a few minutes before the meeting was due to start and we got some coffee. Charles appeared with Greg, who initially seemed a bit flustered. Stephen explained to Greg that it was alright for us to discuss matters with me and then he started things off. "Peter, since you saw Greg last time they have done two trips in the search area. We really need to think what's been going on. The Australians are clearly hiding something. We've got a sub trying to monitor things, the French have a sub in PNG waters and the Chinese have a sub close by in international waters."

"Stephen, being rather obvious, have we asked the Australians what's going on?"

"Several times and they say they wish they knew but I have to say I feel they know a lot more than they're saying."

I turned to Greg. "I know it will be a bind but could you go through once more the loss of the memory modules for the cameras?"

Greg agreed and he told me what had happened including the search in his room while he was having breakfast. He was very thorough and it took some time but when he had finished I started asking some questions

"Did anyone report back to you on how the search was going?"

"Not at all."

"Well do you think it is possible that it was the Australians themselves who broke into the aircraft and searched your room?"

There was complete silence for a moment and then Stephen looked at me. "That's why I wanted you to stay and listen."

Greg looked stunned. "But in that case Alan Nguyen must be the best actor in the world. I'm sure he was as surprised as I was when he was told the memories had been taken."

"My guess is that he was not in on the scheme. You mentioned Group Captain Bob Acton, he probably knew the score and a guy called Dominic Brown in the ASIO building."

Stephen had been thinking about what I had been saying. "But why would they want the memories?"

"Because they didn't want us to find out."

"Find out what?"

"That is what we need to know. Tell me again what you photographed."

"A whole load of boats and some sort of stationary boat with a helicopter on the back. We tried to see some markings but there was nothing to be seen."

"On these last two trips did you find anything interesting?"

"Yes on the first trip we think we heard a French nuclear sub and there was something underneath the boat."

"What boat?"

"The one I mentioned that was there before or it looked like the one that was there before, the one with the helicopter."

"Did you get a picture?"

"Yes we got lots but we had to give the hand held camera memories to the Australians; however, since it was dark the pictures weren't much good. We copied the mission memory to UK using the Mission Support System but we were also able to show the Australians the MX20 pictures from the MSS."

"That must have pleased them."

"Yes it did. Apparently the quality was better than their system. I think they are using the MX15." He paused. "I forgot to mention we also saw a RAN Hobart Class Destroyer about 20 miles away."

"What was it doing?"

"Don't know. We were brought back just as we saw it."

"I wonder if that was because the destroyer reported that they had been spotted. What happened on the second trip?"

"Mary, the radar operator, you know the girl who was with us last night," I nodded, "suggested we try to get pictures of the area in daylight in case there was something to be seen and also have visual lookouts."

"Why did she think that was going to be a good idea?"

"Well she pointed out that the Aussies had been using us at night so it had been impossible to have a visual check. She suggested that we fabricated an excuse so that we couldn't return immediately and then we would be able to inspect the suspected area in daylight before our fault cleared and we could climb and return to Townsville."

"That sounds very smart but surely you'd get found out when the Aussies saw the film."

"Yes, you're right. We'd thought of that. We changed the camera modules in the recorders and then reloaded the originals before landing. Also, we'll only show them up to the pressurisation problem when we replay the mission."

"So where are the memories and what did you see?"

"They should be in UK by now. Maybe Stephen here knows what's in them. Interestingly the boat wasn't there this time but there appeared to be a small sub of some type lying on the bottom where the boat had been anchored; we checked and it was completely silent."

Stephen nodded. "We've got the details back with some good pictures; there does appears to be a small sub of unknown type on the bottom, probably inert judging by the sonobuoy returns. The sub they heard on this last trip was the same one as on the first flight."

"Well my guess is that the unidentified boat with the helicopter was an Aussie one but not sure what to make of the submerged one underneath. If it was a Chinese boat surely they would have said something. Maybe it's North Korean. Wish we knew the nationality of the first sub you spotted."

Charles came in on the discussion. "Perhaps it was a RAN sub."

"Hardly. Think of the next of kin. They would never have been able to hush it up."

Greg added. "Anyway our system would have recognised it."

A thought occurred to me. "Where was this sunken sub and boat?"

Greg got an aerial map out. "Stephen asked me that when I was here before. It was here," he pointed "close to Anchor Cay, definitely in PNG territorial waters."

Stephen looked around and brought our discussion to a close. "Well that's great. Thank you all for coming."

We all got to our feet but Stephen indicated I should stay. We sat down again when the other two had gone. "That was very useful. Greg seems to be doing a good job though I thought he looked a bit tired to-day."

I grinned. "That's easily explained. His radar operator is a stunner and as you know they had dinner with us last night. We took them home to the Novotel."

"You should be a detective, Peter. Anyway is that allowed? Captain fraternising with crew. Must be bad for discipline."

"I'm sure they were discreet. Still you're probably right. He'll have to fish or cut bait. Nothing can be kept secret."

"Not quite as simple as that, Peter. The stunner, as you call her, has a considerably higher security classification than Greg."

I looked at him and shook my head. I wondered what I was getting into. "Let me guess. You surely wouldn't have put her on the aircraft just because it was doing the William/Kate thing?" Suddenly I saw the light. "She was on the aircraft to try to discover what was going on." Stephen nodded. "No wonder she kept on telling Greg what to do. Must be a very difficult role to play and not upset your boss. A regular Mata Hari perhaps?" Stephen was listening to me. "I wonder. I think she clearly has feelings as well as intelligence and a TOP SECRET security rating. Would it help if I told you that she said last night that her boyfriend was threatening to come out to see what was going on?"

"No, it definitely wouldn't. Obviously she's not an agent if you know what I mean; she's just particularly well qualified and is on the Cheltenham payroll though currently seconded to the RAF. To be honest I know she's good but in my opinion there's always a danger of using young people who are highly sexed. I'm afraid in this world nothing is ever simple, like your having an American wife."

"I wondered when we were going to come round to discussing that. But I don't have to tell you, Stephen, of all people, that life is all about balancing risk. You've taken a view that we are both discreet and that's why you're talking to me now. Which brings us back to the situation here. What the hell is going on? And let's not forget, we still don't know who shot the aircraft down."

"UK are telling us that they are getting a buzz that Al Qaeda are going to claim that they shot it down as a penalty for having troops in Afghanistan."

"Why don't you go full frontal with the Aussies? Tell them what we know and ask them what really happened?"

Stephen nodded.

***

Fotheringay looked at Stephen, "Who is this guy, Talbert? This situation is TOP SECRET. We don't want any Tom, Dick or, what did you say his name was," Stephen muttered Peter in a rather long suffering voice, "Peter coming into the act."

"Peter Talbert isn't a Tom, Dick or even a Harry, High Commissioner, he is an expert in accident investigation. Probably one of the world's best. He was offered Chairmanship of the UK's new Transport Safety Board."

"Well if he's that good why didn't he take the job instead of wasting his time down here on the other side of the world?"

Stephen swallowed before replying. "High Commissioner, as I'm sure you know, down here, even if it is on the other side of the equator, is an economy which is probably one of the best, if not the best, in the World. Australia does not have enormous overseas borrowing and their banks are more than adequately funded. Surely Mr Talbert has chosen very wisely to select Australia with Canberra as his base."

Fotheringay realised he had overstepped the mark. "Stephen, I phrased that badly. The big airlines are based in Europe and the States, on the other side of the World. Surely that is where he should be working."

"Well Sir, if I may say so things are changing. Singapore and the Middle East airlines are becoming more and more important, if not dominant. The conventional European airlines are finding it harder and harder to compete and QANTAS has had to do a deal with Emirates in order to stay afloat."

"Alright I apologise for questioning your judgement. Sometimes you remind me of my wife." Fotheringay permitted himself to smile and Stephen raised his eyebrows. "You're invariably right. Alright, what does your Mr Talbert say?"

"He believes that it was the Australians who broke into our P8-U and that the anonymous boat which was present on two of the three visits our aircraft made to the scene of the accident was probably an Australian as well."

Fotheringay considered that for a moment. "Well if he's right what are you recommending that we do?"

"I think you should have a chat with Jack Smithson."

"By myself?"

"Well he will want someone with him. You might like to have a witness if nothing else."

"You've got yourself a job. I'll get Vin Partridge to arrange it."

***

Maureen looked at the report in front of her. "Harry, this latest sortie of our P8-U. They seem to have found a dead submarine on the ocean bed where that mysterious boat with the helicopter was anchored. It's not clear whether this sunken sub is actually in PNG or Australian waters, but it looks as if it is just in PNG. They also suspect that the boat might actually have been an Australian one. The report adds that the submarine our aircraft found when they were searching the first time for the RAAF aircraft was back again. The previous trip there was a French Nuclear sub. Where is our sub at the moment?"

"Keeping well clear, Minister."

"Good. How are we going to sort this lot out?".

"I think the High Commissioner is going to see the Australian Minister of Defence."

"Well I hope he doesn't go in by himself. How he ever got that job beats me."

"I didn't hear that, Minister."

"Good."

"Minister, he is going to be accompanied by our very experienced head of security in the Commission who has been monitoring the whole situation."

"Excellent. How long are we leaving the P8-U out there? The crew went out for a competition didn't they? Not to take part in a war."

"Being in the Services, Minister, means that you have to be ready for anything. It is up to the Captain to keep his crew on the alert and of course he will be helped by the High Commission and the Defence and Air Advisors."

"Splendid Harry. My husband was in the Army as you know. You always know the correct answers. I wish you were with me sometimes in the House when the going gets rough."

"Thank you, Minister."

Chapter 11

Charlie called me when I got into my office after seeing Stephen. "I've got to go to China to try to borrow some paintings for a collection of early original Australian work we're trying to arrange here. How about coming with me and taking a few days holiday?"

"What about the children?"

"I've arranged for our nanny, Jill Evans, to come in while we're away."

"That's really great. When do we leave?"

"As soon as we can get visas."

"I don't think I need one. It'll be a holiday."

"Well, we working US citizens do. I'm going over to their embassy now in Coronation Drive. I'll let you know the answer as soon as I can."

Charlie rang off and I worked out my priorities for my regular jobs in anticipation of our China trip. Mike called me. "I wondered if you had any more ideas about the crashed aircraft? Who shot it down? The official release hasn't said what sort of boat it was. Could have been anything I suppose, even a submarine though in that case it would have been on the surface and the RAAF P8-A would have reported it."

For the first time I realised that having signed the Secrets Act I had to be careful what information I shared with Mike.

"No idea. Anyway it's good news for you. At least you don't have to worry. The RAAF will be reimbursing you. However, there must be a problem for the Australians deciding what sort of boat it was. I can't believe the P8-A would have let a sub shoot it down but if it was a sub then I suppose it narrows down the countries which could have done it; Iran, China or North Korea maybe."

"More likely China if it was a sub as they build their own."

"Not necessarily, Mike. They could have sold one, or the Germans I suppose. If a boat fired the missile then it could be a terrorist organisation which is probably the most likely in my opinion, though in that case why aren't they flaunting their success?"

Charlie arrived home triumphant flourishing her passport with a visa stamped inside.

"How on earth did you manage that?"

"It's who you know that counts. You remember the other trips I did importing those paintings? I got to know their Cultural Advisor quite well so I asked for his help, bearing in mind we shall be showing off their paintings.

"That's great. When are we off?"

"Siow Hui Tan, the guy with the paintings lives near Ningbo and I've asked to see his man in Ningbo in two days time, the day after the day after to-morrow, so why don't we fly to-morrow night?"

"Just as well you're not going to see him the day after to-morrow as there are no direct flights to-night. It will be very tiring."

"No it won't. I'm flying business class with flat beds so I'll get a good sleep. You can join me if you like."

I raised my eyebrows. "Is that going to help you sleep?"

"In business class, I meant. I sometimes think you have a one track mind. Why don't you book the tickets now? And a decent hotel. Remember the Gallery prefers me to travel QANTAS if possible, even if it costs a bit more."

I bought two tickets for Ningbo via Hong Kong and then joined Charlie for a drink and a sandwich. "Thank goodness we can now fly to Hong Kong direct from Canberra. However, there's quite a long lay over there. We have to leave here at 10pm but we don't arrive at Ningbo until 1pm."

"Yes, the direct flight is a relief, at last. It seemed to take an unreasonably long time getting international flights from Canberra operating."

"There's always a lot more to be done than it seems to the outsider. People see the building completed but don't realise all the work required on the supporting systems. And the same goes for the airfield and the runway extension; the lights, Instrument Landing System, markings etc. Then all the details of the airfield have to be promulgated. Air Traffic has to rearrange the airways and again all that information must be globally available. And finally the airlines have to arrange their schedules and the schedules have to be internationally approved. The list seems to go on for ever. Anyway how did your day go?"

"Not bad. Arranging this exhibition, like all exhibitions, will be a very time consuming task. Rather like Canberra going international, it takes ages to get everything organised and get agreements from other galleries and benefactors to lend paintings; we have to have an enormous planning chart for collecting and returning the items, setting up the rooms, advertising and a host of other actions."

"Surely you don't have to do all that?"

"No, but I have to do the negotiating for the agreement to borrow the paintings with dates which have to allow for their collection and return."

"Well at least its predictable, unlike aircraft accidents which are rather like earthquakes --- you know they are going to happen but you can't forecast when."

We finished our drinks and in the morning we broke the news to the children, which didn't go down too well though they really like Jill who comes in to look after them. In the office I called Stephen. "I forgot to ask you if you knew what the special equipment from 'Discover the World Inc' was doing on the RAAF P8-A?"

"You're giving me new information, Peter. How do you know about this?"

I told him about Mike and how Discover the World Inc refused to tell him what the equipment did.

"I told you you should be working for us."

"It was pure luck I got involved. Let me know when you find out what it did."

"You may have to come here to find the answer."

"Well I'm off to China for a few days holiday accompanying my wife. She's got some work to do in Ningbo."

"I hope you don't think you're going on a beautiful scenic tour. Ningbo is where quite a few of the bidders came from at the ASC meeting you were at. The place is definitely not a thing of beauty or a joy for ever. It's really a huge deep water port with a large research and development complex, feeding off one another if you know what I mean."

"I'll have to look at the paintings. I'm not working."

"You're always working, Peter. It's the way you're made. By the way the people we talk to in the States say that Hank is genuine."

"I'm still puzzled why he came to see me. Obviously wanted to know how much I knew, for some reason; maybe he thought I worked for you. Anyway you mean he is employed by the United States Government."

"That's what I mean. Anyway let me know when you get back from China."

As the conversation finished I wondered if he would know anyway, not that I could see how.

We were both home early to pack and were early in the QANTAS lounge since neither of us liked having to hurry, not that we couldn't if we had to. The flight left on time and we arrived at dawn in Hong Kong, went to the lounge to have a shower and then changed terminals for our flight to Ningbo which was full so that we boarded quite late. It was mostly full of locals and I still found it difficult to distinguish Chinese faces quickly but as I sat down I felt that I recognised one of them, I just wasn't sure from where.

Again the flight left on time and on arrival we soon had our bags and found a taxi, making me realise how quickly China had upgraded her airports and terminals from when I used to go there as an airline pilot; of course, they were still relying on Boeing and Airbus for most of their aircraft but there were already signs that this was just a temporary phase. The Marriott was like most Marriotts in the world though it reflected a definite Chinese influence. We unpacked, showered again and then Charlie started telephoning the representative of Siow Hui Tan, making certain everything was organised for the morning and that the shipping agency had been notified; she also explained that I would be accompanying her. Once she was through we went to the River Café with an American style menu as we didn't feel we were ready to spoil ourselves in the Emerald Sea Chinese restaurant.

Later, in the middle of the night my mobile phone wouldn't stop ringing. I rolled over and picked it up. "Peter, it's Mike here. Have you heard?"

"Mike, I don't know where you are but I'm in bed, in China and I was fast asleep so I haven't heard anything."

"My apologies. I'm at Farnborough. A brand new Independant Transport Aircraft Company 970 of Boomerang Airlines, VH-BGZ, touched down and all the tyres burst on the port main landing gear and the aircraft swung off the runway towards the chalets. The port landing gear sank in the grass and collapsed. It was a blessing in disguise as the plane swung round and stopped with its left wing tip bent up on the ground facing the crowd. Unfortunately we're insuring it and I'd like you to find out what went wrong."

I pulled myself together and managed a few words. "That's really thoughtful of you letting me know so quickly. I'll check in the morning."

"No, wait. I haven't finished yet."

"You're still at the SBAC show?"

"Yes, of course I am. I told you some time ago I was going. I went straight from the airport to Farnborough to a meeting. The weather was foul and they had to stop the flying."

"Was any one hurt?"

"Yes. Two spectators had to go to hospital."

"Surely you weren't insuring the aircraft for flying in the Show? The premiums would be enormous, particularly for an airline."

"Quite right. It was going into the static park. It had flown straight in from Karachi."

"What was wrong with the weather?"

"Very poor visibility. Only the helicopters were able to fly."

I tried to think. "Mike, Boomerang? It's a new airline to me. Where are they based?"

"In Perth. As you say, it's a brand new airline and they persuaded me to insure their aircraft."

"What was it doing in Karachi then?"

"It was actually a 970-200, a brand new variant and Pakistan Airlines were considering purchasing some. They wanted to have a look at the engineering, seating etc."

"Well send me a letter authorising me to act for you and I'll see what I can do and when. I'm going to be stuck in China for a few days."

Charlie rolled over. "What was that all about?"

"One of Mike's aircraft had an accident landing at Farnborough. From what he says it might have been a lot lot worse. Only two people injured."

"That's bad enough. What happened?"

"Undercarriage collapsed. Sounds as if it might have been a disaster but wasn't. I suppose I'll have to go to England and see what it's all about. Can't believe it was a design fault but it's possible I suppose."

We tried to settle down again but just as I was dozing off my mobile rang again. "Peter Talbert?" I acknowledged my name. "It's Jeremy Prentice here, Al Jazeera, QATAR. I called you because I knew you were working in Australia. A terrorist guy, Akbar Pervez, who works with Al Qaeda has been on the phone to us and claims they have shot down an RAAF aircraft. We don't want to run the story unless there's some element of truth behind it."

I had got to know Jeremy some years earlier when QATAR Airways had a crew problem and it got into the media. "Did he say how they did it?"

"Yes, he said they fired a missile from a boat between Papua New Guinea and Australia."

"Well Jeremy, the RAAF did lose an aircraft in that area recently so it sounds plausible."

"Do you know what aircraft it was?"

"Yes, of course. It was a Boeing P8-A but maybe you should ask your friend."

"I don't suppose he'll know but we can but ask. By the way have you heard a 970 undercarriage collapsed while landing at the SBAC show?"

"Yes I did. It sounds a bit unlikely. I gather all the tyres burst on the port undercarriage on landing."

"Well the same guy I was telling you about claims that they made it happen by weakening the undercarriage. Apparently the aircraft had just flown in from Karachi."

"They must have a very very knowledgeable engineer to make the brakes lock on touch down without a warning to the pilot. What do ITAC say?"

"Nothing at the moment."

"Sounds more like the pilot having his left foot hard down on the brakes."

"Would that cause the tyres to burst?"

"You're right, good point. No it shouldn't, but maybe there was a genuine electrical fault as well."

"Well thanks for the info on the P8-A. I'll let you know if I hear anything else."

As I tried yet again to go to sleep I did wonder why Al Qaeda had not claimed shooting down the aircraft much earlier.

In the morning, after breakfast in the River Café, Siow Hui Tan's man, Chua Chuen Hou, appeared in the lobby and we were whisked away in a large car to a huge house about 15 miles outside Ningbo near the Tiantong National Forest Park. After the normal courtesies Chua Chuen Hou took us into a huge air conditioned room where the walls were covered with paintings; Charlie and Chua Chuen Hou discussed three of them in some detail while I wandered round the gallery and then sat down to read some magazines and documents I had brought with me. After about an hour or so a very smart Chinese man appeared dressed in a dark blue European style suit who I guessed correctly was Siow Hui Tan himself. Chua Chuen Hou introduced Charlie to him, then me and then, in immaculate English, he discussed his paintings with Charlie. Apparently in the gallery there were three paintings by Australian artists which Charlie needed for the exhibition, two by Tom Roberts and one by Frederick McCubbin. Charlie went through the dates and then Siow Hui Tan started asking about the packaging and transportation of the pictures. He seemed very knowledgeable and I discovered later from Chua Chuen Hou that he had made his money owning a Chinese freight airline. Siow Hui Tan then left and we had a break. Later the agent of the freight company arrived and the transportation of the paintings was discussed in greater detail. We were able to leave by 3.30pm and were back in the hotel by 5pm.

Charlie was understandably very pleased and we agreed to have dinner in the restaurant. "And I've got just the job for you. Let's leave the day after to-morrow and have a couple of days in Hong Kong. We can keep the same flight back to Canberra. All I've got left to do is organise the contract to-morrow with our lawyer. He's coming here though it may prove easier to go to his office."

"Good idea and you're right about the Canberra flight. They are not daily and they are normally fully booked. We were lucky to get our flights at such short notice. I'll try and get a reservation at the Renaissance Marriott on the Island looking over the water. Then to-morrow I think I'll go on a tour of the harbour while you're working."

All went well as I was able to change our flights to Hong Kong and get a good room in the Marriott. Charlie had dressed up for dinner and looked great. On the way down to dinner I booked my tour with the concierge, leaving at 0930. We ate off the set Chinese menu and the portions were sensibly moderate. Charlie looked at me as we got up. "You know what I feel like?"

I looked at her. "So do I. It must be the lobster. Or maybe the ginseng in the chicken. Anyway it's a good idea. We don't have to have coffee."

She ignored me. "Let's go to the lounge and I'll have a Drambuie. But get a real one, not one home made in Beijing. And you'd better get some bromide for your coffee. I've got a long day to-morrow."

I woke up in the middle of the night. I had a feeling that the Chinese guy in the plane was the one I had been talking to at the ASC though I couldn't be absolutely sure.

Next morning after breakfast the coach came round to pick me up with some others; after two or three more hotels the coach was full and we were on our way. I was staggered by the size of the docks. The port seemed to be all deep water, unlike Shanghai; the guide said that it could handle ships of 300,000 tonnes and it was being expanded. As we were leaving I noticed what looked like a naval dockyard; I kept looking and was just able to get a better view as the coach climbed up away from the harbour. Right at the last moment I thought I saw a submarine but it was difficult to be sure. We finished up by driving through the Ningbo National Hi-Tech Industrial Development Zone before going back to the hotels.

Charlie was in our room when I get back. She had finished at lunch time and gone for a swim in the inside pool. Next morning we had breakfast in the café and then took the courtesy bus to the airport. As we boarded I started looking at the Chinese passengers to see if I was being followed but none were looking my way.

We had two very nice days relaxing in Hong Kong and not buying anything. However just before leaving when I did my routine check to see if anything in the room had been tampered with, I was disturbed to notice that my laptop which was inside my bag had definitely been moved. I tried to tell myself it could have been the cleaner but it left me feeling a bit uneasy.

It was Saturday morning when we got back to Canberra and we were able to chat with the children instead of rushing off to work which was nice. I kept on thinking of the Chinese guy on the aircraft since I had never believed in coincidences.

On Monday when I got to the office I found an email from Stephen asking me to call him. He asked me to go over but I had a lot to catch up with so he said he'd come over for a sandwich.

I went on to the internet to see what was the latest news on the Farnborough show and the Boomerang Airlines 970. Apparently the fixed wing part of the Show had already been stopped because of bad weather before the aircraft touched down and swung off the runway, which set me wondering about how bad the visibility had been when the 970 landed. To try to keep the show going the helicopters had been given extra time, which would have had to be done anyway after the landing because the 970's tail was far too close to the runway and would have been an obstruction for fixed wing aircraft.

The 970 was still at Farnborough and apparently the intention was to repair the wing and undercarriage and then fly it to European Aviation's factory in Hamburg with the landing gear down. I decided to signal Boomerang Aviation in Perth and get clearance for a visit to Farnborough; I copied the email to the UK TSB at Farnborough, the Air Accident Investigation Board, AAIB that was, to warn them I would be visiting them.

I did a good morning's work before Stephen arrived. We decided it might be better to get sandwiches from the Canberra Centre and eat in his car. We drove up to Mount Ainslie and looked down at the town.

"Ningbo was very impressive. Did you know they were building a naval facility?"

"Yes. satellites are wonderful."

"You didn't tell me. I think I saw a submarine there."

"They are harder to spot without 24hr surveillance."

"Why would they build a submarine base there anyway? They've already got one in Hainan which has underwater access so we can't see the submarines coming and going."

"It's probably for their new surface boats. You were lucky to see a sub. Was it a Chinese built one?"

"No idea. Even if I had had a good look I could never have told from where it was manufactured; might have been Glasgow from what little I know. But what is worrying me is that I thought I recognised a passenger who was on our plane both ways --- Hong Kong to Ningbo and return; I think it was one of the Chinese people I was talking to at ASC."

"What are you thinking?"

"Well if the sub the RAF saw was being operated by the Chinese and they shot the RAAF aircraft down, then they might think that I was working for you and I was trying to find out what had really happened."

"Surely they wouldn't care if you were working for me. They would be more worried that you were working for the ADF."

"I'm worried they might think I've found out something and they don't want me to tell anyone."

"My friend, if that were the case I'm not sure you would be here now." `

We watched a 747 manoeuvring for landing.

Stephen nudged me. "Which reminds me, presumably you've heard that there was a problem with an Independant Transport Aircraft Company landing at Farnborough?"

"Yes I have. An ITAC 970 of Boomerang Airlines from Karachi being positioned for the Static Park."

"Was your man insuring it?"

I smiled. "He's not my man but unfortunately for him he was. Did you know Al Qaeda are claiming they did it?" Stephen shook his head. "Well I think they're going to. Incidentally Al Jazeera are going to run a story that Al Qaeda shot the P8-A down."

"We were expecting that but not anything with the Boomerang aircraft."

"I'm not convinced that they could do anything with the Boomerang Aircraft --- it would have to be a very sophisticated rewire I think to make it happen. It's easy to claim credit for something you didn't do. Which brings us back to the P8-A."

"Who did shoot it down?"

Stephen's phone rang. "I don't know but Al Jazeera have just announced that Al Qaeda did it." He carried on. "You know Peter, it's very odd. Why have they left it so late?"

"Maybe they wanted to make sure their boat was safe or maybe their communications are poor between here and there."

"Possibly, but news like that normally travels very fast."

"Well no doubt we'll hear some more from ABC and in Parliament."

We drove back to Canberra and went to our own offices. I switched on the radio. All the channels were full of the news of the RAAF P8-A and Al Qaeda but there were no more details. Later I heard the Minister being questioned in the House of Representatives. Lucy White started it off. "Can the Minister for Defence confirm that Al Qaeda shot down our P8-A?"

"No. The only news we have is the one we have all heard on the radio and TV. We are trying to get some form of confirmation but it is most unlikely that it will be possible."

"What action is going to be taken to punish Al Qaeda?"

"If we can get confirmation that they did shoot our aircraft down then we will try and locate the people concerned, but it would be wrong of me to pretend that this will be very likely."

"Will the Minister explain what action is being taken to prevent another aircraft being shot down?"

"All our P8-As carry an electronic warfare self protection system, EWSP, which detects threats from attack, with a Missile Warning System and a Counter Measure Dispensing System which automatically fires flares and chaff as required."

"Why was there no such equipment fitted to the aircraft that was shot down?"

"It did carry flares and chaff but it is possible a different form of missile was being used. The system does not and cannot deal with every conceivable threat. Of course a shell or bullet with no sensing might not trigger the protection system but the chances of an ordinary bullet or shell hitting the aircraft are very unlikely."

"Would the Minister please tell us the exact location where the aircraft was shot down?"

"We only know where the wreckage was found. I will arrange for the wreckage position to be passed to the Member for Wakefield."

"Clearly there is a very serious threat to all our aircraft in this area. What does the Minister intend to do?"

"Appropriate instructions have now been given to our aircraft which should avoid any repetition of the sad loss of our P8-A. The defensive equipment will be armed at all times."

There were a few more questions but nothing substantive.

Stephen was on the phone again. "What do you make of all that then?"

"We know that the P8-A was not on a straight line between Townsville and Port Moresby. He ducked the exact position of the shooting down very neatly."

"Possibly. Depends how closely Lucy White examines the information. Wonder what she'll say when she finds out it was well into PNG waters?"

***

Jack Smithson listened to the Prime Minister.

"Lucy had a point, Jack. Why didn't the flares and chaff protect the aircraft?"

"Prime Minister, we don't know. As I said, the system cannot deal with every threat. It has to be upgraded all the time as new weapons are introduced; it's like detecting submarines, a never ending leapfrog keeping ahead of the game. Of course we've given instructions it must be armed at all times from now on when searching in this area but I suspect it always was armed. A missile without its own sensing might not trigger the system."

"Are you going to give Lucy the actual position of the wreckage?"

"We'll have to."

"Well that surely is going to make the proverbial hit the fan?"

"We are proposing to say that we are as puzzled as they are with the P8-A position. The Captain must have been making an unplanned diversion."

"Jack I must advise you that you are in a tricky position. What did you tell Fotheringay yesterday?"

"I didn't tell him anything, PM."

"How did that go down?"

"I don't think they believed me. They asked me if I knew the owner of the boat with the helicopter."

"What did you say?"

"I asked Vin if we had had an answer from the Naval intelligence team and he said 'No', which wasn't surprising as we hadn't asked them."

"Who was with Fotheringay?"

"Someone called Stephen. Apparently he's their security ace."

"Did their P8-U discover anything? The submarine?"

"Yes, they realised there was something under our guard boat but they weren't able to investigate as it was covered by our boat on the first flight. There was a French submarine sniffing around and another submarine which our guys thought might have been a Royal Navy sub."

"What were the Poms doing having a sub there without telling us?"

"I think they worked out that we were doing something that we hadn't confided to them and sent a sub to have a look around."

"But that's disgraceful. In our territorial waters."

"Papua New Guinea, PM."

"I'll get Geoff Smith to complain. We look after PNG's interests."

"Are you sure they didn't ask PNG?"

"If they did PNG should have told us."

"At the moment PM they may have decided not to."

There was a pause. "Jack, you could be right."

"Just as well they didn't go near it on the second flight as our guard boat was restocking in Cairns. Incidentally our two guys were very impressed by the British P8-U on their flight."

"You told me they were going to be on both flights."

Jack wondered if the PM ever forgot anything. "There was an airline problem and they missed the second flight."

"Why wasn't the flight delayed? I don't trust those Poms."

"And they're not trusting us at the moment. The flight should have been delayed, PM. Operations made a serious mistake and they've been told."

"Did they say if there were any more submarines?"

"We're waiting confirmation but they thought that first one they found, the AIP submarine on their first flight, was probably back."

"Jack, I'd like to see the flight reports. You know we're in an awkward position."

"Yes, Philip."

Jack put the phone down. He knew his position seemed to be on a knife edge but he also knew the Prime Minister would be very reluctant to make him resign. He called Vin Partridge in. "You'd better send the wreckage position to the member for Wakefield, Vin, and let the Prime Minister see the reports of both flights."

"Minister, the second is by the RAF crew."

"Well that's all we've got; I suspect the Poms have been very selective in what they've written down."

"I could send our analysis of the last flight or of both flights as well."

"Good idea. You might as well send all three and see if he reads them."

Chapter 12

When I got home I checked my email and there was a reply from the Chief Operations Officer of Boomerang Airlines asking me to contact Dick Skipton; there was an email address, a UK mobile number and I noticed that Dick Skipton had been alerted with a copy of the message. The other email was from Martin Foster, Deputy Head of the UK Air Accident Investigation part of the TSB, who I knew well from working with him on previous accidents; he suggested I call him giving details of my intended arrival date and telling me that the Independant Transport Aircraft Company hoped to get the aircraft to European Aerospace for repair at Hamburg in two or three days.

Charlie quizzed me. "How long will you be away?"

"Not sure. Can you come with me?"

"In fact I could do with visits to both the Royal Academy and the National Gallery. I'll have to check with the Director and see if I can get away."

"And with Jill Evans, she may have some commitments. Mind you the children will be furious."

The following day Charlie called me in the Office and said it would be alright for her to come with me but she could only stay in London for three days. I booked our flights with QANTAS via Dubai leaving the following night. We arrived in the afternoon twenty four hours later and I waited with Charlie in the non-EU immigration line for an hour before we got through. Luckily our bags were still on the carousel going round and round and we got a cab to the Royal Air Force Club where we were staying. I called Dick Skipton and arranged to meet him at Farnborough in the terminal where he had rented an office. Charlie had already made her appointments and just emailed confirmations. We didn't want to go to bed straightaway so we walked to the Bomber Command memorial in Green Park. It was every bit as good as I had expected and I thought the sculptures of the crew in bronze were fantastic. It was a complete contrast to the Australian War Memorial video of the Lancaster raid G for George but in my view it was just as memorable.

We walked back thoughtfully and then had a meal in the restaurant before going to bed.

I had decided I'd try to manage without a car and so caught the train from Waterloo to Farnborough Main station and a cab to the business terminal. I had called Dick Skipton from Waterloo so he met me and we went to his office. He was about my age but much more sunburnt from the West Australian sun. He was wearing a jacket over a blue shirt but no tie.

"You've made good time from London, Peter. The aircraft is still here because the wing repair isn't finished; the moment its been done it will be ready for the ferry as the new port landing gear has been fitted."

"The landing must have been horrifying?"

"As you know the weather was bad. We only saw the aircraft at the last moment in front of us, at that point it hadn't quite touched down. Apparently it swerved immediately after touchdown someway down the runway which meant we couldn't see what was happening. The next thing we saw was fire engines streaming down the runway with a couple of ambulances following a minute or so later. The tail of the aircraft was just visible from where we were but at that stage we didn't know what the score was.

"After about fifteen minutes there was an announcement saying that the aircraft had just cleared the runway and the helicopter show would carry on.

"As you can imagine the moment the aircraft came to rest the SBAC organisers were going crazy wanting to get it moved so that the flying show could carry on the next day. I don't know exactly what occurred but the show organisers must have spoken to the boss man of ITAC who were exhibiting the aircraft. Presumably ITAC came to a deal with European Aerospace at Hamburg who flew a repair crew to Boscombe Down in one of their huge transport aircraft with jacks, lifting bags, wheels you name it, the lot which was here by midnight."

"What about the weather?"

"Luckily that had cleared by about 7pm. Somehow the EA team managed to lift the wing and get the gear clear of the ground by about six in the morning. They managed to stop it collapsing again on a very temporary basis, got fresh wheels on and by eight o'clock the aircraft was being towed away to the location on the airfield where it is now while the repair is being carried out. Fantastic job."

"How do you know all this, Dick?"

"By good luck I was at the Show so I was told to stay here and look after our interests."

"When do you think it can go to Hamburg for repair?"

"In a week or so. The engine nacelle got crushed and there is an engine change going on right now as well as a wing repair. The systems will all have to be checked very carefully even though the flight will be with the landing gear down."

"That all sounds splendid but what happened, how did it all go wrong? Is there any truth in the Al Qaeda claim?"

Dick looked at me. "It's a mystery to me. As you can imagine there are at least two facets to this accident; the weather was bad and the brakes were suspect. Luckily the sterile area between the runway and the spectators prevented a disaster but because the aircraft is so large it still got very close to the public."

"I'm surprised the undercarriage collapsed."

"The ground was very very soft."

"Presumably the anti skid was not working. Wonder if it was sabotage?"

"But Peter, you know as well as I do it would need a brilliant design engineer to remove the anti skid braking and ensure the brakes on the left side were fully on at touch down without the pilots knowing there was something wrong."

"Yes, I agree. AAIB or whatever they are called now must be heavily involved."

"I would imagine EASA and the FAA are watching very closely as well to see if there have to be any mandatory mods."

"Can we go to the aircraft?"

"Of course."

We drove to the aircraft via the taxiways. I hadn't seen a 970-200 before with its increased wing span over the -100; it was a very impressive sight in spite of all the ground equipment surrounding it. It looked very nearly ready to fly since the wing appeared normal with a clearly new wingtip fence. The engine nacelle was in place though work was still being carried out at the nacelle attachment. It was clearly pointless my trying to talk to anyone as they were all so busy and Dick took me back to the station.

I called Martin Foster before boarding the train and he agreed to see me in his office the following morning. Back in the RAF Club Charlie had returned from the National Gallery and she was clearly all ready to go out. "Peter, I've managed to get a couple of tickets for the new Andrew Lloyd Weber musical. You've got fifteen minutes before we need to leave and catch the tube from Green Park."

"What's wrong with a cab?"

"It'll be quicker by tube. We're going to the Palace."

I did as directed and we had a good evening but somehow I did not feel the same excitement as when I had first watched Evita as a young lad. The Club bar was still open when we got back and we enjoyed sitting in comfort, having a rest from the seemingly endless throb of the multilingual city.

In the morning I walked with Charlie down Piccadilly towards the Royal Academy but left at Green Park to catch the tube to Waterloo, train back to Farnborough Main and a cab to the TSB office. Martin took me up to his office. "Peter, have you made your mind up what happened?"

"Not likely. That's your job. I don't understand it at all. I find it difficult to believe that Al Qaeda had anything to do with it, despite what they say. What was the weather really like?"

"As I'm sure you know it was not good. Variable very low cloud and the Show had virtually come to a stop. However, it was within limits for landing but no good for an air show.

"What do the aircraft records show? And what do the pilots say?"

"The aircraft accelerometer showed 2g on touchdown which is not unreasonable. The pilot said he was in two minds whether to carry out a missed approach but then at the last moment he saw the bottle neck of the runway and decided he could land. He says he didn't have his feet on the brakes as they touched down but applied them very soon afterwards. The next thing that happened as far as he was concerned was that the aircraft swung uncontrollably to port and the undercarriage leg collapsed in the mud. They shut off the engines and the aircraft came to rest with the nose leg hitting the crowd barrier."

"It could have been a disaster, Martin."

"Absolutely. Luckily the aircraft touched down some way up the runway."

"You know I watched the A380 take-off and land a couple of years ago at Farnborough and it struck me then how close the wing tip was to the crowd barrier. The span of the 970-200 is about the same if not slightly greater. Problem is that the show organisers don't want to move the barrier further back since it would impinge on the layout of the halls and chalets."

"You've been reading our recommendations! But it doesn't explain what happened."

"What do ITAC say?"

"Not a lot."

"What happened to the damaged landing gear?"

"Apparently it went back to Hamburg without our permission so we're having to send our engineers over to have a good look at it."

"All very messy."

"Yes, Peter. I'm forced to agree with you. Give you something to do working out who is liable."

"I've got quite enough to do, thank you, wondering what happened to that RAAF Boeing P8-A which was shot down in the Torres Strait."

"Surely that's not your scene?"

"I got involved when Mike Mansell was insuring some special gear on the aircraft. That's another accident that Al Qaeda has taken credit for, if I may use that expression."

"You know I was in the RAF flying Nimrods as a young lad before I joined the AAIB. I've been following the story as best I can though I get the feeling the Australians are being very cagey."

"Too right. I can't say too much but I can say that I'd love to know what the Australians aren't telling us."

"I thought we were great buddies and only compete at sports, Olympics, Test Matches and that sort of thing."

"Yes you're right. However, I do have a theory but I'm not ready to talk about it yet as I need more facts."

We talked a bit more and agreed to keep in touch. I decided to call in on Dick before going home. I told him where I had been.

"What did they say?"

"They definitely don't know. Not too pleased I think that the undercarriage was sent back to Hamburg without permission."

"Wasn't that breaking the law? EA must have been told to let AAIB have a good look at it before it was taken away."

"You're right." I looked at Dick. "Were the maintenance crew at Karachi on board when the aircraft landed here?"

"No. We had ITAC people lined up to support the aircraft all the way as it was programmed to go back to Seattle anyway to be finished. ITAC paid for the SBAC debut."

"But not apparently for the insurance."

"That was because it was only going into the Static Park and Boomerang were operating the aircraft."

"Well who looked after it in Karachi? How long was it there for?"

"I'll have to check. I'll let you know."

I went back to London and met Charlie at the Royal Academy. There was a new exhibition of Turners about to be opened with some special ones being borrowed from the States and Germany. She arranged for me to go in with her to have a brief look at the paintings as the final adjustments were being made; it was great not having to duck and weave round the normal appreciative crowds. From there we decided to have afternoon tea across the road in Fortnum and Masons before going back to the Club.

Chapter 13

Jack Smithson called Vin Partridge and Max Wilson in to his office. "Max, you've seen this paper about laser buoys replacing acoustic buoys. What do you think? If they work it would give us some advantage over the subs for a year or two."

"Yes, Minister. But we've got to test the buoys to see if they do work and unfortunately they are not immediately compatible with our P8-As and the systems in our aircraft."

"Well why don't you go to the UK and let the manufacturers, *Total Systems*, demonstrate them to you?"

"I'd prefer to do a proper test here, Minister."

Vin had been listening, "How about using the RAF P8-U in Canberra? Presumably the buoys will interface with their P8s. I happen to know the crew are going mad with boredom."

Jack looked at him. "You should be in the ASIO. You always seem to have your ear to the ground."

"Thank you, Minister." Vin smiled, "I assume that was a compliment."

"Yes it was and it sounds like a good idea to me. Presumably they'll know all about these new buoys?"

"We're not but we can find out. However there may be a problem."

"You mean that they think the unmarked boat in the Torres Strait was ours?"

"Yes, Sir. We need to brief our guys not to chat to them. If we use those two who flew with them before it should be fine."

"Well get someone to chat up Fotheringay's office and let's see what we can arrange. I don't think the US Navy have ordered these laser buoys yet. It would be nice to beat them to it if they are any good."

Vin left the office with Max and they decided to approach Dominic Brown who had good contacts in the High Commission.

A few hours later Stephen Wentworth's phone rang.

"Stephen, Dominic Brown here. Is your RAF P8-U still here?"

"Dominic, you know damn well it is. What do you want? Not more chasing your own boats?"

"I'll ignore that remark. There's a UK firm called *Total Systems* selling a new kind of active sonobuoy. It uses light instead of sound and they claim all sorts of good things about it. We assume you guys know all the details. We'd like to evaluate it and our P8-As are not compatible with your Pom buoys but I guess yours must be."

"What is the security classification of these buoys? It must be pretty high."

"Well they're not TOP SECRET or anything like that though their performance will be classified. You can read all about the blue green lasers in the United States DARPA development programme, you know the Defence Advanced Research Projects Agency. What *Total Systems* has done is to make the frequency variable with the sea condition which apparently improves the range of the buoys significantly. If there is any security besides the performance it will be in the mechanisation, not the concept."

"Alright Dominic. Leave it with me and I'll get in touch with you in the next day or so, hopefully."

Stephen looked at his watch. It was still a bit early 5pm, 6am London time. He knew Maureen Chester and her team started early so at 7pm he decided to call Harry Brown and sound him out. Harry passed him straight over to the specialist branch in Portsmouth who knew all about laser buoys.

"You've called at a good time. We're about to get ten buoys to evaluate and were planning to do the work here. However, in the circumstances there doesn't seem any obvious reason why we can't do it with the RAAF down under and it will save some money sharing the expense. We'll need to agree how the work is to be done and the crew will have to be briefed. You've got a secure conference room, haven't you?"

"Yes we have. It was upgraded about three months ago. Will you sort things out your end with your heavy breathers and let me know? If they don't go tilt then get Northwood to advise the aircraft commander and then we'll need a crew briefing conference. We need to move quickly before the aircraft is sent home."

Stephen decided not to discuss anything else but he wondered whether in view of the likely close co-operation during the trials they might be able to find out a bit more of what was going on in the Torres Strait.

* * *

Maureen looked at Harry Brown. "Is it really sensible to test these new buoys with the Australians? Things are a bit difficult over the loss of their aircraft and the games they are playing up there."

"The RAF thinks so, Minister. In fact it is hoped that we might possibly learn not only about the performance of the new laser buoys but also a bit more about what's going on up North." Harry then added what he hoped would be the clincher. "It will save a lot of money and the Treasury is very keen."

"I know you think mentioning saving money will switch me on, Harry. Forget it. You spoil your case by mentioning the Treasury. It interferes in everything without having the necessary expertise."

"Yes, Minister"

"Alright I suppose it will be OK." She thought for a moment. "What about the crew. Isn't it time they came home? Shouldn't they be swapped?"

Harry was always impressed the way Maureen Chester thought about people as well as about Defence.

"Well Minister we've got a very good crew out there, some with special qualifications I'm told."

She looked at him. "Well it's not really any of my business but I know what being in the services is like. As you know my husband was in the Army and got killed in Iraq."

Harry nodded sympathetically remembering that Maureen's husband had been the second-in-command in Baghdad and had been killed by a suicide bomber who believed in goodness knows what.

He left the office and called the Chief of Defence Staff's personal assistant. "You can go ahead sorting out those RAF trials. Hopefully it will happen quickly before the aircraft comes back or you may have to swap the crew. Can you get *Total Systems* to get the buoys out to-night? I'm sure if you're quick you can avoid a crew changeover. You'd better keep Boscombe Down on side."

* * *

Greg got a call from Charles to come over to the Commission. They went up to Stephen's office who produced coffee and started straightaway. "I've got a job for you."

"Thank goodness. I'm having trouble keeping the crew motivated. I was about to ask for a crew swap which I didn't want to do."

"This is a special trial with the Australians."

"With the Australians? That's good. It's all been a bit difficult. What are we going to do?"

"*Total Systems* have produced a new type of active buoy using lasers instead of sound."

"I've read about the concept in the DARPA briefings but I didn't think there was any practical application yet."

"There may not be in the States but Total think they've got something usable."

Greg thought for moment. "But even if the buoy works the subs will work out a defence."

"Of course. They always do but it takes time and the third world subs, which are very dangerous at the moment, will take a lot longer than the Allies, if I may use that phrase."

"These buoys are active ones, aren't they? What we need is a way to find the silent subs."

"I'm sure you're right but I expect that is many years away. I would imagine these buoys would be great at relatively short ranges since at the moment anyway the subs won't know they're being pinged. Anyway here is the plan, as far as I know it, for testing these buoys but it may change. The buoys should be here to-morrow morning. In the afternoon at 5pm you must bring your crew here to our global conference room to be briefed on the buoys and how they interface with your equipment. An expert from Total will be coming here plus an engineer from Boscombe Down."

"But we'll need a formal test plan won't we and a submarine?"

"That's why these guys are coming out. It will save both countries a lot of time and money doing it this way. By the way the UK security level of this will be TOP SECRET; everybody knows about the concept but the performance of the lasers will be critical. We don't know who will be flying with you and who you will be talking to so make sure your crew keep conversations strictly on the job. The current programme, which needs confirming, is that the day after to-morrow there will be the briefing with the RAAF over at Russell and, hopefully, the next day the submarine will be in position and you can start the testing."

"Am I cleared to start briefing my crew?"

"Absolutely."

Greg drove back; he had hired a car because there was so much toing and froing around Canberra and out to the airfield. He still hadn't got over that night with Mary; he wasn't complaining, quite the reverse, but somehow he felt guilty; probably because as captain of the aircraft he shouldn't be having an affair with one of the crew; not that it was an affair, he kept telling himself. In fact the following afternoon when he'd got back to the hotel she had treated him as if nothing at all had happened, which was good in a way as he didn't want the crew to know that there was anything special between them. However, she had certainly surprised him with the erotic way she made love; he clearly hadn't been the first. Anyway it was all over now and they had all better settle down to work.

Back at the hotel he saw Mary in the lobby. "Can you let everyone know I want to brief the whole crew in the aircraft at 9am to-morrow morning?"

She nodded and then got into the elevator with him as they went up to their rooms. She grinned. "That was fantastic the other night – you're a wow."

He wasn't sure he wanted to be a wow but he felt himself stirring as she kissed him softly on the cheek. He found himself saying "Hope there'll be time to have a return match sometime."

She looked at him thoughtfully. "It would be nice but who can tell?"

Greg watched her disappearing into her room leaving him feeling uncomfortable and a bit empty. He quickly got his phone out and called Wyn Williams, warning him of the likely flying programme. He spent the rest of the day looking at the internet to find out what he could about underwater lasers. Their efficiency appeared to depend critically on the frequency of the laser but understandably the information seemed to be restricted and it was coming from Universities which were not receiving US Government funding. The UK didn't seem to be a player in the technology so he was a bit surprised that *Total Systems* were apparently so advanced.

He got a message from Northwood that a Jeff Almond from *Total Systems* and a Walter Brownland from Boscombe Down would be arriving in the morning and going to the Novotel; the message requested him to make suitable arrangements with the hotel. He went down to the lobby and was relieved to find he was able to get two rooms which he reserved for a week hoping, he realised, that the trials would then be over and they would be able to go home.

In the morning he was still asleep when his phone rang. Jeff Almond announced that he and Walter were in the hotel and were going to have breakfast. Greg was a bit surprised they were so early until he realised they must have flown direct from Singapore with Singapore Airlines. He put on his uniform and soon spotted them in the far corner of the room with Mary and John Sefton.

Mary could see the slight surprise on Greg's face as she made the introductions. "We all arrived together to sit down and it wasn't too difficult to guess who they were. We introduced ourselves."

Jeff proved to be the shorter of the two, very black hair and, Greg noticed, quite small hands. Walter looked every bit a scientist with thick glasses and a notepad on the table. They were both unshaven and looked as if they had not had much sleep.

Greg sat down. "When will your rooms be ready? You must want to freshen up if not grab some sleep."

Jeff nodded. "They said we could have our rooms at 9am. Luckily some guests have already checked out and the rooms are being cleaned. When do we have to start work?"

"We've got a briefing meeting with the MoD procurement people at 5pm this afternoon and then a planning meeting with the Australians in the morning. We hope to fly the following day."

"When do we go down to Edinburgh?" Greg looked puzzled. "That's where we've got to operate from and that's where the buoys are. Their P8-A Squadrons are based there, the Operations

Room and all the experts. There's obviously been some confusion. The meeting with the RAAF is scheduled at Edinburgh, not here."

"I was told Russell but no problem. We can fly down to-morrow evening or the following morning. I'll need to check with the Air Advisor here and probably with Northwood." He turned to John. "Where are we having our meeting?"

The crew assembled and Greg explained the plan, the need to move down to Edinburgh in the morning and the 5pm meeting at the Commission. Then he went back to his room, called Charles Grainger and told him of Jeff's news. Charles said he would check but the meeting with UK at 5pm was definitely on. Greg decided that if the aircraft had to move then an early start the following day would be good.

He invited Jeff Almond and Walter Brownland to come with him in the car to the Commission; Charles met them and the rest of the crew who had arrived by taxis at the gate to speed up the signing in. The conference room was quite small and Greg decided to have Walt McIntosh and Bill Bailey on either side of him since they would be operating the equipment. The others sat behind him and were spread out so they could see the large screen at the other end of the room.

Charles operated the connection but it was impossible to tell where the other conference room was, though Greg assumed it was in the UK. There was only one guy visible, dressed in civilian clothes, shirt, trousers and no tie.

"Good Morning. I'm going to show you the equipment you will be using and some key features. I understand you have two experts with you to help. Basically you will be dropping submersible buoys just like sonobuoys and they will transmit and receive on the same radio channels as the sonobuoys so that should not present a problem." The speaker held the buoy in front of the camera. "As you can see the buoy is smaller and lighter than an acoustic buoy. The beam is very directional, both transmitting and receiving, so to get the increased detection range it is necessary to rotate the buoy using these jets when searching for a submarine." The speaker indicated how the buoy could be rotated in the water. He then carried on describing the buoy in more detail. When the briefing was over the crew with the two experts from the UK returned to the hotel.

They left at 8am the following morning with Jeff Almond and Walter Brownland in the look-out seats. The morale of the crew had been restored because at last they were doing something and not hanging around drinking beer, sampling every bar in Canberra. They would have preferred to be going home but everyone was pretty certain that once the laser tests were done they would be on their way.

In fact, the aircraft had already stopped once at Edinburgh field on their way out, for the full briefing on the Fincastle before they went to Amberley. It was about 15 miles north of Adelaide and was the home of the RAAF P8-A squadrons as well as ARDU, Aircraft Research and Development Unit, so it made good sense to carry out the trials from there.

After landing they were met by Shane Morris and Fred Cooper; Greg told the crew to leave their gear in the aircraft with Wyn Williams as the briefing for the tests was at 1030 am. The room was already fairly full when they arrived with the RAAF sonobuoy experts, RAN operations and a test team from ARDU. Alan Nguyen welcomed the crew, made the introductions and then invited Almond and Brownland to join him at the front.

Walter put a memory stick into the computer and gave a short PowerPoint presentation showing how he thought the trials should be carried out, looking at the submarine from different angles and at steadily increasing ranges. "We've only got ten buoys so we don't want to waste them. We need good communication with the submarine and it needs to rotate at a fixed position so we can see the varying responses at a fixed range but with different profiles. The first buoy of each flight will be used for the echo measurements and then we will drop another buoy for triangulation tests. We'll gradually increase the ranges on each flight and repeat the whole exercise. In this way we can soon establish if the buoys will be of any use. As I think you know, the communication radio frequencies between the buoys and the aircraft are the same as our acoustic buoys and the display is very similar. However we're going to have to update the acoustic software so that the laser buoys can be controlled in orientation, depth and some other parameters which Jeff will explain to the Acoustics team."

At this stage a RAN Commander got to his feet and broke the news that the only submarine available to support the trials was the one that had been used for the Fincastle competition and it was still at HMAS Cairns. Reluctantly it was decided that the aircraft would have to go back to Townsville and carry out the trials from there.

The meeting went on all day with a break for a meal. All the procedures had to be worked out in detail with great emphasis on getting rapid communication with the submarine. In addition a joint system of assessment had to be agreed so that both countries got the benefit of the trials and it was decided that copies would be made of the memory sticks holding all the results. Four flights were planned using two of the laser buoys per flight with two spares. Walter summed up the meeting. "The first two flights will be very basic. The real performance will only become clear on the final two flights."

Alan Nguyen then closed the meeting. "The performance of these buoys is TOP SECRET. We don't want the news to get out to the Chinese or anyone else" he paused "including the Americans."

With the meeting finished the crew collected their gear and went to their hotel in St Kilda. Greg didn't welcome returning to Townsville but at least they would be able to go straight home from there. He spoke to Nguyen and they decided not to leave for Townsville the next day but wait until the following day, as besides updating the software which Jeff had brought with him, they needed to agree the exact position of the submarine and time when it would be on station. Greg also wanted to be sure the communication system was in place so the orientation of the submarine would be known and could be changed. The trials would start the day after their arrival and the aim would be to get two sorties in each day.

The next day the acoustics team of Walt, Bill and Fred Cooper spent most of the time with Jeff Almond and Walter Brownland loading the control software and making sure they understood how to launch and operate the laser buoys. They had been designed very cleverly so that the response from the buoys were shown on the standard displays and the buoys could be controlled from the keyboard, though understandably with different key combinations.

They left Edinburgh Field at 1000 local time having loaded the buoys and all their gear, hoping they would be able to go back to UK when the trial was finished. They were off airways and able to fly the 1,032 nautical miles direct to Townsville. Edinburgh admin had booked them in a modern multi storey hotel, the Oaks M hotel on Palmer Street in the centre of the town instead of at the Beach House. While Greg was sorting out his messages the crew were getting their rooms and Mary came up to him and gave him his key. "I signed in for you. You are on the top floor and your bags have gone up to your room."

"Sounds great. Thanks."

She looked at him, straight faced, with no sign of any other agenda. "There were only two on that floor, Sir, and I managed to get the other one. The view is great and yours should be the same, since it's next to mine with a communicating door."

Greg wondered what to say and tried not to be sidetracked. He settled down to look at his messages as Mary went back to the others. It had been agreed that Squadron Leader Shane Morris would conduct the trials and the debriefing and that there would be an Australian naval officer at Townsville to liaise with the submarine. After each flight the whole sortie would be replayed on the MSS and the information sent digitally to UK. After the UK had confirmed satisfactory receipt of the mission, the memory drive would be sent to Edinburgh to be converted so that the RAAF could run the mission again on their MSS. Greg spent the rest of the day making absolutely sure the aircraft was ready and at 4pm there was a final briefing making certain that all the crew knew the procedures.

Greg had a drink with the crew after a meal and then retired to his room. He'd rechecked for messages on his computer when he heard a knock; he realised that it came from the door obviously connecting to the adjoining room. He hesitated for a moment and then undid the lock and opened the door. Mary was there, smiling, offering him a beer. "I thought it might be nice if we had a night cap together before we went to bed." She came in and made herself comfortable in his easy chair.

"Mary, how on earth did you arrange these rooms? Surely the rest of the crew must suspect? What about Jane?"

"She and Pat are far too busy together to notice anything else. Anyway it was luck really but it seemed a good idea at the time. What do you think?"

Greg looked at Mary knowing what was going to happen. "We've got a long day to-morrow."

"Then we'd better not waste any time."

"I thought you didn't like rushing."

"Needs must when the devil drives."

He got up and moved towards her. "I wouldn't have put it quite like that."

She got up and undid her skirt, dropping it to the floor; Greg could see that she was more than ready for bed. She came towards him and helped him undress but he wasn't convinced that it was speeding things up, though the last thing he felt like was complaining. He sat on the bed and she sat on his knees with nothing between them. He held her very close and then just as the climax came he heard a phone ring. He thought of letting go but she pulled him more tightly towards her and the phone eventually stopped. Slowly they recovered, Mary pulled back the bedclothes and they lay down together.

Greg realised there was something strange about the mobile phone he had heard ringing. "Mary, I thought I heard my mobile phone and yet I'm sure I switched it off." He looked at her in a questioning manner. "It sounded just like mine."

She lay on her side looking at him, her breasts falling down slightly in a way he did not find unattractive. "My fault, Sir. It was my mobile phone – it would sound like yours."

Greg looked at her and tried to work things out. For a moment nothing made sense.

She stroked him. "I know. I didn't mean you to find out. I forgot to turn mine off." He looked at her, dumbfounded. "They should have told you. It never occurred to me at first that you didn't know. It was stupid of them."

Greg slowly worked out the solution. "I suppose you were put in my crew because of the Royal Flight."

She didn't reply but got out of the bed and went towards her room. "I'd better check to see if there were any messages."

She came back after a few minutes, still without any clothes on as she got straight back into bed and turned the lights out. "There may be problems to-morrow." was her final offering as he put his arms and legs round her so she was very close.

Chapter 14

Buster Briggs, director of DARPA, looked out of his office window in Arlington, Virginia and wondered what he should do. He had just been reading a report from the United States defense advisor in Canberra which said that the Australians were about to test a laser activated buoy which could possibly replace the standard acoustic sonobuoy. They were planning to do it with the RAF because it was a British buoy made by *Total Systems* and that way they could share the costs of the trials.

He called in Jimmy Foster, his chief of Research. "You've read this, I know. I'm amazed they've managed to produce a buoy in such a short time."

"I'm not surprised. I think they got some key information from a Brit with a Green Card who worked for one of the firms we funded to develop this technology."

"I remember that case. Wasn't the firm *Undersea Lasers* in San Diego?"

"Yes, and we managed to extradite the guy from UK in spite of the evidence being very flaky. He's been waiting trial for about eighteen months while we try to prosecute him, though the lawyers are being difficult."

"Spinning it out as usual to get more money, I suppose."

"No, trying to get the actual evidence. We suspect but can't prove anything at the moment."

"Have you let him go?"

"No. We've allowed him out but he has to keep within 15 miles of the local federal police station."

"How long can you do that for? Isn't there a limit?"

"Not sure. There may not be a limit."

"Really." Briggs decided not to carry on down that route. "Can we stop the trials in Australia?"

"We're getting legal advice. We're hoping we can apply to prevent *Total Systems* allowing the Limeys and the Aussies to use the buoys."

"But Jimmy, these buoys are probably better than ours. They are claiming they've solved the problems that have prevented

Undersea Lasers producing a workable buoy. Shouldn't we be trying to find the answer instead of stopping the trial?"

"Buster, we don't want people to know the performance of these buoys. If we allow the trials to proceed the news will be bound to leak out. *Undersea Lasers* will get there in the end; probably hire a guy from *Total Systems* when we stop the trial."

"How much time have we've got to stop them?"

"Well apparently they've got to go to Queensland where the test submarine is located so we've got about a working day in the UK. We're trying to get an injunction to stop *Total Systems*."

"But the brief here says they've already delivered the test buoys to Australia. Even if we stop Total System surely the tests can still go on?"

"We're thinking of getting the Secretary of State to try to persuade the Limeys and the Aussies not to go ahead."

"Sounds unlikely."

"Well we can threaten the Australians with not supplying them with the missiles they need for the F35."

"That sounds a bit drastic."

"We'll wrap it up."

"What about the UK?"

"BAE Systems are bidding to provide the next generation electronics on the F35."

"But I read a brief saying their technology is by the far the best and their price is the best as well. We don't want to shoot ourselves in the foot."

"We don't want them to test the laser buoys. We think the Limeys will realise that they had better toe our line. In fact even if we can't get the injunction on Total System we're pretty sure the trials won't go ahead. The UK defence industry relies on getting contracts from us."

"OK Jimmy, sounds as if you've got things under control. Blackmail is always the best policy in these matters. Let me know how things work out straightaway, as soon as you get any news.".

***

Maureen Chester had the phone on loudspeaker and waited for the Foreign Secretary to finish. "Alastair, I don't like being told what to do by the Yanks. Anyway it is probably too late to stop the trial now. They ought to be pleased we're getting some measurements."

"Maureen, if we carry on we'll never get any more defence business."

"I don't believe that. I'm told BAe's technology is just as good and possibly superior in certain ways. And it's very price competitive. We've agreed to do the test work with the Australians so I propose to let the crew carry on."

"I think this is sufficiently serious I shall have to discuss it with the Prime Minister."

"Alastair, I understand your worry but let's stand up for ourselves for a change."

She turned the phone off and called Harry Brown in. "I thought these laser buoys were our technology, Harry? Can the DoD really stop us using *Total Systems'* buoys? Anyway how come they are so well informed?"

"Well Minister, there's no such thing as a secret these days. I'm surprised the news of the tests hasn't been announced on wikileaks."

"They'll have to get a move on if they are going to leak it. When do the trials start? When is the first flight?"

"I've been told they should start about midnight to-night." He paused. "By the way, Minister, Total Systems strongly deny that they are using United States technology. They say that they have been helped by research at Imperial College here in London and also by some work being done at Southampton."

"But surely I remember the Americans persuaded our Courts to extradite someone who had worked for a firm in San Diego and who they said had given secrets to *Total Systems*?"

"Yes Minister. That's what happened and the person concerned has been held in prison for nearly eighteen months; he has finally been released on bail for a surety of $1m with his passport taken away. However, there seems to be no sign of a trial."

"But that's scandalous."

"Well Minister, since you mention the problem, it is generally thought that the extradition law we agreed with the United States makes it very easy for our nationals to be extradited with very little reciprocity on their part. There is a large body of opinion that is hoping the Government will change the law."

"Well that's as maybe." She looked steadily at Harry. "Should I stop the laser trial?"

"Well Minister, you could tell the DoD that the laser buoys are UK design and therefore we see no reason why we should not carry on. By the time exchanges are over the trials will be finished."

Maureen nodded her head and was about to agree when her red Prime Minster's phone buzzed. She picked it up and Harry made as if to move. She waved him to stay and listened for a bit. "But Prime Minister, it's not an American buoy and it's been developed without their help."

"That's not what they say. They seem very agitated. I'm not sure whether it's because they don't want us to know how well it performs or because they are frightened their enemies will find out."

"Prime Minister, I think we should stick to our guns and tell them to release the guy they extradited from here."

"But Maureen, BAe systems know what's going on. I think the DoD told them to get some local support to stop the trials."

"Well they haven't been on to me."

"That's because you're a hard nut to crack, Maureen."

"Thank you, Prime Minister. That's the nicest thing you've ever said to me."

"Well I'm going to give it another coat of observation but I may have to pull rank."

"Perhaps we could discuss it at Cabinet to-morrow?"

"Maureen, only two for trying. You know as well as I do we've got to make a decision to-night."

She put the phone down and looked at Harry. "I wonder what the Australians are doing? I bet DoD are leaning on them as well."

***

Jack Smithson didn't looked pleased. Geoff Smith as usual was trying to tell him what to do.

"Jack, apart from those Collins submarines which never seem to be serviceable when we need them, all our defence equipment is purchased from the States." He paused as Jack started to argue.

"Alright, those Airbus tankers were a good buy but we need more than just those and if we don't do what the DoD wants we're going to find it difficult to get equipment."

"Geoff, we're the customer. They need our business. Their defense contractors can't manage without selling overseas. These laser buoys seem good because the submarines won't know they've been found. It looks as if it will take some time before the subs have an answer. But we need to know if they really work. My guys tell me the DoD are jumping up and down because they think they thought of the idea first and because that firm in San Diego hasn't yet made the buoys work."

"Alright, Jack, if that's the way you want to play it I'll get the PM to stop you."

Jack called Vin Partridge in. "When does the trial start? I can't think what the fuss is all about."

"My contacts tell me that the aircraft is in Townsville now and is scheduled to do its first sortie to-morrow."

"Are the Yanks trying to stop the Poms, do you know?"

"We think so and they are trying to get an injunction to prevent *Total Systems* supplying the laser buoys to anyone. Bit late for that now as we've got the buoys."

"Well the Poms are in a much more difficult position than we are as they need to sell stuff to the States. I expect they'll cave in which will make things impossible for us to carry on in the short term until we get our system modified to be compatible with the buoys. Do you know how long that will take?"

"About three months I believe but if the Poms knuckle under to the Yanks. then *Total Systems* may not be allowed to give us the software and hardware modifications. We'll just have the buoys which won't be a lot of use."

"What a mess, Vin. I wish we could manufacture all our defence equipment but it is so expensive, the technology needs to be so advanced it takes a fortune to get to get to a production standard. Look at the Collins submarine and the ongoing costs we've got, not to mention some other projects."

"Should we warn the crew that we may have to call the whole thing off?"

"Certainly not. I don't like giving in to the Yanks or to Geoff Smith."

* * *

Greg's alarm went off at six but Mary had already left and the intercommunicating door was closed. His mind was buzzing, trying to work out why they had posted Mary to his crew without telling him and why she had a special security clearance, though what clearance she had was a mystery. He knew she was very bright and was probably destined for other things. She couldn't have been a radar operator for long but she was very good. Why it was necessary to attach her to his crew he couldn't imagine. He hadn't realised that William and Kate were so important though on reflection William would be King William one day. Maybe Kate was pregnant again but that was hardly a reason for a secret service guard.

His mind wandered as he had a shower. Hopefully Mary wasn't pregnant; that was the last thing he needed. He wondered why they had given Mary a security classification when she was so attractive, but maybe that was one of the reasons they employed her. Suddenly he realised he has turning Mary into an Ian Fleming character. In his view she was just a normal human being with normal sexual urges. However, he reflected, she shouldn't have forgotten to turn her phone off before coming into his room; he had remembered and she should have done. Apart from anything else it had spoilt things, but only very slightly, he reflected.

He went down to breakfast and joined John and Pat. Everything went as planned and they started up on schedule. Once airborne he took the aircraft to the first waypoint.

"Captain to Acoustics. Stand by to drop laser one." Each buoy had been marked and numbered so there would be no mistake.

"Acoustics to Acoustics2. Check laser one loaded and identified."

"Acoustics2. Laser one ready."

"Captain to Tacco2. Five, four, three, two, one drop."

"Acoustics2. Buoy gone."

"Captain to P1. 360° turn on to North and I'll vector you to position."

Greg felt the aircraft turning as John pulled the aircraft round tightly onto due North, hopefully pointing at the submarine.

"Acoustics to Captain." Greg could hear Walt sounded excited as they came over the planned waypoint since the recorder showed the actual signal strengths. "Strong contact one mile ahead."

That was all that was required for this part of the trial.

"Captain to IM. Instruct sub to turn 30° onto 120° and advise."

"Captain to P1. Turn 360° slowly onto North again, expect vectors again to reach waypoint."

Greg manoeuvred the aircraft back to the waypoint, helped by the knowledge that the pilots had selected the same display as he was using for this procedure.

"IM to Captain. Submarine in position heading 120°'"

"Acoustics to Captain. Contact sub."

"Captain to Acoustics. Take measurement now."

Slowly twelve measurements were taken of the submarine at one mile range with the aircraft rotating 30° starboard each time.

"Captain to Crew. One mile measurements complete, proceeding to two mile submarine range."

Greg took the crew through the next twelve two mile measurements and they then proceeded to complete the three mile measurements noting the loss of signal strength as the submarine range increased.

The next phase of the trial was to drop a second buoy and carry out triangulation measurements on the target submarine and Greg positioned the aircraft for the drop of the second buoy.

"Captain to Acoustics. Load laser buoy 2 and check."

"Acoustics2. Laser buoy 2 in position."

"IM to Captain. Message from OZOPS. Abandon trial."

Greg remembered Mary's words last night. She obviously had been warned but hadn't told him. "Captain to IM. Acknowledge. Captain to crew, prepare to return to Townsville."

"Acoustics2 to Captain. Laser 2 buoy inadvertently launched while preparing to cease trial."

"Captain to Acoustics2. Copied."

Greg reckoned it didn't really matter if the buoy had gone if the trials were going to be abandoned though he was surprised Bill had made such an elementary mistake. Still he certainly wasn't about to give Bill Bailey a hard time.

The return flight was uneventful but he felt the sense of excitement which they had had was rapidly deteriorating. Back on the ground they assembled for debriefing which turned out to be very unsatisfactory with the flight plan incomplete. Nobody knew why the trial had been stopped but Shane announced that he had received instructions that the complete trial had been abandoned and there would be no further flying.

Greg had a message to call Charles Grainger at Canberra, who gave him a brief explanation of the situation with the Americans.

"Greg, too difficult to explain in detail over the phone. You'll be getting orders to return to UK."

"Are we leaving from here?"

"Yes but await instructions from Northwood. All the best and hope we meet up again sometime in UK."

Greg called his crew together and gave them the news. "I know it's disappointing we didn't finish the trial but I'm sure there are very good reasons. I'm expecting instructions from UK to-night but we are definitely on our way home."

Greg then looked for Jeff and Walt. They were in the bar with Shane and Fred looking very glum. Jeff gave Greg the news. "The Yanks instructed the UK to stop the trials."

"But what has it got to do with them?"

"Well they think that we learnt the technology from them with an unauthorised leak which is completely untrue. However the UK Government didn't dare say no apparently. The Australians are furious. However they've got the buoys and hope to do the trials later when we've modified their aircraft."

"That's great. Good luck. When are you going back."

"I've just arranged that. We're off to Darwin in the morning, then Singapore and home. What are you doing?"

"I hope we'll be off in the morning as well. Awaiting orders." He looked at Shane. "When are you off?"

"Not sure. I think there's a P8 coming up in a couple of days and we've been told to wait."

Greg went up to his room. There was a knock on his main door and Mary was there wearing her uniform. He let her in and closed the door; it was clearly going to be a business meeting. "How much did you know last night?"

"Not a lot but they warned me there was a political argument over the buoys and to be prepared."

"What did that mean?"

"Well they said that if we managed any trials at all then to try and get hold of the results. And also to try to keep the buoys."

"By swimming, I suppose." He looked at her as realisation dawned. "Did you warn Walt and Bill? That must have been tricky?"

"I was forced to explain that I had a special clearance. They were very good and they were as keen as we were to get our hands on a buoy as we knew the Australians would keep the ones they had."

"So Bill dropped an acoustic buoy, did he?"

"Yes, we didn't want Fred to know so I chatted him up as Bill did the switch. The laser buoy is buried under our other sonobuoys."

"I suppose I should be cross having my authority undermined but you were brilliant." Suddenly the penny dropped. "You were put on my crew to find out what was happening in the Torres Strait. It was nothing to do with William and Kate."

She grinned. "You couldn't possibly expect me to comment."

A thought struck him. "Pity we can't examine the results of what we did."

"Don't worry, I asked Walt to switch the mission memory drive when Shane and Fred had gone."

"How did you manage that."

Mary smiled and undid the top of her uniform. "I've got an inside pocket. If you put your hand down you might be able feel something."

"Why don't you just hand it to me?"

She came a lot closer and Greg got distracted.

She grinned. "It shouldn't be that difficult to find and it's in the jacket."

"You mean this, the one from the recorder?" He showed her the drive and moved away shaking his head. "You're out of my league."

"It wasn't difficult to switch when everybody was busy doing the landing checks. I'd got Walt to give me a spare drive just in case."

"The Aussies aren't going to be too pleased when they run their MSS."

She grinned. "Hopefully we'll be in the UK."

"You seem to know everything. When do I get my instructions for us to go home?"

"We may have to do a side trip on the way home via Darwin."

He looked at her. "I ought to be very cross, your giving instructions to my crew behind my back. But you got away with it."

Suddenly her manner changed. "Is there anything I can do to get you to forgive me?"

He grinned in spite of himself. "Not to-night, Josephine. I've got a headache and more to the point I'm not sure I'm strong enough."

"You could try." She took her uniform top completely off. "I've opened the door between the rooms."

"Mary, I need to communicate with Northwood and not through the door."

She carried on undressing until she was just in her bra and panties. "Well if you change your mind you'll be very welcome." She stopped and looked at Greg. "Don't look so worried. I'm protected, there's more to life than working."

Greg closed the door and started to concentrate. He'd left the memory drive on the table where his laptop computer was placed. He couldn't decide whether he ought to send it to Charles in Canberra or take it home in the aircraft but finally decided he would send it registered post to Charles in the morning. He checked on his computer and saw there was an ops immediate message for him. He downloaded the message and unscrambled it. "Return to base via Darwin, Butterworth, Bahrain and Akrotiri. Overflight clearances being arranged. Special operation Townsville Darwin to be advised. ETD +24 hours."

Greg looked at the message but was puzzled about the Townsville Darwin leg. He thought he might ask Charles or Stephen in Canberra but it would have to wait until the morning. He was just getting into bed when there was a faint knock on the intercommunicating door. He couldn't decide whether to open it but the knock was repeated. Mary was there wearing a very thin dressing gown but he could see there was nothing else underneath. She was holding a piece of paper. "Have you got the details of the flight to Darwin?"

"Not yet. I'm beginning to wonder whose in charge of the aircraft. What have you got?"

"They're suggesting that we should fly over the crash area again."

"What on earth for? We know there's a sunken sub down there and not much else."

"I think they want more details of the sub."

"Well they should send a Royal Navy sub to have a look. We took some very good pictures. How can we possibly fly to Darwin on an approved flight plan and then let down over the Torres Strait? What's so important about the sub anyway?"

"Don't shoot the messenger, my love."

Greg was expecting Sir, the 'my love' unsettled him. He slowed down and pulled her close. "Well Mary, no doubt I'll be getting my instructions sometime soon. We'd better get some sleep."

"You're right, lovely."

He went back to his bed but didn't mind when Mary followed. However, they both went straight to sleep, not surprisingly absolutely tired out. In the morning he got up first and brought her a cup of tea. She took it from him and drank it slowly, considering the situation. "Have you checked yet?"

"Yes. My message was no different from yours. It just says 'if possible re-examine crash area and sunken submarine'."

"We can't leave until to-morrow because of clearances. We can think about it to-day."

Greg called all the crew together, gave them the return news which went down well and then discussed how they might look at the Torres Strait on the way to Darwin. John Sefton pointed out the problem that as currently planned they would have to land in Australia after possibly being caught out transgressing their air traffic clearance. He suggested flying to Butterworth direct to avoid any possible repercussions. Greg agreed after getting John Sefton to check that with their extra fuel tanks they could manage a short stay at low level. After the meeting he immediately signalled Northwood and requested re-routing direct Butterworth.

Chapter 15

Greg woke up and, after logging on, he was relieved to find the aircraft had got clearance to fly direct to Butterworth. However he knew that they needed to leave at 1pm that day to ensure daylight. To his slight surprise Mary hadn't knocked on his door last night and he wondered if it was all over between them. She had mentioned she had a boyfriend and she was almost certainly getting ready 'to change ends'. He realised that he was going to miss her, not just sexually but because she was becoming more and more a pleasure to be with.

Suddenly his mobile phone rang. It was operations at Northwood saying that the RAAF wanted them to do a sortie urgently as they had no aircraft immediately available. Then Stephen came on line telling him to expect Shane to contact him with a request for a flight. Greg barely had time to warn John to tell the crew of the change of plan when his room telephone rang.

"Greg, Shane here. Have you heard? Can you do a rush job to the old search area? One of our patrol boats thinks there is a strange sub hanging around on the surface. We'd like to get positive identification if we can."

"No problem. I've just got authority to do this special sortie."

He rang John Sefton and asked him to contact the rest of the crew. "You'd better tell the hotel we won't be leaving and tell everybody to leave all their personal gear behind in their rooms. He called Wyn Williams, explained the change of plan and checked the aircraft was ready; however quite reasonably the aircraft had full fuel on board ready for the flight to Butterworth which clearly would make things much more difficult manoeuvring around the buoys because of the high weight.

A coach arrived in record time and the crew plus Shane and Fred went out to the aircraft. Greg gave Wyn the mission memory drive which Mary had given him and instructed him to post it to Charles Grainger while they were away. They were quickly airborne soon after 10am though Greg wished they hadn't got so much fuel on board; he knew it was going to make it much harder for John. They discussed jettisoning the fuel but decided they would try to carry out the sortie with the extra fuel and only jettison if they had to.

"Captain to P1. Commence descent. ESM, check EWSP armed and start sniffing for any submarine radar. Tacco 2, can you carry out the Tactical Checks please - off intercom as much as you can; we don't have much time. Acoustics, scan the area for stray RF that might interfere with our buoys and Radar, I need a surface plot of the area ASAP!"

John let the heavy jet down through some wispy clouds and quickly became visual with the surface as he carried out some light manoeuvring to get a feel for the aircraft. Anything more would have prompted the usual groans from the rear crew as they had plenty to get on with without having to cope with it all under the influence of excessive g-forces. He decided to fly the aircraft manually and follow the steer indicated by the flight system as the aircraft was so heavy – letting the computers do all the work was not always a good idea and certainly not at high weight when the bank angles demanded to track the targets would be too high and the aircraft might get too near the stall and buffet. Greg positioned the aircraft for a run overflying where they had previously found the wreckage of the Australian P8-A. They levelled at 500ft where the air was thicker, a little bumpier perhaps but Greg knew the entire crew felt ready, purposeful, happy.

"Captain to Tacco2. Happy with the channel check, the buoys have been reset away from the blocked frequencies so standby to drop passive sonobuoy channels 14, 24, 28, 29, 41, drop on the waypoints indicated. P1 360° port stand by for vectors. ESM to port look-out."

Greg felt John turning the aircraft, more vigorously now to avoid wasting time getting back over the sonobuoys.

"Acoustics to Captain. All sonobuoys serviceable, faint contact 090° from channel 29. It's a little garbled being mixed in with some marine life on a similar bearing but I'm pretty sure its our guy."

Greg vectored the aircraft so that the second row of buoys would help locate the submarine.

"Captain to Acoustics. Prepare passive sonobuoys."

"Captain to Tacco2. Standby to drop passive buoys 15, 17, 33, 39, 52, drop."

"Acoustics to Captain. Channel 17 has come good right next to the target, I've got definite hull popping sounds and air blowing into the tanks - I think he's coming shallow. He's changing speed too, going a little slower now, its too soon to say but I'm guessing at less than five knots."

"Captain to Acoustics. Can you give me a classification, we need to know your assessment of the target!"

"Well Skipper, we've got some very interesting plant noise with this one which I'm really not sure of but we've got enough information to call it – probably the original AIP machine again.

"Captain to Tacco2. Prepare active sonobuoy. P1, prepare for MAD location"

"P1 to Captain. Too heavy for MAD. I need 30 minutes to burn off the excess gas."

Greg was not surprised but he was hoping that with the latest active sonobuoy he'd be able to get a bearing from the buoy as well as distance to locate the submarine.

"Acoustics to Captain. Active buoy is just settling, contact two miles at 015°, several good solid returns."

"Radar to Captain. Strong return 010° one and half miles."

"P2 to Captain. Submarine surfacing, conning tower half out of water."

"P2 to Captain. Submarine now submerging."

Greg switched his screen to the Acoustic display and vectored the aircraft slightly starboard of the target."

"Radar to Captain. Contact dead ahead. Suspect only periscope."

"P1 to Captain. Only periscope in sight."

"Captain to P1. Remain visual if possible. Turn 360° for another flypast. Port look out, get some photographs."

"Missile, Missile, left 11 o'clock. Break right."

"John. BREAK OFF, make climbing turn to starboard, evasive manoeuvres! Fire decoys"

Greg felt power coming on from the engines and the aircraft doing a climbing turn. He heard the anti-missile system operating, the decoys firing and the chaff dispensing. The next thing was a loud explosion and he knew the aircraft had been hit.

"Look out to Captain. Port tank hit and on fire."

"MAYDAY, MAYDAY, MAYDAY Tango Golf 32 hit by missile...." Greg heard Jane calling out an emergency message. He leapt to his feet and had a look. It was difficult to see the situation exactly as the engine nacelle blocked the view but clearly there was a raging fire near the front of the tank.

"P1 to Captain. Front of the port tank is alight and it will only be a matter of minutes before the port wing is alight. Crew, prepare for ditching. Transponder at emergency. Turn on locator beacon, select float mode."

Greg felt the aircraft descending rapidly.

"Look out to P1. Fire still burning and wing appears to be disintegrating"

"Ditching in 15 seconds."

Greg felt the aircraft slowing down as John raised the nose. There was a sickening impact as the aircraft hit the water and he could feel the aircraft breaking up. Water started pouring into the cabin from underneath the floor. He saw Mary and Stan climbing out of the port wing escape hatch but the water was rising incredibly fast. Walt was ahead of him and somehow managed to get out but as Greg felt the water rising up to his throat he knew that for him it was too late.

***

Vin Partridge came into Jack Smithson's office carrying a piece of paper. Jack read it and then read it again. "What's happening. All it says here is there's been a MAYDAY from the British P8-U stating that it has been hit by a missile and is ditching. For God's sake, who did it? How many survivors? Where was it? What's going on?"

"That's it, Minister, that's all we know at the moment. We're getting one of our P8-As to fly to the Torres Strait but it will take about four hours before it reaches there. We've got the routine asylum seekers naval patrol boat somewhere in the area and it's being sent to the spot. Don't know yet how long it will take."

"What the hell was their P8-U doing there? I thought the Poms had stopped the laser buoy trials and were now on their way home?"

"Apparently a submarine suddenly appeared and our Operations asked the UK for their help as we didn't have an aircraft immediately available."

"Did Max give permission? We've already lost one aircraft there which we can't explain and now we send another. I shall lose my job over this."

"Max did know as we had to get permission from UK."

"Well he'll have to be the fall guy. Tell him he'd better have a bullet proof reason for asking the Poms for help again. I want to talk to the Prime Minister."

"Minister, it's even worse than I've told you. There were two of our people on board."

Vin left the room and a moment later the phone rang. "Prime Minister. Bad news I'm afraid. The British Boeing P8-U which we were working with until they stopped the trials has been shot down in the Torres Strait near the sunken submarine with two of our people on board." There was a pause while Jack listened. "I agree PM, I'm as appalled as you are that we asked for their help again. Apparently Max Wilson knew and gave approval. There was a submarine close by and he thought if we could establish whose it was it might help explain what happened to our aircraft. I've warned him he may be in real trouble by using the Poms." Another pause while Jack listened. "Yes I know you might want me to resign but don't you think that might lead to an undesirable knock on effects for us all? " Another pause. "Philip, of course I'm not threatening you."

Jack called Vin back into the room.

"Do we know where the aircraft crashed?"

"Yes, Sir. The aircraft had one of the latest floatable crash recorders and it's transmitting its position by satellite.

"Well then where's our patrol boat which is patrolling the area?"

"They've just told me it's back in Brisbane getting equipped for going back on patrol."

"Surely we have more than one to check these asylum seeking boats?"

"I believe not, Minister. It's not like Christmas Island in the Torres Strait, there's not that many boats because North Queensland is very inhospitable for would be asylum seekers."

"What about our boat guarding the sunken sub. Did it see anything. Can it help? Surely it has a boat it can launch?"

"I'll get Max to find out, Minister."

"Straightaway. There may be survivors. Time is of the essence. It will be dark very shortly."

"I know, Minister, everybody is doing their best."

"What about helicopters? Can't we get one there? The guard ship has one."

"We haven't got a rescue one with the range. Its about 600 nautical miles from both Darwin and Townsville. We're getting one to go to Cairns and refuel. It might be able to help but it will be dark. Let me talk to Max. Your idea of the guard ship helicopter and boat might work."

Vin left rapidly and returned a few minutes later. "A couple of guys on the guard boat saw a flash and thought they saw an aircraft ditch but apparently they were not good witnesses. The helicopter is currently in Cairns on a routine transfer and Max is arranging for it to come straight back and search. We've alerted all ships on the general and emergency channels to be on the look out for survivors and given them the position of the crash."

Jack was silent for a few moments. "Vin, do you think it is the same boat or submarine that shot our P8-A down?"

"Presumably. That Al Qaeda story was just a fabrication."

"But we still don't know who shot down our aircraft. We're going to look like absolute idiots in Parliament."

Vin decided that luckily the last remark was not a question so no answer was required.

***

Maureen heard her special phone ring. She looked at the time and saw it was 3.30am. "Harry, yes I can hear you. What's the matter."

"Minister, very bad news. Our Boeing P8-U out in Australia has apparently been shot down in the Torres Strait."

Maureen tried to get her mind working up to speed. "Harry, I thought we had cancelled the trials and it was on its way home."

"You're right but there was a last minute request to identify a submarine where the Australian P8-A was shot down and apparently Northwood agreed."

"Do we know what happened?"

"We don't yet. There was a MAYDAY call and that was it."

"What about survivors?"

"Minister, we don't know anything more. Whether it ditched or just sank on impact."

"But that's terrible. Surely the Australians are doing something? They've got aircraft, boats, helicopters."

"We're sure they are doing everything they can. To make matters even worse there were two RAAF aircrew on board. Luckily the Australians know where the aircraft hit the water as we had equipped it with the latest type of pneumatic ejectable emergency beacon/crash recorder which would have floated on impact."

"But why was the aircraft hit? Surely all our aircraft have anti ground missile defence?"

"Yes, the aircraft was fully equipped. It should have worked but these systems are not perfect. I'm told they could have fired a visually tracked missile which wouldn't be detected."

"Apparently." Maureen was silent for a moment. "Harry, who did it? And why?"

"We don't know."

"Did the Australians ever find out who shot their aircraft down?"

"Not as far as we know but they tend to be a bit secretive these days for some reason."

"Well the Australian press won't stand any nonsense. They'll find out as soon as the Defence people know."

"Only if they are allowed to say so, Minister."

"What are you saying, they've resurrected their D Notice system?"

"It's very difficult, as you know, Minister, to find out if a D notice system is in place by definition, though the Australian system is a voluntary one."

"Does our Prime Minister know?"

"We've told his Chief Secretary."

***

Robert Fotheringay picked up his phone.

"It's Jack Smithson here. I'm afraid that your P8-U has crashed in the Torres Strait."

"Say that again. I don't understand what you're talking about."

"Robert, that RAF aircraft that was here in Canberra and flew William and Kate."

"OK. I know the one you mean. The one that was doing some trial with your people. I thought the flying was cancelled and that it had gone home."

"Well it should have done but it was asked to do a last minute search for a submarine in the Torres Strait."

"But that was where your aircraft was shot down, wasn't it?"

"Yes. And it looks as if your aircraft was shot down in the same area."

"Are there any survivors?"

"We don't know yet. All we know is that the aircraft gave a MAYDAY call and that's all."

"When will you know?"

"We've got no assets there. We're trying to get one of our P8-As there as quickly as we can. Also a naval boat and a helicopter but it's all taking time."

"But it will be dark soon."

"We know that but we hope to have something on the spot before then, assuming the aircraft crashed somewhere near where ours did."

"Did you ever find out who shot your aircraft down?"

"No we didn't but presumably it's the same submarine as last time."

"I didn't know it was a sub."

"We're not sure but your aircraft was looking for a sub so we're assuming it was the same one."

"Do the people in the UK know?"

"Yes, my people have been talking to the Minister's head civil servant, Harry Brown."

"Fine. Please keep in touch when you know anything. It's a terrible loss and I'm thinking of all the families."

"There were two of our people on the flight as well which makes matters even worse for us."

***

I had just come home from the Office when I saw there was a message. I turned the sound on my mobile, looked at it and sure enough I had missed a call from Stephen. "Stephen, you called."

"Our P8-U has called a MAYDAY and the emergency beacon is transmitting. Presumably it's crashed."

I couldn't believe it. "But I thought the aircraft was on its way home."

"It should have been but apparently the RAAF suddenly saw a submarine in the original crash area and our P8-U was the closest asset available. Someone in UK approved the sortie and off they went."

"But what happened?"

"The MAYDAY message said they had been hit by a missile. That's all we know."

"Survivors?"

"Hope so. I'll let you know the moment we get any news."

Chapter 16

Mary gasped for breath as she surfaced and to her horror saw the aircraft starting to sink. The nose suddenly rose in the air with the main part of the port wing and the engine still attached to the fuselage; the outer part of the wing was missing and a mixture of smoke and steam was coming from the burnt end of the wing. Then silently the aircraft seemed to be sucked down and the last she saw of the plane was the silver tip of the nose.

She looked around her and could see one of the wing dinghies about twenty yards away; the other was much further off. She swam towards it and then she saw two others wearing life jackets by the dinghy. As she came closer she could see she was looking at John and Pat. She was thankful that the water was relatively warm, she guessed 75°F.

John spluttered "We'd better try and get into this thing." but it definitely wasn't as easy as in the training pool at Waddington in spite of the calm water. Somehow they pulled themselves into the dinghy and then they looked for the rest of the crew. Pat pointed to a life jacket about thirty yards away which proved to be Walt and then on the other side they found Stan. They swam towards the dinghy and were hauled in. They looked around for more survivors and they saw a life jacket floating with a body inside. With the paddle that was lashed to the inside of the dinghy they managed to get alongside and were horrified to see the lifeless body of Jane. Between them all they got her aboard but there was nothing they could do; Mary suspected she had been injured in some way before she was drowned but it as impossible to tell.

Apart from the noise of the dinghy rocking in the water and the noise of gulls wheeling and circling over their heads there wasn't a sound. They all looked around. Mary broke the silence and pointed to a spot about a hundred yards away. "Look over there."

John gasped. "That's a periscope. And a very modern one. Let's hope he doesn't surface."

The others knew what he meant. If the sub was prepared to shoot the aircraft down for some reason then presumably it wouldn't hesitate to kill them all. The submarine didn't surface but suddenly close to the periscope a mast appeared followed by a gun. As it stabilised at the top of the mast it rotated towards them. Mary yelled "Swim" and leapt in the water throwing off her life jacket. She took a deep breath and dived down about four metres. Even underwater she could hear the bullets hitting where she had been a few seconds before. She stayed down as long as she could and then as slowly as she could she came to the surface. She could see what was left of the dinghy and positioned herself next to it but trying to keep it between her and the submarine. She surfaced just long enough the get some more air and dived down again. She could tell there was more firing going on but not at her. Six more times she did this and the last three times the firing seemed to have ceased.

She slowly rose and looked around, trying to get her breath back. She couldn't see the periscope and hoped that the submarine had dived and gone away. She spotted a life jacket still inflated, swam towards it and carefully put it on. She saw with horror an inert body bleeding which she recognised as John's. She looked around again and as she did so she saw an arm waving about 250 yards away. There was no sign of the first dinghy but she could see the other one some way away half inflated; she swam towards it, grabbed the light line trailing in the water and towed it slowly as best she could towards the waving figure. As she came close she saw it was Pat who had clearly escaped by swimming a long way away. Mary's greeting was terse. "We'd better try to swim away from here; there's blood in the water and the sharks will be coming. We can't get into this dinghy but it will be more visible than we will."

They stayed together knowing their chances of survival must be very slight. Three hours later it was beginning to get dark and they were both beginning to tire when they heard a noise, not of an aircraft but of a boat. They blew their whistles as hard as they could and saw an open boat overloaded with people coming slowly their way. At first they thought they had not been spotted but then they could see the boat turning slowly towards them. As it got closer Mary saw it was an old ship's lifeboat full of people who she guessed were potential asylum seekers, desperately trying to improve their lives by getting to Australia. She wasn't certain the boat could take two more bodies as it was so overloaded that the freeboard was almost non-existent, but they were pulled in to be greeted by dark Semitic looking people, she thought almost entirely men, who she took to be Arabs from Africa or the Middle East.

The boat was moving at about three knots driven by a tiny outboard. In poor English Mary and Pat discovered that they had each paid $1,000 to a man in Djakarta and had then boarded a ship going to Papua New Guinea. They had been loaded into the lifeboat the previous day and told to head south. The engine had failed but they had managed to fit a tiny outboard. There was a man who seemed to be in charge but he looked completely lost. There were a few people holding mobile phones who were trying to call for help.

Mary and Pat reckoned that a search aircraft would soon be on the scene since the P8s emergency beacon would be transmitting but it was getting almost dark. They hoped they might be spotted in the morning and sat squashed together in the bottom of the boat surrounded by the asylum seekers who looked resigned to their fate. However, some of them suddenly got very excited and Mary quickly realised why; they could hear an aircraft coming close and low. Pat recognised the noise of a P8 and then as the noise got even louder a searchlight came on bathing them all in daylight.

The light was gone almost as soon as it had appeared but the aircraft came round again and shone the searchlight. Mary smiled "Well they were probably looking for us but they found an asylum seekers boat instead. Don't know what happens next. I thought they had a naval patrol boat in these waters. I don't know about you but I'm cold and hungry."

The aircraft carried on searching with the noise going further and further away but then they heard a new noise, the thump of a large diesel vessel getting louder and louder and soon they could see its navigation lights. It clearly knew the exact location of their boat and presumably could see it on its radar. It seemed to be a large coastal vessel, the black rusty hull towering above them. It stopped almost on top of the life raft with a searchlight fixed on them. A boat was lowered amidships and came alongside with three men it.

"Anyone speak English?" and before the so called captain could reply Mary yelled "Over here. We do."

The asylum seekers made way for Mary and Pat to speak to the crew and they quickly explained the situation. Half of the asylum seekers got into the boat with Mary and Pat and were ferried to a long ladder which had been put out of an access door in the side of the ship. Slowly they climbed out one by one clearly tired out with exhaustion. Mary and Pat were the last to climb up and as they clambered up they realised how weak they were. All the asylum seekers had been led away but there had clearly been communication between the boat crew and the Captain as they were taken straightaway to what looked like the officer's mess or canteen.

The Captain appeared carrying some brandy. "Better drink this. It's meant to be good. We were alerted on the radio that an aircraft had crashed and to look for survivors. Then an air force plane told us about these asylum seekers and asked us to pick them up and take them to Cairns which is where we're heading. Luckily we were able to help as the depth where we picked you up was just alright. As you can imagine finding you on board was a real bonus. We've told them that we've got two crew and they need your names." He wrote the names down. "Were there no other survivors?" Mary shook her head. "Right, off you go for a shower and we'll get you some dry clothes, then food and bed. We've got a trained medic on board who'll check you over but he's busy at the moment with the seventy asylum seekers."

Mary looked amazed. "No wonder the life boat was crowded. Seventy. I thought there might have been forty."

They were shown the shower and given some clothes and returned twenty minutes later feeling almost human again but then the full enormity of what had happened to them began to sink in. They were given bacon and eggs and though they were hungry neither of them felt like eating a lot. The Captain reappeared. "We'll be in Cairns in the morning and I understand a plane is being positioned there to take you to Canberra."

They were shown to cabins and went straight to sleep but later Mary woke up and relived the last few hours. She knew she had to accept it all but it seemed worse than any nightmare.

***

Mary woke up again at 7.00am. She could tell from the lack of movement and thump from the diesel that they were in harbour. She looked round the room and saw to her surprise that her flying overalls, trousers, jumper and underclothes had been cleaned and ironed. There was a knock on the door and a man dressed in a medical uniform appeared. "Can I check your blood pressure, lungs, and pulse?"

"Are you a doctor?" He shook his head. She grinned for the first time. "Well you can do my blood pressure and pulse."

When he had finished she decided to show off her lungs and breathed in vigorously; to her surprise it hurt a bit and he noticed. She lifted the back of her jumper and he listened with the stethoscope. "Well you be careful my dear. If it doesn't get better you'd better see a doctor."

She showered and got dressed. Another knock on the door and Pat appeared also wearing his flying suit. "Mary, let's have a quick breakfast before we go. I'm starving."

Mary nodded but realised she was feeling the whole event even more than Pat, who on his part was clearly shattered with the loss of Jane. Being shot down was bad enough but the loss of the rest of the crew was hurting and, she knew she must face up to it, she was missing Greg. He had been a capable captain and he had really excited her sexually. She didn't normally let herself go completely when she made love but with him she hadn't cared. She knew she hadn't thought things through but she hadn't planned on his leaving her suddenly, tragically, like this.

Alan Nguyen suddenly appeared as they were having breakfast. "Good to see you both."

Mary didn't know what to say. "What on earth are you doing here?" She stopped. "You must have been up all night."

He smiled. "We did leave rather early this morning."

"The Captain said there was a plane coming but I didn't believe him."

"Well he was right. It's one of our VIP planes."

"But it must have cost a bomb." He didn't argue. She realised that their predicament was clearly not a secret; Alan must have got authority from the very highest level to be allowed to come and collect them. "Have you found any more survivors?" She knew the answer before she asked the question but she wanted to ask anyway.

"We've got an aircraft looking and there's a boat on its way from Cairns which should be in the area about now."

"Alan, they had better be careful in case that sub is still there."

"Yes, you're right. We need to talk about that later."

Mary certainly didn't feel like talking about it right then but she knew everyone would be wanting to know what happened. She managed a smile. "How much later?"

"Could we have a preliminary debrief when we get to Canberra?"

"Not until I can get out of this flying suit."

Alan look uncertain but clearly wanted to move on.

"Alan, we've got to say our farewells first and then we can go." Pat led the way to the Captain and they thanked him.

He looked at them. "Be careful as you go out. You do realise you're front page news and your photos will be in every newspaper, probably all over the world." He showed them the Sydney Daily Telegraph which he had clearly printed on the boat. Mary could see a terrible library shot of her on the front page with another one of Pat. The headline blared out. 'Another plane shot down in Queensland' and underneath 'Are we defenceless?'

As they went down the gangway Mary could see a lot of photographers and there was no way they could be avoided as they made their way to a waiting car. She ignored requests for posed shots, as did Pat, but she was afraid that the Captain was going to be right; the photos they did manage to take were going to appear all over Australia and then probably, globally, which was the last thing she wanted.

The car whisked them away to the airport where they were treated as VIPs avoiding more photographers and were driven straight on to the ramp and stopped by a Bombardier Challenger VIP jet transport.

"Alan, this is ridiculous. Why couldn't we travel by airline?"

"Mary, you're not strong enough for one thing and what are you going to use for money, identification, passport and clothes? You can't wander about like that."

"But we need to go to Townsville to collect all our belongings."

"Your crew chief, Wyn Williams is arranging all that and it's all going to Canberra where you can help sort everything out. We arranged one of our regular transport planes to pick it up."

Mary gave up and they sat in comfort in the VIP seats. Then she pulled herself together. "Alan, give me some paper and a pen and I'll try and put something down."

Alan opened his brief case and produced paper and pens for them. For the next two hours until they landed at Canberra she wrote down the events as best she could remember while Pat, after a brief start, fell asleep. She had to wake him up as they taxied in next to the terminal. Charles Grainger met them at the aircraft. He looked distraught and admitted to having had very little sleep, having been on the telephone almost from the moment of their MAYDAY and the emergency beacon being transmitted to the world. "Look, we've got no rooms in the High Commission so Brigadier Timothy Whetstone, the Defence Advisor, has agreed that you can stay at his house. It's completely secure so you shouldn't have any problems. Hopefully there you won't get bombarded by the media."

"But what about Pat?"

"Well we reckon that the press will be after you rather than him and so we think it will be alright if we put him up in the Novotel. He's been there before so he knows his way around."

"Seems a bit unfair on Pat."

"I don't think you realise the media pressure you're going to be under. The whole world is following the story, if I may call it that, and you're a very attractive lady. Pat will be interviewed of course but he won't be hounded." He thought for a moment. "If it's alright with you I've got my wife with me and we'll take you both shopping to get some clothes until yours arrive. Then, if you can manage it, we ought to have a debriefing." Mary realised it was no good arguing about money and she did want to get out of her flying suit. An airport car took them through the barrier into the normal car and passenger area and into the car park entrance.

Mary was still holding her report and looked to Charles for advice. "I've written a brief account but I'm not sure who I should give it to."

Alan looked at them. "How about this. If you all wait here I'll get it copied at the airport and then we'll all have copies. Then let's plan on a full debriefing at 1700."

Charles agreed and Alan was away about twenty minutes. He gave the original to Mary, a copy to Charles and kept one for himself. He left and Mary and Pat went with Charles to his car where his wife Fiona was waiting. They drove over to the Mall and then split up, Mary going with Fiona to Myer where she rapidly chose a pair of slacks, a jumper, a skirt and a blouse. From there she went to the lingerie department where she decided that utility was the order of the day rather than femininity; she knew full well that the next few days would definitely not be the time to display her figure.

They all met up at the car park and Charles dropped Pat off at the hotel. When they got to the Brigadier's house Fiona introduced her to Jacquie, Timothy Whetstone's wife. Mary was very concerned at the extra work involved in looking after her.

"Look my dear. We often put visitors up and nobody could be more deserving than you with all you've been through."

Fiona had to go back home and Jacquie took Mary up to her room. She showered and then lay on the bed thinking of everything that had happened in the last twenty four hours.

There was a knock on the door and Jacquie handed her the phone.

"It's Stephen from the High Commission."

Mary listened. "Mary, its Stephen Wentworth here. I don't think we've met. I'm in charge of security here and Charles has just given me your report to be typed up. How about our meeting up? If you agree I'll send a car over and meet you in the lobby. Get your photo taken as they are giving you a proper pass."

She put on jumper and trousers, looked in the mirror, shook her head, did what she could with her hair and went down. She gave Jacquie the phone who in turn gave her a key of the door and told her the security number to get through the gate. "If you get a car just park it in that slot over there."

The Commission car was waiting and, after getting through the gates, Mary got a pass. A man came over and introduced himself. "I'm Stephen. I recognised you from your photograph."

Mary raised her eyebrows. "What photograph?"

"The one they sent me from Cheltenham."

She nodded. "I should have known. Well I expect there are going to be a lot more of me after the photographers send their shots in so I'll be on the public record I'm afraid."

Stephen led the way to the lobby and up to his office where they sat in the easy chairs.

"I've scanned through your report. It's horrifying, the shooting of the survivors."

"They clearly didn't want anybody to recognise them. Must have been the same reason why they shot down the Aussie aircraft. Wonder what it was?"

"Very good question. They've got to be found. If only there had been some markings on the sub."

"We need to find it and sink it before it can fire back. Another sub or a boat might be best."

"Well it's not up to us. We can only hope. What we have to decide right now is how to handle the publicity. You appreciate your rescue is a double whammy?" She looked at him curiously. "I think this is the first time we've had a ship launching a boat load of asylum seekers in this area. It puts another dimension on where they can land. And of course the media and the papers can't wait to get hold of you --- have a look outside."

Mary could just make out two or three photographers outside the gate. "What do you suggest? I think I've agreed to an RAAF debriefing later on to-day."

"Well it all happened in their territory or the PNG's so it is an Australian incident. However, in the circumstances they have agreed that Charles can be with the interrogation team. But that doesn't solve the media problem."

She looked at him. "Do the media expect us to go through all the agony and inconvenience of being interrogated for free?"

Stephen looked at her in surprise. "I suppose they do. Why do you ask?"

"Because I want us to be paid and the money go towards supporting the families of the people who've been killed. No money, no interviews."

Stephen looked at her and began to realise for the first time what he was dealing with. "That's a great idea but you do realise that if they pay money you'll have to co-operate with them? You won't be able to just walk away."

"I'll willingly do that in exchange for getting real money for the families."

"But you're in the Services Mary. You can't be paid."

"I don't mind if the money goes to the Benevolent Fund but I'm not going to be hounded by the media for nothing."

"Sounds as if you need an agent to negotiate."

"An agent will expect to be paid."

"Wait a moment. I've got an idea. Let me ask someone."

He dialled Peter Talbert. "You've caught up with the news?"

"Yes, only two survivors. The girl and the co-pilot. What a shambles."

"There were two female crew, Peter, and the one who survived is with me now. I'm calling on her behalf, really. She says she's not going to give interviews to the media unless she gets paid and the money is all to go to the families of the people who died in the crash."

"Good girl. Must be the one we met in the Club. I knew she was a goer." Mary heard the reply and smiled. "Well, why have you called me?"

"You know your way around. Who is going to negotiate for her? How much for an interview? Actually it won't be for her, it will have to be to the RAF Benevolent Fund."

"Well if she goes for a UK paper and does a special interview plus only talking to agreed people she might get a £100K. News of the World has gone now but the Sun would probably do it." Peter paused. "On second thoughts my advice would be for her to do the deal out here, quickly, before all the lawyers in Whitehall interfere. No-one is going to criticise her if the money goes to charity and it would be a brave politician to try to do her down. Tell her to go for it."

Stephen looked at Mary. "Peter, how about you negotiating for her. Quick as you can." Mary nodded and Stephen hung up. "Let's leave it like that for the moment. Interviews may be tough."

"Well they did give us a bit of training on the course at Cheltenham in not answering the questions, just in case."

"Alright then, change of subject." He gave her a box. "Here is an ordinary mobile phone, it's yours from now on. I assume you no longer have the your special mobile." She nodded. "Well this is a regular one, nothing clever. You will need to get your photograph taken so we can give you a new passport. Do you have your credit card and bank card details?"

"It's all on my computer which hopefully will be here somewhere."

"Yes, Charles is dealing with Pat and the crew chief. All the gear was loaded first thing this morning and should be here any time at all. We agreed I'd look after you because of your security situation. I expect your stuff will be in your room fairly soon. Charles will give you a float but you'll have to deal with your bank and credit card people to get new cards."

"But who knows when I'm going home? They'll never send the cards here. I may need a lot of money. However, I've got my bank card reader in the car so maybe with the phone you've given me I will be able to transfer back to you from my bank account any money that you or Charles give me."

"Mary, you won't need to do that. Charles ought to be able to keep you in funds from the Commission until you get home. Excuse my asking, do you have dependants? Are you married or have a partner?"

She smiled. "My parents live in Cambridge. I'm foot loose and fancy free." She looked at Stephen. "I know you hear a lot of gossip but we're not bespoke." She thought for a moment. "I'd better speak to Pat and tell him the plan about the media and make sure he doesn't object. Also Charles to make certain he's on side."

Peter Talbert called back and Stephen put the phone on speaker. "Look, I've kept the lawyers out of this. The Australian volunteered to donate A$40K to the RAF Benevolent Fund for an exclusive article and interview and Sky similarly agreed to give A$50K but a quarter of each will go to an RAAF nominated charity." Mary looked as if she wanted to say something but Stephen raised his hand as Peter continued. "However they wanted global exclusivity so The Australian will have to pay A$300K and Sky the same. My view is that for better or for worse your story is going to be covered Worldwide and doing it this way both The Australian and Sky can charge. Perhaps I should have charged them more as they may make a killing. They won't backtrack on the payment because they will announce it to show how munificent they are before they publish the article and before either of you appear. Hopefully you'll go along with that."

Mary nodded to Stephen. "Peter, that's fantastic. It's not a lot but it's a lot better than nothing. Here's my new mobile number 041 2343 4573 but it may be better to double check with Charles Grainger for our availability. Not sure when I'm going home so we'd better get the interviews over. I'll amplify my report for the Australian and they can have it to-morrow. We're having a full debriefing at 1700 but not sure when it will finish. It may be a bit late for Sky and for me for that matter."

Chapter 17

Charlie was dealing with the kids when I got home. I brought her up to speed.

"My love, I see I'll have to watch you."

"What do you mean?"

"That girl who survived. You took a shine to her."

"I'm old enough to be her father."

"Nonsense, her elder brother at best and you should have argued with me."

"Well a thing of beauty is a joy for ever."

"I don't mind for ever, it's while she's out here I'm thinking about."

"Sometimes I think you're just a little bit suspicious."

"Wrong yet again. I'm a lot suspicious."

"You can't say that. Very suspicious would be OK."

"Shut up, you can kiss me and get us two gin and tonics."

As I poured the drinks I decided to ring Stephen. "How did the debriefing go?"

"Don't know yet but I do know it's finished."

Charlie had been listening. "Are you on the ASIO payroll yet?"

"You've got it wrong. It's Cheltenham or some other clandestine place or even MoD and I'm not."

"Well I'm not sure we can afford you spending your time on charity work." But she leant over and made it quite clear she would live with it.

We turned on the TV and I switched to Sky for the news. The crash was still front page news and suddenly there was an interruption and the announcer proudly announced that they had decided to donate not only to the RAAF but also to the RAF charities as a help to the dependants of the crew killed on the RAF P8-U. This was immediately followed by an interview with Mary French. She was wearing her formal uniform and handled the questions very well indeed. Charles Grainger had warned me it would be a harrowing experience and understandably the most dramatic part of the interview was the machine gunning of the survivors. She didn't pull any punches and told it, blood, bodies and all.

Then she was asked about the asylum seeker boat and here the emphasis was not so much on the rescue but the method the asylum seekers had used to try to get into Australia. The whole thing lasted for about thirty minutes and Mary was incredibly composed.

Charlie looked at me. "That was fantastic. How on earth did she remain unmoved?"

I knew she had had training but didn't feel I need tell Charlie. However, I did tell her about the charity dimension.

"Peter, I did wonder. It seemed so out of character for Sky. However I can understand their wanting global exclusivity. It will be a front page news item for several days. What about the co-pilot. Why didn't they interview him?"

"They probably have but I doubt he was as good. To-morrow morning, perhaps?"

"And I have to admit in spite of wearing uniform she did look quite smart. Why don't we ask them round?"

"I'll try them to-morrow. I've got her mobile number."

Charlie couldn't help smiling. "What took you so long?"

***

Maureen Chester looked at the TV clip which Harry Brown had brought in. "That girl is very good, Harry. What a terrible experience. I've read her report but somehow hearing it from her first hand really drives things home. How come I couldn't see her on the BBC but only on Sky and ITV?"

"Apparently she refused to be interviewed unless the media contributed to charities to support the families of the dependants. So Sky and the Australian have got a global exclusive."

"How absolutely splendid. Pity it had to be News Corporation, but they are based in Australia."

Maureen thought for a moment. "Does that mean that all the world's media have to pay Sky or The Australian to use her story?"

"That's the way I understand it and presumably the BBC hasn't paid Sky yet."

"In that case I would think they're on a real winner though I suppose it depends on how much money they had to pay for the exclusive."

"A total of £400K, £300K to the RAF Benevolent Fund and the rest to an RAAF equivalent."

"That's brilliant and no agents' fees. Did she think that up?"

"I think she got a friend to do the negotiation. I'll try and find out."

"Shouldn't she get something for bravery in front of the enemy?"

"Yes, Minister. It is being looked into but there are rules and the experts aren't sure where her actions fit in. However there's not much doubt she must get something."

"Why?"

"Those laser buoy trials that the Prime Minister cancelled."

"Harry, I'm not sure you should put it quite like that."

"Well Minister, she managed to get hold of the recorder module and we now have it in the UK so we can start analysing the performance of the buoys."

"That really is brilliant." She paused. "But I thought the deal was that the Australians collected all the modules."

"Apparently the one they got was not the one that was actually used. She managed to switch the modules before they landed."

"No wonder Cheltenham think highly of her, Harry. That's really good. I'm determined we continue to develop these buoys if they've got the right performance."

"Yes, Minister."

"It's a triple whammy, Harry. The shooting down, the laser buoys and her handling of the media getting money. Mind you with regard to the media, it's just as well it wasn't in UK or the lawyers would somehow have got themselves into the action and got most of the money that was going."

"If you say so, Minister, but I'm not sure your view reflects Government policy."

They looked at one another and laughed. "Harry, I wouldn't be without you." She became serious. "But now we have a responsibility to find this submarine as well as the Australians. Is there nothing we can do? Our press is going mad not to mention the media. And I've got to answer questions in the House."

"Well our submarine is still out there but the chances of finding and identifying the other submarine must be very remote."

"Well it must try. I suggest we tell the Australians that our submarine has just arrived in the area and we are offering it to help."

"There has been a suggestion that we should send out another P8-U."

"No, I don't think that would be a good idea. Attack helicopters which carry Martels[3] or whatever they are called these days sound a better bet."

"That would mean sending out a boat, Minister."

"I'm not serious, Harry. The Australians have got plenty of boats and helicopters out there. They'll be trying like hell to sort things out. Apart from our sub they don't need any more help."

***

I made a list of likely countries that would not only shoot aircraft down but also machine gun survivors in the water. I called Stephen and he decided he'd better come round.

"Look, that sub is not nuclear so it must need to get refuelled and get supplies. In fact it probably refuelled between the two dates when it shot down those aircraft. How good are your satellites?"

"Since you ask me, not as good as the American ones."

"Can't you ask them?"

"We have and they haven't spotted anything unusual."

"Where have they looked?"

"All the usual suspects. China, North Korea, New Caledonia."

"Won't be the French. I favour North Korea but I don't think they've got AIP submarines unless the Chinese sold them some. Anyway the distances are large and the navigation not all that easy. Could be Chinese I suppose but they wouldn't start shooting. Even if it was theirs we wouldn't be able to spot it because of the underwater sub harbour. Have we asked all the AIP sub owners?"

---

[3] Anti shipping missile

"Apparently we did immediately after our aircraft was shot down but as I said we don't know all the countries that have these subs."

"You know, Stephen, we still don't know what's so fascinating about that sub that our P8 found. Besides this AIP machine, the French have had one of their nuclear subs there and so have we. Have you forgotten to tell me what makes this area so hot?"

"Well, I believe there was some garbled emergency message which was transmitted on the satellite emergency network which the people in Cheltenham heard."

"When was that? Let me guess. Was it just before the Aussies intercepted that inflatable?"

"Apparently it was, but the experts couldn't decode the message though for some reason the latitude and longitude was transmitted in the clear. Presumably all countries that monitor the emergency channel must have copied the message as routine and those which had relatively local submarine facilities like the French, Chinese, North Koreans must have been particularly interested. What puzzles me is why was the position sent in the clear?"

"Probably because the position came from a standard inertial navigator and it was easier just to send it in the clear because it would have been difficult to code using a 'one time pad' which is changed each day. The details of the sub and the emergency would be precoded. I suppose only by going to PNG could the UK actually legally send a sub somewhere close without telling the Australians; the others could go to the entrance of the Bligh Channel but would have to surface to get near the sub."

"Peter, it was the inflatable and the RAAF P8-A activity that encouraged the MoD to send the submarine out. Of course, we didn't know then that there was a submerged sub lying on the bottom. We knew the Australians were up to something but they hadn't told us what. That's all."

"Have we asked them?"

"Of course, but they just look puzzled and say we'd like to know as well."

"But they admit it was their boat that was hanging around?"

"Not really."

"Well I'm afraid I may have to go to the States for a few days in connection with that accident at Farnborough. Hopefully you'll sort it out before I come back."

Stephen left and I scanned through my emails. Mike was chasing me again about the Boomerang aircraft and the accident at Farnborough. I decided to send a message to Roger O'Kane of ITAC in Seattle, we had worked together before[4] and I trusted his judgement. 'Am representing Boomerang Airways in connection with the accident to your 970 at Farnborough. Would like to visit you and others to discuss situation.'

Mike Mansell called.

"Mike, relax. I'm planning to visit ITAC."

"Great. But that wasn't why I phoned. Have you heard of that UAV that has hit a 737 in the States? Terrible. All killed."

"What was the UAV doing?"

"It was a small cargo plane. It had clearance apparently in accordance with the latest FAA rules."

"But the normal ATC conflict warning should have operated."

"I know. I think the safety rules may need tightening with UAVs. Maybe the UAV pilot didn't hear Air Traffic."

"That shouldn't matter. The UAV should have taken avoidance action automatically. Were you insuring the 737?"

"No thank goodness. But I might have been doing that UAV. I've started insuring them."

"Rather you than me. I'll let you know when I'm off to Seattle."

I tried to do some work but that story of the UAV unsettled me. It was a sign of the ever changing world and the remorseless advance of technology. Were we going to have passenger aircraft without pilots on board and instead have the pilots sitting in comfort in some darkened room trying to keep awake? I decided I didn't want to answer that question! Instead I called Mary French "You were great last night."

"Thank you. It wasn't easy in the circumstances. I still can't believe it all happened. Writing the Australian piece wasn't easy either. It's in to-day. Have you seen it?"

---

[4] ***Blind Landing*** by same author

"Not yet but you've given me an idea. Why don't you and Pat O'Connor join us this evening and you can bring the copy of the Australian with you?"

"That's sounds like a great idea. I'll have to check with Pat as I'm not sure when he is going home. And I've got to fit in another interview with The Australian."

I gave her our address and then texted Charlie to warn her. 'Great. What are you going to give them?' and I contented myself with 'a surprise.'

They turned up at 6.30pm and I sorted out some drinks. Pat was wearing a jacket and tie and looked rather subdued. Mary surprised me slightly by wearing slacks; however, on second thoughts I realised it was probably a wise choice since she had met Charlie a couple of times and knew she kept an eye on me. Mary gave me the paper and I decided to read it later.

Charlie was very supportive. "Did they come through with the money? I thought that was a splendid idea."

"They said they had done so and I'm pretty confident they will as I politely asked for a contact to check before handing over my report and I saw the editor rapidly make a note to send me an email."

"Mary, what I don't understand is how they managed to fire at you without surfacing?"

"I didn't either but luckily I recognised it was a gun at the top of the mast. I've checked with UK and the experts think it is a development of the German submarine Muraena gun. It has to be recoil free, of course, mounted at the top of the mast and the Germans use a Mauser gun. Why anyone should want a gun like that on a submarine goodness only knows but the sub Commander knew what he was doing alright."

"Did you recognise the sub?"

"I never saw it but the pilots did briefly. It was just surfacing then, as we approached, it dived again."

"Did the pilots recognise it?"

"Don't think so. I think what happened was that they intended to surface but the moment we pinged them they dived."

"Not wanting to be recognised."

"Yes, I suppose."

"Mary, the sub commander was worried that you had recognised his sub and wasn't taking any chances. Something like that must have happened with the Oz P8."

She nodded and then stopped, I suspected trying to put the whole thing behind her. After a long pause she looked at me. "Did you read about the accident in the States with the UAV cargo plane?"

"Not yet though an insurance colleague mentioned it to me."

"Well it's in the paper here as well as my bit."

Charlie looked questioning and Mary explained the details. "Peter will know the procedures to make UAVs safe flying in airways. I think the rules are that as long as communications are triplexed to the controlling ground pilots and the UAV has a UAV certificate of airworthiness then it is permitted. Oh, there are extra rules for avoiding aircraft automatically if they are in close proximity and possibly on a collision course. That's why all aircraft which fly on airways that allow UAVs have to transmit their position at all times. The Traffic Control system has had a continuous alerting program for any possible collisions for many years but obviously extra safety procedures are required for UAVs."

Charlie looked horrified. "Sounds terrible. What's wrong with having a pilot?"

"Pilots need space for seats, windows, controls and coffee. It adds to the weight of the aircraft. It's cheaper to keep them on the ground."

I looked at Mary with a respect I hadn't anticipated. I had spotted the fact that she was very attractive and reacted as a superior male; I should have realised she clearly was a lot more knowledgeable than I had given her credit for, which was very stupid of me because I had known that she had a special security clearance but hadn't tried to find out anything else about her.

She turned to me. "I'm surprised you're not involved with UAVs."

"You know I only get called in if anything goes wrong but, in fact, you're right in that I have to keep up with the certification rules, as you clearly have done."

"Wasn't Antipodean Airline Insurance covering the UAV?"

"What do you know about Antipodean?"

She smiled. "Not much, but I know you work with them."

"Do you now?" I thought for a moment. "He wasn't covering the UAV but you raise a very interesting point. Should he be covering a UAV if he's covering commercial aircraft as well? "

"Peter, surely its no different from insuring aircraft from two different airlines? They can still hit each other. The accident investigators try to find out what went wrong, you try to find out whose fault it was and who is going to pay whom."

"Yes, you're absolutely right. I bet the NTSB are going hairless over this collision. A terrible tragedy and liable to set back UAVs in controlled airspace for years unless they can find an immediate answer."

Charlie said fervently "I hope so."

"Peter," Mary came in again, "has it occurred to you that if you'd taken on the new UK Transport Safety Board as Chairman you would be really worried now? "

"I'm not sure you're right. It could be that the 737 was at fault or even Air Traffic. On the other hand the UAV should automatically have avoided the collision."

I could see Charlie looking a bit concerned. "Mary, you seem very knowledgeable about Peter's affairs?"

As usual Mary was quite unabashed. "There's nothing that isn't in the public record."

"Surely not the UK TSB appointment?"

"It was reported in both Flight and Aviation Week. Your husband is as well know in the aerospace industry as you are in the Art World."

I decided it was time to change the subject so I gave Mary and Pat an Italian menu for a very good delivery service. I did the same with Charlie who shrugged her shoulders in mock despair. "I don't need one, thank you, unless they've changed the menu." I rang the order through and produced more drinks. We had an interesting evening though it was overshadowed by the loss of the RAF P8. Before they left I asked them when they were going home. Pat said he was leaving the following evening but Mary considered the question. "I'm not sure. I've got a friend who may be coming out so I may wait for him before going back."

After they left Charlie was a bit uptight. "That girl is after you. She's been studying all about you."

"Rubbish. You heard her say that her boyfriend is coming out."

"How do you know it's her boyfriend?"

"She mentioned him the other night. You were there."

"Somehow she seems a little bit out of character for an RAF Officer. Certainly no USAF officer would behave the way she does." I toyed with the idea of telling Charlie about Mary and her special clearances which I didn't really understand but decided I'd better not until I had discussed it with Stephen. "She seemed an expert on unmanned aircraft."

"Yes she did. Caught me by surprise. However you can see now why she was really put on the aircraft to come out here on the Fincastle competition."

Charlie thought for a moment. "I thought it was because William and Kate were on the aircraft but you're telling me that she's involved with what's going on in the Torres Strait."

"Yes, I'll explain a bit if you like."

"Not now you won't. Come on Zebedee, time for bed."

"I didn't know you were old enough to remember that. Surely they didn't have that children's programme in the States?"

"My Aunt married a Limey and she bought the DVD when they published it."

"Now I understand why your English is so good."

She decided to practice. "Would you mind frightfully if we went to bed?"

"I would be absolutely thrilled."

Her practice was soon over. "Don't bet on it. I'm still suspicious of your Mary and what she grows in her garden."

But in spite of Charlie I woke up in the middle of the night with my mind racing. I thought about the conversation the night before and the UAV hitting the 737; perhaps there might be an explanation after all for the peculiar Australian reticence and Mary, with her high security clearance. But I wasn't sure about the shooting down of the two P8s.

Chapter 18

I arrived in Seattle in the middle of the afternoon, about the same time that I had taken off from Sydney. I had flown Air Canada non-stop to Vancouver, business class and managed to get some sleep on the 14 hour flight. I rented a car and decided to stay in Everett where Roger now had his office. I had chosen the Tulalip Resort Casino which seemed to be OK and went straight to my room. My appointment with Roger was not until the following morning so I showered, dozed and then had some soup in the coffee shop. The TV was full of the 737 accident and there were many aviation experts discussing the desirability of having UAVs flying in the airways while the FAA was justifying the concept in principle. There was also a man from the NTSB not committing the Board to any conclusion.

In the morning I had a swim, breakfast in the coffee shop and was in the ITAC lobby by 9am. I signed in, got a pass and the girl telephoned Roger's secretary. In fact Roger himself came down to greet me and took me up to his office. Coffee appeared almost before we sat down. "Now then, Peter, it's good to see you but why did you need to come all this way? Couldn't we have sorted it out by email or over the phone? The pilot burst all the port tyres having his foot on the brake pedal when he touched down."

"He says his feet were not on the brakes but that he did apply them the moment they touched down. Then, the moment he did so, the port wheels locked on, the tyres burst and he couldn't keep the aircraft on the runway." I looked at Roger. "Surely the tyres shouldn't have burst. Why did the brakes lock on?"

"Well to be honest we're not sure exactly what happened. You may be right because there was a fault with the main braking system."

"Wasn't there any indication that the system was faulty?"

"Yes, there was a warning message on the systems display."

"What did it say?"

Roger looked a bit uncomfortable. "We're not sure of the exact words. We think it said 'Brake System fault. Stand-by selected'." I looked surprised. "The problem is that this aircraft was first the -

200 and there were later modifications to the systems with corresponding changes to the warning system. The aircraft had a certificate of airworthiness but it hadn't been cleared for passenger service. At Hamburg, after the accident they incorporated the latest revisions to the warning system during the repair and we can't find out the exact modification state of the aircraft at Farnborough and what was on the displays, even though the recorder has told us the state of the systems."

"I haven't read the pilot's report. What did it say?"

Roger passed me across the pilot's official report. Apparently the master caution light had been on and there had been more than one warning on the system panel. He did know there was a fault on the braking system and that the stand-by system had been selected. He hadn't known that there was no touch down protection on the stand-by system. The weather had not been good and he only saw the start of the runway at the last moment. He was not aware of having his left foot on the brakes and he was taken completely by surprise when he did apply them and the aircraft swung violently to port. He tried to correct but it was to no avail, presumably because most of the tyres had burst; then the aircraft left the runway and the undercarriage immediately sank into the grass and the left leg collapsed.

"Roger, it looks like it was a typical accident. Mix of several things. Poor warning, poor reversionary brake system, bad weather, very soft ground. I'll have to advise my client that the warning system did not make it clear that there was no anti-skid protection on the reversionary system."

"The pilot should have know that the back-up system had no protection."

"Possibly. There may be room for your firm to negotiate but you're going to find it embarrassing not knowing what the warning system actually said. Does the latest system make it clear that there is no protection?" Roger nodded. "Well then in that case you may have a problem in the negotiations."

"Aren't you going to talk to the pilot?"

"I may do but from what you've told me there's no need. Mike will handle the situation and negotiate with you. He may want me to testify also if the going gets tough. The people who got hurt may have a go as well but luckily I'm not representing them."

"I can't believe you came all the way over here just to talk to me and discuss braking systems. We could have done all this on the phone or even by email."

"You're right. I'm going to see a friend of mine in Bremerton and it seemed a good opportunity to see you first."

We talked some more about the accident and then the 737 accident with the UAV cargo plane before I left. Back in the hotel I rang Tyler Hammond of AM! International. "Did you get my message? I plan to catch the 8am ferry to Bremerton from Seattle to-morrow."

"Peter, I'm now a freelance so you'd better come to my home. It's a bit of a drive." He gave me his address which was in Colchester overlooking Seattle Sound. In the morning I checked out at 6am, found my way down to the ferry in the dock area and got in the car loading line. It was a lovely day with very little wind and I spent most of the crossing on the deck enjoying the view. We were soon off the ferry and forty five minutes later I found my way to Tyler's house overlooking the water.

"I'm afraid Marie, my wife, has already gone to work in Bremerton. She's an accountant and works for the Bremerton City Council keeping my taxes up so you'll have to put up with my catering. Anyway it's good to see you again after twenty years."

We had been at University together both reading electronic engineering at Imperial College in London. We communicated irregularly, usually when my name was mentioned in the press in connection with some accident. I knew he was an expert in naval matters which was why I had decided to contact him

"Tyler, I didn't want to tell you too much by email on the reason I wanted to talk to you but I've had a wild hunch and thought I'd run it past you. I've got involved with trying to find out what happened to an RAF P8 that got shot down in the Torres Strait."

"I've just been reading about that. Didn't the Australians lose one as well? Shot down by a submarine? Sounds like North Koreans to me."

"But Tyler, what were the submarines doing there?"

"Is that a rhetorical question? Do you want me to guess?"

"Go ahead."

"Well there must be something there that is particularly interesting."

"How about a sunken submarine?"

"Possibly, but I haven't seen any reports of submarines being lost."

"Maybe because the loss is highly classified? When did you leave AMI?"

"About a month ago. Why do you ask?"

"Well AMI specialise in knowing about projects worldwide. You must be right up to speed on submarine technology. Were you privy to classified stuff?" Tyler didn't respond. "Let me say that I'm subject to the UK Official Secrets Act over this but my current thinking is just blue sky. I've told no-one."

"I know a bit about modern submarines but nothing really highly classified."

"Good. You know I've come to the conclusion that there's only one explanation for a sunken submarine that nobody talks about."

"What's that?"

"I think that sunken sub is an unmanned one. Is it possible do you think for some country to produce an unmanned sub?"

"Well I don't know a lot about unmanned submarines. Obviously there are a lot of short range ones about but surely this one would have to be a long range one which would be an entirely new departure."

"Who could manufacture one? They would have to be very advanced technically."

"Obviously we could. We all read where DARPA is giving funding and why. What makes you ask?"

"I'm getting convinced that the sunken sub in the Torres Strait is an unmanned long distance submarine being guarded by the Australian Navy."

"But surely the Australians would not be able to manufacture such a submarine?"

"Well I think they may be thinking of having a go at a short range unmanned sub but I don't believe they've actually made one yet. I had a tour of ASC a few weeks back and noticed the place next door which you probably know about, South Australian Boats. I think the unmanned submarine in the Torres Strait is a long range one that didn't follow its pre-planned programme and went on walkabout."

"Why such high security?"

"That puzzled me but then it occurred to me that the Australians could be guarding the sub, if that is what it is, for your Navy. Maybe you people are trying to recover your sub and you don't want the world to know you have such a device with such great capability?"`

"Well we would have had to tell the Australians."

"You didn't have much of a choice. You probably swore them to secrecy and bribed them by some sweetheart deal on F35. What I want to know is if it is possible to make such a submarine?"

"Absolutely, though I think it would have to report regularly to get instructions and give a position report."

"Would it have to surface or is the low frequency communication system good enough?"

"No, the performance of underwater long range communication systems is not fast enough. However, the sub wouldn't have to actually surface as it could release a floating satellite antenna and then wind it back again. Of course coming into harbour there would have to be special arrangements. If there was an underwater entrance like the Chinese have then it would probably have a special short range underwater system."

"How about fuel?"

"To be effective it would have to have a very long range."

"How about nuclear powered? With no crew on board it would be a very powerful machine, depending on what sensors or weapons it had on board."

"Well I suppose it's possible. There's been a lot of work recently on making the reactor smaller and still give adequate shielding. Mind you, the systems would have to be immaculate and cater for every possible contingency. A lot of the work is still classified but the trick would be to ensure that the uranium is sufficiently 'poisoned' that the total system cools down. There would have to be an immaculate shut down procedure."

"It sounds like a very dangerous thing to do because it's impossible to cater for every occurrence. A collision with another ship for example."

"I agree, Peter. Presumably the design would have an almost immediate close down capability if excessive accelerations were experienced or damage occurred to the outer sheathing of the reactor."

"Surely it wouldn't be possible to build such a machine in complete secrecy?"

"I reckon it could be done, possibly more than one if they were all done at the same time. Rather like many years ago when Lockheed used to build secret aircraft in the Skunk Works. And remember an aircraft could be seen whereas a sub can be launched without anyone seeing it."

"Did your firm get any clues?"

"I don't think I can I answer that."

"The thought of an unmanned nuclear submarine roaming the world fills me with horror."

"But Peter, surely it is like aircraft, the vehicle would have to be designed to meet a particular risk level."

"Well as we said, there would have to be some very sophisticated autonomous built in safety features to avoid other craft and the ocean bottom, rocks, etc."

"You're right. And in an emergency the operator would almost certainly want the machine to transmit its position and its current shut down status."

"Tyler, the fault might make that impossible."

"Most unlikely. It would automatically release a radio buoy which would transmit a message on the satellite emergency frequency."

"But the whole world would hear the message?"

"Of course, but the message would probably be in code so no-one would know what it said and I expect it would be very short."

"What about electrical power to manage the cooling?"

"I'm no expert on nuclear power but I imagine the reactor would be designed so that in the event of any fault which necessitated it having to shut down completely there would be sufficient battery power to run the cooling system until the temperature had dropped to safe levels."

"But surely the submarine couldn't be allowed to lie there indefinitely with the nuclear fuel on board?"

"You're right, but there would be no immediate hurry if the reactor unit with its shielding in the submarine was not damaged."

"What sort of time are we talking about?"

"Years, not days."

We carried on talking for most of the day only breaking to go to a local café for a sandwich. I left in time to catch a midnight flight back to Sydney from Vancouver arriving at 8am having lost a day.

***

Charlie had taken a day off which was great and we had our second breakfasts together; my first had been on the plane and hers had been with Peter, who was at school, and Francie who Jill had taken to nursery school.

"Did you learn anything?"

"Yes I think so. The Farnborough accident was just a typical accident, nothing to do with Al Qaeda."

"Surely you didn't need to fly all the way to Seattle to find that out?"

"Absolutely right but I went to see an old University friend who is an expert on Naval power and submarines."

"Don't they have experts here?"

"The experts may already be signed up with the Department of Defence here."

"What is that supposed to mean?"

"Well there is some skulduggery going on somewhere and I've got to be careful."

"Why?"

"Because I'm not a citizen here and my work permit could be revoked."

Charlie thought about that. "Well we could work in the States, or the UK for that matter."

"Of course, but let's face up to that if it happens."

"If you stop investigating the P8 then there won't be a problem."

"You're right."

"But you still want to know the truth. Oh well, don't say I didn't warn you. Peter won't be pleased if he has to change schools." There was a change of note. "You must be tired. Don't you want to go to bed."

"What a splendid idea. I hadn't thought of that."

"Sometimes I think you never think of anything else."

She leant over to kiss me and as I held her I realised she would have needed to have put on more clothes had she been going to work.

We got up later on and while Charlie found some food I rang Mike." "You may be liable but the brake warning system wasn't very good. I think you should negotiate with ITAC. I'll send you a full report and if you want me to do anything more let me know."

"Peter, well done. I knew you needed to get involved."

"Don't count your chickens but ITAC will have to settle in my opinion"

I had barely put the phone down when Stephen rang. "I was just checking on your return. Welcome back."

"What's been going on? Anything new come to light?"

"Not really. The Australians are still being very cagey about everything. Did you sort out your Farnborough accident?"

"Yes thank you. It was just a typical accident, nothing to do with Al Qaeda. Combination of poor design and pilot error with poor weather thrown in."

"So why did you go to Seattle?"

"To see a US Naval expert and exchange ideas."

"Did he tell you much?"

"A little but he didn't rebut my suggestions."

"Alright then, when are we going to meet?"

"How about to-morrow morning in your office?"

Charlie was listening. "You're not taking my advice then?"

"Maybe. I'll see what Stephen suggests.

In the morning I got the car out and drove over to the High Commission. To my surprise Mary was with Stephen. "Shouldn't you be back in the UK?"

She smiled. "Shouldn't you be writing a report on the Farnborough accident and getting on with your work?"

I looked at her. "Yes, you're absolutely right," there was no doubt she was a very attractive lady and used her charms to good effect, "but I've been thinking about you instead."

"That's nice," she grinned and then added "I hope."

"I thought at first you were put on board the P8 to monitor William and Kate which surprised me, but of course it was really to try to find out what the Australians were doing. Things didn't go quite as planned; all of a sudden you were propelled into the front line of the action to find the Aussie P8. I guess it was your idea to wait until daylight to find the sunken sub and it was probably also your idea to look for a submarine near the wreckage. Unfortunately, the pilots caught a glimpse of the sub which immediately submerged when you pinged it. The sub commander thought you had recognised his boat and where it came from so he shot you down, like the RAAF P8." She didn't deny or confirm my remarks so I carried on. "Now then, you seem a mine of information, whose sub was it?"

Mary shook her head. "I wish I knew."

"Presumably it was the original AIP submarine?"

"Yes, I think it might well have been."

"Well how are we going to find out?"

I looked at Stephen. "I'm going to have to be careful. If I upset the Aussies I could lose my work permit and have to leave."

"How could you do that?"

To my surprise Mary interjected. "If he discloses what really is happening in the Torres Strait against the wishes of the Aussies."

Stephen though about that and looked at me. "Do you know what is going on up there?"

"I've got an idea or two which the Aussies wouldn't want advertised."

"Well why was our P8 shot down? Or theirs for that matter?"

I looked at Mary expectantly and she responded. "As Peter explained, because they didn't want their identity to be discovered."

I considered her idea. "I think that is probably the right answer but we still need to decide why the Australians were guarding the sunken submarine. But there's another thing. Mary, the crew saw only the periscope when the missile was fired. How the hell did it manage that?"

"I wondered about that and so when I asked about the gun I queried the missile as well. Apparently it must be like the German IDAS system developed by Thyssen where a torpedo tube is loaded with four fibre optic guided missiles and the missiles can be fired singly. The sub sees the target through the periscope and then fires the missile guiding it to the target. The German system was optimised for bringing down ASW helicopters and clearly the system in this sub can cope with close flying aircraft as well."

Stephen joined in. "Two German systems, but it can't be a German sub."

"No way, but maybe some German engineers. Perhaps we should ask Thysssen if they lost any key engineers and, if so, where they went." I paused. "Going back to the sunken sub, of course it was no secret that something was there, as we discussed the other day, Stephen. The sub would have transmitted a satellite message on the emergency satellite frequency which would have been picked up by all the defence communities such as China, Russia, North Korea, Iran, Australia plus the UK at Cheltenham. Incidentally all the world's search and rescue organisations would have got the message but it would have been in code and indecipherable." I looked at Mary. "It must have happened at least two months earlier. Presumably you might have been advised at the time?"

She didn't argue or agree and Stephen said nothing.

I carried on. "Anyway, why were the Australians there? Mary discovered that they had an anonymous boat sitting over a sunken sub but the strange thing is that no-one had announced they had lost a submarine. No country in the world could have kept that quiet these days with crew aboard, however closely they tried to control the internet. To my mind there can only be one solution, the submarine was unmanned."

"Mary, when you came round to us the other evening and we discussed that UAV accident, it was only then that I realised that the sub could be unmanned."

"I remember, but I never thought of an unmanned sub. Anyway, Peter, the range would be too short to get there."

"I'm coming to that. I seem to remember that you told me, Mary, that the sub was quite small?" She nodded. "Now we suspect that the Australians were trying to build some special submarine without telling anyone so one solution might be that they were guarding their new submarine until they could salvage it."

Stephen thought about what I was saying. "That sounds plausible but extremely unlikely. What about the shooting down of the P8s?"

"Possibly the sub wanted to look at whatever the Australians were guarding or even damage it but I think not. Returning to the sunken sub I think it's impossible for the Aussies to have already built a sub. Now my understanding is that an unmanned sub would not be transmitting all the time. It would probably only transmit if there was something wrong. Maybe the Australians heard the coded distress message from the sub and decided to find it."

Stephen considered that. "Well that is a possible scenario but again it doesn't explain the shooting down."

"Right. It's important to note that people only started to notice the RAAF monitoring the area about the time their naval patrol boat intercepted the semi rigid inflatable which sank; we need to check that the interception of that inflatable event was after the distress message, assuming we know when that was."

Stephen made a note. "I'll ask Cheltenham for the exact date and time. Incidentally what do you think the boat was doing?"

"I think it was carrying some very powerful depth charges with delayed fuses to destroy the sub. That's why it blew up so spectacularly when it was fired upon. And that was when the RAAF started searching for subs with their P8-As"

I looked at Mary. "Interestingly the Australian boat was not being guarded as far as you could see though on your second trip there was a Hobart destroyer not too far away. It struck me, Stephen, that the Australians were being very tight on security and, unusually, telling you absolutely nothing. So how about this?" I had their full attention. "The sunken sub was a USN machine on trials, it went wrong and sank. Unfortunately it was in Australian or PNG waters, though the good news was that it was recoverable. The problem for the USN was that the sub had transmitted what was in effect this MAYDAY message and a lot of countries might have heard it, as the message had to be on the international frequency to ensure worldwide satellite coverage. The USN soon discovered that the Australians had found the sub and so they told the Aussies what had happened and asked them to keep mum but guard the sub until they could get their salvage vessel over to recover it. The Australians agreed and, as I said, after the inflatable interception the RAAF kept looking for submarines in the area to prevent anything happening to the sunken sub."

"Well it's certainly a scenario but I'm not sure it covers everything that happened."

"I agree, Stephen, but it could be helpful in that we know what we might say to the Australians and your friend Dominic. The large inflatable dinghy situation and the shooting down of the aircraft seem to follow on logically but it would need to be some country trying to get at or destroy the submarine."

Mary shook her head in frustration and joined in. "This thing has really escalated. I came out to try to find out what the Aussies were up to and now we want to know who shot our aircraft down."

Stephen pointed out that the Australian public had still not been told any details about the people who had been killed in the inflatable boat. Nor had there been any details of what had caused the damage to the Australian P8-A in spite of large lumps of wreckage having been discovered.

I looked at him. "Then why can't we, I mean you, ask the Australians? Stephen, you've obviously got a contact there. Dominic?"

"Yes and he won't tell me anything. Instead he tells me he doesn't understand what I'm talking about."

"OK. Tell him there's a rumour going around that Al Jazeera have got some story of an American unmanned nuclear sub sunk in the Torres Strait and being watched over by the Australian Defence Force; you've been asked for a comment."

Mary look at me in surprise. "Nuclear?"

"How else would the machine have the range without a supporting boat? I think it has to be unmanned as it is the only explanation of a sub being lost without the world trying to rescue it. The Australians would never have agreed to guard it if it had been full of dead bodies, nor would they have agreed if it was nuclear powered."

"But if it was nuclear that would be terribly dangerous."

"Not necessarily. The thing would have been designed to fail safe. However, just as well this thing is clearly TOP TOP SECRET."

Stephen thought about that. "Why do you think they might respond to your ideas?"

"Clearly once you mention nuclear they will realise that they have to be particularly careful that the Australian press or any media for that matter doesn't get hold of the story. They will also realise that the Americans have been misleading them. They just might agree to talk about a hypothetical situation. Clearly we both want the same thing, to find out who shot our aircraft down. By the way, were the other crew members of our P8 ever found?"

Mary sadly shook her head. "Apparently they did search for a couple of days but it was unsuccessful."

"Why don't we try and salvage our aircraft? We know it's not deep there and the pilot did a great job ditching it so it's largely in one piece and it sank very quickly." Mary nodded and I turned to Stephen. "At the same time as you discuss Al Jazeera you can tell them that we shall be asking PNG if we can salvage our aircraft."

"Peter, they will go hairless if I say that."

"Why? It is in PNG waters, not Australian."

"They think they control the whole Strait."

"If they do it is only because the PNG government asks them to. Surely if we want to salvage our P8 we need to ask the PNG government?"

"I think you're right but the Australians won't like our discussing anything like that with PNG."

"Well that will make it even more likely that they'll talk to us."

Stephen agreed and I went back to my office; to my surprise Mary suggested accompanying me. However, I pleaded other appointments. I reckoned if she had something important to say she would soon find a way of telling me and I was very conscious that Charlie would not be over the moon if she found Mary had been with me in my office.

Chapter 19

Dominic looked at the Defence Minister. "Well those UK security people in the Commission seem to have guessed what's going on. But it's worse than that. They say the sub might be nuclear."

Jack Smithson reacted quickly. "Nuclear? The US Navy said it was diesel and had the range because no systems were required to look after the crew. You didn't admit anything?"

"I told Stephen, their chief guy there, that I didn't know what he was talking about. He virtually threatened me with telling Al Jazeera of their suspicions. He also wanted permission to salvage their aircraft and they were going to ask the PNG Government. I said they needed to ask us but Stephen said that this was a special situation and our agreement with PNG didn't cover it. I didn't agree but he's probably right. The last thing we want is the UK chatting up their government; for a start I think the sunken sub might be in PNG waters by a metre or two."

"The public will go mad if they learn there's a nuclear sub in our waters liable to go off. I think we ought to recheck with the Defense Department."

"Yes, Minister, we'll check again but the US Navy people said it's completely safe."

"They would, wouldn't they? But they didn't tell you it was nuclear."

"Minister, is it perhaps time we told the Poms what's going on?"

"We can't because the Americans won't allow it."

Dominic looked unconvinced. "Surely they can't prevent us. It's possible that the Yanks are lying to us."

"They can be very awkward and they've got Geoff Smith in their pocket. He'd try to stop us telling the Poms what day it is."

"Too late for that. The Poms are telling us it's disclosure day."

"How the hell did they find out?"

"Well we know they found the sub on the first search flight with our two crew on board but somehow I think they've now managed to get a better look even though we tried to prevent them going there again. On their last search flight I think they pretended they had a mechanical fault and it was daylight before they left the area. We can't be sure but they almost certainly took pictures of the subs and did more tests. We know this because when we looked at the camera memories there was a big gap while they had their so called mechanical fault."

"But they don't know it's a US sub. And why are they suggesting it's nuclear?"

"Not sure why they are saying that. Maybe just to get us to agree to talk to them. Of course, what they really want, Minister, is to know who shot their aircraft down, just as we want to know who shot ours down. If we can co-operate on that they will back off on talking about the sub."

"But we can't separate the issues, Dominic."

"Well Minister, if we can't offer something they'll talk to PNG, Al Jazeera or wikileaks; someone will disclose something and then, if you will permit me, you'll be up to your back end in alligators the next time you go into Parliament."

"Thank you for that, Dominic, but you're probably right. I'll chat to the PM."

Dominic left but Vin Partridge, who had been present but had remained silent, stayed in the office.

Jack looked at him. "What should we do?"

"I think we should talk to the Poms so that we can control the situation."

"Get me the PM when he's free."

Five minutes later Vin managed to get the PM on the line. Jack explained the situation.

"Well PM, I think we should ask the US Defense Department to see if they will allow some relaxation."

There was a pause while Jack listened.

"You know my views on Geoff Smith, Philip. He's In their pocket. We should tell the Yanks what we're going to do and get on with it, whether they like it or not. If we don't do that then goodness knows what the Poms will do."

***

Maureen Chester looked at her Chief Secretary. "I'm all for good intelligence Harry but this stuff from the High Commission seems very flaky. They are suggesting that not only is there a United States unmanned submarine in the Torres Strait but that it's nuclear powered; furthermore it went wrong and is now inert on the sea bed. They asked the Australians to keep an eye on the sub until they could salvage it and swore them to secrecy."

"Yes, Minister."

"Well no-one is going to believe that."

"Minister, who was it who said 'truth is stranger than fiction'?"

"Look, even if it's true how does that help us in finding out who shot our aircraft down? That's what we've got to do, whatever those Aussie defence people are playing at. Perhaps we should ask our people in the States to help?"

"We've tried that and got nowhere."

"Who is this guy Talbert? I gather we asked him to be Chairman of our Transport Safety Board and he turned it down."

"He was appointed and then the EU said we couldn't have the Board so the previous Government cancelled the appointment and then, after the last election, we told the EU to mind its own business and recreated the Board. By that time Talbert was committed to going to Australia because his wife had been appointed a director of the Australia National Gallery."

"Well he seems to be pretty sharp. Was it his idea, this nuclear unmanned sub?"

"Yes Minister, but there is also a very smart lady out there, Mary French, who was in the RAF and who we were able to put on our P8 before it left so that she might help investigate what was going on. Luckily she was one of the survivors. You remember watching her talking to Sky TV in Australia after she made them agree to pay money to the RAF Benevolent fund. By the way I discovered that it was Talbert who negotiated the media exclusivity for her."

"I'd really like to meet her when she comes home; and Talbert of course. Make a note of that Harry. We need more people like her, and him for that matter."

"Yes, Minister. I have heard it said that she is quite friendly with the Deputy Director down at Cheltenham."

"Is that the one who is very smart and very attractive?"

"I think you must mean Rupert Carstairs. He's very good at his job."

"You make that sound like a criticism, Harry. Anyway it all sounds very incestuous. She must be attractive as well as knowledgeable."

"If you say so, Minister."

They both allowed themselves to smile.

"Who does Talbert think owned the submarine that shot our aircraft down?"

"He doesn't know."

"What about Rupert's partner? Does she know?"

"Minister, as usual you're ahead of me. I didn't know he had one but he does move very quickly."

"Harry give over, you know I mean the girl out there."

"Minister, she isn't his partner and she doesn't know either but as a general comment I think **we** should value Talbert's opinion rather than hers. She's not very experienced."

"Didn't you tell me she had a fling with the P8 captain? She sounds pretty experienced to me. I wonder if Rupert will find out?"

"Minister, if I may be bold enough to say so you're digressing, but I would imagine so. Not that he is in a position to complain, by all accounts."

"I'm not so sure about the digression. Wasn't it Christine Keeler who got Profumo into trouble all those years ago. And there's been a recent resignation from the head of the CIA. Sex can cause all sorts of problems."

"So they tell me, Minister."

***

Back in the Office I went over the situation. I felt that we were on the right lines with our explanation but something was missing. My phone rang. It was Dominic Brown who I had spoken to when I was representing Boeing and who I now knew was the main RAAF contact for Stephen. He asked if he could visit my office and see me and I agreed that he could come straight round.

"Peter, I thought I'd come round to see you in your office rather than making things official."

"Thank you, but I haven't the faintest idea what you're talking about."

"Well I believe you are still taking an interest in the loss of the RAF P8-U?"

"I'm still a British citizen so of course I want to do all I can to help find who shot it down."

"Well we understand that but we feel all the investigation should be done by our agencies..."

I interrupted "And not by amateurs?"

"You know very well that's not what I meant. Even though it was an RAF aircraft that was shot down it was shot down in Australian waters and Australian security is affected. We are responsible for the investigation"

"I don't understand what you're saying. For a start the aircraft was not shot down in Australian waters, it was shot down in PNG waters. I'm not at all sure you are responsible. It is the country where the accident happens who has the responsibility for investigation. I'm sure you are responsible for investigating the loss of your aircraft in PNG waters because they will have asked you to do the investigation but it doesn't follow you are responsible for our aircraft."

Dominic was caught completely off balance by my response but rallied as best he could. "The PNG will want us to have complete authority on investigating all air accidents in their territory."

"So you say but I'm sure you won't mind us checking and discussing the whole situation with them."

"What do you mean?"

"Well the sunken sub is in their territory as well."

"All that is irrelevant. We believe you are actively investigating who shot the RAF P8-U down and we are warning you that your work permit does not allow you to investigate military aircraft accidents."

"Look Mr Brown, or whatever your rank is, if you try to revoke my work permit I shall take you to court and I will disclose a lot more than you would like. At the moment we are trying to co-operate with you but you are pretending you know nothing. I don't particularly like wikileaks or whatever it's called but there are other ways of disseminating information. I've left instructions with Al Jazeera and other media telling them what to do if I suddenly became incommunicado. However, listening to you I think I'd better go to Port Moresby anyway and discuss everything."

Brown clearly didn't look very enthusiastic at the thought of my dashing of to PNG. For a moment he looked unsure of himself, probably something he wasn't used to. He did his best to recover.

"We are responsible for looking after their interests."

"So you say but I'm sure they'll be happy to talk to me or Stephen and let us explain all the issues." Dominic clearly didn't relish that prospect. "Anyway I've been thinking and have come to the conclusion that things aren't what they seem to be."

"What do you mean?"

"All I can say is that you need to consider your agreements with the US Navy. Your media wants to know who shot your aircraft down."

"Do you know?"

"Not for certain but I'm working on it."

"Well you must let us know all your ideas."

"Not at the moment because they are just ideas. However, if you start working with the UK it might be possible to sort out the real situation."

Dominic realised he'd been wrong footed but decided to recover. "I don't believe any of this. You're just making things up. Guessing wildly."

"Perhaps. Who shall we decide to be the judge? Wikileaks?"

"Well Peter, I've warned you."

"And I've warned you. Do you want you and your politicians to be shown to be complete fools? With a nuclear sub in Queensland waters?"

"What do you mean, nuclear?"

"What word don't you understand? You know perfectly well we suspect that it must have been nuclear powered."

"You're making things up. It's diesel."

"How do you know? You only know what you've been told. Have you tested the sub for radiation?" Dominic involuntarily shook his head and I decided to twist the knife a bit more. "And another thing. Has it occurred to you why you couldn't find any survivors of your P8-A?"

Dominic looked at me apprehensively. "Go on."

"Maybe the sub machine-gunned the survivors just as they did with the UK plane."

He looked at me with horror and said "You're crazy," but his heart wasn't in it. He got up to leave and then sat down again. "Peter, in all the circumstances we won't challenge your work permit and in return I'm sure you'll agree there is no need for you or yours to talk to PNG."

"Dominic, hopefully I can persuade Stephen to agree with that. Perhaps you'd better get his agreement as well."

This time he did leave and I called Stephen and gave him a flavour of the conversation.

"Have they really got things wrong?"

"Stephen to be honest I'm not sure but there has to be a reason why the aircraft were shot down."

"You did well over the work permit. He won't like having to ring me and ask me not to go to PNG."

"Hope he keeps to his word and not try to arrest me. He clearly didn't fancy me or you having a chat with PNG. However if they did gag me or detain me I trust the High Commission would try to rescue me and get a court order. Incidentally I'd be very happy to talk to PNG. Anyway, I reckon you've got Dominic by the short and curlies over this one."

***

"Who is this guy Talbert?" Jack Smithson looked at Vin Partridge.

"He is an aviation accident investigator who normally deals with commercial accidents and air safety. He is very well known in the aviation community."

"Well how did he get involved with our problems? He's a Pom isn't he?"

"He works from here and of course the RAF P8-U was shot down."

"But why did Dominic Brown decide to see him?"

"He felt he knew about the submarine and our agreement with the Defense Department."

"Well if he does then so will the UK High Commission and the UK Government. There is no point in hounding him."

"What is worrying Dominic is that Talbert said things may not be the way we think they are. I think he threatened Talbert with getting his work permit withdrawn and Talbert retaliated by saying he was going himself to PNG anyway and discussing the whole situation, sunken sub, the lot. He also threatened going to Al Jazeera and wikileaks talking about sunken nuclear subs in the Strait."

"Vin, the last thing we want is the Poms talking to PNG. The whole thing will get into the media."

"Dominic knew that alright. He was forced to ask Talbert not to go to PNG in exchange for not trying to withdraw his work permit and Talbert said that Dominic would have to ask Stephen which he didn't relish at all. He had to retire hurt, which didn't do his pride any good."

"Well I think Dominic screwed up for once. It's all perfectly obvious. The Americans have explained things very clearly. Our problem is that we don't know who shot our aircraft down or why; we've got to find that out soon or the press will annihilate us. We might lose a vote of confidence and have to have an election."

"But Minister, we're beginning to think that this Talbert guy might be on to something. The Yanks may not be telling us the truth. There is a view that it might be helpful to confide in the Poms. After all they lost an aircraft as well while trying to help us. It is just possible that the US Navy is not telling us the whole truth."

"We are committed to the Americans. We agreed not to disclose to anybody their submarine and its whereabouts."

"If they are lying it could be argued that that releases us from the agreement. We need to know who shot the aircraft down and the Poms might help. Surely our agreement with the US Navy doesn't stand if they haven't been telling us the truth."

"The PM will have to give permission and Geoff Smith will never agree."

"The PM might, rather than lose office. You can be very persuasive with the PM if you have to be, Minister."

Jack looked at Vin's face which was completely impassive and wondered what he knew.

***

Charlie took my drink away and handed me the phone. "It's your boss who isn't paying you any money."

"Peter, Stephen here. Can you be in my office to-morrow at 10am. Dominic has asked to come over."

"No worries. Did he say what he wanted."

"Yes. He wanted a chat."

"I'll be there."

Charlie took the phone back and returned my drink. "How much an hour are you asking?"

"I know I could have said no, but if I can help find out how and why those people lost their lives I'd like to do so."

"I'm sorry. I know I'm being a bit of a bitch. I think I'm jealous of that blonde you've taken a fancy to."

"I haven't seen her since I last saw Stephen. For all I know she's gone home. And I haven't taken a fancy to her, we're not even just good friends."

"I should hope not; we all know what that means. Anyway I know she's still here. She phoned me yesterday and asked if she could take up my offer to show her round."

"Did you agree?"

"Of course. 9am to-morrow."

"To-morrow?"

I looked at her and she grinned. "Yes, my love. I suspect there will be a cancellation." We finished our drinks and went to bed.

In the morning we got up as usual and all had breakfast together. I was half expecting the phone to ring but it didn't. Charlie and I left together at 8.30 am; she drove to the Gallery and I went to my office. I was with Stephen just before 10am.

"Peter, I found out about the equipment that *Discover the World Inc* rented to the RAAF. It was a complete acoustic library of all the world's submarines regularly updated by the USN who agreed that the Aussies could have it while they were searching for subs as part of the deal on the sunken submarine."

"Well that solves that little problem. No wonder they would have liked it back. They wouldn't want it to fall into enemy hands."

The secretary came in and said that Dominic had arrived and Stephen went down to collect him. He had clearly decided that he had not excelled himself when we'd last met and shook my hand cordially.

Stephen explained that Dominic was expecting a tête-à-tête but had agreed immediately that there would be no problem if I was present. We both waited for Dominic to start.

"What I am going to tell you is between our Governments and strictly on a need to know basis. On no account should what I'm telling you go any further."

Stephen reassured Dominic as I did. "Dominic, like you we want to know who is responsible for shooting down our aircraft. We also want to know who murdered the crew who escaped from our ditching aircraft and maybe you people are in the same position, as I believe Peter told you the other day."

Dominic hesitated and then started to describe the situation. "About a week before our patrol boat intercepted that inflatable which sank, one of our monitors heard a signal on the emergency satellite frequency which she thought was very odd. She couldn't make any sense of it; all she could make out was the numbers which looked like a geographical position. Later she realised it was in a sort of morse code at a very high transmission rate. So she slowed it down but it was still gibberish. Strangely it was impossible to tell if the latitude was north or south of the equator and whether the position was east or west of Greenwich. So she investigated on which satellite path the signal had come in and discovered it was heard by one covering northern Australia and Borneo. To cut a long story short the position on the message was in the Torres Strait.

"So we sent a P8-A there and in the relatively shallow clear water the crew saw the sunken boat which turned out to be a submarine. We put a very high security grading on the event and decided to send a survey vessel out to assess the situation and possibly raise the vessel with a salvage boat. The next thing that happened was that the US Navy came on line and told us that they had developed a long range submarine which didn't have a crew. Apparently while testing the sub it malfunctioned and sank. They said the whole project was TOP SECRET and they asked if we could protect the sub until they were able to bring a suitable vessel to rescue it. We agreed but decided not to use a naval vessel; instead we wet leased an old salvage boat using a Naval crew. Then there was the discovery and loss of the large inflatable boat and so we decided to monitor the area for subs on a regular basis and the rest you know."

Stephen started the discussion. "Can you run through the timing again."

"This all started about three months ago. Then we caught and sank the inflatable going towards the sunken sub area. We were unable to find out where it came from though we suspected Mongols rather than white Caucasians. However we couldn't be certain because of the severity of the explosion. We suspected the boat came from a submarine so we started regular searches which resulted in the loss of our P8-A. Then your P8-U came out and the rest you know."

Dominic stopped for a moment and I joined in. "Didn't they ask you to lift the sub?"

"No. We would have had to get commercial help which the US Navy didn't want. They said that they planned to bring a floating salvage vessel over and lift the submarine themselves in due course. It was going to be tricky because the sub had gone aground on a shelf between two reef islands but not centrally which made it difficult for the salvage vessel to get close."

"So why do you think other countries were or are interested in this machine?"

"Well the initial message went global being on the emergency channel so presumably lots of countries heard it. Maybe like us they decoded the position and decided to look around. Problem was that the moment we started patrolling the area looking for subs all the other countries who were interested spotted the activity and got curious. There was the French nuclear sub, the Chinese nuclear one, the unknown AIP sub probably twice and a recent one which we believe was yours according to our crew on your P8. They didn't come into our waters of course so we couldn't formally complain."

Dominic stopped for a moment. "So I've brought you up to date which won't please our American friends. What are you bringing to the party?"

Stephen looked at me inviting me start questioning.

"Well we have similar interests with regard to our P8. Have you asked the USN what propulsion the sub had?"

"Yes we did and they said conventional."

"Have you tried to get the same answer through the DoD?"

"Yes, we have and there is a deathly silence. They haven't confirmed it was diesel."

"When are they coming to collect the sub?"

"They haven't told us yet."

I wasn't sure what Stephen wanted but I kept on asking questions. "Dominic, do you have a Collins sub you could use in the area? It seems a bit risky to use another P8."

"There's one patrolling there right now."

"That's good because I have a feeling that there's going to be some more activity before this thing is over. Hope your sub is fully armed to defend itself."

"Of course."

"There is one other thing you should do which I mentioned the other day, if you haven't done it already." Dominic looked at me suspiciously. "Check for radiation. If the sub is nuclear you might want to make sure it isn't damaged."

Our meeting came to an end and I went back to my office. Later, at home, Charlie asked me how things went.

"It was fine but we haven't solved things yet. How did your meeting go with Mary?"

"No problem. I think she really enjoyed it. By the way she knew she had been included out of your meeting with Stephen."

"How do you know?"

"She told me where you were."

"Glad she knew and wasn't feeling left out."

"Wouldn't bet on it. I wouldn't like to play poker with her."

"No comment."

She looked at me. "Don't even think about it." I grinned and had to duck to avoid getting my face slapped.

Chapter 20

The Secretary of Defense sat in the small presentation room next to his Pentagon Office and Admiral Cooper introduced the briefing.

"Mr Secretary, we asked to see you urgently because of an unexpected situation and we need your authority to proceed. Captain Sheila Reynolds will explain where we are at."

Sheila Reynolds dimmed the lights slightly so the screen next to her could be seen clearly showing the approaches to the Torres Strait.

"We picked up a submarine from our hydrophones between San Cristobal and Nendo in the Solomons. It was very quiet but our experts judged from the pump noise that it was nuclear. We were able to track the sub from a carrier we had visiting Point Cruz using Sea Hawk S60 helicopters and then we rushed up one of our Virginia attack submarines, the *Delaware*, which was conveniently operating in the Coral Sea off Cairns preparing for some anti-submarine competition between the Allied air forces. The *Delaware* managed to lock on to the sub which was by then going south in the Coral Sea travelling at 12 knots at a depth of 150 feet. All of a sudden the machine accelerated to 30 knots but turned west and then north west. Our sub followed it and the commander got increasingly concerned as it was heading for the shallow waters between Papua New Guinea and Australia where compulsory pilotage was required from the Bligh Entrance down the two way channel." Reynolds indicated the route with her laser pointer. "In any event the maximum depth of about 72 feet was far too shallow for the *Delaware*. The sub went dangerously close to the Portlock reefs leaving them to port and then headed for the Bligh Entrance to the two way channel south of the Bramble Cay light.

"The next thing that happened was the sub turned south south west and started to weave erratically from side to side making it very difficult for the *Delaware* to follow. Then as the sub approached an island called East Cay it veered to starboard heading towards Anchor Cay and then ran into a shelf wall which stopped it very abruptly and it dropped down about 20 feet to the bottom. The *Delaware* went into listening mode and the acoustics team advised that the engines of the sub had closed right down but pumps were still running. The commander organised two divers with cameras."

The room lights were dimmed further and reasonably good pictures of the sub were shown. One of the divers stood on the hull of the machine for several of the shots.

The Defense Secretary couldn't contain himself. "It doesn't look all that large and there's something strange about it." His face cleared. "I know, it hasn't got a conning tower."

"Right, Sir. But it still has torpedo tubes by the look of it and the design seems very novel. We think it's very important to get a much closer look if we can. Because the sub is quite small we wondered whether it had been programmed to go down the channel between PNG and Queensland but then the navigation systems malfunctioned."

"There couldn't have been a very big crew, Captain and they must have been very uncomfortable. Did any of them escape?"

"We don't think it had a crew, Sir".

The lights went up and Sheila Reynolds looked as if she was expecting more questions. The Defense Secretary did not let her down. "No crew? Who could have built and operated such a machine?"

"We don't know, Sir, but we think it must be Chinese or North Korean. We understand that the Secretary of State has asked both countries but has not yet had a reply."

"Was it really unmanned?"

"We don't think there could have been a crew, Sir. We think it really must have been unmanned, especially as we saw no signs of escape and no country has announced a loss of a submarine which we feel they would have been forced to do if lives had been lost."

"What about propulsion?"

"We agree with the initial hydrophone assessment that it must have been nuclear powered because of the pump noise. We think the nuclear power plant shut down but the pumps kept running while the uranium cooled down and we believe it has been designed to fail in a completely safe mode. Of course it would only be really safe if the boat was physically undamaged."

There was a long silence. "Captain, that's horrifying. We must find out its attack capability."

Admiral Cooper decided to help his Captain. "We agree, Mr Secretary. As you know we are developing a similar machine but we have at least eighteen months to go and that's being optimistic."

"What are we going to do now? What's happening to the machine? What do the Australians know?"

"With your agreement we plan to tell the Australians that we have lost a submarine and would they look after it until we can get a salvage vessel in position to collect it."

The Defense Secretary swallowed and considered the suggestion. "Is that wise? What about the real owners of the sub? Won't they be trying to reclaim it?"

"We don't think so. We wouldn't want to admit that we had such a machine and similarly we don't think whoever has made this one will want to advertise it. As you said, Mr Secretary, what we need to know is what armament, if any, it was carrying."

"Can you get at the sub in the shallow water?"

"In fact we can, Sir. As you saw it lies between East Cay and Anchor Cay in about 80ft. We can get a salvage vessel close enough so that it can half submerge to facilitate getting the sub on board."

"Tell me. Will the owners of the sub know what's happened? Will they know where it is?"

"We believe so. We've checked with our communication people and a signal on the emergency channel was transmitted exactly at the time the sub scuttled itself. We can't read the message because it is very short and in code but we're pretty certain the sub released an emergency floating transmitter."

"If we heard the message surely we know who owns the sub?"

"Unfortunately not, Sir, as we can't read the message, only the position."

"That's ridiculous. We have all the experts in the world."

"Yes, Mr Secretary, but we believe that the code used a daily code book so a short message would be impossible to decode."

The Defense Secretary considered what he had been told. "Alright then, are we going to tell the Australians the sub is nuclear powered?"

"We see no reason to do so and anyway it isn't powered at all now."

"How certain are we that the pumps will run until the fuel is safe?"

"The pumps have already stopped according to our submarine. It stayed in position submerged for twenty four hours before going to Cairns. We believe that the design is fail safe."

"But surely the pumps must run all the time?"

"We think not with the latest design but of course the sub must be raised sometime since the nuclear fuel can't be left in it indefinitely. But we're talking of years. That's one of the reasons why we want to look at it."

"What about radiation? How badly was the sub damaged?"

"We think the nuclear unit was undamaged and is intact, judging by the operation of the pumps and the way they shut down."

"Alright Admiral, please go ahead but clearly this project must have the highest security imaginable. We'll have to advise the Secretary of State but no juniors need know. Absolute minimum number of people. And you had better make sure that the Australians don't tell anyone, anyone at all. Not even their Limey friends if they want to get a good deal on the F35 including mods."

***

Matt Fraser looked at Hank Goodall. "When did you get back from Australia?"

"A couple of days ago. I never thought I'd say this but it's good to be back in Washington. There are worse places than the CIA."

"What was wrong with Australia?"

"Canberra's so boring and sitting round in a car just waiting for something to happen is deadly. The weather doesn't know what to do; either freezing or boiling hot. And their security is so tight. I found it very difficult to decide how much they knew about the sunken sub and the submarines they discovered nearby."

"Good for them. Maybe that white mausoleum they've built is doing a good job. Anyway I've read your report. You think they're talking to the Limeys in spite of being told not to?"

"Yes, I do. I've been watching the UK High Commission and I've seen a Limey accident investigator going in there several times and, more importantly, an Oz military security guy. In addition there's a smart blonde who was in the crew of the British P8 which was shot down; she's been in and out of those gates like there's no to-morrow."

Matt raised his eyebrows. "The real problem for us is judging whether they believe our story."

"Well I think they did at first but after the Brit P8 was shot down they may have changed their minds. I spoke to the Limey accident investigator I mentioned some time back and he struck me as being pretty sharp. He'd already worked out that there might be sub down there. My contact says they keep wondering why the aircraft was shot down. What are you going to do? Threaten them with not providing what they need for the F35?"

Matt realised why Hank was not penetrating the corridors of power. "I don't think that would endear us either to Lockheed or the Australians. Now that they suspect the sub might have been nuclear we've got to be more careful."

"What have you told them?"

"We haven't answered their question, which I suppose is tantamount to saying yes."

"Have you checked for radiation? Wasn't the sub damaged?"

"No, we don't think it was damaged but we can't get near it without being discovered."

"If it's leaking radiation the ADF will not be pleased. There could be a class action against us."

"We are aware of that, Hank."

"When are you going to try and recover it?"

"We haven't made up our minds yet." He decided that Hank had done his job. "Anyway thanks for the report and we'll let you know what happens."

Hank got the message and left and Matt pondered what to do. He knew the US Navy wanted to get the sunken submarine to San Diego but he was worried about the submarine which had shot down the two aircraft. So far, amazingly, the truth about the unmanned submarine had not got out but he wondered how long that situation could last.

***

Stephen looked up as Mary entered his office. "Presumably he's told you?"

"Who's told me what?"

"Rupert Carstairs is coming in to-morrow."

Mary showed no surprise or emotion. "No, I didn't know. Why should I?"

"Mary, we may be in an organisation with high security clearances but there are some things which tend not to be kept secret."

Mary permitted herself to smile. "I don't know what the gossip says but I told you that we are just good friends. What's he coming over for?"

"I think he wants to talk to the Oz head security lady, Jessica Butt, to try to persuade them to let us salvage our P8. Mind you I think he'll be wasting his time. She never gives away anything. Hard as nails."

"Presumably that's why they've sent Rupert out. He'll do it if anyone can."

"I think he will have met his match with her. He also wants to talk to Peter Talbert since he thinks he might have views that are worth exploring."

"Surely Peter has told us what he believes?"

"I don't think so, Mary. My reading of him is that he holds back what he really believes is the final solution until he can prove it. I suspect he is a lot further ahead in sorting things out than we give him credit for. Did you notice when we all met he let you say what you thought first? Mind you he did add nuclear to the situation. But I still think he hasn't told us everything he suspects."

Mary considered Stephen's remark. "You're probably right. Changing the subject, I was going to suggest, until you told me about Rupert, that it was time I went home. I'm not contributing anything new here any more. However I suppose I'd better wait and say hello to Rupert. By the way, I assume they've got me posted away from Waddington."

"Yes, you're no longer on the squadron's books. And you don't have to wait for Rupert if you don't want to."

"I'd better stay and say Hello. Where is he staying?"

"The Defence Advisor is putting him up as well."

Mary left the office and decided she'd take advantage of her membership of the RAF Club and go to the Commonwealth Club for lunch. She went into the bar and to her surprise saw Peter Talbert with a person she didn't recognise. "Hi, we must stop meeting like this."

Peter smiled. "That's exactly what my wife says." He turned to make the introduction. "This is Mike Mansell ..."

"Of Antipodean Airline Insurance."

Mike looked surprised. "You're very knowledgeable, young lady."

"Wish. But it was your equipment which had the submarine database that the Australian P8-A was carrying when it was shot down."

Mike looked at Peter and then at her thoughtfully. "Not mine, but we were insuring it."

Mary realised she might have given out information which was not in the public domain. "But you got paid presumably?"

"Yes, thank you. We were able to give *Discover the World Inc* the money though I think they would have preferred the actual machine back."

"I can imagine. The US Navy couldn't vouchsafe that the data was secure."

Peter Talbert thought about that. "But it must have given them a lovely excuse to come over here and try to find out what's going on."

Mary decided that she'd better not carry on this line of development with Mike present. She found herself musing about Peter; she definitely fancied having him or someone like him. He had that splendid combination of intelligence, common sense and being attractive sexually; he was older than she was but it was just as well they weren't away working together because she wasn't sure what might happen. She'd always found that abstinence made the heart grow fonder, or keener anyway.

She joined them for a light lunch and then Peter dropped her off at the Defence Advisor's house. Later, she got a taxi and went to the Dendy cinema to watch a worldwide release of a Wagner opera with Bryn Terfel singing. She went back in a dream hearing leit motifs and Bryn Terfel's voice in her sub conscious.

In the morning she was awakened by her new telephone. "Hello my love, Rupert here. I've just got in and having breakfast"

She looked at the clock which said 7.15am. "Great. I'll be down later in time to be at the Commission by 9."

"I'm seeing Stephen then. Shall I come to your room when I've had breakfast?"

"Why don't we meet for lunch if you're free? My flight's not until 2030."

She thought she could hear the lead balloon dropping. "Fine. See you then."

Perhaps she had been a bit ungracious bearing in mind their relationship in the UK but she realised that meeting Greg, then the crash with her lucky survival and finally encountering Peter had made her think a bit and wonder what she should try and make of her future. Up to now perhaps she had been a bit too free sexually and certainly knowing Rupert hadn't done her career any harm. But she knew she wouldn't have been able to start climbing the ladder without being very competent; of course, having good looks was a bonus. Anyway, though Rupert was good at his job he was not a person with whom one could consider have a long lasting relationship.

She didn't hurry getting up as she wanted to make sure Rupert was with Stephen before she appeared. In the event she got a cab to take her to the new restaurant opposite the Supabarn in the Mall before going to the High Commission.

***

I was in my Office when Stephen called. "I've got a visitor from the UK who would like to meet you. How about coming over here for lunch?"

"Are you going to give me any clues?"

"He's a heavy breather from Cheltenham. Rupert Carstairs if that means anything to you."

"Nothing I'm afraid but then I'm not in your business."

Stephen's call actually suited me very well as I had had an idea, an avenue which I, for one, had not explored. I was at the Commission at noon and waited in the lobby. Mary appeared wearing a very business like grey suit and skirt. She joined me.

"Peter, I hope they won't be long, I only had a light breakfast."

"I assume you're talking about Stephen and the man from Cheltenham, Rupert something."

"Carstairs, he's the deputy director. He came in at dawn this morning."

"He must be tired."

"I've no idea as I haven't seen him yet. Anyway he'll have been travelling first class and should have had plenty of sleep."

"What on earth is he doing here?"

"He wants to flush out what the Aussies are up to and get permission to raise our P8."

"Then he has come to the wrong place. He should be in the States. The Australians only know what they've been told, though now they suspect the sub might be nuclear they might be more challenging to the Yanks."

"Are you going to tell him where to go?"

I couldn't help smiling. "Perhaps you should rephrase that but since you ask me, I'm definitely not sure. He'll have to be delicate over the salvage since, as you know, it is in PNG waters." Mary returned the smile. "Mary, my dear, forgive me for being nosey but is this the friend you told me might be coming over?"

"I might have told you it was on the cards."

We were interrupted by Stephen and Rupert Carstairs appearing from the lift. He was about my age, obviously a high flier in the world in which he moved. He was immaculately dressed with a very smart shirt and tie that must have come, if not from Savile Row, very close by; I wasn't sure how we were going to get on but I could see he might be quite attractive to the opposite sex. Maybe there would be an opportunity for Charlie to meet him and give me her impression.

Stephen did the introductions and I watched with interest the greeting between Rupert and Mary. He wanted to be effusive and she clearly had the shutters up. We decided to have a quick lunch in the Hyatt and Stephen drove us since walking would have taken too long. We started talking about all the issues. Rupert looked at me and was very charming "Mr Talbert, we really appreciate the help you are giving us. I plan to see the chief of their intelligence organisation this afternoon and I wondered if you have any advice for me?"

"Best of luck. I expect Stephen has told you that Jessica Butt gives nothing away. Have you met her?"

"I haven't had the pleasure but I'm sure there won't be a problem as we have a common interest."

"Well Rupert, re salvaging the RAF P8 and their's for that matter the wreckage is in PNG waters so it will require some finesse. By the way have you seen a copy of the signal from the sub before it sank?"

"Not personally."

"You know it wasn't in English or American?"

"I read the brief of your meeting with Dominic Brown. Surely we don't know that; it was in code so it could be in American or any language."

"You're right of course. The message was bound to be encoded. Do you have any ideas why the P8s were shot down?"

He looked at me again. "I wish we had."

"Surely that's the point. We need a theory that explains not only the sunken sub but also the aggressive nature of the submarine that shot down the P8s. If it were me I'd look more closely at the emergency transmission from the sub. It really needs translating if it's humanly possible." I grinned. "Maybe with a computer."

"What do you recommend then?"

"I would give the original message to a UK decoding expert --- Bletchley Park and all that. See if the experts can hazard a guess at the country of origin. You see I'm beginning to think that the sub is not a US one at all. I think the Americans found it somehow and now want to get hold of it; they've asked the Australians to look after it until they can get their hands on it by refloating it. I'm coming round to the view that the owners of the submarine would like to destroy it since they don't want anyone to know whose sub it is."

Rupert looked at me and I could see his mind was racing. "If you're right that puts a completely different dimension on the situation."

"Perhaps the Australians will take that view as well."

The lunch didn't last long as Rupert needed to get over to the ASIO building in plenty of time and his car was waiting. Stephen left with him and we decided to have coffee. For once I thought Mary looked unsure of herself. "What are you thinking? Aren't you looking forward to going home?"

She looked at me thoughtfully. "I am, of course, but I'm not sure what I want to do when I get back. I think I've had enough of secrecy and security."

"Well presumably you are still in the RAF even if you're not in the normal career structure."

"Yes I am, but that's the problem. I don't have a career in the RAF."

"What was your degree in?"

"Mathematics, but I'm not a dedicated mathematician. Navigation interested me for a bit and I joined the RAF on an impulse since university graduates got accelerated promotion."

"Well how did you get involved with security?"

"I was on a specialist course studying some new equipment and I was asked to go for an interview in Cheltenham. I think I was approached because my mother was half Russian half Swedish and she liked to talk to me in Russian."

"Did you ever use your Russian?"

"I did a bit looking at the equipment on their latest fighters. I did a short exchange tour in the States on Lockheed P3s as a radar operator and then got sent to Seattle to give an opinion on the ease of operation of the P8 radar."

"You've covered a lot of ground in a short career. No wonder you were sent out here to see what was going on."

"But I haven't found out what's going on."

"Well you found the sunken sub which was brilliant."

"But got shot down by another one and what worries me is that it was my fault in a way. I encouraged Greg to go after the machine."

"But that was your job."

"Well I should have foreseen the danger."

"Nonsense. The problem is that we don't know who owns the sunken sub. As I said I'm getting convinced it's not an American one."

"Could it be the Chinese? Hainan is not too far away for a nuclear sub."

"I agree. That's the logical solution."

"But Peter, you don't think so?"

"I can see the North Koreans shooting you down but not the Chinese."

"Well what happens next?"

"We wait for your Rupert to return."

"He's not my Rupert and you said that just because you wanted me to argue."

I grinned. "Maybe to help you. You clearly find yourself at a watershed in your life and are having to think things through."

She looked at me. "You really are a lovely man. It's just as well you're happily married. You understand me."

"Well my dear. I wish you every success when you get home. Maybe you should volunteer to join the UK Transport Safety Board. It's a relatively new organisation and oversees both aircraft and marine accidents. With your language skills you could be especially useful."

"You know that's not a bad idea. Would you give me a reference? One from you would make it a shoe in."

"Of course, I would be delighted but it won't be a shoe in. My recommendation could be counter productive. The head guy must be smarting that I was offered the job and turned it down. Anyway that's your decision. Send me an email when you get back so I know how to contact you and let me know how you get on. Maybe one day we'll work on a case together."

"That might be fun," and there was no doubt what she had in mind so I decided a formal handshake was what was required when we said goodbye, though I couldn't help admiring her walk as she left to take a taxi back to the Defence Advisor's house. I went back to my office but I had barely got there when Stephen called. "Rupert's returned. Would you like to come over?"

"Stephen this is costing me a fortune."

"Well you'll be pleased to know I've now got agreement to pay you as a consultant."

"Well I have to admit that's welcome news and my wife will be delighted. I'm on my way."

As we sat down he handed me a small telephone. "You had better have this secure phone which works in Australia. I can't afford to pay you to keep coming over to my office. Use it as your main desk phone; it's very clever as it recognises if the caller wants the conversation to be scrambled and this red light comes on. If you need to call me securely then you operate this switch."

"Well this means that the Aussies will know I'm working for you."

"Of course. But they know that already so it doesn't matter."

"What happens at home?"

"We just discuss the weather."

"Someone could pinch the phone."

"Wouldn't matter as it has to be used from your line but in fact if you took it home it would work once we had set up the number. However it's too heavy to do that. We have a couple of lighter phones which are transportable but they are expensive and might be pinched. Obviously these phones must not be taken out of the country. We've got other ones for worldwide use which are software controlled and look like regular phones."

A few minutes later Rupert came in and we sat in the easy chairs while Stephen remained at his desk.

Rupert looked at Stephen. "You're right. Jessica's not a chatter-box. I had to work really hard. She clearly was under orders not to divulge anything more than we had been told already but she looked really uncomfortable when I pointed out that they really had no idea who owned the sub and that she was probably guarding a trophy which the Americans wanted to capture. I could see her fitting all the slots into place. She then asked me who I thought owned the sub and of course I couldn't help. But I pressed home the advantage and asked if we could salvage our P8 and she agreed. I said we would try and use an Australian vessel if we could. I added 'did we have to ask the PNG' which made her cough."

"What did she say?"

"No! They would arrange the necessary permissions."

"Well that's good. Not sure if there'll be any crew members left in the aircraft. Maybe there will be a trace of the missile that hit it. I think it was fibre optic guided and could get through the aircraft decoy systems. Incidentally, Mary told me that there was a laser buoy on the aircraft that was hidden to take back to UK and wasn't collected after the flight so we might find that useful."

***

Jack Simpson watched Jessica Butt sit down in the chair opposite him. She was definitely overweight but managed to carry it without any noticeable shortage of breath; he knew he was biased but he tried not to let it show. There was no doubt that she was first class at her job and she treated him like an equal and not like an employee who partially worked for him.

"Had the Pom's deputy head of security in yesterday. He told me that the US Navy could be lying to us and that the sub is not one of theirs at all. They are just asking us to stand guard over it until they can get their hands on it. Worse than that, they're convinced it's nuclear."

"Well presumably their theory is that the sub shot the P8s down because they didn't want to be discovered." Jessica nodded. "Sounds plausible though very drastic. Have we tried this explanation on the US Navy?"

"I've sent them a long message to see how they would react to the Pom's theory. Clearly they must know the identity of the sub and we wanted to be told immediately. I added that we didn't like the idea of nuclear and possible radioactivity and that we were planning to raise it ourselves anyway."

"That should do it."

***

Stephen hadn't phoned me for three weeks which was great and I had more or less got things under control. Then to my surprise I got an email from Mary. 'Hi! Thought you'd like to know I've just started with Transport Safety Board as a temp. They'll take me on their team when my service release comes through in a few weeks. As you might expect they log all reported accidents including military ones, national and international. There's also a space for comments if the TSB is not involved.'

I replied 'Congratulations. What were the comments?'

' P8-U shot down by sub, nationality not known.'

I decided to ring Stephen using the phone he had given me. "I'd like to know a bit more about the morse code message that was received. Presumably they have it at Cheltenham. Do we know how it was decoded there?"

"Peter, I'll find out but something occurs to me. If your theory is correct surely the US will know the nationality of the submarine?"

"Not sure. If it was a genuine malfunction then they may have realised that this was their chance to grab the submarine. Alternatively they may have been tracking it through one of the monitored passages, damaged it and the country owning it didn't want to admit it was their sub. However, in that case the sub must have come a long way out of control. Your point is a very good one and I'm sure the Australians are asking the US Navy what they know."

In the morning Stephen called. "Would you believe that they never managed to decode the signal in the UK apart from the position? As we know, they noticed the incident with the dinghy exploding and of course we were telling them about the RAAF P8-As flying in the Torres Strait. As a result they sent out the *Audacious*. Anyway I decided to ask Dominic if you could talk to the girl who realised that the message was in morse code. To my surprise he said yes and that you should ring him to fix the meeting."

The moment we had finished I called Dominic and went to his office after lunch. With him was a fifty year old brown haired lady wearing a brown trouser suit and rather formidable steel glasses. Dominic introduced me to Sarah Johnson who smiled cheerfully and I asked her to tell me about her discovery.

"There isn't much to tell. I was on nights when at about two in the morning we got an emergency signal. I looked at it but it made no real sense at all. The transmission only lasted a few seconds. I played it back many many times and for many days and looked at the modulation on a screen. I could recognise some numbers which turned out to be in the Torres Strait but the rest was indecipherable. It looked like a type of very fast morse code but it wasn't morse code and the words seemed rather long. Then I found that if I substituted a dot for each dash dot, a dash for each double dot and a space for each dash dot it was nearly morse but it had some extra characters I didn't recognise. Having said that the actual message was still encoded so I gave up."

"That's brilliant. You seem to have outsmarted our experts in the UK and also, I suspect, the Americans even if you weren't able to finish the job. So where is the message now?"

"I've got copies here. We found the sub so it didn't seem to matter."

Dominic looked at her. "Sarah, did you never give your decoded morse to anyone for proper full decoding?"

"No. It seemed pointless since we had the sub."

I could see Dominic searching for words but not wishing to upset Sarah. "But we need to decode it to try and find whose submarine it is. Let me have it straightaway."

I looked at Dominic. "Can I have a look? Not that I know anything. It is years since I did any serious morse code."

He gave me a copy which was a single piece of paper full of code that superficially was mainly morse code but clearly wasn't. "Is this the original code or your transposed code if I may call it that."

"You've got both, Peter. The code in bold type is Sarah's decode. What I don't understand is that the numbers were in the clear and the rest is in this quasi morse code."

"We had that problem as well. I think it was because the emergency message used the output from a standard navigation computer while the rest of the message was pre-coded." I pointed. "Notice that the position is right at the end of the message and there is a few milliseconds time gap after the code finishes. Is this what you gave your experts?" She nodded and I turned to Dominic. "I'd like to give this to the experts in the UK to have a go to decode."

He looked surprised. "They must have tried already."

"Yes but I don't think they were as clever as Sarah, here. They might be more successful decoding the text. Mind you the message is short and if it was done on a 'one time pad' basis it would be indecipherable."

I went back to my office and called Stephen to tell him of my conversation with Sarah Johnson and Dominic. "I think we now need to get the message relooked at."

"It must be very difficult because presumably the United States people will have had a go."

"Stephen, nobody has had a go at Sarah's decoded morse. You'd better send it to Cheltenham."

I looked again at the coded message that Dominic had given me. The problem was that there were morse characters I didn't recognise which set me thinking. I decided to send the page to an old colleague of mine who specialised in cracking codes for fun and on an impulse I copied the email to Mary. 'Thought you might like to see the emergency message since Cheltenham missed it.'

To my surprise she sent me a reply the following morning. 'Be very careful. Can't read bold code but looks like it's in Russian.'

I rang Stephen. "I've been very stupid. I sent the half decoded emergency message to Mary and she clearly recognised the non UK morse code characters in the message even though she couldn't read it. I'm sure you remember her Mother was half Russian. Tell me, do we track Russian naval ships and support vessels?"

"Not 100% but there will be a database that is constantly updated. Why do you ask?"

"Well this submarine we've been looking for. It's an AIP machine, not nuclear. If it's Russian there must be a support ship somewhere. There may be pictures of the ship and the sub together."

"I'll find out what we've got."

Chapter 21

Matt Fraser went over to C Street in Washington DC and signed in to see Brett Nelson, Head of Operations in the Office of the Secretary of State.

"Brett, what are we going to say to the Australians? They've realised that the sub is not ours and they've discovered it's nuclear. We're definitely not the flavour of the month. Are we still hoping to raise it?"

"Yes, the Navy say our boat should be there in a couple of days. Why do you ask?"

"Are you still convinced this submarine is North Korean? I'm surprised they've got the technical ability to develop a nuclear power plant, let alone unmanned."

"Well it did fail."

"But we don't know what failed."

"The navigation system by the sound of it."

"Well what is very concerning is that another submarine, presumably from North Korea if you're right, has already shot down two aircraft, presumably to try to hide where the unmanned sub came from. They're not going to be pleased when we start lifting it, they might try to stop us. They seem to have got very advanced anti ASW armament since they've destroyed two P8s both of which carried defensive packs. Goodness knows what their torpedoes are like. Brett, why is it so important to get the sub?"

"Primarily the Navy wants to look at what weapons it's carrying, together with their associated fire control systems. They need to know what sensors are on board, whether they're primarily passive sonar systems or if they've got the new laser arrays developed. They would also like to check on their nuclear power plant but that is the second priority."

"Well I think it's not worth the risk. Have we told the Australians or the Brits who we think owns the submarine?"

"Yes, we had to when we admitted that it wasn't ours."

"Have they challenged the North Koreans?"

"Don't know. I would have thought so."

"What precautions are we taking against interference whilst raising the sub?"

"The Australians have a destroyer in position, a submarine at Port Moresby plus continuous air cover in the area using P8-As."

"But surely we need our Navy there? This thing could go horribly wrong. We don't want to lose another P8."

"The Aussies don't want to advertise what's going on, particularly if this sub might be nuclear."

"Brett, it all sounds very dangerous. The North Koreans are very unreliable. Goodness knows what could happen. I think someone should call the whole thing off."

"The Defense Secretary is committed."

"Well the President needs to step in. We could be starting a war. Suppose it's a Chinese sub?"

"Well we've asked around and nobody claims it."

"That's ridiculous. The most advanced submarine in the world and the owners are prepared to kill for it rather than admit that they own it?"

***

Stephen called me the day after I had got Mary's message. "I've just heard that the USN hope to raise the sub in a couple of days.

"I think they are being very foolhardy. If it's a Russian submarine they are asking for trouble. We've lost two aircraft already."

"Dominic has been told by the US Navy that it's a North Korean sub. But you may be interested to know that there has been a Russian convoy of ships in the Pacific near the Coral Sea visiting some of the islands trying to increase their influence."

"What sort of ships, Stephen?"

"An aircraft carrier, two escort destroyers and two fleet auxiliary ships which apparently could support AIP submarines."

I considered the situation. "Is our submarine still in the area?"

"Yes. The *Audacious* hasn't gone back yet. Why do you ask?"

"I think it should try and see if there's a Russian sub about."

"More likely to find Chinese or even French."

"Well in my view the Australians may need some help. It should be in a support position when the salvage vessel is raising the unmanned sub."

"What could it do?"

"It might be able to help if this other submarine appears. At least we might get a positive identification."

"Surely not if the sub remains submerged?"

"It's quite shallow close by the sunken sub and Mary told me that there is only one deep water channel to the salvage vessel past where the P8s were shot down. It might have to surface and then it should be possible to identify it. Alternatively we may be able to get an acoustic signature using the passive sonar arrays on the *Audacious*."

"Well we'd better talk to the Aussies and offer our services; they've already probably guessed that the unknown sub detected when the RAAF crew were flying on our P8 was a RN one so they won't be surprised that we have a submarine asset in the area. Meantime perhaps we should accuse the Russians of shooting our P8-U down."

"Definitely. Once they realise that we know it's their submarine they might stop trying to protect it. It ought to defuse the situation. However, I can't see how they are going to admit their sub massacred our crew, not to mention the Australian crew as well."

***

"Harry. This thing is getting really serious." Maureen looked at her notes. "The Americans think that the sunken submarine is North Korean but your man Talbert thinks it's Russian. What makes him think that?"

"Minister, Peter Talbert is not my man but he seems to be fairly clued up. He discovered that an Australian in the communication part of their security organisation actually managed to decrypt the code into readable morse code but because it didn't look right she didn't pass on the decrypted code for analysis by their intelligence team. We are now working on it and I understand it was the lady who escaped from our P8-U and made the media pay for her story who immediately recognised that the code was Russian even though she couldn't read it."

"Well good for her. We clearly need the message decoded as quickly as possible but our immediate problem is what should we do? "

"I'm advised that it is most unlikely that the code can be cracked because of the way it is generated and the fact that the excerpt is so short. However Talbert suggested that we checked our satellite database and we found that in fact the Russians do have a support convoy not too far from the Coral Sea which could be supporting a Russian sub. George Swinburne says we still have a sub out there and that he has had a message from the High Commission asking if it would be possible for it to monitor and guard the area when the US salvage vessel comes in."

Maureen looked suspiciously at Harry. "Then what? What rules of engagement are we going to give to our submarine commanding officer?"

As usual Harry admired the way she saw the essentials. "Minister, that's the critical question. Talbert and our ministry legal team are suggesting that if a Russian sub appears and starts a hostile attack it would be quite in order for our submarine to defend itself. Presumably the submarine commander is always authorised to defend his own ship if it is attacked? In view of the loss our P8 and the machine gunning of the survivors, it is being suggested that the Russians would be in a difficult position to complain."

"Harry, is your Mr Talbert suggesting that given cause we could just sink their sub killing goodness knows how many submariners?"

"Minister, the Russians declared war when they killed our people and, probably, the Australians as well."

"I'm going to get the Foreign Secretary to approach the Russians. We don't want to start a war."

"I'm sure you're right Minister though I have heard it argued that in this case the fighting has already started."

"Well asking the Russians can't do any harm."

"Yes, Minister, you're quite right. But maybe you shouldn't rush the question."

Maureen looked at Harry and shook her head. She hadn't anticipated being a wartime Minister.

***

"The US salvage vessel has arrived to raise the North Korean submarine."

Jack Simpson looked at Vin Partridge. "What are we doing?"

"We've got a destroyer standing by."

"What about the media? Are they aware of anything?"

"Not at the moment but at any time a ship going down the two way deep water channel might report something."

"Are we looking for submarines?"

"Yes. We're trying to keep a continuous patrol of P8-As."

"Is that wise? That damned sub has shot down two P8s already."

"Our specialists and the UK experts agree that the missiles that shot the aircraft down only work at short range; they were designed to deal with helicopters but our aircraft got so low and close that it was a no-brainer for the sub captain. We've given instruction for the P8s not to go below 6,000 ft. As a back-up we've got a Collins sub at Port Moresby which we are going to put very close to the salvage vessel. In addition you accepted the offer of help from the Poms and they now have a nuclear attack sub patrolling the entrance to the deep water channel, near where their P8-U was shot down."

"That screw up on the emergency message from the sunken sub. Have we decoded it yet?"

"Not yet and I'm not sure it will be possible. The Poms are having a go as well."

"What about the Americans?"

"We haven't given them the stuff we're trying to decode yet. We'll tell them of course the moment we find out but as I said, we don't think it can be solved because it was so short."

***

"Captain - Sound Room. Faint submarine contact, bearing approximately 270. Acoustic signature suggests possible AIP-powered submarine. Bearing moving very slowly right, signal strength increasing."

"Office-of-the-Watch, order submarine to Action Stations. Bring torpedo tubes one and two to immediate readiness to fire".

Tom Benson considered how he should respond. His RAN Collins submarine, *Rankin*, had been submerged at periscope depth for two days, ever since the US salvage vessel arrived. It was on station about five miles north east and pointing at the salvage vessel and the sunken sub which they were guarding on behalf of the Americans. The crew was on high alert following the loss of the RAAF P8-A some weeks earlier. Activity on the salvage ship had been readily detectable by *Rankin* as the salvage ship used its bottom-scanning active sonar to locate accurately the sunken submarine and then proceeded to deploy lifting hawsers from its massive stern-mounted lifting derrick. *Rankin* meanwhile was operating in 'Ultra Quiet State', its crew instructed to switch off all unneeded equipment and to avoid making any unnecessary noise. In the Sound Room, the sonar operators monitored multiple sonar systems linked both to their main bow sonar array and to further hydrophones along the full length of the submarine hull. In addition they were streaming a towed-array sonar, designed to detect low-frequency noise-signatures both from surface and submarine contacts at long range. As was now the norm for submarines, *Rankin* was operating totally 'passively', listening for the acoustic signature of its targets. Tom didn't dare use active sonar as it would immediately announce their position to any intruding sub.

"Sound Room - Captain. Status update on the salvage vessel?"

"Captain - Sound Room. Salvage operations appear to have ceased at sunset, Sir. Still have a trace on their generator machinery.

There was a pause.

"Captain! Submarine contact signal strength now increased, engine revs 150, indicating small increase in speed. Now bearing 290, moving slowly right. Tracking towards the salvage vessel."

Tom didn't need to say anything. He knew the whole crew would be listening and ready for action. The intruder was approaching in the deep water channel north of East Cay. The problem was that he couldn't take offensive action unless he knew that the submarine they could hear was confirmed hostile. Furthermore the area where they were operating was very close to the shore and protruding reefs so there was very little room to manoeuvre.

"Captain - Sound Room. Submarine contact continuing to close. Very quiet, probable AIP-powered. Estimate speed – three to eight knots."

"Action Plot - Captain. What's your estimated target solution?"

"Action Plot, Sir, contact now bearing 300, estimate range 4800 yards, speed 8 knots, course 300. Heading directly for the salvage vessel. Probably at periscope depth."

Tom knew there was little time to think through the options. The unknown had been detected very late and was much too close to the salvage vessel for comfort. It was probably still unaware of the *Rankin*. He decided that the only thing he could do was to announce his presence by accelerating across the sub's bow and to attempt to deter it from closing further. This was a risk, but his rules of engagement limited his choices. And there was no time to winch in the towed-array.

"Sound Room - Captain. Emergency -- sever the towed array cable."

"Ship Control. Full-ahead, both engines. Steer 200. Keep 120 feet. Shut all watertight bulkhead doors".

"Fire Control. Prepare to fire torpedoes, tubes 1 and 2. Open bow caps 1 and 2".

Almost instantaneously they heard the intruders's bow sonar go active, acoustic sound pulses radiating through the *Rankin*'s pressure hull to establish its range.

"Captain - Sound Room. Sub increasing engine revs, now 220. Estimated speed 20 knots. Bearing 350."

Tom realised it was going to be touch and go whether he could get between the intruder and the salvage vessel. He could easily launch torpedoes but he dare not do so without cause. The *Rankin* was accelerating but so was the other sub and he was pretty sure it would have a ten knots advantage.

"Captain - Sound Room. Sub Bearing 355. Revs 300, speed estimate 25 knots.

"Action Plot - Captain. Latest target solution?"

"Action Plot Contact course still 300, speed 25, range 2600. Closing directly on salvage vessel."

The two submarines were on a fast-converging course but Tom decided he would continue for a few more minutes hoping the intruder would change speed or direction.

"Captain - Sound Room. Discharge signatures on target bearing. Firing torpedoes. Two launched".

Tom had no confirmed identification of the submarine but knew he could delay no longer. "Fire Control, open torpedo tube flap valves 1 and 2. Select sub as target. Standby by to fire in 1 minute. Two weapon salvo. Track plan 4".

"Fire 1!". Pause. "Fire 2!". In short succession, two thuds shook the *Rankin* as its water ram torpedo discharge systems ejected the two 21 inch diameter Mark 48 homing torpedoes. It seemed like forever but in reality only a few seconds before both torpedo electric motors started and could be heard over the control room hydrophone relay speaker.

"Captain-Fire Control. Torpedoes 1 and 2 on intercept track. Estimate 3 minutes 30 seconds to run.

" Torpedo 1 - in contact! Now homing.

"Captain - Sound Room. Discharge signatures on target bearing. Firing decoys. Three launched. Bearing 020."

The intruding sub was now taking evasive action. By firing these acoustic anti-torpedo countermeasures, *Rankin* and its torpedoes were now presented with multiple contacts, and these completely masked the target itself. They waited for an impact but the decoys had diverted the *Rankin*'s torpedoes and both weapons had clearly locked onto the countermeasures before they could go active and home in on the intruder. They were going to miss with no opportunity for a re-attack until they could re-establish its new position.

A moment later they heard two muffled explosions, clearly audible through the pressure hull.

"Sound room. Loud explosions heard, bearing 090". This was the bearing of the salvage ship. The sub had clearly hit its target.

"New contact on intruder. Bearing 040. Bearing moving rapidly right." Getting an exact target track on the intruder was now going to prove hard as it abruptly changed course, presumably to seek the deep water and escape.

"Target has now reduced power slightly and sounds as if he's turning starboard. Bearing 070."

Tom wanted to try again before the sub escaped. He guessed the sub was trying to regain the deep water channel. "Captain. Helm full port. Reload and bring torpedo tubes 1 and 2 to immediate readiness to fire."

There was a pause as the *Rankin* turned port as fast as possible.

"Sub bearing 350"

Tom was relieved to see the bearing reduce so they could have another chance to launch torpedoes.

"Helm amidships."

"Captain - Sound Room. Sub Bearing dead ahead. Revs 300, speed estimate 25 knots."

"Action Plot - Captain. Latest target solution?"

"Action Plot, Sir, contact now bearing 360, estimate range 2900 yards, speed 25 knots, course 140. Still periscope depth. Proceeding deep water channel."

"Fire Control, open torpedo tube flap valves 1 and 2. Select sub as target. Standby by to fire in 1 minute. Two weapon salvo. Track plan 4".

"Sub bearing dead ahead"

"Fire 1!". Pause. "Fire 2!". Once again two thuds shook the *Rankin* as its water ram torpedo discharge systems ejected the two 21 inch diameter Mark 48 homing torpedoes to get them on their way. Again Tom was relieved when he heard both torpedo electric motors start.

"Captain-Fire Control. Torpedoes 1 and 2 on intercept track. Estimate 2 minutes 15 seconds to run."

" Torpedo 1 - in contact! Now homing."

Once again the Sound Room reported decoys being fired and, despite all efforts of the men steering the torpedoes, they locked onto the decoys while the intruder was taking evasive action. They could hear the unknown sub, now travelling at full speed, moving away from them. Tom knew there was nothing more he could do since it would be useless trying to chase the enemy as there was no way he could match the speed of what he was pretty sure was a very modern high speed sub with some very effective decoys. He decided to try and help at the salvage vessel. "Immediate surface. Full speed ahead. Port on to 200."

***

The crew of the *Audacious* could only just hear a submarine entering the deep water channel towards the salvage vessels and sunken sub; they were on the bottom about a mile from the channel keeping their pumps as quiet as possible. The sub was moving very slowly and Jim Sherburn, Captain of the *Audacious*, wondered if the intruding sub had heard the pumps of the *Audacious* running as it went by; he knew he couldn't keep his sub as quiet as the AIP boat. However, Jim was sure that even if the intruding sub could hear his submarine the captain would not be diverted from attacking the salvage ship; nevertheless, he realised he might be attacked as the intruding sub returned trying to escape, assuming that the *Rankin* had not caught it.

Fifteen minutes went by and then they heard the sounds of torpedoes and decoys being fired as well as two loud explosions which Jim guessed were torpedoes probably hitting the submerged sub or the salvage vessel. They had not heard any sounds suggesting a submarine had been hit so Jim's crew were on high alert waiting for the returning AIP sub. In fact, they had no difficulty hearing it as it had gone to full power as it turned, trying to avoid the *Rankin*'s torpedoes and escaping down the channel towards them as quickly as possible.

"Captain – Sound Room. Sub bearing 020. Speed 25 knots. Range 4000 yards. High rpm. Course 130. Periscope depth."

Jim gave the order to power the turbines, accelerate to 15 knots , head towards the target and rise to periscope depth. Then as the *Audacious* picked up speed he ordered the preparation of two torpedoes and also to be ready to fire decoys. Suddenly they could all hear the sound of their submarine being pinged very loudly by the intruding submarine which was closing them at very high speed. He gave the order to prepare to fire both torpedoes.

"Captain - Sound Room. Two discharge signature on bearing 005°. Torpedoes".

"Sound Room – Captain. Fire four decoys. Helm full starboard."

They felt the *Audacious* turning to avoid the torpedoes. Tom decided that if he kept the his sub turning he might be able to fire at the target as it escaped.

"Sound Room report target bearings when able."

The decoys had done their work but it seemed to take a long time for the *Audacious* to turn back towards the target.

"Captain – Sound Room. Target bearing 030."

"Helm amidships. Steer 180"

"Action Plot - Captain. What's your estimated target solution?"

"Captain – Action. Contact now bearing 020, estimate range 2000 yards, speed 25 knots, course 130. Heading towards end of deep water channel, periscope depth."

Jim immediately prepared to fire at the intruder as it crossed his bows but the torpedo needed to be fired well ahead of the target even though they were close. After listening to the earlier exchange between the intruder and the *Rankin*, he reckoned that the target might have expended its decoys or not have had sufficient time to have reloaded fresh ones, depending on the decoy system being used on the target submarine. So he decided he would fire one torpedo to see what happened before firing the other. Jim waited until the sub stopped turning.

"Bearing 350"

"Fire 1."

"Captain - Sound Room. Discharge signature on target bearing. One decoy launched".

"Torpedo 1 -- in contact! Now homing."

Jim waited but there no explosion. The decoy had done its work and the Mk 56 torpedo had clearly missed.

"Contact bearing 360"

"Fire 2."

"Captain-Fire Control. Torpedo on intercept track. Estimate 3 minutes 30 seconds to run."

"Torpedo 1 -- in contact! Now homing."

A long pause and then ,"Torpedo 1 – still homing on contact! "

Jim felt the whole crew holding their breath waiting to hear if any decoys were fired. Then suddenly there was the sound of an enormous explosion.

"Captain – Sound Room. Sound of severe structural damage and air bursting to the surface."

They were rapidly approaching East Cay and he ordered the submarine to turn. "Helm full starboard. Course 045."

Anti-climax set in. Jim realised that they had severely damaged the submarine, perhaps sunk it, but he had no idea from where it came. He decided not to surface as he didn't want to be identified by passing ships and so set course eastwards at periscope depth to get away from the Torres Strait.

***

As the *Rankin* approached the salvage vessel they started to hear an exchange between two submarines behind them, presumably the intruder and the RN Submarine *Audacious* which Tom knew was located monitoring the approach to the deep water channel.

"Captain - Sound Room. Two discharge signature on 180°. Torpedoes".

"Captain – Sound Room. More discharge signatures on 180°. Three decoys. Different decoy discharge noise. Not intruder."

Tom reckoned that had to be the intruder firing at the *Audacious.*

"Captain - Sound Room. One discharge signature on 180. Torpedo."

"Captain - Sound Room. More discharge signatures on 180. Three decoys. Probably intruder."

"Captain - Sound Room. One discharge signature on 180. Torpedo."

There was a long pause and then, suddenly, they all heard the sound of a torpedo exploding.

"Sound room. Sound of sub breaking up with severe structural damage."

Tom felt sure that it was the intruder that had been hit but there was nothing he dared do without knowing which one had been sunk. As he looked at the salvage vessel he could see in the glare of searchlights that the vessel was very badly damaged and seemed to be sinking. The RAN destroyer was already rescuing survivors and the Captain advised *Rankin* that its help was not required. He reported to operations and was told to return to

Cairns. Tom decided that it would be permissible to stay on the surface as it was dark and follow the track of the unknown sub for a few miles before turning East. He ordered the hatch to be opened and climbed up until he could see outside into the starry night and surrounding sea. Suddenly he could just make out that they had started steaming through oil and debris. He slowed the boat right down and had a careful look with the searchlight. He could see large pieces of wreckage which could only have come from a submarine. He got his camera crew to take photos using the searchlight and they all saw Russian Cyrillic script on some of the floating pieces. There were no signs of any survivors or bodies and he shuddered, thinking of all those men drowning or suffocating in their metal prison. Of one thing he was certain, the sub was no longer a threat.

* * *

Jack Simpson reached out for his telephone. He heard the news, put some clothes on and drove as quickly as he could in the dark to his office to find Vin and Max Wilson waiting. "This sub. Did it surface so we could identify what it was?"

Max had a signal in front of him as he replied. "No, Minister. It just fired two torpedoes and the salvage vessel is now sinking."

"Why didn't our sub prevent the attack on the salvage vessel earlier?"

"Well Minister it couldn't fire until it was attacked. The commander of the *Rankin* quite rightly decided to make its presence known and draw the sub away. It tried to go between the sub and the salvage vessel but the sub was too fast. They were on a collision course when the intruder fired its torpedoes so the *Rankin* immediately manoeuvred and fired two torpedoes. But of course it was too late to prevent the target's torpedoes hitting the salvage vessel."

"Apparently the enemy sub fired decoys and the *Rankin*'s torpedoes missed. The *Rankin* had another go turning inside the intruder sub as the other sub was leaving but again the torpedoes missed because of the decoys."

"So the sub got away? We still don't know if it was North Korean?"

"No, Minister. We're confident the sub didn't get away and we know that the sub was Russian."

"Good God. How do we know that?"

"In his message the *Rankin* Commander says that shortly after the intruder escaped the *Rankin*'s second pair of torpedoes, they heard more torpedoes and the firing of decoys. Then there was an explosion followed by sounds of submarine structural damage which caused the *Rankin* Commander some concern as they couldn't tell for sure from the acoustics which submarine had been sunk but the Commander was fairly sure it was the intruder. All the *Rankin* could do at that stage was to surface and try to help the damaged salvage vessel. However our destroyer had the rescue under control and so the *Rankin* set course for Cairns."

"How many casualties on the US Navy salvage vessel?"

"Not sure but luckily very few. The crew had finished all the preparatory work and were in the bow waiting to lift when it got light when the torpedoes hit amidships. Our destroyer had most of the crew on board already. I'm told that the salvage vessel will almost certainly be on the sea bed by now, apparently right on top of the sub."

"So we don't know about the other explosion?"

"Yes we do, Minister. The *Rankin* Commander decided to go back on the surface since it was night and nobody could see them. They started going through wreckage and they could see Russian Cyrillic script on some of the pieces. The Commander thinks the sub was destroyed."

"What about bodies?"

"The *Rankin* had a very good look but the Commander thinks it must have gone down with all hands. The damage must have been very severe."

"Have we heard from the Poms"

"Not yet but we should do any time at all as their sub has been working very closely with our naval operations."

The phone rang and it was Geoff Smith.

"Geoff, it's no good yelling at me." It was clear from Jack Simpson's demeanour that he was finding it very hard to control himself. "The PM authorised this operation. Unless you shoot your mouth off to all your mates in the press, we can probably keep everything under wraps. Your American friends are not going to advertise that they were clandestinely trying to pinch the sunken submarine. And the owners of the sub are not going to want to admit that they shot down two P8s and murdered the crews. If you take my advice you'll talk to the Americans and agree a cover story for the loss of the salvage vessel should the need arise. Everyone out there is in the services and must keep their mouths shut. Just say nothing if you can manage that, Geoff."

Jack listened some more. "Geoff, for God's sake forget the Russian submarine. It's sunk. I told you, the owner is not going to say anything if you don't. It won't want to admit that they shot down our aircraft and murdered the crew."

He had hardly got rid of the Minister for Foreign Affairs when the Prime Minister came on the line; Jack started to listen and then waved for Max and Vin to wait outside.

"Prime Minister, I see no reason why I should resign. If you can stop Geoff Smith shooting his mouth off and telling the press then we can keep the whole thing quiet. The Americans won't want to advertise what they were up to and neither will the owner of the sub. Anyway it was you who agreed with the Americans that we would guard the sub and you knew they were going to send their salvage vessel. The ADF was only doing what you had agreed. Your immediate challenge is shutting up Geoff."

Jack listened for some time. "Philip, I know I gave permission for the Poms to have their sub there and it was just as well I did. The enemy sub is sunk but we don't have to tell anyone. I'm not going to resign. If you want to fire me that's up to you but your majority will be down to one and the papers are liable to find out about that affair in Melbourne."

Another pause. "No, Philip, I'm not threatening you but there's a reporter who is very close to finding out the truth. If you're thinking of making changes to your cabinet I think you should look elsewhere."

Jack listened and then decided he needed to change his tone. "Philip, pull yourself together and stop panicking. The priority is to check the level of radiation from the sunken sub. Unless Geoff tells the media they won't know about the salvage vessel and they won't have to if there is no radiation. I told you. I don't suppose the USN are going to advertise that their salvage vessel has been sunk trying to raise a sub which wasn't theirs. What you had better do is make sure that if there is the slightest press leakage then you are ready to redo the D notice."

He put the phone down and called Max and Vin back in. "I've just told the PM the priority now is to check that there's no radiation from the sunken sub as a result of the torpedoes sinking the salvage vessel. Of course, if there is then we may have to get the Russians to remove the sub. It will have to be removed sometime but there's no hurry for that as long as it's safe now. If there's no radiation then I think we can wait until all the dust has settled. Meantime, make sure that all service personnel involved know that there is to be absolutely no discussion of what happened with anybody."

***

My phone rang. I managed to find it in the dark. It was Stephen.

"Dominic has just been on the phone. A sub has just sunk the USN salvage vessel and it appears to be Russian, as you thought.

"How many killed?"

"If you mean on the salvage vessel don't know yet but apparently it will only be very very few."

"What happened after the torpedoes hit? Did the Aussie sub sink it?"

"No. Apparently it all happened too quickly; the Aussie sub fired two lots of torpedoes but they all missed because the intruder fired decoys. Then the Australian sub heard more torpedoes and decoys followed by an explosion but of course the Commander couldn't know for sure which sub was hit. Very sensibly he decided to start going back to Cairns on the surface and the crew saw oil, debris and they recognised Russian Cyrillic script on bits of the wreckage. Presumably our sub sank it but we haven't heard yet."

"What about bodies?"

"Apparently no bodies were sighted."

"Well it looks as if our sub did a good job."

"Peter, it's not as simple as that. The USN will have lost people. The enemy sub crew will all be dead."

"Well the USN shouldn't have tried to steal the boat, whoever it belonged to. They knew they were taking a gamble."

"But they thought it was a North Korean boat."

"Well maybe they did but does that make it alright then? And what about the two P8 crews?" I paused. "Stephen, there's nothing we can do now. It's up to the Australians to keep it quiet; my guess is that the Americans and the owner of the sub will say nothing if they can get away with it. Not sure how they will handle the dependants of the dead and injured; presumably they'll have a cover story and look after them financially, not that that will bring the dead back again. What a mess. I'll come and see you in the morning."

I put the phone down.

Charlie muttered. "I heard all that. Is it serious?"

"Yes, very. But maybe it will all sort itself out though a lot of people have been killed."

She pulled me towards her. "You'd better get some sleep before you try to help in sorting it all out."

"I can't do anything. It's way out of my hands. I'm worried about the unmanned sub and its nuclear reactor. It may have been damaged and giving off radiation."

"I'm sure you're right but there's nothing you can do about it now. You can hang on tight to me and tell Stephen in the morning."

I managed to drop off to sleep but called Stephen first thing. "You'd better get on to Dominic and make sure they are going to check if the unmanned sub has been damaged and emitting radiation."

"I've done that already and Dominic tells me that they are trying to keep the whole thing quiet."

"Just as well it didn't happen in Sydney Harbour."

***

Maureen looked at her briefing sheet. "Have we heard from *Audacious* yet?"

"Yes, Minister. The Commander heard an unknown submarine go by approaching the salvage vessel. The crew could hear torpedoes being fired and exploding. Then they heard more torpedoes being fired together with decoys and the Commander,

Captain Sherburn, guessed that the RAN Collins sub *Rankin* must have been firing torpedoes at the unknown sub as it was turning round. Then they heard the unknown sub approaching them at full speed with its pinger going. Clearly it must have realised the *Audacious* was there as they heard two torpedoes being fired at them; Sherburn ordered decoys which caused the ongoing torpedoes to deviate; then he managed to fire two torpedoes, one at a time at the Russian which by this time had run out of decoys. So the second torpedo scored a direct hit; the sub must have been completely wrecked because the Australian sub saw oil and debris confirming the loss but no bodies."

Maureen thought about Harry's briefing. "But why didn't the Russian sub counter with more decoys?"

"Not entirely sure. Apparently some subs only have a limited number of externally mounted decoys; alternatively the other solution might be that it didn't have time to reload the decoys if they were fired internally."

"How do we know it was a Russian submarine?"

"The *Rankin*'s Commander identified the wreckage with Russian script on it. Of course our sub commander had no idea of the sub's nationality when he had to defend his submarine."

"Yes, Harry. He did that brilliantly." A pause. "Well it's clearly out of our hands. The Foreign Secretary will have to decide what to do."

"Minister, luckily there's no rush. Nothing need be done unless the submarine owner complains."

"What about the Americans, Harry?"

"Well they won't be in a rush to complain either since they were pinching some other country's sub."

"But if we know it was a Russian sub that killed our people we ought to do something?"

"But why since we don't know? It may be better to do nothing, Minister."

Maureen nodded but Harry could see her mind was racing.

"Harry, you told me it was an unmanned nuclear sub that was being salvaged."

"Yes, Minister."

"Well the torpedoes might have damaged it and the reactor might be emitting radiation."

Harry once again marvelled at his boss.

"You're right, Minister. Talbert is already getting Stephen at the Commission to make sure the Aussies are checking."

"But surely the sub can't be left there indefinitely with the uranium fuel on board?"

"My understanding is that there is no immediate hurry to raise the submarine providing it is intact and the reactor is not damaged. The reactor is designed to be 'fail safe' but you are quite correct, Minister. Sometime it will have to be raised and the uranium removed. Presumably the Australians will get the Russians to do that in a few years time. Alternatively they might have to do it themselves.

"But the media? Won't they get hold of the story?"

"They won't know if they're not told. But it will be harder if the sub is radiating and its got to be fixed."

"Your man, Talbert, expected something like this."

"Yes, Minister."

"He deserves a KBE."

"Possibly Minister, but there would be too many questions asked. A CBE at most but an OBE would be safer.

"But the girl would only get an MBE."

"Yes, Minster."

Epilogue

We met upstairs in the lounge of the RAF Club. Mary looked really great in a very formal grey dress which seemed to accentuate her figure rather than confine it. We kissed and I was glad I had had a good shave as she felt very smooth. I looked at her appreciatively. "Mary, lovely to see you." I looked at my watch. "We've got time for a coffee. We're not on parade until one o'clock."

"You look pretty good yourself. When did you get in?"

We went over to sit in a couple of easy chairs by the window.

"Yesterday afternoon and I'm just beginning to feel that I might survive. Have you checked in yet?"

"Yes, they let me in early." She looked at me and grinned. "Room 309 if you're interested but it's only got a single bed."

"Mary, give it a rest. Quite apart from the fact that I'm very happily married you need a younger man. I'm not sure I'd be strong enough for you."

"Nonsense. Anyway we could have fun trying. What room are you in?"

"Never you mind but I'm surprised you don't know. You booked the room."

I had remembered that Mary had rung me about two months earlier telling me she had received a letter saying she was being awarded an OBE. She had been a bit embarrassed to find that I had not received a similar letter. However two days later I was able to return her call when my notification arrived giving her the news that I had been awarded a CBE in the Foreign Office List. I had complained to her that I was puzzled as I had never been near the Foreign Office and so she asked me if I preferred to be promulgated in the Navy list with a commendation saying 'For helping to destroy an enemy submarine and killing all the sailors.' I had shuddered and remarked that I didn't like to be reminded of that aspect of the affair. She had replied that I might have a different view if I'd been shot at by a Mauser machine gun.

Mary had explained to me over the phone that it was the usual thing for people from MI6 and those who travelled from

Cheltenham to be recognised on the Foreign Office list so that no explanations were required but that it only happened normally on retirement. I had pointed out she had retired, perhaps a little early, but anyway I had expected her to have got an AFC or DFC for courage in the face of the enemy. She said those awards were not really applicable and again, for them, explanations would be required.

It had been then that I had suddenly realised that I would need to get a room in the RAF Club and that it was probably too late but Mary, typically, had thought it all through and had booked a superior room at the front for Charlie and me when she got her letter. When I pointed out that that was taking a gamble she countered by saying that if the worst had happened I could have always gone over as her guest.

"You're right." Mary nodded. "I did try to get room 400 for you when I booked but they couldn't promise. Anyway, I'm not serious about us any more as I'm thinking of advertising on the net for a partner before it's too late."

"Now I know you're joking." I poured some coffee. "How are you getting on at the TSB?"

"Absolutely fine but what I find strange is the complete openness. It's so different from Cheltenham. There's no secrecy except for firms trying to hide their mistakes, given half a chance."

"Do you want to go back to GCHQ?"

"In a way but I got too much coverage when we were shot down and I wouldn't like to be chained to a desk there. At least here we move around getting briefed and kept up to date regardless of whether there are accidents."

I checked on the time. "It was just as well you let me know about this lunch to-day with the Minster of Defence. Something must have gone wrong with their system."

"Yes. I had my invitation about two weeks ago and then her office rang in a panic asking how they could contact you."

"Someone must have been on leave. They could have called Stephen. Anyway we'd better go."

We arrived at the MoD main entrance, had our identities checked, photographs taken and passes issued. We were taken up to the Minister's office and then shown into a small room which looked like a meeting room but on a side table some sandwiches, plates and coffee had been had laid out. We were joined by Jim Sherburn, a naval captain in uniform who turned out to be the commander of the *Audacious*, the submarine which had sunk the Russian submarine. Maureen Chester, the Minister appeared accompanied by her Chief Secretary.

"I wanted to meet you all. I must apologise for not arranging lunch in the House but in view of the still very high security classification of what you've all been through I thought it would be easier just to have a chat here."

She paused and we helped ourselves to the sandwiches, coffee and sat down. "I'm not sure people understand what it is like when an incident like yours occurs on the other side of the world. Apart from anything else the timing is invariably in the middle of the night and the news comes in very infrequently in dribs and drabs. Harry, here, has to decide whether to wake me each time something happens. And, to make matters worse, when it does come in it is very often horrific and one feels virtually helpless as events unfold."

She looked at Mary. "It was dreadful for you, my dear, being shot down but at least you knew what was going on. Sitting here waiting for news of survivors was very difficult. Obviously we were very relieved that you and the co-pilot survived but the loss of the rest of the crew was heart breaking. And then I saw you on the TV telling the terrible story of your colleagues being shot. It was unbelievable and you were so composed. I could hardly believe it when Harry told me that you had done that deal with the media; it was the one thing which cheered me up a little. What a brilliant idea."

Mary chimed in. "Thank you, but we were very lucky to survive."

"Not luck, just very quick thinking."

Mary turned to me. "And it was Peter who actually did the negotiation with the media and advised me how to avoid getting trapped with the lawyers and all the rules."

"But it was your idea and I'm glad you're both going to the investiture to-morrow. Very well deserved." She turned to Jim

Sherburn. "You had to make a very tricky decision, Captain, to save your submarine."

"Not really Minister. We did what we are trained to do. We had been well briefed."

"But I gather you worked out that the attacking sub would be running out of decoys."

"It's standard procedure to consider these things, Minister. Of course, it was very unusual to be attacked by a submarine and having to reply without knowing the nationality of the boat."

"Yes, the Americans thought it was the North Koreans but as you know Peter Talbert, here helped by Mary, were convinced that it was a Russian one." She nodded towards Mary. Maybe she'll tell you about it sometime." She turned to me. "And as for you Mr Talbert, thank you for all your support helping us to find out what was going on."

"It was a pleasure, Minister, but of course this is not the end of the story."

"You mean that the submarine will have to be raised sometime?"

"Yes but there is no rush. Maybe when everything cools down the Australians will get the Russians to take the sub away or maybe they'll have to do it themselves."

"Perhaps, but it may be a different Government, Mr Talbert. They have to change rather more frequently than we do." She paused. "I gather a couple of years ago you turned down the chance to run our new Transport Safety Board."

"Not at all, Minister. I accepted the job and then the European Union interfered."

"But we told them to mind their own business for once and offered you the job again."

"Yes, that's true, but by then my wife had been offered a job as a director of the National Gallery in Australia at Canberra."

She smiled. "Well it's all over now. I hope you feel you made the right choice."

"Australia is a marvellous place and it doesn't really matter these days in my sort of job where you live."

"Are you going to stay there? I'm sure we could find you a job."

"That's nice to know, thank you. However my wife is an American and an international art expert. To be honest we don't know what we may do."

"Is she here to-day?"

"Not yet unfortunately but hopefully she will be able to make it for to-morrow."

The Minister turned back and started chatting to Mary and, quite understandably, it was clear that it was Mary who really fascinated her. The sandwiches were great but as usual on this sort of occasion I was so busy concentrating on the conversation that I realised as I left that I couldn't remember what was in them or how many I had eaten.

We walked up Whitehall to Trafalgar Square. "Mary, that went well. I was surprised she didn't offer you a job."

"Actually I have been offered a job but I don't think I want to get involved with the MoD again. I want to be able to do what I want to do without consulting anybody."

I smiled. "That checks perfectly. I think you're very sensible."

She stopped, turned and hugged me then kissed me. "Yes, you're right. Just like that because I felt like it."

We caught the No 9 bus back to the Club, crossed the road and as the doors of the Club opened we could see Charlie checking in with a tall slim handsome looking young man aged in the early thirties. She turned to us, hugged me and kissed Mary. "Am I glad to see you. It doesn't seem to matter how many times I go from Oz to UK and however well I sleep, I still don't think clearly when I escape from that overcrowded mess at Heathrow." She turned back to the man standing next to us who was looking at Mary. "This is my brother Andrew over from LA. I only found out he was going to be here just before I left."

I turned to him. "Where are you staying? I think they're fully booked here."

"No problem." His accent was East Coast and fairly soft. "I'm staying in the Hilton up the street on the next block."

Charlie looked at me. "We've managed to get a seat for Andrew this evening, fairly close to the three of us in the stalls but Andrew wants to come to the investiture to-morrow; he wants to see what happens. I've told him it's too late"

I looked at my watch and then turned to Mary. "Why don't you ring the admin number we have and say you want to bring your partner who has just returned from overseas. You might get away with it."

Mary hit me, then asked Andrew for his passport. He produced it with great alacrity, clearly rather liking the idea. She found the contact number and went outside the door to make the call.

Charlie shook her head at me. "Only you would have thought of that solution."

I turned to Andrew and smiled. "You'll put up with it to get in won't you?"

It seemed to take some time but Mary finally returned looking triumphant and handed Andrew his passport back. "I'd better not tell you what I said but you should be on the list to-morrow."

We went up to the lounge to get some tea and Andrew kept looking at Mary. "I'm sure I've seen you before. Where do you work?"

"I work for the UK equivalent of your National Transportation Safety Board. How about you?"

"Oh, I just work for Apple."

Mary looked at him thoughtfully. "Do all Apple employees stay at the Hilton?"

He smiled. "It depends."

"I'm sure it does."

"How long have you been with your NTSB."

"About three months, before that I was in the RAF"

I could see Andrew had worked it out. "I knew I'd seen you before. You were on the television quite recently recounting how your aircraft had been hit by a submarine missile and then you were shot at in the water. Charlie told me a bit about it. Australia wasn't it? I remember thinking how marvellous you were as you were telling the story but I never thought I'd have the chance to meet you."

To my surprise Mary turned slightly pink. I thought she never showed that sort of reaction but Andrew had clearly touched the spot. She mumbled thank you and tried to change the subject but Andrew had switched on. "Did you ever find out who owned the submarine which shot you down?"

For once Mary needed help and I chipped in. "No we never did. As you heard, the whole thing was unbelievable."

He looked at both of us. "Well then, why are you two getting awards here to-morrow?"

"It's a long story and maybe Mary will tell you sometime when she can."

We left Andrew in the lounge while we all got organised and then we went to the theatre. It was a good evening though we only saw Andrew at the two intervals. However it was rapidly becoming very plain that he wasn't minding the deception of being Mary's partner.

As we were going to bed I turned to Charlie but she knew what I was going to ask. "He was married for about a year and then got divorced when his wife started an affair with some guy every time he went away on business. And there were no children."

"How did you know what I was going to say?"

"I'm your wife and you've spent the whole evening watching those two enjoying each other's company."

"My love, the girl needs a break and maybe your brother could be the answer."

Andrew joined us for breakfast and the time soon came to get a taxi even though the distance was short, since the girls didn't feel that walking in high heels down Constitution Hill in their best frocks would be a good way to arrive.

At the palace Charlie and Andrew disappeared to get seats to watch the ceremony, Mary went into the OBE line and I was ushered into the room for CBEs. While waiting I couldn't help noticing the walls which were plastered with Gainsboroughs and other well know artists. My turn came to get my decoration put round my neck and then back outside. I met up with Mary and we waited for Charlie and Andrew to reappear. I started telling Charlie about the paintings.

"What a waste on a Philistine. We couldn't see any at close range."

"You'll have to wait for your DBE and then you can have a proper inspection."

"I'm not sure what a DBE is but it won't be this time round."

"It might be if you got a job in the National Gallery or the Royal Academy."

"And pigs might fly."

"That would be a good painting. Isn't there a special painter who does things like that?"

We all had our pictures taken in various combinations with Mary and I holding our medals and then, as it was a bright day, we decided to go back through the Park and look at the War Memorial. Charlie produced ,as if by magic, some walking shoes for her and Mary. We led the way followed by Andrew and Mary who seemed to have a lot to talk about.

I put my arm round Charlie as we arrived at the Memorial and again I couldn't help swallowing thinking of all those thousands of lives that were lost defending the United Kingdom. We were all very quiet and even Andrew stopped talking.

After a bit we decided to go back to the RAF Club. As we went underneath the road by Hyde Park tube station Mary picked up an Evening Standard, glanced at it and then stopped. She passed it to me without comment but looking at it I could see there was no need. 'Russian lost sub in Pacific' stood out at the top of the page and below the narrative quoted a Russian spokesman who had said that a long range submarine was missing somewhere in the Pacific, position unknown. Regrettably it was assumed that it was lost with all hands.

I passed it to Andrew who had got his answer on the nationality of the enemy submarine rather earlier than he had expected.

Appendix

Mission system in the *Dire Strait* Boeing P8-U

In this fictional book, unlike the real world, the Royal Air Force has bought the Boeing P8 anti submarine aircraft which, at the time of writing, has only been ordered by the Indian and Australian Governments. The imaginary mission system described in this book is based on the one that was being developed by Boeing for the Nimrod MRA4 aircraft until the programme was cancelled by the UK Government. However, the system is a mythical one and has no firm connection with any existing commercial system.

The system records the flight navigationally together with the sensors --- the MX20 electro optic/infra red camera, radar, sonobuoys and electromagnetic radiation. In addition the system is pre-loaded with known information on submarines and naval ships, friendly and hostile. During the flight the system will indicate whether the targets discovered by the sensors can be identified by reference to the database and if a target is friendly or hostile. The capability of the aircraft is enhanced by the crew having multi-functional displays, capable of being switched so that each crew member can select and look at what is being shown on the displays of the other crew members ; for example the pilots can select what is in front of the radar operator and perhaps see targets ahead which were not visible immediately to the naked eye.

After the flight the portable Mission Support System can replay the flight on its own displays, make a copy of the mission memory and also send secure information over the internet to its base in the UK.

Milton Keynes UK
Ingram Content Group UK Ltd.
UKHW040659111224
3598UKWH00035B/259